Mars Knight is a retired widower living in Belen, New Mexico, a place where you can wash the car, and it still won't rain. He is writing under the pseudonym Mars Knight, because he doesn't want to embarrass his family. Mars loves his four dogs, the great outdoors, and writing stories, not necessarily always in that order.

Man Ki... ... ...ssed will live li... ...g in Belen, New Mexico, a pl... e where you ca... ...dom be... ...like a pin... ...like a whinpo... le... he...pe...bat... age... ...pen... be ca... wanto an... ...a life unti... Mi... ...on... ...w cop... ...h... and... ...ion... ... h... ...des you rare... ify... s... ... ...ce...

Dedicated to the memory of my late wife Lucretia, who inspires me still, to count my blessings, and not count my troubles, because "Things could always be worse."

Mars Knight

THINGS COULD ALWAYS BE WORSE

AUSTIN MACAULEY PUBLISHERS™

LONDON * CAMBRIDGE * NEW YORK * SHARJAH

A CIP catalogue record for this title is available from the British Library.

ISBN 9781035803491 (Paperback)
ISBN 9781035803507 (ePub e-book)

www.austinmacauley.com

First Published 2022
Austin Macauley Publishers Ltd®
1 Canada Square
Canary Wharf
London
E14 5AA

I offer thanks and gratitude to all those at Austin Macauley who worked with me and for me to publish my first novel.

On Earth's sister planet, Gaia, in an alternate universe…

Chapter 1

Melanie watched closely, peering through the wet windshield, as two blocks ahead, the two alleged aliens Robulus and Jeemis, strode towards the waiting Carry Van. She wondered why the driver was holding on to his open door, standing in the rain, as if he'd seen or heard something.

Then Melanie saw it too! From the opposite direction, a white Tanki accelerated towards the idling Carry Van, as if aiming for it. The van driver appeared to be frozen in place, perhaps he was praying, as the enormous white Beast Utility Vehicle sped towards him.

Robulus and Jeemis ran down the walk, but they could not arrive in time to be of any assistance, so they stopped and watched in horror, as the Grand Pissan Tanki slammed into the Carry Van's open door, narrowly missing the driver. Sgt Crankace dove onto his van's front seat in time, before the door slammed shut. The door fell off onto the road, crumpled like paper. The Tanki slid to a halt, about thirty yards beyond the damaged van, skewing to one side as the oversize tires slipped on the wet pavement.

A block and a half away from that bad scene, Sgt Slappus, Melanie's driver, depressed his brakes and slowed down, undecided about what to do next. He was torn between fleeing to get help, and fleeing to protect his passenger. He quickly chose door number two. He could turn right at the next corner, one block away from the crime taking place ahead. His passenger Melanie felt his decision nearly before he did. She knew that he was going to drive off, and she was having none of it.

"Like Hades, Sgt Slappus!" she said angrily. Melanie reached over to the steering column, turned off the ignition and tossed the keys down onto the floor. The surprised sergeant yelped in fear. Melanie unsnapped her safety belt, threw the passenger door open and began to run towards danger.

Sgt Slappus, sweat beading on his forehead, found the keys on the floor mat near his feet. He drove off and accelerated to high speed until he reached the air base's Max Beefburger outlet. He needed a cheesy egg croissant, and a medium coffee to help calm his nerves. After breakfast, he would go and get help as fast as he could go. "Demn! That was too close!"

Robulus and Jeemis watched in stunned amazement, as a black boulder, tumbled out of one of the Tanki's four doors and rolled towards them. They couldn't identify the frightening apparition until it stopped, at the appropriate six-foot, polite, social distance from them. Their amazement only increased, when a head and four limbs, in all of the appropriate places emerged. It was a person!

The Vometta Wilde person opened her left hand, and aimed with her fingertips. She fired her Stoppem Stayser twice; first hitting Jeemis, then Robulus. VW only needed to borrow one of them, so she randomly grabbed up Jeemis. She folded him under one thick arm and tucked him in-between folds of fat on her torso, and rumbled towards the damaged grey Carry Van.

Donut, another of the Tanki's occupants, had trotted back to that doorless vehicle to snatch up their second hostage, Sgt Crankace, who still lay across the front seat, his crotch warmly wet. Donut pulled the shocked driver out the door by his wet shoes, and Cranky was unable to react, let alone resist the man. His head cracked down onto the pavement and he immediately lost consciousness.

Meanwhile, Loser, the getaway driver, had shifted the huge Pissan Tanki into reverse, so as to get closer to the kidnap victims and his fellow BEWBs, and expedite their exit from Onnitt Air Power Base. Loser had seen a second grey Carry Van turn off, and breathed a big sigh of relief. He was armed, but he didn't want to kill anybody today.

Loser used the truck's interior rear-view mirror as he backed the behemoth up, but he happened to glance down, and saw through the windshield, a vision of loveliness. A gorgeously wet woman was running down the street. Towards him! It was a fantasy come to life. This beauty didn't want him to leave the area without her. She wanted Loser, and Loser wanted her. He was transfixed, like when he used to watch the Pimpsons cartoons.

Barump! "Waa!"

Loser slammed on the brakes, but it was too late. The Tanki's back wheels had rolled up on top of something! He shifted into park, and got out of the truck to see what he was parked on. He didn't want to move it and run over somebody. He stared at the bizarre sight. The massive truck's position, reminded him of a child doing push-ups, with its grille nearly touching the ground and its rear end stuck high in the air.

While Loser was thus occupied, Melanie was running hard, with her head and one shoulder held low. She slammed into Donut's hunched back, as he struggled to drag the unconscious Sgt Crankace out to the Tanki. Donut shot forward, and like a piledriver he rammed headfirst onto the puddled roadbed, and dug out a new pothole with his skull. Melanie fell down too, atop the prone, still form of Sgt Crankace. She was dazed badly.

Meanwhile, Loser had observed that all four rear tires of the BUV, sat atop a huge black hill named Vometta Wilde. Jeemis was untouched by the vehicle, and after he clawed his way out of Vometta, Loser grabbed the alien by the arms. He dragged him out from beneath the truck, and Jeemis let him. Loser saw what had happened to Donut too, and urged him to action. He yelled, "Grab the girl. Hurry, before she recovers!"

Donut's head was uninjured, but he'd skinned a knee. He shook it off and recovered his few senses before the woman did hers. Donut stumbled to Melanie's side as she struggled to rise to her feet. Donut tried mightily, but could not hoist the woman onto his shoulder.

Loser had boosted the very tall, but lightweight alien, high up into the raised back seat of the extended truck cab, shut the door and then ran back to help Donut. "We'll put her in the driver's seat!' Loser said.

Loser climbed in first, and pulled on Melanie's flailing arms, and Donut pushed her up and in from underneath. She screamed for help, and Donut slammed the door shut. He ran around the front of the truck to get in the back seat with the alien. Donut sat behind Loser, and Jeemis was behind Melanie. Donut was proud of himself. He was a star, and hadn't needed to use his stayser glove!

Loser propped Melanie up in front of the steering wheel, slapped her once and said, "Drive, Sow!" in his best movie villain voice. "And no funny stuff!" he added. Loser felt certain that this was a classic line.

Loser poked a sharpened screwdriver up under her chin and drew blood. Melanie jerked her head back, and viciously slapped his hand away. She set the transmission in drive, and pressed the accelerator. The rain came down harder now, and the sky had darkened. "Where to?" Melanie asked dreamily. Jeemis surreptitiously observed it all. His extended helplessness act had passed the test.

Loser turned his head to remind Donut, "Use your stayser on him if need be. Keep him covered." Donut didn't need reminding, and he pointed his fingers at the alien sitting beside him on the wide bench seat in the rear of the cab. Melanie regained her senses slowly, and found the Beast Utility Vehicle rather easy to handle and drive. She followed Loser's directions, and soon they were off Onnitt Air Power Base. Melanie expected that police would quickly put an end to this kidnapping, or whatever it was. She breathed deeply and tried to stay calm. Police must soon arrive. The white Pissan Tanki should be easy enough to see and identify. It stuck out like an honest lawyer.

Traffic, slowed and befuddled by rain, clogged the Ohaha streets, but the BUV seemed to push the cars away and to either side, like a bow wave in front of a moving boat, and so they kept rolling. Still, there was no pursuit. Melanie kept glancing up into the rear-view mirror, hoping for once to see a cop behind her.

Melanie was scared and angry but back in command of herself again. She screamed at Loser, "Not only kidnapping, but murder! You killed that, that…"

Donut was pissed off too, and saddened. He cried out in rage, "You killed the Sperm Whale! Wasn't supposed to be no killin', Loser!"

"Everybody just shut the poke up!" Loser felt the same demn way that Donut did. Vometta was like a convenience whore, open twenty-four hours a day, three hundred and sixty-five days annually, except in leap years. He'd often wondered if it was the enormous volume of sperm input, that caused Vometta to bloat up into the great black whale she'd become, but that was before his time. Loser only joined the BEWBs three years ago and Vometta was already entertaining the troops back then.

From his seat behind Melanie, Jeemis screeched, "She's not dead. In fact, that creature seemed unhurt, because she was eating some kind of cakes or donuts down under the truck before you pulled me out from there" The alien's voice was like a sledge hammer on the eardrums, and both Loser and Donut cringed in pain, clapping their hands to their ears. It was unfortunate that Loser still held a sharpened screwdriver in one hand and he stabbed himself in the temple with it. Crime was painful sometimes.

Melanie was furious with her situation. She refused to be a victim. If the police didn't rescue her, she would take things into her own hands, like her mother had. Her mother Pamela died while fighting off an attempted rapist, six years ago.

Mrs Gryzolski was getting into her car, after a night shift at the hospital where she worked as a nurse in ER, when she was attacked. The rapist used a knife, but Pamela wasn't getting in her car with him. She pulled away from him and ran, but was stabbed in the back repeatedly. When he was arrested, it was learned, that he had been released without bond the day prior, for rape; his third charge. He served three years for Pamela's murder.

Melanie vowed to emulate her mother. No son of a sow was going to victimise Melanie! No one! She looked into the rear-view mirror at Jeemis. He appeared unperturbed. Loser turned his head to the alien, and said, "You might be immortal and all, but you do as I ask or the chick gets it." Melanie wanted to hurt the man, badly. She would get her chance.

Jeemis said, "That's well thought out. She gets it, and who drives?"

Loser said, casually. "You or Donut do."

"Without your hostage, you have no hold over me, "Jeemis shrieked.

Melanie caught the attention of Jeemis in the rear-view mirror, and asked him a question with her blue eyes. He understood. He winked, but shook his head no. Melanie didn't know or understand why Jeemis didn't want to end this charade here and now, but she decided to trust him. She would behave, and drive on. For now.

Blood flowed from the right side of Loser's skull, but he didn't let that stop him from turning in his seat, and announcing to his current audience, "Listen up! I'm in charge here, and this is how it's gonna be; right? Everybody follow my orders, and we'll all come out of this alive." Loser always kept in mind his future portrayal in the movies, and his biography in the Who's Who of Crime.

"So, here's the deal," Loser said. He tried to snarl, but it came out sounding like a fart. Melanie rolled her window down a few inches, just in case. "The alien tells us how to get to the TDS or the chick gets it," Loser repeated his threat, but now added a disclaimer, "And I don't care if we all die, including the immortal alien back there! "He jabbed the screwdriver at Melanie's unblemished cheek as an exclamation point. Loser had to show that he was very serious, had to maintain strict control. He enjoyed creating fear too, because that was always fun.

Melanie was ready this time. She saw the weapon coming. She jerked her head to the side, reached up with her right hand and snatched it from his grasp before he could react. Melanie flung the screwdriver out her open window. It bounced off the pavement once, and landed in the median, where it stuck into a lonely, discarded shoe.

Loser was stunned by her beastly behaviour! It was uncalled for! Victims needed to know their places in a crime. Submission was always best for everyone. He pulled a switchblade out of one of his calf-high, leaf green, wool socks. His green feet were shod with red sandals, which gave his legs the appearance of squashed tomato plants. He said, with a note of triumph in his voice, "I have a lot more weapons where that came from."

Jeemis redirected Loser. He shrieked, "Get on the Interstate Melanie, I-800 westbound. If we're going to the TDS, we need to drive to Poke's Peak, Colorotta. "His voice was like a hammer on the eardrums.

Before Loser clapped his hands to his ears, he made sure that the switchblade was closed. Loser found a few napkins in the glove box from Taco Bill's, and stuck them to his self-inflicted screwdriver head wound. He berated Donut in frustration. "You're a poking numbskull, Donut. For the brains of this outfit, you leave a lot to be desired. You know who will play you in the big screen version of our crime, Donut? Probably Lem Kerry, or that other poking idiot, Harley Skeen."

"Oh yeah?" Donut said. "Well then I guess that Pee Pec Garmon could be you." Donut said it weakly, as if he wanted to insult Loser, but without hurting his feelings.

Melanie was sick of the bullscat. She said, "I hope you enjoyed your big scene, because this movie is going to end badly and it's going to end soon."

Loser replied, "It ends when the credits roll, Baby." Wow! He impressed himself with that line. Like something from Stakespeare. Loser remembered that playwright's name, from an English teacher he once had. She tried to tell him about a play called, 'Queerio and Julian'; a tragic love story of a gay mobster from Sicily and his tranny cousin from Pairuss, who is imprisoned in the Basteelle. He never understood it, and preferred, 'Lady Chatternot's Lover'.

Loser had sort of identified with Queerio though, because he was a loser too. Lou Snert had always complained and maintained that he grew up a victim of society, and now he had turned the tables. It was his turn to make a victim out of society. There was nothing personal to it. Simple payback is all, a bit of retribution.

Lou Snert was born in Hurlon, Kentucker, into an extended family of jolly incest. The Snerts made up most of the Hurlon community, which was best known for its fabulous KKK picnics. Lou could recall the evening campfires with crosses, and the bomb-making, arts and crafts classes at Biblo Study.

The Kruel Kuks Klub thrived as a popular community of like-minded gentlemen, who enhanced civic pride, by ridding the county of various pests. This iconic clan of country lords, quiet arsonists and patrician terrorists, had originally formed in response to losing the Uncivil War. The motto of the KKK; 'It ain't over until we win', struck many however, as evidence of bad sportsmanship. No one wanted to play with them, so they played with themselves.

Little Lou began his adventurous career in crime, as a dedicated panty thief. He would stroll into the ladies underwear section of a store, and lift panties from their shelves. By the time he reached adolescence, the teenaged Lou had elevated his game, and was lifting panties from the elevated legs of his classmates. It was during a boring lecture, on the great General Napolean Fallaparte, when Lou fell in his own Otterloo.

He was on his knees at the time, under a girl's desk. Her jeans and a pair of panties were being passed around the class by frivolous classmates. The girl panted and gasped audibly, but the instructor Miss Kneedy, continued to drone on and on, oblivious to her surroundings, utterly lost in her own world of names and dates.

Lou's downfall came, when the girl did. Her screams of ecstasy were heard two classrooms away, and curious students filed in to see the cause of the commotion. They found a flipped over desk, where a bare-legged girl wearing a huge smile, was cuddling a backpack. The teacher was yelling and screaming one question, "How did you do that? How did you do that?" Then she demanded, "Show me!"

Lou's papa was secretly proud of his expelled son, but he entered the brat into an all-boys military institute in Muddlesboro, Kentucker. Lou knew that this move was a waste of time and his dad's money. By the age of sixteen, he was already stupid enough to graduate anyway, he figured. He didn't need two more years of dumbing down; he was there early, like a prodigy.

Lou dropped out of school, and opted for an apprenticeship in street crime, after the military failed him. He joined the Career Criminals Union, as a dues paying member. Lou Snert took the street name Loser, and raised his crime game to include such nefarious activities as cattle mutilations, bicycle thefts, urinating in public and not paying his parking tickets. Lou met Buster Monk in a Destroyt city jail cell. He'd been arrested for fishing in a family's backyard Koi pond, using a crossbow.

Loser hated and feared blacks. Buster Monk changed all that. Once Monk made Lou's intimate acquaintance in jail, Loser grew to appreciate certain advantages of the race. Crime, sex and mutual distrust, led them to meet again, after their release from jail the next afternoon. Their relationship reminded Loser of his parent's marriage, which had lasted twenty-seven years, and was only marred on those frequent occasions, when Ma chased Pa around, chopping at him with an axe. Buster Monk was the head of the Ohaha BEWB chapter, and had planned this kidnapping, but had called off with a toothache at the last minute.

Melanie couldn't understand why the police hadn't stopped them yet, but she had a strong feeling that she knew who might not want them stopped—the Department of Defence and Offense. DODO had the two aliens in its grasp, and lost them. They wanted to retain ownership.

And why would DODO want to find the TDS location, and risk her life to do so? The answer hit her hard. Immortality! The idea of immortal soldiers to fight in future wars must be irresistible, and well worth whatever she endured. "Like Hades," she said under her breath. She wasn't playing. Melanie wished and hoped and prayed that her father and the second alien would combine and come for her and Jeemis.

Melanie was driving westbound on I-800. Rain continued to beat down, in fast, fat drops. Traffic was sluggish and unpredictable. Melanie understood that drivers freaked out with every rainfall, as if seeing a new and frightening phenomenon of nature for the first time, and she made allowances. OTR truck drivers were different though, and they sped past her in the left lane, creating waves of water that one could surf upon. These professional big rig drivers always accelerated as the weather declined, attaining record speeds during the most intense of whiteout blizzards.

Loser switched on the satellite radio, and tuned in to his favourite country gangsta rap music station. Melanie hated the nasty noise, but it was the latest pop music fad. Loser tried to sing along with the song that was playing, in a thick nasal monotone that made Melanie want to blow her nose. Loser turned the volume up higher, to help cover his accompaniment to the famous drawling, soprano voice of the Cowboy of Colour, Lil Papa Hoppa-long Cassidy Nelson. It was his big hit, 'Mama Don't Let Your Cowboys Grow Up To Be Gangstas'. It was from his platinum CD, 'Ho Is in Horse, Hooker, and Horny'.

17

Melanie endured the instant acid reflux that sprung up, when Loser rapped along with Papa Hoppa. Background music, such as it was included electronic percussion, and what sounded like a rabbit jumping up and down on a steel guitar, while a raccoon played with a broken record on a turntable.

The lyrics to the hit song were enough to make your mama puke. Loser sang along. "Mama don't let your cowboys grow up to be gangstas, rustling up hos and jacking pickups. Mama don't let your cowboys grow up to be gangstas. They'll chug malt liquor and do train robbery stick-ups. They'll beat on their women, steal your money and drugs, and they'll take all your bullets and have gunfights with thugs."

Melanie switched off the radio. She couldn't bear such idiocy at such a stressful time. Yesterday morning at the secret inquiry, she'd heard enough stupidity to cause her nightmares. Now, she needed to concentrate on the traffic and the wet road conditions. Her thoughts drifted however; she wondered which one of the four men on the panel with her, had leaked?

Chapter 2

"If stupidity was a game show, this is what it would look like," Melanie thought.

"Please take your seats, this secret committee to investigate the alleged existence of alleged aliens will commence in sixty seconds; allegedly," said Chairman Aaron Chip. The recording engineer Draco gave Aaron a thumbs up sign.

"This is a clusterpoke," Melanie decided. She sat down in her assigned place on a cheap, foldout chair. Melanie didn't swear out loud in public, but no one could hear her thoughts. She hoped. She looked at the four men serving on this panel of inquiry with her, and wished she could tuck her tail and run. They looked like geriatric judges for a television talent show. The two try-outs faced their judges from six feet away.

Melanie was science advisor to President Crumm, but the four men consisted of two career politicians, one lifetime bureaucrat and an ancient academic. It seemed an unlikely bunch for this particular inquiry into the alleged existence of alleged aliens.

The four men were anxious, and they fidgeted in their assigned seats, tapping pencils, toes, teeth and microphones as they waited for the opening gavel. Melanie was simply amused at the proceedings. Each of them sat a small card table, and the five tables adjoined the other in a straight row; to look professional she supposed. They held court in a disused viewing theatre, two storeys underground, on the Onnitt Air Power Base in Ohaha, Nobraska.

The five interrogators faced off against the two alleged aliens, who looked like normal, albeit, very tall men. They sat on the hot seats, ready to be grilled, sans lawyers. One bare table, with a single microphone was provided for them, plus two bottles of tepid water.

Posturing at the centre table of five grillers was the reigning chairman of this committee, Califoreignya congressman of the Demolist political party, Aaron Chip. He was a needle-necked, goggle-eyed goose, known familiarly as the

Prince of Prevarication. Congressman Chip always insisted that he was important, and made continuous efforts to demonstrate it.

Sitting to Chip's immediate left, was Brenny Comeon. His head reminded Melanie of a cauliflower, with a face drawn with crayons, by a kid with both eyes closed. Brenny was the current Adjunct Assistant Associate Administrative Deputy Secretary of F.I.B.B.; the Federal Investigative Bureau of Bureaucracy.

Next to Brenny, the shapeless form of Professor Felix Polyplastis dwelt. He overflowed his chair. Professor Polyplastis was seated at the far left of the proceedings. He taught Modern Cultural and Social Anthropology, at the University of Califoreignya, Berzerkley. Felix resembled a duffle bag full of cats, with ears on top. Several stiff grey hairs, hung down like icicles, from an area where his chin should have been located, and his bottom lip seemed to merge with his tire-stack neck. He drooled.

To Chairman Chip's right, sat the eminently execrable senator from New Yank; Huck Choomor. The spectacles on his face, balanced precariously on the bottom of his long sloping snout, defying the laws of physics. Observers often speculated on these anti-gravity eyeglasses, and how Huck secured them to his face. Conspiracy theorists offered a variety of explanations, including one that said he was a magnetic cyborg from Shyna, wearing iron glasses. Another popular idea suggested that the spectacles were actually a parasite that fed on his brain. Melanie thought that explanation most believable.

Melanie Gryzloski sat next to Senator Choomor. She was the thirty-nine-year-old presidential science advisor. She'd earned a doctorate in evolutionary biology and a master's degree in zoology from Horvord. She'd written four books on those two subjects since then. The blond-haired, green-eyed beauty was recognisable to many Shamericans, due to her several appearances at press conferences with President Crumm. She was single, and always had been, by choice. Her career was her passion.

This secret inquiry would be recorded for posterity. Three audio and video technicians, who'd all signed No Leak Agreements, stood ready behind the alleged aliens, and the director for this production was Draco. He announced, "Ten seconds! Nine, eight, seven…" Chairman Chip took up his gavel, clenched his teeth and popped his eyes out, so as to express the gravitas of this situation. He tried counting backwards with Draco in his head, but lost his way at number four.

"You're on!" Draco announced.

Chairman Aaron Chip banged down his $2.99 gavel onto the tabletop three times, and in a voice that made one imagine a gargling rooster, he squawked, "Thank you all for your rapid responses, and appearances here today, to this hastily called emergency investigation with serious national security implications. Our mission here today, is to determine the alleged existence, of the two visitors who face us."

The visitors thus referred to scowled, allegedly indicating their displeasure at these proceedings. They were as sceptical as Melanie that anything useful could come out of this investigation.

Aaron Chip continued expostulating. He said, "May I remind you all, that today is mostly a get acquainted session. Each of the five members of this secret inquiry, will be allowed to ask three questions only this morning, with the understanding that tomorrow, Friday morning, we will have sixty minutes each for follow up. Remember, only three questions!"

Aaron licked his thin lips and scratched an ear, as he surveyed his fellow committee members on either side. He cautioned them, "Keep in mind that we have all signed an NLA, and that what we learn here today is to remain a secret." Chip's head bobbled about on his skinny neck, like a balloon on a stick in a windstorm.

"First, prior to our inquiry," Chip said, "we will watch this curious video, which first brought the two oddities before us to the attention of the entire world."

The two oddities in question went by the names Robulus and Jeemis. When standing, they measured more than seven feet tall, and looked dry and lanky like thin strips of jerky. Robulus wore short, black curly hair atop his narrow head, while his companion Jeemis, had a head topped with long brown locks. Their skin was as pale as egg shells, but had a granular texture, like fine sandpaper. They wore black coveralls and size 22 shoes.

The studio techs brought up the video requested by Chairman Chip on a large TV screen, which was situated laterally, so that all could watch the action. The usual jumpy, jittery selfone video was recorded two days ago, inside of a Max Beefburger fast food restaurant in Ohaha, Nobraska, and eleven miles north of the Onnitt Air Power Base. The incident occurred during the restaurant's busy lunch hour, and the action began with a noisy crowd of hungry people waiting in lines, ordering food at the service counter.

A large, hairy man entered the picture, wearing white hot pants and halter top. Suddenly, he reached down into one of his matching white knee-high boots, drew out an automatic pistol, and began to shoot indiscriminately into the crowd.

Two tall, pale men in black coveralls ran directly towards the mad shooter, absorbing bullet after bullet. Flesh and blood formed a pink mist in the air around them. The men were unfazed, and moved steadily forward until they reached the shooter. The pair disarmed the maniac, and secured him to a commode, with his white belt wrapped around the nape of his neck, pressing his face into the toilet bowl. They vanished before police arrived.

According to witnesses, although the clothing of these two heroes was wet with blood from obvious bullet entry and exit wounds, they never faltered. Police investigators later found eleven flattened, distorted bullets on the floor of the burger joint. The shooter said he was dealing with menopause, and was just letting off steam. Two of his victims died, and four were wounded. He complained that the two tall guys had messed up his mascara.

This video was first posted on Spewtube, and soon found its way onto Phasebook, Tooter and even Soonagram. It went mega-spiral, with over 10 million views in the first twenty-four hours. Thus, the two heroes were easy to spot, recognise, and report to authorities, which is what happened the next day.

The two tall, bulletproof men operated a booth at the Ohaha Convention centre, where an exhibition showcasing drone technology was taking place. Throngs of admirers and curious people surrounded the booth, where these two hero celebrities, described the many amazing drones they'd designed and built. Robulus and Jeemis were picked up at the exhibition within hours, and detained by the Department of Defence and Offense, better known as DODO. Three armed military police officers, from the nearby Onnitt APB, took custody of them, moments before the FIBB, and the Department of National Surveillance arrived with the same objective in mind. The unattended booth of the popular, admired heroes was stripped bare of drones and controllers within minutes of their absence.

As expected, the Make-Believe Media journalists, as they were popularly known, had reported on, and analysed the shooting video non-stop, in the two days since it occurred. For example, an editorial in the newspaper of the nation The New Yank Times, opined that the entire episode was a bad public relations stunt for Max's Beefburger, and speculated that President Crumm owned the parent company.

The editor of The Swampington Post wondered if the dynamic duo in the video were enforcers for a secret government drug cartel. The writer also made the strange claim, that the two men were wearing armour, and using fake blood. Lastly, the same genius said, that he could prove that the shooter was a whistle-blower who could damage President Crumm.

The twenty-four-hour news networks like CON and MNBS, made a hash smoothie out of the video. It's as if they put all of their craziest ideas into a blender, and selected puree. Then they served it up to folks without taste, who claimed to like the flavour. The Conscience of News network for instance, downplayed the video as nothing more than a poorly produced trailer, for a made-for-TV-movie about gun violence in the fast-food industry, while on the Mainly Non-Biased Stuff news network, one reporter said it was related to Rushin election interference. He gave no details.

The closest that any of the national media came to the actual truth of the matter, was found on one of the celebrity tabloids seen at supermarket checkout lanes. The Globe Weekly Inquirer blared out three separate stories on its colourful front page the morning after the shooting. What first caught the eye, was a file photo of celebrity actor Don Crews, with the bold caption; 'Don's Lifelong Acting Coach Discovered to Be a Mannequin'. The second story to draw a second glance, showed an ancient picture of singer Elvin Parsley, with the caption, 'The Duke's Face Seen in Sunspot'. Finally, at the bottom of the front page under a picture of the great, iconic golden globes of Max Beefburgers, one could read, 'Immortal Aliens Stop Slaughterfest in Ohaha! Page 11'.

Of course the Inquirer was more trusted than most of the major news organisations, but that didn't amount to much. Nobody believed the dreck that passed for gourmet journalism anymore; not even the journalists. The MBM had gotten lazy, and their on-air talent simply served up reheated, leftover meatloaf, night after night, knowing that most people will swallow anything if it's easy to chew.

The shooter video ended, when the selfone videographer was stampeded by the panicked lunch crowd. Some of the terrified customers, wanted their food first, and vaulted over the counter to grab it, before fleeing out the back door.

"Lights up!" Chairman Chip clapped his dainty hands, which hadn't seen a day's work since he changed a flat tire on his bicycle back in the eighties. "Damn, I am good at this chairman thing," he thought. "I am a born leader." A born liar was more appropriate, according to his friend and family.

The hot overhead lights, which were dimmed during the video, were returned to their former blinding whiteness. Chairman Chip stared with hostility at the two visitors, and his eyeballs protruded like a road-killed frog's. 'So!" he cawed loudly, pointing a finger at the alleged aliens. "This proves it! You identify as superheroes!

"We saw chunks of flesh fly from your bodies," he ranted. "Yet you sit here before us now, unharmed. This is un-Shamerican, and I for one, will not stand for it!" Aaron chirped. "Now," he continued, "follow my logic." Aaron Chip glanced to both sides, to see whether his colleagues on this secret panel were paying attention, or awake at least. Satisfied, he said, "Number one; you are immortal. Number two; immortals are not human. Conclusion: you guys ain't human!"

Chairman Chip smacked his lips together in appreciation for his acumen, and he said, "Therefore you support President Crumm! Am I right?" he asked.

When Robulus replied, it was in that deep bass voice so beloved of TV advertisers, but was twenty-five decibels louder. Its powerful, seismic rumble caused the audio technician to rip his headset off and shout in pain. In answer to Chip, Robulus asked the chairman, "Is that your first question?"

Chairman Chip's neck elongated like a night crawler, and his eyeballs extended from their sockets like a crab's, anger coloured his face purple, and altogether he resembled a mouldy eggplant. "No, it is not!" he squawked. "This is my first question: have you, or any of your associates, ever been associated with President Crumm, or anyone associated with him or his associates?" Yellow foam oozed from his lips, like pus from a wound.

Jeemis replied this time, in a voice just as ear-shatteringly loud as that of Robulus, but in a shrill tone, like a million fingernails on a blackboard. Answering in a screech capable of breaking mirrors, the alleged alien replied, "No."

Chairman Chip, and the other three males on the panel of inquiry, looked as if they'd swallowed a dumpster. They were stunned! It was disrespectful, despicable behaviour! It was uncalled for! Perhaps the two were real aliens after all.

Melanie smiled at Jeemis' reply, and she was tickled by the shocked response it evoked from the others. Utter silence reigned for several seconds, while Chip regained speech function. He finally recovered enough, to pound his gavel down onto the card table, again and again. He was nearly apoplectic when he yelled, "You are out of order, Sir!"

His sour face expressed his disdain for these two weirdos, and their unacceptable behaviour. He said gravely, his face dark, "I have been in politics for twenty-eight years, and I have never, not once ever, heard someone answer a simple yes-or-no question, with a simple yes-or-no answer!

"It's unheard of. It's just not done!" he declared angrily. "Now, let us continue", he said softly, "If we may." Aaron forgave them this once, but he cautioned them." Please try to answer all questions fully and completely in the future," he implored.

Aaron posed his next zinger, he said, "Answer this: How many of you alleged beings, are here on Gaia, or in its immediate vicinity?"

Robulus looked at Jeemis, and Jeemis looked back. They each pointed at themselves and said, "One," then at each other, and counted, "Two." The power of their combined voices, bought some pieces of plaster raining down from the ceiling, and a lightbulb popped too.

After the shockwave had passed, Chip angrily retorted, "I cautioned you about the need to provide complete, over-explained, irrelevant answers! If this shameful, one word answer behaviour continues, I will suspend these proceedings until cooperation can be obtained!"

Anger contorted Aaron's face, so that his eyes filled with blood, and looked ready to burst. He barked, and Melanie thought for a second that someone had stepped on a dog. Spit flew from his lips, "Do I make myself clear?" he asked.

"Is that your third question?" Jeemis screeched.

Aaron's body went rigid, as if turned to stone. One eye took a timeout, and went out back for a smoke until it could calm down. An exorcist would have fled from him in terror. His face turned from purple to bright red, which matched his tie nicely. Melanie was at pains to keep from breaking out in laughter, and she covered her mouth with a delicate hand, and turned her face away.

Draco and the audio video engineers were younger and less able to restrain themselves. Draco clutched his belly in laughter, tears streamed down his eyes, and he courted injury to his ribs.

Aaron ignored the help; he couldn't acknowledge such little people. He resumed his professional, chairman-like persona, and said, "This is my third question: "Who is funding your invasion? And, answer properly!"

Robulus replied, his enormous voice a force of nature, "This question makes illogical assumptions and therefore it is one that cannot be answered properly. You have wasted your third question too."

"Obstruction!" Chip choked out. "This is outrageous!" He beat down his cheap little gavel as if driving nails, until the head broke off and bounced up into the air. It flew in a pretty parabolic arc and crashed to the floor several yards away.

Melanie could contain herself no longer, and she burst into jolly laughter. Four grave, surly male faces turned her way, and tried to make her vanish by force of will. She'd been called in on this secret panel, less than twenty-four hours earlier as a substitute for Demolist Califoreignya congresswoman Fanny Neurosi. Fanny had a hair appointment that was more important.

Melanie had flown in from Dunfor, Colorotta on last night's red-eye. She'd been accompanied by her father, who was interested in attending the drone exhibition in town. Melanie knew that this committee was a secret, but she didn't realise until much later, that it was a secret from her boss the president too. Melanie would not have participated had she known.

Aaron Chip did not want to accept that he had to abide by his rules, but he reeled in his eyeballs anyway, and gave in for now. Tomorrow he would bury these two upstarts! He tapped the stick handle of his broken gavel down and said, "Very well, but tomorrow is a new day." That seemed profound, he thought, so he added, "So, be on your toes, if you have any."

Chairman Chip looked to his left, and said to the AAAADS of the FIBB, "Mr Comeon, the table is yours."

Brenny Comeon said, "No thanks, I've got nicer ones at home." With bloodshot eyes, he looked out over the tall heaps of dark bags piled up beneath them. The lines creasing his ancient face created the illusion of geologic layers, tinted, textured and eroded by time. In a buzzing whine, and sounding like a Shynese motorcycle stuck in second gear, he addressed the alleged aliens, "Good morning and welcome to my world. These are serious issues we face, and our national security, perhaps our very existence, depends on your answers to my three questions. Please treat them with the appropriate respect. Thank You."

He swept a hand, through the last lonely strands of hair residing over his left ear, and spoke again, "My first question is this: What is your purpose in our country?"

Jeemis replied, his voice piercing skulls, "We live here and operate several businesses."

Brenny looked up from his notes, a crack opened up between geologic ages, and words came forth from between the layers, "You operate businesses in our great nation, but were not born here, and are probably illegal aliens." He shook his head, without causing a facequake, and said, "And you probably pay no taxes; right?"

"Yes, we do," Robulus thundered. "Last question please."

Comeon and Chip came out of their chairs at that remark! They were appalled at the perverse, alien behaviour exhibited by their guests!" Chip slapped his gavel handle down hard, and pinched a finger between it and the table. He reacted by swinging his hand up to his face, to stick his sore finger into his mouth. He whacked his forehead with the gavel stick. It was audible, a perfect cowbell sound.

Aaron pretended that he meant to do that, and tried not to wince in pain. He said, venomously, with a hiss, "I am in charge here, and I will decide whether a question is a question or not a question." Aaron Chip looked over at Brenny Comeon again. He suddenly recalled a time, fourteen years ago this very month of Septober, when that smarmy cat turd had remarked on a tie that Aaron was wearing. Comeon had joked that Chip's pink paisley necktie, looked like, "…dog vomit on a tongue".

Ha! He would show that son of a sow! Chip lightly tapped his stick on the table and said, "I judge in favour of the alleged aliens. You have one question remaining."

Brenny farted in irritation, and said, "Fine! Last question." He looked down at his notes again to see what it was. "Oh yeah," he lifted up his large, heavy head and asked, "What is your SIGN?" Although it was a stupid, throwaway question, Comeon acted as if he'd go down in history with such famous Greke philosophers as Playdo and Socitoomies. He licked his fingers, and preened his bristle brush eyebrows.

Robulus' stentorian voice erupted with a geyser of sound, "Of course! According to the United States of Shamerica's Department of Categorisation, federal law MT6660, section fourteen thousand eight hundred and two, paragraph nine hundred and forty-six, we are required to be registered, and to carry our Special Interest Group Name identity card at all times. You have copies of all such documents of ours on the table in front of you. Perhaps you can read there, that we are registered as LIARS; Legal Illegal Alien Resident Squatters. I hope that this satisfies your requirement for a fully and completely irrelevant answer. Thank you. Next human please."

After the echoes of his answer faded away, Brenny raised those tired eyes up from the depths, as if fossils from an ancient limestone cave. He said, "Tomorrow you will face the fire, and I will have all the matches. I warn you to dress in asbestos."

Chairman Chip announced for the record, "The esteemed professor of important stuff at Berzerkley, Felix Polyplastics will ask the next three questions."

"It's not plastics! Polyplastis!" The professor harrumphed several times, and readjusted himself. The chair that his amorphous form occupied was invisible. His body folded around it like a hungry amoeba that was eating lunch. With a line of mustard and a few onions on them, his fingers could have passed for hot dogs. He opened a thick folder on the table, and pulled a half ream of paper from it. On the first page was his handwritten list of questions, but the rest was blank filler material to advertise his stature as a famous academician.

The iconic Professor Felix Polyplastis was a fixture at Berzerkley. He taught subjects that were found nowhere else on the planet. He was a maverick, who offered studies in progressive courses like, 'Social Injustice as a Consequence of Climate Change,' and, 'Making the Best of Being an Idiot,' and 'Diversity and Superheroes', among others.

"Welcome to Gaia, and good morning to one and all," Felix said. His voice sounded like a rasp against steel, as if his larynx was trying to escape from the prison bars of his throat. "My three questions are important, intelligent and interesting. Please answer them honestly and completely." Whenever he spoke, Felix's head wobbled, as if on a spring. His hair resembled sheep's wool, and his barber actually saved the clippings to make blankets.

Professor Polyplastis picked up a handful of paper sheets from his stack, and shook them out importantly. He held the pages up to his face, and read his first question. "My initial focus of serious inquiry and pertinent question of vital importance is this; are your genitals congruent with those of humans in any of its many genders?"

Robulus and Jeemis had expected stupid questions from stupid people. Most humans couldn't help being stupid, it was beyond their control. They scanned the five faces of the humans in front of them. On four visages, they found the same inane placidity common to napping sheep. The fifth face belonged to Melanie, and they expected three intelligent questions from her at least, during the course of this farcical investigation. They had much that they wished to reveal. Perhaps tomorrow would prove more productive.

Jeemis piped up to answer the professor, "No."

Felix gasped, Brenny howled and Aaron smacked his stick on the table, over and over, as if punishing the table for some unforgivable sin. "Order! Order," he crowed. "This is your final warning," he said, "I want no more, one-word answers. Period!"

Polyplastis pulled at his colourful tie, which looked tiny upon his bulky torso, and seemed as ludicrous as a peacock feather on a hillside. He wrinkled his scruffy eyebrows, and resumed his questioning. "Try this; on your home planet, how much does the top one percent pay in taxes?" he asked. "Relatively speaking," he added lamely.

Jeemis shook his head and Robulus head-butted the tabletop in frustration. Jeemis answered with a blast of sound. "These are neither serious nor important questions. They're idiotic," he replied. He added, "I am beginning to think that the endemic stupidity virus on Gaia has become more virulent in its latest mutation."

Robulus boomed, "There were no taxes levied on our native planet, when we departed from there sixty-five million Gaian years ago." He answered more than was asked, but he knew that it would pass by unnoticed, like facts to a journalist.

"Final question;" Felix said, "how many races in your race of beings?"

If this race of beings had been capable of crying, tears of pity would have dripped from their dark eyes. Jeemis replied, his voice like a shriek of pain, "One, same as humans!" He added, "Professor, my ass!"

Aaron played a short, one-handed drum solo on the card table with his chairman stick. These stupid aliens were turning this entire investigation into a monumental clusterpoke. Less than usual was being learned! The needle-necked chairman looked to his right side now, at the decrepit Huck Choomor, who sat with pursed lips, as if humming to himself. Chip introduced him to the aliens, in case they didn't know. "New Yank State Senator Huck Choomor will ask the next three questions," Aaron announced.

One could not have straightened out the scowling, terminally-downturned mouth of Huck Choomor, with a team of horses pulling at the corners of his lips. He still looked as pissed off today as he did sixteen years ago, when his favourite housekeeper tested positive for pregnant. The last time he was reported to have smiled, he denied it, saying it was only gas.

Huck's lips parted, and the voice of a cigar smoking seal barked out from between them. He read from his notes, holding them at arm's length as he tried to focus on the letters, "Do you support a woman's right to be right? Do women earn as much as men in your job? And, would you vote for a woman president?"

Huck slapped his notes down onto the tabletop, as an exclamation mark of sorts. Following this, a hushed silence, a purposeful absence of sound, made Huck glance down at his notepad. A red flush turned his head cherry-red, and he cried, "Wait! Those aren't my three questions! Those are my wife's! They're for her middle school math class!"

Robulus thundered, "No, no, and not applicable."

Huck's nose twisted as if trying to unscrew from his face. He moaned, "I object!"

Chairman Chip considered siding with the senator for a moment, but his stomach growled at the same time. Aaron realised that he'd gone without breakfast, because he'd run out of time. He'd stopped at the Dollar Fifty Store to buy a gavel, and he couldn't find anything there, except for the toy thing he had broken. He needed food now, so he ruled against Huck. It was nearly time end to this inquiry. He tapped his stick and said, "Next questioner please," without introducing Melanie Gryzloski. She wasn't one of them. She worked for President Crumm!

Melanie smiled. It was dazzling. "Good morning," she said. Her voice was syrup for the ears, and sent warm shivers down a man's spine. Her blonde hair and green eyes shone with sharp intelligence and she looked great in her blue jeans, a casual white blouse with green vest and white hiking shoes. Blue-green dolphin earrings dangled from dainty lobes.

Melanie was intrigued by the two alleged, immortal aliens. Oh, she didn't believe they were real for a second! It was ridiculous to think otherwise. They looked too much like humans to possibly be alien beings. This was the real world, not some Hollowood sci-fi movie. Melanie couldn't explain the shooting video, but she didn't plan to ask the men about that. Melanie wanted to hear their story. They'd made some incredible claims, and she wondered what this was really all about.

Robulus and Jeemis turned their dark, beady eyes in her direction, and returned her greetings, which shook the walls with the powerful volume. They smiled as well, certain that finally, they would field some good questions. Melanie asked them;" What more can you tell this august panel about the virus you mentioned; the stupid one?" Her sarcasm went unnoticed by the four other committee members.

Robulus boomed, "This sounds as if it should be a follow up question, but we are prepared to answer of course." Jeemis nodded his long narrow head in agreement. Robulus explained, "Nineteen years ago, a laboratory in Huwan, Shyna was experimenting with viruses, and they created a hybrid monster germ. Sloppy lab practices led to cross contamination between the common cold virus and two other viruses they'd been studying.

"Combine these reckless techniques with poor security, and several lab workers soon caught colds. No one worried about it, because they caught colds every year, so thought nothing of it. This virus could do something else however, something nearly unheard of. It found a way to pass through the blood brain barrier, by inactivating the protective cells and bacteria in place to prevent such an invasion of the skull. Once inside the brain, this virus clogged up neural pathways, and impeded new synapse production."

Robulus continued uninterrupted and said, "The infected lab workers slowly, gradually, became stupider and stupider. Their average IQ dropped by more than twenty points over a period of a few months. They never noticed. They'd become too stupid to realise that they'd become stupid.

"The stupidity virus spread like wildfire around the world, a pandemic that everyone was too stupid to look for. Within three years, ninety-five percent of the world population had been exposed to this mutated cold virus, and, like the numerous cold viruses, one can catch them year after year after year."

Melanie was horrified by this tale, and her face showed it. Jeemis piped up shrilly, and said, "Bear in mind Melanie, that four-point eight percent of humans, have proven immune to the deleterious mental effects of the stupidity virus." She understood his meaning and took some comfort in that idea. Then she scanned the ovine faces of her fellow panel members, and wondered if what Robulus and Jeemis had said was perhaps true.

Melanie was unnerved, but moved on to her second question. She needed no notes. She pursed her full pink lips, and asked, "You mentioned something about being on Gaia for sixty-five million years; how can this be so?"

"That's a tricky manner of asking such a question, "Jeemis screeched. "I wonder if you ask how we happened to arrive here on Gaia, or how we can have lived so long. It's like asking two questions in one," He shrieked. He winked at the woman and grinned.

He said, "Our apparent immortality is a product of super advanced nano-technology, which we can explain in fuller detail tomorrow during follow up questions. As for our arrival here, I will tell you this much; we crash landed on Gaia, and triggered a massive catastrophic chain of events, that resulted in the final demise and ultimate extinction for your dinosaurs. Sorry about that."

Melanie didn't believe it. It was absolute nonsense! No being could live through crashing into Gaia at many thousands of miles per hour. No one could live for sixty-five million years. Of course, getting shot half a dozen times without suffering injury wasn't possible either.

Melanie asked her third and final question, "How can your story be verified or corroborated? This is astounding." She held her breath as she awaited the answer.

Robulus replied this time. He said, "Everything we have revealed, can be corroborated by a fantastic lifeform that we call the TDS."

Melanie's face asked the obvious follow up question, but Robulus merely offered up a scat eating grin. Jeemis, after an excruciating pause, said, "If all of cosmic knowledge was held in a tank, the TDS would be the tap. It's not far."

Silence, almost. Aaron's stomach growled angrily, but Jeemis shattered the quietude. He shrieked, "Th...th...that's all folks!"

Chapter 3

What Melanie didn't know was that twenty minute after the echoes of Jeemis's final shriek faded away, a man named Al Darkly hung up his office fone in slow motion. Al's thoughts sped towards destruction like a drunk driver on a ski jump. Somehow though, Al always landed on somebody else, and walked away unscathed. Darkly was well known in Hollowood as Pitch Al; a play on his last name combined with the pitch blackness of his heart. Pitch Al was like the mythical King Midals of the golden touch, everything he grasped made him richer. The five foot four and a half inch tall, fifty-seven-year-old, billionaire business tycoon was a model of corruption to lawyers everywhere. His resume was impressive, and included; talent agent to the stars, ownership of Papa Al's Pizza Parlours, and owner of Darkly Cinemas.

Darkly Cinemas owned and operated twenty-two movie theatre complexes, which boasted twenty-four screens each. The company even filmed, directed, and produced several popular movies of its own, such as the adult feature, 'Zombie Massage Parlour' and the horror flick, 'Gay Vampires Raid the Harem'. Pitch Al ruled his empire from his corporate headquarters building in Scaldsdale, Aridzonea. He was registered under the SIGN of BEER; Billionaire Egotistical Entitled Rich.

Highly sensitive about his short stature, Al liked to do things bigly. Currently he sat on a large throne, at a desk he could have parked his Jagwire on, in an office of gymnasium proportions, minus the bleachers. Al could see the city of Scaldsdale, fifty-two floors below his penthouse suite, through the window walls which wrapped around his office.

Al pressed a button on his business fone to summon his secretary, who worked in a closet converted to office. His secretary, prompt as always, appeared at his desk. "What's up boss?" Torkel Berndt asked. Al's secretary stood six feet, four inches tall and weighed a muscular two hundred and forty pounds. He wore his long, greasy black hair in a ponytail, and a long heavy beard draped from his face. Tattoos covered his bare arms up to the shoulders, where the torn off sleeves of a jean jacket began. Below the waist he wore a pair of ragged denim jeans and two dirty boots on his feet. He didn't like the name Torkel, and preferred that people called him Torchy.

"Hey, Torchy," Al said, to regain his secretary's attention. Then he said "Did you happen to overhear any of that fone call? That was Professor Polyplastis on the line. He owed me a favour named Roxie, so he told me about a top secret inquiry that he participated in this morning, on the air power base out in Ohaha, Nobraska." Al's voice squeezed out from between tight teeth, because he clenched an unlit ninety-nine cent cigar between them while trying to speak. His flat skinny lips formed a perpetual fake smile, like a used car salesman's, perfected and frozen in place after decades of rigorous practice.

Torchy leaned against Al's dance floor-sized desk, and casually replied in a voice, that rose up from deep inside his beer barrel chest, "No Chief; you know that I never listen in to your fone calls. But what was all that talk about immortality, and that TDS thing?" He slurred like a tired drunk, after decades of rigorous practice.

Pitch Al brayed like a jackass, catching the unlit cigar as it fell from his open mouth. "You're funny Torchy, real funny," he said. Al's throne and desk, sat up on a platform, raised eight inches above the rest of the office floor, so that he could always look down on others. He surveyed his office kingdom, with its putting green, swimming pool, tennis court, sauna and unused, dusty gym.

Al Darkly was a Shamerican success story. He had triumphantly tumbled, a long, long way downhill, from his honest beginnings as a new-born baby, and he was very proud of that fact. Al had grown up as an only child, in an unstable gypsy life of constant road trips, and short stops, in town after nameless town. After a while, every demn town looked the same. His petite mother, Moochkins; Gawd bless her cell, managed heavyweight boxers for a living; names like No-Nads Norman Falls, who wore his boxing short's waist so high up on his torso, that any blow below the chin was a low blow, plus Buttercup Bronson and Waldo Pigeon-Toes Atchoo. After every introduction of Waldo, half the crowd would yell gesundheit.

Al's father Corgi was a diminutive tyrant, who designed and sewed costumes for Dizzyworld characters, like Ricky Rodent, Sinnerella and Sleeping Booty. Corgi didn't believe in education and said it was a scam, so he sent Al off to public schools instead. But the small family of small people, never stayed in one town for very long. The townspeople wouldn't tolerate it.

The Darkly family lived out of a Hoaxwagon van, adorned with peace symbols and flowers, interspersed with images of boxers getting their bloody heads bashed in. Young Al was a genius of sorts. He turned con games and scams into an art form. He learned early, after a couple of serious beatings, that the best scams paid off just moments before one had to leave town. Al's schemes grew in style and complexity, as he gained painful experience.

By Al's fifteenth birthday, both of his parents were behind bars, and they weren't serving drinks. They were both serving life sentences in Fedup Penitentiary in Califoreignya, for second degree murder convictions. They were found guilty of killing a boxer who refused to flop, on a heavily wagered bout. Moochkins seduced their prospective victim first, after getting him drunk. Her husband Corgi first watched the seduction, then sewed the drunken boxer into a Trannie Mouse costume, and threw him off a bridge. Unfortunately, he chose the bridge overlooking the police department in town, and the body landed on Sgt Rook, nearly crippling him.

Young Al Darkly was sent to a reform school outside of Nowins, Lousyanna, but he was expelled the following year for blackmailing the school principal. Al had stolen some compromising photos from his married English teacher, after she had fallen asleep in the principal's office, following a nooner. Apparently, she was cheating on Al with the principal, and now he had the pictures to prove it.

Al was both smart and cunning however, and after he applied at law school as a minority of Shamerican Indian descent, he was accepted. He graduated, passed the bar exam, and began grabbing up as much money, power and influence as possible. Through various intrigues, Al gained enough damaging information on the judges who he appeared before, that he began to win case after case in court. In fact, Pitch Al holds the record, for getting criminals he defended; back out onto the streets to prey again. That fact appeared in his resume.

What Al wanted now was immortality. He'd seen the shooting video. It was incredible! Imagine living through a shootout! The possibility opened up all kinds of criminal doors. Dying was bullscat; there wasn't any future in it. He did not want to die with so much left undone. There were so many people to con, so much money to be made. Pitch Al was a wizard at predicting trends and capitalising on them, and he figured that immortality would sell well too, if he could obtain it first and get it patented.

Al Darkly could honestly boast of his market prescience, and in fact, boasting was the only honest thing he ever did. Pitch Al founded the 'hate market' in the early years of the century. He capitalised on the divisiveness created by the Make-Believe Media and the Demolist party, and made millions of dollars with such mail-order gifts as Scat on a Shingle, which was dog crap on cedar roofing, and was sold as a Mother's Day gift. For Valentiny's Day and wedding anniversaries, he made millions, selling long stem Rushin thistle by the dozen, with a plastic vase shaped like a toilet.

Al had so many more ideas, but he needed so many more years to implement them. Immortality would give him power as well as longevity. If this TDS thing could give him the formula, then he needed to buy it or steal it. With immortality, all things were possible, especially if he owned the rights.

The fetid miasma of a slimy plan began to bubble up to the murky surface of the stew cooking in the cauldron of his skull. His fake smile morphed into a sardonic grin, his teeth clenched his smokeless cigar, his lips parted wide.

"Oh Burnie!" Al shouted for his secretary. Burnie was his pet-name for Torchy; a familiarity he used, when he wanted a special favour that he wasn't going to return. Torchy exited the porn site on his selfone, stuck his head out of the closet office he worked from, and answered, "Yeah Boss?" Al required the titles of Boss, Chief, Sir or Czar.

"Burnie," he said, removing the cigar from his teeth, "I want to call in the BEWBs. There's a branch in Ohaha. I know them, because I used their services once. They slashed some tires for me on an ex's car. Get them on the fone for me."

Torchy stared at his little big man employer in surprise, and growled, "Those idiots couldn't steal their own piggy banks without screwing it up, Boss." Torchy spoke up when he disagreed with Chief Al. Al appreciated that. He enjoyed the exchange of diverse opinions.

"Just poking do it" he ordered.

The national HQ of the Basement Elite Without Breakfasts was located in the heart of Porchland, Oreogon. The BEWBs were founded in the late nineties, by the professional, mercenary protester Polly Graf, as a protest-for-profit organisation. Their oath, as recorded in their request for a federal grant, went like this: "I, as a sovereign ruler of the basement I dwell in, do hereby swear, from this time forward, to eschew the most important meal of the day, to observe a morning hunger strike, so as to demonstrate the seriousness of our cause, whatever it may be this week, and I pledge to protest and to support protests, depending on what pops up, so help me, Mom." Mostly, they skipped breakfast, because it was too early in their day.

It was a tough code to live by, but the BEWBs grew in size, and the union of protesters even had a hotline now, at 1-800-LUV-BEWB. The enterprise was organised into regional chapters and local branches, and had expanded into thirty-six states. The Ohaha branch was more like a twig, with only the four aforementioned members in it, but Ohaha didn't attract a lot of street criminals, when so many government jobs were available.

Torchy placed the call to the BEWB branch of Ohaha, Nobraska, from his office. The four members of the Ohaha BEWBs were slow to answer the tinkling selfone, for they were working hard at eradicating social injustices, in the large unfinished basement of their leader's mom. Answering the fone was Monk's job anyway!

Buster Monk aka Felonious Monk, was the boss of the outfit, because it met in his mother's basement. When their business fone rang, the four activists were racking up big scores, burning and looting, while playing their favourite video game, 'Unity'.

The other three BEWBs were, in order of no importance: sergeant at arms, Lou Snert aka Loser, a white refugee from Destroyt, Mushagain; Ido Notno aka Donut, from the eastern Yourapeein country of Khookistan, who was schemer in chief; and finally, the fourth member of the band, enforcer and party girl Vometta Wilde, aka VW the Love Bug, or alternately the Sperm Whale. Monk paused the video game, and in his best Hollowood criminal voice, he answered the ringing fone, "Ohaha BEWBs, how can we hurt you?" Torchy transferred the call.

Al made all of the necessary arrangements with the BEWBs, and forced Monk and Donut to repeat the instructions back to him twice. Darkly now needed to raise funds for the payday that he'd promised the BEWBs. He had a patsy singled out too. Pitch Al picked up his office fone handset again and placed a call to the most innocent, gullible bankroll he knew.

Al's call was answered by the four-foot, eleven inch tall, tough-as-gristle, Kate Armstrong, who was chauffeur, bodyguard, secretary and masseuse to acting legend, Don Crews. "It's for you Mr Crews!" Kate hollered, like when her mama used to call in the pigs. Her high-pitched whining voice, echoed through the seventeen thousand square foot cottage, and finally reached the ears of her boss Don Crews.

Don was pleasantly engrossed in a bondage flick, on his one hundred twenty-inch plasma screen TV. He watched his pornography with the sound off, as he preferred to read the closed captioning. This was the sort of serious acting that he wished he could have broken into.

Don heard Kate yelling about the fone, so he paused the action, kicked off his high heels and took the call. He saw that it was from his long-time agent Al Darkly, and hoped that it was related to a new movie role.

"Hello, Don. How's my favourite actor?"

Even sheep can smell a wolf, and a frown pulled Don's lips down, when he caught the scent. "Whaddya want from me Al?" he sneered.

"Oh, don't act like that Don," Al scolded his client. "You know that I always have your best interests at heart. Look, I am offering you and only you, an honest chance at true immortality. Physical immortality Don! Your career could last forever!" Al insisted.

"What in Hades are you babbling about now Al?" Don asked, snuggling down into some of the twenty-four pillows on his sofa. "I was just getting to the golden showers scene, and I don't have time for these games. Get to the point Al."

"It's like this Don; listen closely. A pair of alien immortals can lead us to this TDS thingy and boom! We're immortal. Forever."

"Al, this plot is dumber than the last Mission Improbable sequel I did." Don knew that whatever Al was selling, it wasn't going to come cheap. "Bottom line; how much?" He began to whimper." You know that I lost money in that asteroid insurance scam."

"I am doing this for you Don. You know that all of my millions are offshore. Can't touch it. Immortality is so you, Dom! You gotta bankroll this. We need forty thousand."

"Okay Al, I'll do it, but only because I know that if I put up forty K today, you will pay fifty thousand back to me in thirty days," Don replied. "It's not because I believe a word you've said."

"That hurts, Don" Al retorted. "You know I don't con my clients anymore, not since I was sued for using a double of Joan Conda, in my X-rated monster movie Wadzilla Versus King Dong"

Don said, "I loved that film. That scene where the Joan Conda lookalike was having a threesome with Wadzilla and King Dong, was worthy of an Ashcan award."

Pitch Al smiled at how simple it was to manipulate the conversation with Crews. He was like cookie dough. He said, "Don, it's not an investment which includes a thirty-day cash return. You are buying the rights to immortality. Do you understand that? If we get the formula for everlasting life first Don, we can control the market, literally forever! It's gotta be worth billions!"

Don Crews agreed to bankroll Al's plan, but didn't want to know any details. He wanted in, if there was even a slight chance that Al hadn't lost his mind. Immortality sounded great; he could make sequels for eternity, and maybe he would find a great porn movie script he could star in. He wondered if there was such a thing as a poker double.

* * *

Four small-time hoodlums sprawled atop a broke back double bed, toking on a zucchini-sized reefer. The BEWBs had emerged from Buster Monk's mom's basement, and had adjourned to the Putit Inn motel. It was close to Onnitt APB, where their assignment for tomorrow morning was located. They were all speaking at once in excited voices, with spit spraying liberally, and fairly distributed to all.

"We've made it to the big crime! Finally!" Felonious Monk yelled. FM threw a fist into the air; the fist that was not grasping a bottle of booze. He belonged to the SIGN of ROOTS; Repeat Offenders Out on The Street, and his skin was black, but he identified as 'other'. He became a career criminal because, "I couldn't not never get arrested for my skin colour, so I done had to resort ta crime." Society was to blame for that.

He didn't mind the time he'd spent in a jail cell, because he could play video games and watch TV all day, without being nagged at by his mother. Plus, jails served breakfast!

"This is epic crime history in the making!" Loser cheered loudly.

Donut shook his head in amazement, and said, "It's unbelievable! A double kidnapping…"

Vometta, an enormous black woman of enormous talents agreed and said "Mmhmm" through a mouthful of pizza.

As the leader of this motley assemblage of society's refuse, Monk most closely resembled a hamster, though nobody said it in front of him. FM's cheeks were often stuffed full of sunflower seeds, and when he lost his temper several times a day, his flat nose twitched, his teeth protruded, and his eyeballs darted about like hummingbirds on meth.

Felonious Monk was made of equal parts petulant paranoia, persistent anxiety and chronic toothaches. He liked to strut his five-foot nine inch, two-hundred-and-fifty-pound form around, looking for trouble, always in a bad mood and daring anyone to speak. He'd lash out randomly, angrily and often violently. FM was unpredictable. When happy, he beamed with bright rays of light, but that occurred only on those frequent occasions when he inflicted pain on others.

Facing Monk from the opposite side of the sad, swayback bed-of-a-thousand squirts sat Ido Notno. Ido came to Shamerica from the country of Khookistan, on a student visa. He was expelled from Midwestern University for rape, so he joined the US Army. Private Notno went AWOL a month later, and had since made a career decision to enter the crime field.

He stood only five and half feet tall, and weighed a mere one hundred and twenty pounds. He was kept around for his cunning and brains, and not for his courage or ferocity. Ido was called Donut, because he was 'small enough to dunk', according to his ex-cell mates. The fact that he was valued by the Ohaha BEWBs for his brains, said much about the state of this decrepit group. With dark eyes and dark hair, Donut considered himself to be a great catch for the ladies, and although he dressed well, the ladies didn't much agree with his assessment. He did have two wives however.

Lou Snert knelt on the mattress at the foot of the crowded bed, and sucked on a cigarette. He was the BEWB's sergeant at arms. He loved weapons, violence and drugs, but not necessarily in that order. Loser was six feet two inches of cadaverous, meanness. He was of the SIGN of BiSOn. The Bisexual Offenders were a popular Special Interest Group Name to belong to, and was just one of scores, that divided Shamericans by skin shades, genders, sexual preferences, political parties, economic classes and diets. All citizens and non-citizens were required to register for one of them. A person could change their SIGN as desired, once every five years.

Loser, at one time in the past, had aspired to be a Navy Seal, but that idea washed out when he realised that he was allergic to water. So, he considered joining an airborne ranger battalion, but soon discovered that he was scared of heights. Finally, he found a temporary home in the National Guardians, where he was assigned to an armoury in the states.

On his first day working in the armoury, Private Snert fell in love with a beautiful piece named Oozie, and she returned his affections. He took that rifle home to bed that very same night, and Lou and Oozie had lived together ever since. It had been seven years now.

Lou was soon dishonourably discharged from the Army, for exposing himself to his female and male co-workers. He was also accused of possessing a tiny poker. Lou Snert felt called to a life of crime, and soon earned the moniker, Loser.

Vometta Wilde lay on her back like usual, in the centre of the suffering bed, chewing on a roast chicken. She supported her head on four motel pillows, which when stacked atop one another, were comparable to four dimes in thickness and comfort. VW had turned twenty-five last week, and she was reputed to have four children by six different fathers. Vometta began her life on the street at age thirteen, after running away from her abusive home. She did what she'd been raised to do, and she made good money at it.

Physically, Vometta resembled the famed Germy car commonly known as a VW, but with five short stubby projections, which most thought were four limbs and a head. She appeared to roll when she ambulated and, was as dangerous as a monster truck if one got in her way. There was only one thing that Vometta enjoyed more than eating or having sex, and that was eating while having sex.

VW, as a rule, never wore clothing. She had tried tarps, tents and theatre curtains, but they were a nuisance to remove, and the food crumbs accumulated to the point, that she once trapped several mice in her clothes. Nowadays she preferred using sequins and glitter on her beautiful black skin to simulate clothing. No one noticed that she was naked when she went out, or if they did, they thought better of mentioning it to her.

She and the other three Ohaha BEWBs had experience in kidnapping, and their sole venture into this federal crime was successful for nearly ninety minutes. The crime, though a failure in the end, had added glamor to their police records. It was eighteen months ago, when the quartet had executed a precision snatch of the oldest of Vometta's three daughters, from the young girl's foster family. Mommy had missed her big girl, and needed her now to earn some money because Mommy was out of cigarettes. "And they ain't cheap girl. By the way, what did you say your name was?"

The BEWB's had gotten about seventy-five miles away, but they hadn't yet rented the girl out, when the police caught up to their getaway car and pulled them over. All four of them were arrested on the spot. The BEWBs had forgotten to check their victim for a selfone, and the girl had been talking to the police, the entire time she was in the trunk of the car.

The criminals paid a price. They were sentenced to unsupervised probation, fined fifty dollars and punished further, with having to perform twenty minutes of community service. The highlight of the entire episode occurred, when the BEWBs made it onto the nightly news for forty-five seconds of fleeting infamy. In recognition, the national BEWB HQ gave the Ohaha branch members a new getaway vehicle; a Pissan Tanki, the largest, non-commercial, production vehicle in the world. It was known as a BUV or Beast Utility Vehicle.

Loser said, "If we pull off this poking caper, we'll get our own demn reality television show fer sure, man."

Donut was intrigued by the idea of a reality show. He asked, "Whaddya think we should call it? I was thinking along the lines of Perp Tank or maybe Kidnap Kings, huh?"

Monk wondered for the zillionth time; how in the poke this idiot was the brains of this poking outfit? "Nah, Nonut; that's dumber than scat. If we is havin' us a reality show, I dun gets to names it. 'Cuz I be the boss man."

Vometta was chewing on a pizza, and she asked, "Whkul fluxazedi?"

Loser hopped off the bed in agitation, and accepted the whiskey bottle from Buster. He drank a big slug and faced his three fellow BEWBs. He pronounced, "That's really the entire poking point VW; the movie, not the TV show." He seemed to know what subject she referenced. "I've been thinking about this," he said. He cocked his head like an owl, as if that would impart an aura of wisdom to his next words, and said, "I think that Woopsie Oldbird would do you right girl, and I'm thinking that Willis Myth could play Monk. And Lonny Doop for Donut."

Monk saw how this was going. "And who be you, Loser? Don poking Crews?

"Hades no!" Loser retorted. "More like Robby Indero."

Donut's plan was simple, which was best for this set of BEWBs. The crew first required some intelligence gathering to pull off their job. They needed to learn, where on the air base the aliens were hanging out. They knew where to look for the information.

The bar was called Spurts, and it slumped less than a half mile from the front gate of Onnitt APB; mere stumbling distance. Its close proximity to the base, and the class of clientele it drew, made it the ideal watering hole for young service members. At Spurts, they could have a beer or twelve with like-minded seekers of oblivion, or lose money playing pool; they could mingle with the local sluts, prostitutes, drug dealers, condom artists, and doctors with penicillin on hand. VW and FM went there.

VW and FM made a great tag team for extracting information. She pried with flirting and he tried with hurting. Neither their tricks nor their kicks were needed this night though. Beer and braggadocio had offered them a gift. They gained the information they wanted, without having to expose themselves. It was perfect.

Monk and Wilde had drifted into a cloud of high people, who hung around a table where two men sat, and played king of the bar, hoping to impress the women. Their combined blood alcohol levels could have powered a factory. They sounded like schoolkids on the playground; drunken schoolkids.

The white serviceman with the walrus moustache loudly bragged, "I did sentry duty there today! I saw the poking aliens!"

His black drinking mate, who wore Spiderman earrings, needed to top this remark, so he slurred with as much volume as he could muster, "I drove all four of you guys out there to Squat House, and I saw the fatherpoking aliens first!" Spit and beer flew from his mouth and created a mist around his head. "I drove!"

"No, you dint! I saw them first!" Walrus retorted. He rose from his chair in anger, and his knees banged the table, spilling a pitcher of beer on Spiderman. Vometta and Buster left the bar before the fight even started, but they saw two police cruisers driving that way, lights and sirens on. The pair of BEWBs headed for a grocery store. The duo had one last item to attend to before they returned to the Putit Inn.

As he drove, FM remarked on their good fortune. He said, "It's as if our crime has been ordained and blessed by the god of crooks."

Vometta, while chewing on a smoked ham agreed, and said, "Qwiddi aflabuu kazxunka."

That seemed wise, and Buster Monk nodded his head sagely, before saying, "Has to be." He repeated her proverb, to help him remember it for later use at parties, "The god of crooks is a poking lawyer...wow!"

They stopped at a grocery store to buy whiskey, a few rotisserie chickens, some donuts, several cakes, and two cases of beer, before they drove to the Onnitt

APB. They had one more errand to attend to. They were allowed onto the base by the gate guard, after they explained that they were picking up a friend, who'd completed his work shift at the Max Beefburger. The nice man even gave them a base map.

Monk navigated to Squat House by the shortest route. The two-story tall, red brick pile of ugliness perched on a corner lot, and Wilde counted four, armed security officers patrolling the grounds. Some lights were on inside the unit, but drapes were drawn.

FM drove past the place, and turned off a block down the road to circle back. He said, "It has a dark guard shack around the corner. There must be a driveway back there or something. I'll drop all the booze in there."

VW said, "Utzal pugapsto wiffi," without losing a crumb of the cake she was eating."

Monk was overjoyed to hear this; two male and two female guards were on duty. Everything was coming their way. He turned off the Tanki's lights and stopped the BUV at the curb, a block away from the abandoned guard shack.

The guard shack was out of use. It would be easy to get the alcohol in there. After that, it was just a matter of getting the guards to look inside. FM turned off the truck's ignition, but left the keys in. He told VW, "Stay here, I'll be right back."

Vometta suggested that he, "Twaku erxequat." She was chewing on a round of cheese.

He did. FM took a blanket out of the back seat and, grabbed a case of beer and a fifth of whisky too. He carried the items, walking in the shadows, to the unguarded guard shack. FM pushed open the sagging, wooden door of the shack with his shoulder and hip. It scraped against the cement floor and gave him access inside.

Monk put the folded blanket down on the seat of a three-legged stool, and balanced the case of beer and whiskey atop that. He lit a cigarette, and pulled a string of firecrackers out of the pocket in his sweatpants. There was a wooden counter inside the guard shack. FM set up his delayed ignition attention-getter on top of it. He set the burning cigarette down on the countertop, and laid the fuse leading to a bundle of a hundred firecrackers across the cigarette, at butt's end.

Felonious Monk exited the old shack and left its door ajar. He returned to the Tanki, where Vometta was taking a few breaths, before finishing a chocolate cake. FM started the truck and idled in place, waiting for the show.

The lights in Squat House were out, and the street was quiet. The four MPs that were on duty were on loose patrols, ensuring only that no one entered or exited the house. When the firecrackers erupted in rapid-fire explosions, it must have seemed like gunshots at first to the startled base cops. They ran for cover behind the stairway, or hit the ground, while drawing their weapons.

It soon dawned on them that the racket emanated from the guard shack area, and they approached it from different angles, with caution. The discovery of the beer and whiskey inside the shack was unanticipated, and its presence there was heavily debated by the four MPs.

"That's Tennishoe Whiskey! That ain't the cheap scat," one of the two men said. He was a body builder type, who loved mirrors more than he loved Mom.

A short, petite woman with freckles on her nose said, "It's probably stolen."

The other woman, a buxom blonde said, "I don't want to get caught with stolen booze, do you?"

"Hades no!" said the fourth sentinel, an aspiring alcoholic, whose greatest boast was that he could touch his tongue to his eyebrows.

"What should we do?" Freckle-nose asked.

"We have to get rid of it, hide it maybe," said the man of the mirror.

Long-tongue loved it when others arrived at the same conclusion he'd come to. "You are all absolutely right, and I am lucky to be working with a group of such smart people. We must do precisely as you all have proposed."

The three others looked at him expectantly, waiting for him to tell them what they'd suggested. He obliged, but added some drama first. He picked up the whiskey bottle and gazed at it in contempt, then growled, and said angrily, "We have no poking choice! We have to drink this crap!" He unscrewed the cap and raised it to his lips. Before he drank, he said, "Duty before all."

The MPs sucked down the evidence.

FM had seen enough. He shifted the truck into reverse, and backed up to the cross street behind them. Then he turned on the headlights and drove away. He navigated the BUV through the air base and out the gate. They returned to the Putit Inn where Loser and Donut played cards, drank whiskey, and smoked cigarettes and crack, while waiting for their return.

Buster plopped down on the droopy bed, and cracked open a cold beer. Vometta sprawled out in the centre of the bed, and pulled open a party-sized bag of potato chips. Donut said, "You sure were gone a long time. I hope that means you accomplished something."

Buster Monk emptied his can of beer, and then flattened it for recycling, using Donut's forehead to crush it on. Loser cackled like a cartoon witch, at the injured expression on Donut's face.

Monk related all that he and VW had successfully achieved that night, and how magically all of the pieces were falling into place. He remembered the wise words of VW. He said, "The god of lawyers is a crook."

Making use of the new intelligence provided by Monk, and the occasional spray of potato chip crumbs from Vometta, Donut formulated the outlines of his new and improved plan, and explained it to the others. He also shut down their last, remaining worry about whether the aliens would be affected by stayser weapons. Donut reasoned that since the aliens bled and expressed pain, the electric jolts of the staysers would disable them, as they did humans.

Loser and FM listened carefully and offered suggestions where needed to complete the fine, detail work. VW finished eating the chips. Once their plans were well laid, that's what the Love Bug wanted too; well laid. The men complied; there was enough of her for all of them.

Chapter 4

A half hour prior to Melanie's abduction, two staff sergeant MPs signed out for and received keys to, identical battleship grey, Dodgy Carry Vans. The two men were at the Onnitt Air Power Base transportation depot, and it was 8:15 AM, Friday morning, September third. A light rain fell. The two men had important driving assignments to perform on this cool, wet Friday morning. Sgt Crankace would pick up the two alleged aliens, and drive them to their assigned building on base, while Sgt Slappus, was assigned to carry out the same duty for Melanie Gryzolski.

The woman and the two alleged aliens had spent the night in separate base lodgings, which were situated a short distance from each other. Drivers for the other four members of the secret committee on alleged aliens, Chip, Comeon, Choomor and Polyplastis, were not needed. They'd brought their own personal drivers with them. These four special people were ensconced off base, in the costliest luxury hotel in all downtown Ohaha. They were spending taxpayer money after all, three of them were career government employees, and Professor Polyplastis was on an expense account from UC Berzerkley.

Personal chauffeurs for the trio of politicians also stayed in "free", sumptuous quarters, at the same location. These pampered drivers, would each drive one public servant in a limousine, to the secret, underground location on the air power base.

* * *

The two aliens did not need to eat, breathe or drink water to survive, but they would suffer horrendous consequences of pain and suffering as any human would if they did not. So, Jeemis had fried up bacon and eggs for breakfast, while Robulus had brewed coffee and made toast. The kitchen was supplied with all of

47

their wants, since they were for all intents and purposes, prisoners in Squat House.

During the night, Robulus and Jeemis had seen four MPs walking the grounds. Their presence was as much to keep the two mystery visitors from leaving, as to keep intruders from entering, but the aliens were in no hurry to go. They'd been on Gaia for sixty-five million years already, and another day was of little concern. The firecrackers popping off overnight seemed curious, but they hadn't lost sleep over it.

Squat House, was once the residence of General Squatsmore, and was named after this infamous officer, who retired in disgrace, after being discovered by MPs one Saturday afternoon, with his pants around his ankles and a private Reardon on his knees playing the pipe organ.

The sordid story of the general spread faster than an escort girl, in spite of attempts to keep it hushed up. General Squatsmore never made a statement regarding the accusations, and the general's poor wife maintained for the rest of her life, that, "He never asked me to do that." 'Knees' Reardon was transferred to the US Navy, where his skills would be more appreciated.

Two and a half blocks west of Squat House, on the same street, stood another lodging residence, where Melanie Gryzloski and her father Matt had spent the night. They were not assigned security of course, and in fact, had dined out last evening.

They were in the kitchen together now. Melanie had washed and dried her coffee cup. Her father was drinking his second helping, and was solving a crossword puzzle. He sat on a stool at a kitchen counter. Matt put his pencil down, looked up at his beautiful daughter and said, "I think you're excited."

She laughed a delightful sound, and said, "Oh, you think so Dad? This is so bizarre! I wish I could tell you about it!" Melanie glanced at her eyefone to check the time. "What will you do all day; go to the Drone Expo?" She walked to the large, rain-streaked picture window overlooking the street and looked out.

"Yes, probably for most of the day," he answered. "There should be some truly amazing technology to see." Matt was fifty-nine years old, and he was six years a widower, a retired power engineer. His wife of thirty-two years had been brutally murdered. Melanie was their only child.

Matt was known as Griz, a moniker derived from his last name, and from his manner of dealing with his daughter's tentative boyfriends a couple of decades

ago. Matt stood six foot two inches tall, and weighed one hundred and ninety –
five pounds, mostly muscle. He was a bear of a man.

He said, "I have my suspicions about what you're up to, my dear. The Max
Beefburger shooting happened, right here in Ohaha, a couple of days ago. And
those two guys, who were shot up and walked away, must be of interest to the
powers that be."

Melanie said, "Dad, if I told you, I'd have to kill you."

Her father rose from his seat at the counter, and said, "I prefer the guillotine.
It's quick and painless."

Melanie said, "Dream on. I'm thinking, burning at the stake."

Matt joined his daughter at the wet window. They watched a grey Carry Van
pass by their unit, and then a few seconds behind it, a second grey Dodgy came
into the Gryzolski's view. It pulled up to the curb, and stopped in front of their
place at Crap View. He kissed his daughter on the forehead. "Good luck," he
said.

"Okay then, Dad," Melanie said, "Have a great day. I know I will. I better
head out."

Matt helped Melanie don a light blue windbreaker. They hugged and Matt
opened the door for his daughter, and she skipped down the wet steps to the entry
walk below. Matt closed the door and watched her from the window above.

Sgt Slappus had driven out of the transportation depot at 8:17 AM, following
behind Crankace, and they drove the wet streets of Onnitt. Their wipers slapped
water from their windshields as they made their ways together, towards the
separate lodge houses. The grey sky hung low, and though it was 55 degrees, it
felt chillier.

Sgt Crankace drove past Crap View, where the Gryzloskis had lodged, and
continued on towards Squat House, two blocks ahead. Slappus depressed his
van's brakes and brought it to a stop, at the curb in front of Crap View at 8:29
AM. He'd arrived one minute early! He'd received verbal warnings, for such
unmilitary behaviour before, on two separate occasions, and he could not afford
a third strike!

Slappus nearly pulled away from the curb again, to drive around the block
several times, but then he saw Melanie descending the steps from Crap View.
Oh my! She was a vision, even seen through his rain-streaked windshield on a
grey morning. She wore blue slacks and matching windbreaker, her blonde hair
was tied back in a short ponytail, and green earrings dangled from her cute ears.

Slappus, or as his ex-wife called him, Slappy, put the large passenger van in park, left the motor idling, and set the emergency brake. He got out to greet, and to open the door for his VIP passenger. The eager sergeant failed to pay attention to his footing as he rounded the front of the vehicle, and so he slipped on a wet, oily patch of pavement, and fell on his butt. Splat!

To her credit, Melanie rushed in to help the man up, rather than laugh at him. Slappy's first instinct after such an embarrassing flop in front of a pretty woman, was to slap away the helping hand, and to get up by himself like a big boy. And once vertical, he would swear and curse until he regained that macho feeling again.

But, Slappy's training kicked in, over-riding his base male instincts. He graciously accepted the woman's soft hand, and rose to his feet. His dress uniform slacks were soaked from heel to buttocks." Thank you, Ma'am," he managed to push out between grinding teeth. He opened the front passenger door for his rider, and Melanie stepped up and into the roomy Carry Van. She smiled and said, "Thank you, Sir"

Slappy closed her door, and turned his head, unclenched his teeth, and spat out a piece of his tongue. That muscle had not retreated from the dental danger zone quickly enough, when his jaw clamped down hard on the swear words that frantically tried to escape his throat. He did preserve his dignity in front of this attractive woman however; otherwise, he would have cursed like an actor. "Demn that hurts!" he muttered. Slappy returned to the driver's seat. Melanie pretended not to notice the blood trickling down his chin, and she looked straight out the windshield.

Melanie watched the first van, which was a couple of blocks ahead of them, through the flopping windshield wipers. It pulled over to the curb and parked at a large brick building on a corner lot. She snapped on her seat belt. Melanie guessed that the van was picking up the two alleged aliens. She had wondered where on base they'd stayed. Slappy released the parking brake, shifted into drive, and slowly pulled out onto the wet roadway. They were heading down the street towards Squat House.

* * *

A white Pissan Tanki was parked on Elm Street. It faced the grey Dodgy Carry Van parked in front of Squat House; at a distance of about fifty yards.

Three BEWBs sat inside of the BUV, swearing and reviewing the latest change of plans.

Donut's original plan called for Loser to drive, and he sat behind the steering wheel now, so that hadn't changed. Vometta's assignment required her to snatch up one of the two aliens, and Monk was supposed to nab the Carry Van's driver. VW was wolfing down a yard long submarine sandwich, and she was ready to roll; literally. Monk was missing however; he had called off sick with a toothache, and Donut was the substitute kidnapper now.

The Pissan Tanki was seven thousand pounds of 'getouttatheway'. It came standard with four doors, and two, five-foot-long bench seats, which sat three adults each, comfortably. A stowaway space, with a pair of small, foldout jump seats, completed the front cab area. The cargo bed measured eight feet long, and six feet wide. Dual rear tires on tall wheels allowed the BUV to carry two tons of weight with eighteen-inch ground clearance, and the rig was powered by a six hundred horse power diesel engine.

The BEWBs were armed with state-of-the-art staysers, which they hoped would immobilise and subdue the aliens, as well as it did human beings, with powerful electric jolts. The Good Homekeeping Stoppem Stayser was worn as a glove. Two compressed air canisters fit comfortably in the palm of most adult hands. Darts could be fired from under two fingers or from all four fingers at once. VW and Donut wore stayser gloves on both hands.

These popular home staysers gave off a high voltage, low amperage shock that disabled victims at various settings. The gloves were thumb operated and could be set to discharge electric jolts at three levels; Low, Medium and Bye. The length of shock time was also adjustable and three settings were available; five seconds, twenty seconds and one minute.

Donut felt anxious and complained, "I'm not supposed to do the dirty work. Violence makes me sick."

Loser was none too happy either, but it was what it was. He said, "Suck it up butternut! And don't poke this up! I'll kill that poking Monk, toothaching son of a sow!"

Vometta made excuses for the absent BEWB with dental problems, she said, "Fweeda looszape. "Chunks of semi-chewed cinnamon roll ejected with each soggy syllable, and Donut thought her syntax awful.

Her comment only served to infuriate Loser further, and he groused, "Are you poking kidding me Love Bug? Monk calls off sick with a poking toothache?

On the biggest day of his career? That's just poking crazy! Some great leader right?"

Donut tried to calm down and console himself, with the idea that now, with his physical involvement in this double kidnapping to come, a major action star would have to play his role in a movie of this caper, rather than one of the brainy actors, if they had those. This double kidnapping, would be the crime of the poking century after all! While they waited for some kind of activity to occur at Squat House, Donut considered various movie titles for their world changing crime.

Donut tried to visualise his movie title ideas, to see how they looked in bright, neon lights. Several clear possibilities jumped out at him right away, titles like 'I, Donut' and 'Dough Day Afternoon', for instance looked good. Other titles dawned on him gradually, but they had their beauty as well, 'The Dough Warrior' for example, and 'Doughface'. He should have been visualising what he was going to do, but … A vehicle came down the road!

Loser saw it too. "It looks the right shade of government grey to be our target, folks. Brace up! It's show time!"

Donut's bladder was waving the yellow flag of cowardice, but he shored it up, with thoughts of the stories he would be able to tell his future cellmates one day. This crime would be the stuff of legends, or of late-night comedy monologues; he hoped the former. Donut thought about girding his loins, but wasn't certain of the process, so he gave it up. He dug down deep, skin deep, and threw caution to the light breeze, and then said, "Let's roll!" He hoped that he sounded convincing.

Vometta was ready, and cookie crumbs blew when she said so, "Heppz toob visch."

* * *

Sgt Crankace sat in the parked van at the curb in front of Squat House, and wondered where in Hades the four sentries were. Nobody came to meet him, no one was in sight. They must be under trees, or hiding from the rain somewhere, he surmised. He was perturbed. Something wasn't right.

A later inquiry, led to court martials for the two men and the two women MPs, who were on guard duty at Squat House on that fateful morning. The disused guard shack was later torn down, because of a fishy odour which issued from the building, and neighbours often complained of the stray cats, and circling seagulls.

The party that happened inside that nasty old love shack on that Septober night was not their clients' fault, the lawyers had maintained. Some wicked person had planted the beer and whiskey in the guard shack, and the MPs had naturally drunk the alcohol, to protect children who may have found it otherwise. It was the only proper thing to do! As for the orgy which followed their altruistic booze party; it was no more than four service members being cordial, and respecting the wishes of others.

Cranky shook his head in irritation. He'd been briefed that his passengers would be escorted by sentries to the car. "Demn it!" Now he had to get poking wet! He kept the engine running, set the brake and opened his door wide. He stepped out of the vehicle, and from the corner of his eye, he saw two tall men dressed in black coveralls descending the steps of Squat House. Those must be my riders, he surmised.

* * *

Sgt Crankace was lying in a hospital bed, suffering a severe concussion, and was being interrogated by MP Captain Morgan. He had a headache but was free; Melanie had been kidnapped in his stead, when she jumped into the fray.

Melanie was far less happy than he, and so when Loser moved to turn the radio on again, the stupid lyrics of the country gangsta rap song crept back into her thoughts, and she slapped his hand way from the control knob.

Loser was appalled at his victim's outlandish behaviour, and made to slap her back; across the face. A wall of sound from behind him stopped his hand. It was the alien's voice. Jeemis said, "Hey, I bet you're on the news." Loser was an opportunist, like a germ. He said loudly, as if in a hopeless competition with Jeemis, "I was gonna turn the news on man, and it was my idea first. Be cool fool."

Donut kept to himself, his mind racing in circles like a dog chasing its tail. He was a born worrier. He worried that things were going too smoothly, and he worried that Vometta may have been injured and lost functionality. Donut worried about the weather and this chick's driving, and this loud-mouthed poking unpredictable poking alien. And he worried about Loser losing it.

Loser tried to avoid self-analysis and deep thought, because during past attempts, he'd always dived down into his conscience. He hated that nag, and stayed out of the abyss now, preferring the comfort and familiarity of a kiddie pool. Loser had concluded that shallowness required much less effort to stay afloat in than depth did, and his puddle was easier to keep clean too.

Loser changed the topic, and introduced himself. He said, "I'm Loser and behind me is Donut." He acted like they were family. "Who do we have the honour of kidnapping?" he asked, congenially.

Jeemis screeched, "You kidnapped an immortal alien, and that's me; Jeemis. The woman was in the wrong place at the wrong time and her identity is of no importance."

Melanie appreciated the gesture, but she could do this better herself. She said, "I'm your worst nightmare punk."

Donut was shocked at such sass from a woman, and he felt like smacking her around to teach her some manners. Loser wanted to backhand the sow too, but she was driving now, and he worried about the alien. He would wait for his chance to tame her later.

Chapter 5

Once the disabling effects of the stayser had worn off, and he'd regained muscle control, Robulus set off at a jog for Crap View, running on the wet sidewalk. He knew that Melanie's father was lodging there with his daughter. Robulus and Jeemis had researched all of the members of the secret inquiry panel, as a matter of common sense.

Robulus skipped up the front steps of the house, and rapped sharply on the wooden door. The tall alien hoped that the big, bearded man had proven immune to the staggering effects of the stupidity virus, like his daughter had.

Matt Gryzolski pulled the door open, curious about the frantic knocks. He was astonished to see a seven-foot tall, stick figure with obvious concern written in his dark eyes. "What?" Matt asked in alarm. "What's happened?"

"My friend, and your daughter Melanie, have been kidnapped," Robulus' voice blasted Matt backwards a step, and the words weakened his knees. "My Gawd!" Matt roared. "What are you saying?" Matt held onto the door, dazed and unsure.

Robulus spurred him to action. He said, "Pack your necessities. We'll take your car." Matt opened the door wider and said, "You'd better come in then." He turned and went down the central hall and into a bedroom. Robulus stepped inside and shut the door. While the alien may have looked bedraggled, and dripping wet, his black coveralls, woven from a waterproof material of his own creation, kept him dry underneath. His hair dripped.

Matt tossed his toiletries and some clothes into one small bag and was ready to depart in under four minutes. It's not like he had any suits to pack, in fact, he'd never owned one in his life, and didn't know how to knot a necktie. At fifty-nine years old, Matt was, and always had been, a dedicated professional, casual dresser, but he did it well.

Matt rejoined Robulus in the entry foyer, and donned a blue jacket, pulled from a coat closet there. He wore a western style, cowboy hat over his full head of grizzled, silvery hair, which matched the hue of his short-trimmed beard and bristly moustache.

The pair exited the house, leaving Melanie's items behind. The government would manage her things until she could retrieve them, if she ever returned. Matt led Robulus around the sprawling Crap View domicile, to the driveway behind it. Matt used a key fob to unlock the doors and start the ignition on his vehicle, a black Fard Burro.

Matt fit his six-foot one inch, one hundred ninety-five-pound body, comfortably behind the steering wheel, while Robulus required some bending, folding and mutilation to fit his tall frame into the front passenger seat. They snapped their respective safety belts closed, and while Matt backed the car out onto the street, Robulus saw why the unit was known as Crap View. Its balcony, complete with BBQ grill, looked down upon the backside of a base mess hall. A plethora of dumpsters and garbage cans, overflowing with food provided an ecological niche for stray dogs, cats, and kids, as well as the usual pigeons, starlings, and land-locked sea gulls.

"Where are we going?" Matt asked as he pulled onto the roadway. The wipers swished across the windshield as Matt drove towards the base exit gates. Robulus boomed, "The Ohaha airport."

Without blinking, Matt said, "If the kidnappers plan on flying out, we simply make a phone call." Then he asked, "What about the police? What in Hades is going on? I'm Matt, but call me Griz." He tried to concentrate on driving, but he needed to understand what was happening, so that his mind didn't stray into dangerous story-telling mode. Matt spoke in a strong, deep voice. "Who are you?" he asked.

Robulus could see and hear the bear inside this hairy man, with his large paws and growling voice. "I am Robulus. My kidnapped friend is Jeemis. We were the subjects of the secret inquiry involving…"

"I know now!" Griz interrupted, "You're the guys from the Spewtube shooting video at the burger joint! Shot full of holes, but no leaks!"

Robulus grinned. "Correct," he boomed.

Griz observed lights and sirens driving in the direction from whence they'd come. He drove off the air base and turned right onto state Highway 75, northbound towards Ohaha's Effmee Airport. Rain fell at a moderate rate, but traffic flowed like cold molasses moving uphill. "What happened back there?" he asked Robulus.

Robulus replied, "Two men kidnapped Melanie and Jeemis. I must assume that someone from the secret committee revealed information to the wrong people. Jeemis has contacted me to say that the bad guys want to find the TDS. He will keep me up to date and will watch over your daughter. I know where they are going. They drive but we will fly." Robulus judged that Griz was immune to the endemic stupidity virus, but he wanted more information.

"Jeemis and I are immortal aliens, not of Gaia," Robulus thundered. "We crashed here on your planet sixty-five million years ago," he added. Robulus wanted to gauge Griz's reaction to his claims.

Griz drove hard without being aggressive, and for the most part, in the left lane. To his credit, he didn't snicker or deride his passenger's comments. Instead, in a voice most disinterested and casual, he said, "So you fell to ground and couldn't get up. And you came all the way here to Gaia, to buy gift cards for some woman on Galactic Phasebook, and got scammed, right?"

Robulus was well pleased and smiled in satisfaction. Griz would do just fine. He rumbled, "It is well that you are sceptical and that you have a rational, alternative explanation for my lack of bullet wounds. However, this is of little concern. What does matter is that I am in continuous communication with Jeemis, and Melanie is doing great. She is driving the getaway truck. Jeemis can and will protect her. Please try not to worry," Robulus said. "I'll talk and you drive, and besides, the crooks are more stupid than dangerous," he added.

Griz wasn't certain what to think or believe. It was so fabulously unbelievable as to remind Griz of what passed for news. His daughter was involved however, and Griz was determined to follow every possible course of action to find her. He wondered where the law was in all of this and he asked the alleged alien, "Hey, Robulus; this is a serious crime. Where are the cops, if you know?" he asked.

Robulus replied, "At Dinkum Donuts."

* * *

The Onnitt Air Power Base MPs, had arrived at Squat House in three cars, followed by a fire truck and an ambulance. Officers found four naked people passed out in the guard shack, which stunk like a shrimp boat, and two additional naked people were discovered on the front seat of a grey, government Dodgy van, that was missing its front driver's door. Rain drummed down on them, and they kept rhythm.

The couple having sex inside the van didn't hear all of the many sirens closing in on their location, or they were too far gone to care one way or another. When the six naked bodies were taken into custody and placed under arrest, the two male EMTs demanded that Vometta, with a visible tire track across her chest, be taken away in the ambulance to the base hospital, to treat any possible injuries.

A fight nearly erupted between the EMTs and the MPs, over custody issues for Vometta, but when the FIBB showed up to take over the case, utter chaos ensued. The local FIBB bureaucracy bureau chief, Clyde Escope, arrived on scene with a faxed order, direct from his own desk, which authorised the FIBB to take charge. This included retaining custody and exclusive interrogation rights of any and all prisoners involved in this sinister plot.

The EMTs were allowed thirty minutes in the privacy of the ambulance, to check the woman's vitals, as they called it. A line formed in the rain, at the back of the emergency vehicle's doors. It seemed that many vitals needed checking and rechecking, by many unqualified personnel. The ambulance rocked like a boat in a storm, and the shock absorbers took a beating. Someone called out for coffee and Dinkum Donuts, and some neighbours popped over to see all the fuss. The scene may have devolved into a block party had it not been for a jealous MP who called the cops to report a disturbance.

At some point later that morning, Vometta was transported to the local FIBB office in downtown Ohaha, according to investigators. A special interrogation room was prepared for the very important prisoner, with mattresses and buffet tables.

Video recordings of the proceedings were made, and copies could later be had for $19.99 plus applicable taxes. A catering company was called in to deliver various food items, including fried chicken, ham, sausage and biscuits with gravy, pastries and a side of beef.

Vometta confessed to a lot of crimes, real and imagined, during these prolonged interrogations. She liked it here. Buster couldn't hurt her, plus they had better grub. "I could get used to this interrogation stuff," she thought.

As she chewed on a pig carcass and had sex with another questioner, Vometta pondered for the millionth time, "Does eating make me hornier or does poking make me hungrier?" She'd think on that. "Shwuga," she hollered, "vigaxico spaloopa wahwah?" Her next interrogator filled her order and bought her a chocolate cake, and then he filled her.

* * *

It fell upon the wide shoulders of Onnitt APB commander General Storr, to inform the next link up in the chain of command, about the double kidnapping carried out by a team of highly trained professional criminals. MP Colonel Musturd had called Storr mere minutes ago with the awful news. On top of the abductions, the second alien, along with the presidential science advisor's father, had also gone missing from the air base; whereabouts unknown. Storr gulped down a shot of brandy and made the call to his boss.

His boss, General Lee Speeking, was sitting in a fifteen-hundred-dollar chair, in an office in the Hexagon. The walls were decorated with photos, portraits, framed awards and other items celebrating him, and his forty-one-year career. His secretary, Randi Muphins sat atop his ample lap, which could easily seat two, and on happy occasions it did. When General Lee's phone rang, she jumped up, ran into her adjoining office and answered it for her boss.

"You have reached the office of General Lee Speeking," Randi answered, "No one is available to take your call at this time, but if you leave..."

General Storr wasn't playing that game this morning, "Knock it off, Randi, and get me the general on the line. This is General Storr."

"Scat!" She replied, "We were just getting warmed up too. Okay, hold on, man."

General Storr shook his head in consternation. One just couldn't find good help these days. Why, in his prime, the gals were more respectful of the officers they screwed for promotions and favourable evaluations. They didn't say 'man', it was more like: 'Would you like to poke me, Sir?' and 'Would you mind if I go down on you, Sir?'

General Storr got down to business immediately, skipping the usual braggadocio pleasantries. He informed General Lee Speeking of the national emergency, and then Lee called up to President Crumm's Chief of Staff, Tommi Gunn, and filled her in on all of the particulars. One can barely imagine the ragged shape of these particulars by the time that Tommi briefed the president.

After passing through four military lifers, and their particular individual, cover-your-ass mechanisms, the distorted mess landed on President Crumm's

59

desk. It sounded like another false news report. The president heard that his science advisor had run off with one alleged alien, and that her alleged father may have eloped with the second spaceman. President Crumm phoned the Onnitt base commander for clarification. He got it and it made him angry. When the POTUS also learned of the secret investigative committee, he was understandably infuriated. He asked General Storr where the four members of this covert panel were.

General Storr said, "I just spoke to MP Colonel Musturd, Sir, and she assures me that the four conspira…er, um, I mean, four committee participants are still underground in the converted viewing theatre below building A-2."

President Daryl Crumm nodded his head in approval. An idea took shape in his busy brain. He replied, "Good, good. Do they know what has happened, and why three of their participants have failed to arrive?"

Storr said, "I asked the same question Sir, and the colonel replied that the four men have not been notified of these developments. She informed me, that those four people knew that these alleged aliens were on base, and they are therefore considered people of interest, in our investigation into their disappearance."

Crumm heartily agreed that one or more could be implicated. He told Storr, "That sounds right to me General. Let's keep them there. I'm on my way."

"Yes Sir!"

Chapter 6

As soon as Winkin, Nobraska police officer Wayne Bruce heard the kidnapping reports on his scanner, he knew exactly what he needed to do. According to the chatter, the kidnappers were on I-800 and driving his way. All police were ordered to stand down; "Observe, but do not approach," was the exact wording. Wayne sat at his kitchen table, with a plate, a fork, and a few uneaten pieces of Whoremel Vegan Bogus Bacon on the table in front of him. An empty glass that once held six fluid ounces of lamefruit juice sat to the left.

Wayne picked up his selfone and called his superior. Wayne was the only black cop in his precinct. His boss, Lt. Dick, best known as 'Big', answered the fone, "What?"

Wayne whined, "I really hate to do this Sir, but I need one week of emergency leave, due to a family crisis."

"Oh yeah, Wayne; what happened? Your mistress got pregnant or what?" `

Wayne loved how the lieutenant took such a personal interest in his officers. He said. 'Yes, something like that. Look, Looey, I need a week off and I've got it coming too."

"Alright, alright already," Lt. Dick said. "We don't need you around here anyway. Get her on the pill you moron." End call.

"Perfect," Wayne thought. Now if only the wife will let loose of me. "Good morning, Sweetheart!" He hollered. He left the small kitchen and went down the hall to the bedroom. His wife Moon emerged from the bathroom, brushing her long golden hair. She knew he was scheming. She could see it in his fawning face, and she'd heard it in his pleading voice. "Yes, Honey," she replied, in her most innocent tone. "What is it dear?" She asked with suitable wifely anxiety.

Wayne faced his beloved wife. He puffed up like a balloon and tried to look big, which was difficult when one was five foot, seven inches tall. He swelled his small chest, sucked his belly in, and raised his pointed chin. He coughed once and said, in the gravest of tones, "I must go my love. Duty calls and I must save the world."

Moon lowered her chin as if in despair, hiding her huge smile. Then, in mock astonishment, and expressed with a gasp of horror, she cried, "Oh, not again, my King! That's twice this month!" She raised her eyes and loudly lamented, "Oh the sufferings of a superhero's wife!" Moon plumped out her lower lip in a childlike pout, while thinking of the delightful night ahead of her, writhing and heaving beneath the body of the young man who serviced her and her car too.

Wayne Bruce marched stoically over to a bare wall in their bedroom, and flipped up a wall switch. A panel slid open, to reveal a hidden cupboard. Wayne gazed in rapture at his latest colourful creation. Hanging there in all its glory was the fifth iteration of his Crime Blaster XL-5 superhero costume. Only his wife knew of his secret identity. He felt sorry for all the sacrifices his poor wife made to support his off-duty hobby. She was left alone at home night after night, while he, CB XL-5 saved the world.

Wayne's specially designed, high-tech, custom costume had cost a small fortune, but one cannot save the world in street clothes. It's not cool. Not only that, but according to the National Council on Superheroes handbook, rule two; "If a superhero saves the world, while not wearing an approved costume, it doesn't count."

In fact, according to superhero theory; "The costume is an extension of the superhero, and increases his or her effectiveness in proportion to its level of coolness." Wayne's was super cool, with its Shamerican flag stars and stripes. It was constructed of nylon and Kevlar and was certain to increase his popularity and fame. When he saved the world in his fancy costume this time, he was sure to score a reality TV show of his own. Once he got famous, there would be Crime Blaster XL-5 action figures, video games, comic books and movies everywhere!

Wayne's work as a patrol officer was great, but he was driven to do more. Call him selfish, but he got a big thrill out of saving Gaia's dumb ass, every other week or so. And better yet, saving it right in the nick of time; well, that was orgasmic. His reality show wouldn't necessarily show that part. It was kind of personal. Fade to ocean waves.

His CB character was locally well known and hated, by the streetwalkers and drug dealers of downtown Winkin, Nobraska. These criminals were embarrassed to transact these vice crimes, in front of a character that looked like he should be the entertainment at a kid's birthday party.

Wayne lifted his costume lovingly off its hangar. He pulled a custom costume luggage piece from the hidden closet. Although his outfit needed no ironing, Wayne kept it wrinkle free in this special carrying case. He placed the costume inside of it, and added his signature weapon, a short, fat club. Wayne tossed a clean pair of socks and underwear into a separate go-bag and went into the kitchen. He added his police scanner and some drinks and snacks to the bag, then he grabbed a jacket and an umbrella from the coat closet, slapped a ball cap to his thin-haired head, and was ready to depart.

Wayne walked into the home office to kiss his dear sweet wife goodbye. She was giggling on her selfone with someone and she tilted her head up for his kiss. She asked, "How long will saving the world take this time dear?"

"Never fear my darling," he said waggling a finger. "I shall complete this mission in three days or less," he reckoned. Standing erect, not letting the heavy burden bow his back, Wayne exited his home, and loaded his gear into his red mid-life crisis car, a sporty Chovey Cumaro. Wayne backed out into the street, and aimed his car through the driving rain towards the nearest I-800 interchange.

Wayne reached the last of the three entrance ramps leading from Winkin to the interstate highway, and parked on the road edge, where he had a clear view of all passing traffic. The great white Tanki would be easy to spot. He felt assured that the Pissan had yet to come this far, and that he was in plenty of time. He turned his scanner on, snapped open a can of Dr Popper and sat back to await destiny.

* * *

Two nationally recognised roving TV news reporters, Barry Porter of CON and Vera Fynne of NFN, were reading the same Bullitico newslog story on their separate eyefones. They were several hundred miles apart. Barry Porter was in Chitowno, Illnoise aka the Windbag City, working the grand opening of its third, Sacred Stars Temple franchise location. He was currently sitting in a wholly uncomfortable chrome chair in room 384, at the famous Rattysin Hotel.

Vera read the story whilst in the passenger lounge Concourse C, of the Lambkins International Airport in St Loozus, Miseri. She was waiting to board a plane home to New Yank City. That's where the No False News network headquarters were located.

Her cameraperson had left the night before, after they'd finished up their coverage of the Miseri State Fair. Vera wanted a break, so she stayed an extra night in town, and now she wanted this story.

The Bullitico newslog ran this breaking news headline—"ABDUCTION!" —and this is what the two journalists read: "Traditional roles were reversed this morning on Onnitt APB outside Ohaha, Nobraska, when an alleged illegal, immortal alien was abducted, along with his moll, presidential science advisor, Melanie Gryzolski. Inside sources tell us that the kidnappers belong to a white nationalist, right-wing extremist group calling itself the Jewish Notsees with a Sweet Tooth. This notorious gang of extortionists and blackmailers abducted the alien, right from under the lustful watch of a horny security team."

The article continued with a second paragraph, "One of the perpetrators of this heinous crime was captured by police in a state of undress. This female suspect is being held in tight seclusion at the Ohaha FIBB building. One eyewitness described a long line of food delivery trucks parked along the curb in front of the entry doors. The alien abductors of the JNWST gang are said to be driving west on I-800, in a white Pissan Tanki, license plate; ALM-101."

These two roving reporters wanted this big, breaking news story. Vera made a decision and acted on it. She would ask permission later. Vera jogged down the concourse and exited the secure airport area. She reached a ticket counter, and breathlessly asked for the earliest flight to Ohaha. "Oh, please hurry!" she gasped. She was glad to be dressed in her traveling clothes; blue jeans, tennis shoes, and a red blouse to match her purse and her lipstick. A sterling silver bracelet ringed her left wrist, and simple red post earrings completed her ensemble. Vera wore her silky black curly hair to her shoulder blades.

Forty-seven minutes later, her plane lifted off for a two-hour flight to Ohaha. Vera had her Pucci purse and a small carry-on bag, the rest of her luggage was flying to NYC. Vera knew that she would pay a price for her impulsive behaviour, and for assigning herself this story without approval from above. She also worried that she'd chosen the wrong city for her destination. If the kidnappers were not detained, and the big truck continued west, she'd be three hours behind the story when her plane landed! Demn it!

Barry Porter was a man, and he behaved with logic and reason, not emotion and intuition. These situations must be done with decorum and aplomb, not in a mindless rush. Barry, the consummate professional, called his editor before he did anything, sometimes even before he thought anything. He would find a way into this alien abduction story though. The publicity would propel him to the tip of the top echelon of false news stars. He would earn his own prime time news show, like Beano Meltzer!

Barry hated to leave behind the local celebrities, who attended these temple franchise grand openings. They were all so genuinely fake, such authentic frauds! He loved them; could relate to them. He lived by the Hollowood motto; "Phoniness is the true reality."

He called the editor's desk.

"Yeah?"

"Hello, Mr Bleeker. Barry calling."

"Barry who?"

"Barry Porter, your reporter."

"Oh, yeah. Okay, what's up, Porter the reporter?"

"Mr Bleeker, as a brilliant program editor and a master of common sense, I believe that you have probably come to the insightful conclusion, and masterful decision, that I should be the one to cover the alien abduction story. And, sir, I must say that I totally agree with you. So, without further ado, sir, I will be on my way. I won't forget to return with a nice gallon jug of Scootch.

"Porter, you say less in more words than a demn politician!"

"Thanks Boss."

"Look, you've got a deal, but make it a two-gallon jug."

Barry packed his bags and checked out of his hotel, leaving a message at the desk for his camera woman, saying, "Thanks for your fine work, Lorna, but glory is a jealous mistress, and she's all mine this time. Hope you understand. Love, Barry"

He caught a taxi to O'Where Airport, and booked a flight using his eyefone while on the way. He made his destination, the Nobraska city of North Flatte. Barry calculated methodically that if the villains continued without apprehension on I-800, he could intercept them, and follow them to their destination. He would rely on his eyefone to document the sights and sounds of this breaking news event once he was on scene.

After he checked his two bags in, and received his boarding pass, he wandered into a Skorbucks. He paid eleven dollars for seven ounces of a frothy, foamy milky drink, with a few droplets of coffee added for colour. He sat at a table and set his hot drink atop the dinner plate-sized tabletop. Barry pulled his eyefone from his jacket pocket, and started eye-scrolling through the hundreds of newslogs, using the spoken keywords, "alien abduction". Barry told his fone to remove all human abductions by aliens from the results.

Vera Fynne's plane was six miles high and an hour away from Ohaha, before Barry Porter took his first two-dollar sip of foam. Vera was drinking coffee too. It was a must for a roving reporter. Her plane was packed full. Vera flew often and it continuously baffled her that, no matter what airline she flew, no matter the destination, no matter the day of the week or whether day or night, the plane was filled with the exact same people! It was downright eerie, and somewhat frightening, but it was always the same demn passengers!

The screaming brat, the belligerent drunk, the idiot who doesn't hear his or her own, loud singing because of their earbuds; the coughing, the crying, the puking, the body odours and the identical robotic staff. It all amounted to another routine flight. Vera shut out the mayhem, and started having second thoughts about her rash behaviour. She knew that somebody, probably several somebodies, were going to raise Hades over her independent, unorthodox, undisciplined, headstrong, overbearing, aggressive conduct. And all the other nasty adjectives they could find in their thesauruses.

Petty, professional jealousies were a perennial gauntlet of bloodletting in television news. She'd run the course, and been scarred. To Vera's way of thinking, traditional journalism meant mining the story, digging for factual gold, and that upset many of her colleagues. Truth mattered to her. She'd deal with it later. Vera dropped down to the next item on her worry list; her relationship, such as it was.

Vera had lived together with Terry Rock as a mostly faithful couple for nine long years. They shared an abominably expensive apartment in New Yank City, and had slowly drifted apart like continents. It was inevitable that they would fail. Terry drove a tractor trailer rig for Lostco, and she was rarely home more than three or four days each month. Those few days were ordained to be the very same days that Vera was out of town, on assignment. Their costly home was mostly empty. It was a poking joke!

Vera was fifty-four years old, and she knew the relationship manual well. She knew by experience. People grow and change every day, but if they don't grow and change together, they'll grow and change apart. Eventually, each party wonders what they ever saw in the other. She and Terry were like that now; utter strangers.

Vera had lost at love twice now, once with each sex. Maybe it was her. She was smart, had graduated fourth in her class, with a master's degree in journalism from Gorgetown. She was pretty too; a petite five feet, four inches tall and one hundred eighteen pounds, with dark hair and eyes. Her hair curled over her ears and accentuated the oval shape of her face. She had a lot to offer, but, perhaps a meaningful relationship was beyond her ability to manage properly. Not everyone found their soulmate.

Vera had returned to her hometown in Imes, Aowa after completing school, and with her innate charm, her graceful delivery and intelligence she soon landed a job. A local NFN affiliate hired her for their daily, afternoon and evening, amuse-news features which followed the hard news. Her short segments were intended to make people smile and think happy thoughts, after twenty-minutes of hearing about crimes, deaths, rapes and murders in their area.

This first on-air gig was where Vera developed and perfected her breathless, on-the-scene, breaking news style and persona. This is not as easy as it may sound, when one considers that Vera accomplished this, while acting inspired by greased pig catching rodeos, and projecting excitement when revealing the secrets of growing a backyard corn crop.

When she was twenty-five, Vera married a man she'd known in high school. He'd been a popular jock. All of her friends, and even his one, warned her not to wed Reddick Knek. He's a brutish, womanising scoundrel, they agreed. Vera had thought that all men were like that, and if they just had enough of the right sort of love, they would reform and become gentle lambs.

They just needed love. That's the final excuse that she'd settled on, to explain why her father and her uncle came into her bed when she was growing up. It had to be because her mother and aunt were so rotten and unloving. Vera often had to explain away various bruises and injuries to her friends and teachers, to protect her violators.

Her marriage broke though. Love and devotion were for nought. Reddick couldn't be fixed. It took twelve and a half years of his affairs and abuse before she got it. She blamed herself. She should have known. Men were savage beasts with a poker for a weapon of domination, and they couldn't be trusted.

Vera thought back to the fateful night that changed the course of her life, and ended the marriage for good. Reddick came home drunk again, but this time with a stripper in tow, rented for the night from a club he frequented. Vera was passed out in her bed. She'd gotten drunk that night too, and was naked, atop the sheets.

Before she was fully awake or aware, Vera found herself participating in a frenzied threesome.

Later, guilt-ridden and depressed by her own depravity, Vera went into isolation. She hated herself for finding pleasure in the caresses of the whore. The prostitute's soft gentleness contrasted sharply with the vicious thrusts of her caveman husband. Vera became lonely and frustrated, and was eventually convinced that she was a lesbian. She applied for her Lesbo in Training or LIT certificate, and soon passed muster, and was registered as a member of the Feminist Lesbian Man Hater SIGN; FLeMH.

The NFN network, hired Vera slightly more than ten years ago, and brought her to their NYC offices. She'd risen rapidly in her field, and had quickly become a recognised, national media star, second tier. Vera was positive that this alien abduction story would set her atop the pinnacle of journalism. Maybe she'd win a Putzer Prize! What a rush that would be! Now, if she could only catch up to the story. That would be a big help.

Chapter 7

Torchy stepped softly out of his mini-office, and into the office arena of his boss. He found Al in front of the large mirror near the bowling alley, where he worked on perfecting his fake smile. Torchy cleared his throat, "Uh, hey Boss?" Al spun around on his heels and said, "Tell me!" His eyes wrinkled with amusement. He hopped into a golf cart and drove back to his desk.

Torchy waited patiently while his boss mounted to the raised desk platform and climbed up into his throne. In a voice as nonchalant and easy as a hooker, Torchy said, "How do you want it Chief? Good or bad?"

Al answered like a regular john, "Give it to me good," he said.

Torchy inhaled deeply and said, "Okay then, the good news first. One alien and one female hostage have been successfully kidnapped! It's a success, Boss!"

"Wonderful! Wonderful," Al cheered. He pushed a button on his chair arm, which made it spin in a counter clockwise rotation once. Al faced his brawny secretary, and asked, "Where are they? Where are they going? Polyplastis said the TDS thingy wasn't far."

Torchy answered, "They're driving a white Pissan Tanki, on I-800 westbound, in a rainstorm. I read it on a newslog."

Al stuck a cigar in his mouth, clenched it between his teeth and said, "My great confidence in the exceptional, instinctual criminal faculties of Buster Monk was not misplaced. I know how to pick winners Torchy. Felonious Monk came through like the champion serpent I knew he could be. I saw the promise. To be honest Torchy, Monk may be my most successful unrehabilitation project ever." Al pulled a lighter from a cubbyhole in his desk and lit his cigar. He splurged, because he'd earned it!

Torchy stood motionless, like a wax museum display of Jeek the Ripper, and listened to his employer brag again, trying to look impressed and failing at it. Torchy was enjoying this. Sadism had its merits. Torchy waited for Al to sit back in his chair, throw his feet up on the desk and puff on his cigar. Then he asked, "Boss, you want the bad news now?"

Al put his hands behind his head. Torchy pretended to study Al's putting green. Darkly laughed, and said, "Are you kidding, Burnie? Everything's going our way. Lay it out."

Torchy raked his heavy beard with his fingers, dislodging some food crumbs. "Well, it's like this; the sperm whale is in custody of FIBB. She got left behind somehow, I don't know…"

Al popped out of his seat, without need of the chair arm's eject button, and his burning cigar fell onto the precious warthog hide rug under his chair.

Torchy was thrilled by the reaction, but he said, "Calm down boss! You know that Vometta won't say a word."

Al spat at his burning cigar, but hit his shoe instead. The acid burned a scar in the leather. He snarled, "She can't say a word! She's always got something in her mouth!"

Torchy said cheerfully, "That's right. She'd choke if she tried. Moaning is the most she can manage," he said, with fond memories.

Al picked up the cigar. Burning warthog leather smelled horrid. He ascended his throne and said, "Get Buster Monk on the fone. He's on the scene, directing and producing this crime drama. He'll tell us what's what."

Torchy shook his head in awed admiration; the brilliance of his boss never ceased to amaze him. He returned to his shoebox office space, sat in his broke back chair, and placed the call to Monk's selfone, from the clunky office fone which sat atop the overturned trashcan that served as his desk." He told the fone, "Call Buster Monk."

Buster paused the action on his favourite video game, 'Female Prison Riot', and answered his selfone. "Yeah, what's up, Torchy?" the big BEWB asked.

Torchy nearly burst into flames. He bellowed in a quiet voice so that Al didn't hear him, and that isn't easy to do. "What the poke, Chipmunk? What's up?" Torchy bounced from his chair and paced in agitation. Back and forth; two steps turn, two steps turn. "Where the poke are you? How are the poking hostages? Scat like that!" His voice rose louder with each word, indicating his increasing anger.

"Oh, that." Monk remembered now. He said. "Look man, my tooth was a killin' me, so I called off. That's what you axen about, right?"

The best thing about landline fones is the satisfaction one can get, from crashing the handset down onto the cradle when done talking. Torchy felt a lot better after his grand slam. He strolled out into Al's office. His boss was vigorously massaging Dr Chia's Hair Growth Tonic into the patch of wispy white hairs on his head, and the baldscape encircling them. He paused in his fruitless efforts when he spotted Torchy. He had anticipated a simple fone transfer. He took the burning cigar from his mouth to be safe. "What?" he asked.

"Monk," Torchy replied. "He stayed home to drink malt liquor and play video games." He didn't know this as a given fact, but he knew the type; his mom for one.

Al's face went dark, struck by a mental power outage. He gritted his teeth, and pushed another of the many buttons on his chair arm. A loud primal scream erupted from wireless speakers hanging from the cathedral ceiling. When the echoes died, Al felt some relief, and said, "Call Loser, and transfer the call to me."

* * *

Vera deplaned, slung her purse over a shoulder, and pulled her wheeled carry-on bag behind, as she hurried through the airport concourse. She plowed through and around the mindless, milling hordes that go to airports to mindlessly mill. While speed walking to the car rental agencies, Vera was frantic. She'd read a trusted newslog that reported the location of the white Pissan Tanki in Bland Island! They had a two-hundred-mile lead on her! She'd never catch up! Demn it!

"Anything can happen," she thought optimistically as she whipped around a corner, and headed onto the final straightaway to a car rental counter. Bam! She collided, head to chest with the tallest man she'd ever seen. She bounced off and nearly fell over her trailing luggage.

Somewhat dazed, Vera stared blankly for a moment at the long, thin man in black coveralls. She also noticed a bearded man in a blue jacket and outback hat, standing off to one side with an amused smirk on his face. She didn't have time for this. Vera regained herself and made to resume her car quest.

Then, with a jolt of sudden recognition, she blurted out, "Wait! You're one of them! From the Spewtube video!" Vera's mind was connecting dots at warp speed, and she liked the emerging picture they described.

Robulus thundered in reply, "Yes, and you are Vera Fynne of No False News."

The semi-pro airport loiterers turned in curiosity towards the explosive noise of Robulus' voice. Then it hit them; celebrities! An amoeba-like flow oozed towards the newscaster and the alleged alien, with individual faces hidden by the selfones they aimed at the two celebrities.

Robulus didn't wish to deal with this and Vera, who was more used to the attention, was not currently in the mood for it. Robulus said, "This way, let's go." He started off at a brisk walk, in long smooth strides, leaving Griz and Vera struggling to keep up.

Griz said, "By the way, I'm Matt Gryzolski, the father of the kidnapped woman."

Vera was impossibly thrilled that she had collided with half of the story, but felt bad for this handsome man jogging next to her. She gasped. "OH, my Gawd! I'm so sorry, Matt. Are we in a race?" she asked.

Matt gave a laugh and said, "It seems so, but we've managed to leave our fans eating dust."

Vera risked a backward glance, and replied. "My bag's wheels are starting to smoke."

They came to a stop in front of a line of storage lockers. Robulus produced a key, unlocked one of them and removed a thick, rectangular black case from inside. He looked at Vera's carryon bag and said, "You won't need that."

The news journalist considered the suggestion, and then nodded her head. Robulus picked up her bag, placed it into the locker, closed the door and handed her the key. She dropped it into her purse. Then they were off to the races again. Robulus carried his black case by its handle. Griz and Vera followed him though the airport labyrinth. Griz told her, "Robulus has an airplane." He'd left his own luggage in his car's trunk.

Vera's heart danced a jig. She'd done it! By accident or by luck, it was like in all the movies, where improbable coincidences accrued more quickly, and in such fantastic numbers, that any semblance to reality usually vanished in the first twenty minutes. However, it seemed that life was a series of crazy synchronicities, like peanut butter and jelly meeting for the first time. Scat happened, and she was here to scoop this pile up. Awesome! Vera hadn't been this excited since her divorce.

They entered the underground, short term parking garage, and soon found Griz's car. Vera was impressed that Griz opened her door, and she slid into the back seat. Robulus sat up front to direct Griz to the private airfield where his plane was located. Robulus turned his head to look back at Vera, and he said, "It is indeed fortuitous for our enterprise that you ran into us. If not for nearly a three-hour delay, behind a jack-knifed tractor trailer rig, and the resulting nine car pileup, you'd have run into someone else near the car rental counter."

Vera laughed, and replied, "Fortuitous indeed. I was chasing this story and took a wrong turn."

Griz glanced up into the rear-view mirror, caught her eye and said, "A wrong turn that turned out right." Griz had little regard for so-called journalists, didn't watch television and, so he was unfamiliar with Vera Fynne. Robulus was directing this show, so Griz couldn't object to her presence. He would try to behave.

Robulus directed Griz to a small, shiny hangar, no larger than a one-car garage. The alien pointed to an entry door and said, "Park there."

"There's a plane that seats three people inside that little shed?" Griz asked.

Robulus said, "We designed it for two, but there is room for us."

Griz said, "I can't wait to see this."

Vera, in reporter mode, asked Robulus, "What did you mean by, 'our enterprise'?"

Griz answered, so as to spare a few thousand auditory cells from damage, and said, "Robulus has endured three hours of grilling from me, and he refers to a plan for mankind, that he and his kidnapped partner from outer space, Jeemis developed. Something about curing man of a stupidity virus. I got little more than that out of him though."

Vera wasn't certain if she knew more before, or after, that answer from Griz. They exited the car and got wet. Rain fell steadily, in big heavy drops. Robulus carried his black case. He used his palm print to open the small side door into the mini-hangar and lights came on when they entered.

A metallic fuselage, dimpled like a golf ball, sat atop a tripod of tires. A pair of wings folded against its sides, like a bird at rest. An engine mount and propeller depended from each wing. All in all, it was about the size of a large passenger van. Griz tried not to laugh; it looked as flightworthy as a penguin.

Robulus flipped a wall switch to open the electric hangar door. Griz and Vera stood like dummies as they watched Robulus go about his pre-flight check.

Robulus unsnapped the sturdy case that he'd picked up from the airport locker, and produced a shiny silver object the size and shape of a television remote. He walked around the strange craft, aiming the diagnostic tool at various parts of the plane as he did so.

"Let's go," Robulus said, after one circuit around it. He pushed a button on his remote gizmo and the cockpit doors opened up. A door panel on each side slid back and a short ladder dropped down to the floor. The tall alien climbed up, and into the pilot's chair. Griz stepped up inside first, to avoid the temptation of looking at Vera's butt had she preceded him. He found a way to wedge himself behind the two cockpit seats, and sat on the floor, with his legs stretched out, feet towards the tail, his back braced against a console between the two seats.

Vera buckled into the co-pilot's chair, and stared in fearful wonder at the cockpit controls. A pole between her legs held a small keyboard on an adjustable arm, and a fourteen-inch computer screen, which displayed a mirror image of the pilot's controls. Robulus' control computer and a manual steering column emerged from the simple dashboard. A microphone and speaker hung down from the ceiling. That was it. The rest was a wraparound windshield.

Vera couldn't decipher any of the keyboard's symbols, and she nervously licked her lips. Robulus touched a few places on his monitor screen, the doors closed and the craft noiselessly rolled forward, out of its shelter. The hangar door shut behind them. Rain clattered down as Robulus called up to the tower. He had filed his flight plan earlier, using his eyefone while stuck in traffic with Griz. A few more screen touches and the wings folded out and clunked into place; the tail too. Soon the propellers were spinning.

Griz heard the wind blown by the propellers, but discerned no engine roar. Robulus identified his craft as Malarkey 17, and soon received permission from the tower. He was directed to the private runway. The air traffic controller asked Robulus, "Are you sure that torpedo can fly? Ha ha." Vera and Griz heard their exchanges over the speaker above them.

Robulus replied, "Pray for us." He told Griz and Vera, "Hold on. Three G forces in thirty seconds. I'll show that smarmy human…"

The Malarkey folded its wings back again and they locked in place, against the side of the aircraft. The two cockpits chairs reclined and Griz scooted towards the tail, to lay flat on his back. The propeller blades flattened against the fuselage. Robulus said, "Three seconds." Griz wished he'd packed a parachute and Vera wanted to pee.

"Two, one." Whoosh! The Malarkey shot straight up into the sky. Vera watched the altitude numbers on the screen in front of her. One thousand feet in the first five seconds, and Robulus continued accelerating for twelve of them, before slowing their ascent.

The air traffic controller screamed maniacally, "You can't do that! It's illegal! Get back here! I'm calling the manager!" Robulus muted the hysteria and smiled in satisfaction. The cockpit seats returned to vertical and Griz sat up and got semi-comfortable. "What in Hades is this critter, Robulus? "Griz asked.

Vera said, "That was amazing! That poor man!" She laughed, excited with adrenalin. That was fun.

"No doubt," Griz said and laughed also.

Robulus answered Griz's question, "Jeemis and I have been designing and constructing these, shall I call them UFOs, for many millennia. It's as simple as knowing how to use gravity to one's advantage. The force is everywhere, pulling in all directions at once. The strongest of these gravity 'waves' emanates, relative to our vantage point, from the centre of your planet Gaia. Jeemis and I harness this gravity power, and use it for many purposes. The wings and propellers arc for looks."

The craft operated on autopilot, and according to Vera's screen information, they flew at twenty thousand feet and four hundred mph. She had a feeling that it was capable of a lot more than that. She assumed correctly, that the alien was simply following the flight plan he'd filed.

She and Griz remained silent, waiting for Robulus to divulge more of this alien plan for man. Griz didn't know any more than she did. Robulus was reluctant to reveal the plan, and while together in a car for three hours, Robulus deflected a lot of Matt's queries like a skilled politician. "We call our project, the Unveiling," he told Matt, "And I will reveal more details at a later hour."

That later hour had come. Robulus told them, "Give me a minute. I have to set the countdown clock." He opened up the blocky case from the airport locker. Robulus or Jeemis kept this case close to them wherever they went, and had been doing so for the last fifteen months. He pulled a silver and black laptop out of it. He opened it up, and Vera saw another odd keyboard with strange symbols. Robulus explained what he was doing, since Griz had his back to them and faced the tail area. He said, "I am setting the clock for midnight, approximately twelve hours from now. This will set activity in motion, for there is much to be done to prepare for the TDS Unveiling."

The alien shut down his computer and packed it away in the black case. He pulled three bottles of water from a bin between the two cockpit seats. After he distributed the water, he said, "Get comfortable. It's eighty-six minutes to Colorotta Springs and I have a lot to tell you."

Chapter 8

At 9: 56 AM, close to the same time that Vera boarded her flight to Ohaha, a white Pissan Tanki passed the third I-800 entrance ramp, leading out of Winkin, Nobraska, where Wayne Bruce sat in his car in waiting. When he saw the BUV, his broad baby face lit up like an LED lightbulb. He believed in saving energy. He started his car, and sped down the ramp and merged with traffic. Wayne turned his wipers on and moved into the middle of the three westbound lanes. Interstate traffic was light for the most part, except for the left lane, which was busy with OTR truck drivers. Before long, Wayne saw the huge white Tanki ahead. He closed to within eight or ten car lengths, and settled in for a long stretch of driving. He estimated two and a half to three hours before they reached Bland Island, if they went that far.

Wayne Bruce had not yet formulated a plan of attack. It wasn't possible. A superhero had to know who the bad guys were first. Secondly, one needed to know their evil plan for world domination. Thirdly, said superhero had to narrowly escape death, and save the world right in the nick of time. It was all there in the manual. If the manual wouldn't convince a person, comic books could!

Wayne Bruce's favourite comic was Super-duper Tarantula Man. The marvellous arachnid was featured in Marvy Comics. The art was fantastic and the dialogue was the absolute best! Wayne remembered a scene from 'Super-duper Tarantula Man Meets Doctor Tick's Parasite People', Issue 32841. It was that awesome! Doctor Tick had robbed the World Blood Bank Vault in Shyna, of Gaia's entire supply of type-whitey blood, and had it delivered on pallets to the Parasite People of Urang. Doctor Tick was dangling a bucket of liquid radioactivity, gleaned from the Urang uranium juicers, over the whitey blood, when Super-Duper Tarantula Man scuttled in and warned him, "You have ten seconds to put that uranium back in its cage before I call in the social workers!"

Tick sucked his face in and laughed! "Go ahead and try it! I defunded them too! Ha ha!"

Tarantula Man winked one of his five eyes and the next two pages were, "Bam! Pow! Kablooey!" Of course, right after he squished the blood out of Tick, and splashed the bucket of uranium juice all over the parasite people, the social workers showed up.

Wayne wanted a comic book for Crime Blaster XL-5 someday. That was his dream. Today could be the day, to make his dream come true! He pitied his lonely wife. Saving the world was a lonely job too, but somebody had to do it. Wayne sighed. He turned on the car radio, and tuned in to a country music station. He'd always enjoyed hearing cowboy drinking songs, about cheating on their pickups and shooting their wives. Or did he have that backwards? He'd ponder on that awhile as he drove.

Several long car lengths ahead of Wayne's red Cumaro, the white Tanki trundled forward, its big tires spraying water far and wide. Donut saw a sign reading, '16 Miles to Yuk'. He announced, "I gotta pee, Loser."

"Me too," Melanie said.

Loser nodded his shaven head and said, "Shut up! I'm in charge here!" After a two count, Loser said, "I think we should stop in Yuk, in case anyone needs to pee. That's how it's done!" His selfone jingled. Loser slipped it from his back pocket and stared at its screen. It trilled some more.

"Demn!" he swore. "Poke me! It's Torchy!" Loser answered his selfone reluctantly and turned the speaker on, so that Donut might hear the call. "Well, good morning, Mr Torchy! And how are we today?" Loser tried for light and happy, but came off dim and stupid.

Torchy snarled, "What's this 'we' stuff, Loser? Are you a doctor now? Get your scat together BEWBie! Mr Darkly is on standby. Hold on."

"Hey, Loser," Al Darkly said, and then for no reason asked, "Is that you?"

Loser was flustered, and answered Al's question with a question, "Who?"

"Who I am speaking with," Al replied, annunciating loudly and clearly for the mental deficient.

"Oh, it's me, Loser."

Pitch Al shook it off. He said, "I think we're past that. Look Loser; I want to thank you for a job well begun. I knew that you were the real force of the BEWB crew, the true leader. Keep up the good work. So, tell me, where is the TDS? Where are you going?"

Loser felt as ethereal as light beer, as airy as a loaf of white bread, the unexpected compliments sprouted an erection. He gazed at the peapod lump in his long shorts with affection. Loser hollered back to Jeemis, "Where is this place at anyway?"

Jeemis shrieked, "The TDS is on Poke's Peak, near Colorotta Springs."

Al's hearing went on holiday for a moment, until his auditory nerves recovered consciousness. Then he heard Loser say, "The TDS thang you hired us to find is in Colorotta Springs."

Pitch Al said, "Poke's Peak."

Loser said, "We be goin' there."

Al kindly corrected Loser's grammar, "We are going there," he said.

"Cool!" Loser yelled. "We be too!"

Al moved on, "Are the victims unhurt? Everybody okay?" He asked.

Donut hollered an answer from the back seat, "Only our bleeding eardrums, Sir! This alien dude shrieks like a banshee!"

Now that Al had slopped praise all over Loser like a coat of paint, it was time to apply the turpentine. He said, "So Loser tell me why Vometta is wearing out the agents of the Ohaha FIBB, not to mention blowing up their grocery budgets, and why didn't you call me you poking moron, I gotta know what's going on out there or I can't manage the situation, from now on call me every two poking hours!" Darkly was speed talking, like a television car adman reading a disclaimer.

"Sure Bossman, "Loser replied automatically, having no idea what was said. He asked, "But the sperm whale is okay, right? No, um, disabilities?" Loser cringed to remember the accident and the truck tires parked atop her mountainous chest.

"Forget about her. She's still poking and choking. You have one goal, Loser! Focus!" Al became subdued and serious, "You know what this is all about, right; the ultimate prize?"

"Yeah," Loser said, confident that he possessed leverage. "I wanted to talk to you about that, Al. You see, it's like this; I think I should get that toothaching bass turd Monk's share of the payoff."

"Shut up, Loser!" Al railed. "And don't poking call me Al! Now listen to me, Loser, and you too, Donut. You are on a quest, a journey, more important to the fate of all mankind, than the landing on the moon. You are going to pop in to see this TDS guy, and pick up the recipe or formula for immortality. Jason and the Golden Piece don't stack up to this. Look, if there's a fee, put it on your BEWB charge card and I'll pay you back. In fact, you guys, I will double the pay for both of you, to twenty thousand dollars each."

Loser said, "Thank you sir. What are we supposed to beat out of this TDS crew? Immaturity?"

Donut shook his head in exasperation. Loser was such a stupid ass. Donut piped up to say, "No Loser, Immorality!"

Loser snarled, "He's got all he needs of that. It's immaturity, right Al…I mean, Sir?"

Call end.

Once they had reached the town of Yuk, Melanie steered the BUV into a Fas-Gas lot. She parked in the most distant corner, relative to the convenience store, as Loser had directed. The Pissan didn't need any fuel, it still held three quarters of its sixty-two-gallon capacity. Loser had already laid down all the rules once. He reiterated, "Behave." He brandished a 9 mm pistol to show he meant business, a Schlock. "Donut, keep your stayser handy," Loser said. "Remember, we stay together or people get hurt. Let's go, Mel."

"Don't call me Mel!" she said. "If you can't assemble the three syllables of Mel-a-nie into one big word, then leave my name alone," she snapped, nerves frayed by the ordeal. Her neck and shoulders were as tight as bow strings.

Jeemis screeched, "We know, Loser. No trouble. Relax and act cool."

They walked through the rain together, Jeemis and Melanie in front of Loser and Donut.

The quartet entered the convenience store, and angled towards the restrooms at the back. A hideous leer stretched across Loser's face as he followed Melanie into the Ladies room, one hand massaging his crotch. Melanie spun around swiftly, and shoved the palm of her hand hard, up under his wispy chin. Loser's head snapped backwards at the same instant that Jeemis barged in. There was a head-on collision. The door and Loser's cranium cracked together with a hollow sound, like a kettle drum.

After the echoes faded away, Jeemis, who was holding the door open, howled, "Leave it alone." Loser pretended to be interested in the damage to the door and avoided looking up into Jeemis' dark cold eyes. Loser said, "Hurry up and pee, Mel. We need to leave." He left and entered the Men's room as Donut exited it. Donut discreetly covered Jeemis with the Stoppem Stayser gloves.

Melanie washed up and left the restroom at the same time that the unwashed Loser exited the men's. He gave Donut three twenties and told him to buy a few snacks, some drinks and a coffee. "Two coffees," Melanie said. Jeemis wailed, "And three's a charm."

Loser hustled his captives outside while Donut stuffed a basket full of junk food.

Wayne Bruce strode into the Fas-Gas in time to see and hear the 'Whomp!' of door meets head. He waited outside the Men's room until Loser and Jeemis came out. He needed to pee. Now he'd seen the craven behaviour of the green sock wearing guy with red sandals, and the mouse-like dude wearing the Brokes Brother suit. He'd showed no direct interest in his two foes, and had pretended to an intense study of the store's assortment of feminine hygiene products.

Wayne Bruce was unaffected by Melanie's mature beauty. He was married. His alter ego Crime Blaster XL-5 had no such concerns however, and he intended to win her heart. After he saved the world and rescued her, she would be his. He had yet to uncover the kidnapper's plot for world domination, but for Super-duper Tarantula Man, that discovery often had to wait until the next issue.

Shopping and bladders attended to, and the Tanki was soon on the highway again. Wayne followed behind the white BUV, in his red Cumaro.

Melanie glimpsed a line of blue sky on the western horizon, and the rain was letting up some. She saw the creepy guy from the Fas-Gas fall in behind them, in the red mid-life crisis car, as she moved into the middle lane of I-800. He'd stared at them and watched their every move in the convenience store. Maybe he was a cop, she thought.

Loser was stuffing one yellow twinkery snack cake after another into his maw when Jeemis asked, "How did you Ohaha BEWBs wind up with an eighty-five-thousand-dollar Pissan Tanki? Surely it was not earned by honest labour."

That short phrase, 'honest labour', pushed Loser's, 'hysterical laughter' button. He howled like a coyote, barked like a dog and trumpeted like an elephant. The two and a half twinkerys of mushy yellow cud inside his mouth and throat were ejected onto the dashboard and windshield of the Pissan, although enough crumbs were inhaled that he coughed, choked and laughed all at once.

"Gross," Melanie said.

Donut had been gulping down boatloads of Fas-Gas sushi, taken from the day-old rack, when Loser's fit made him bust out in a hyena laugh. He spewed out a missile of porpoise poker, which struck Loser in the back of his very sore head. Melanie pushed buttons, to roll down all four windows, to overcome the horrendous stench of rotted fish. The car on their right side rolled their windows up, and swerved onto the shoulder so the driver could stop to vomit.

Loser stopped laughing to breathe, and finally remembered that Jeemis had asked him a question. He worked back, and then recalled what the question was. He answered, "We got this here Beast Utility Vehicle, from the national headquarters of the Basement Elites Without Breakfasts, in Porchland, Oreogon. Them nutjobs who live up there in the specific northwest, raised like a zillion dollars, with all them BEWB Lifts Matter riots a couple years back."

Melanie was sickened by the memory of the BEWB Lifts Matter death and destruction, which was enabled by Demolist party politicians, and promoted by the Make-Believe Media. All of the hatred fear and resulting destruction of the riots was triggered by a pair of big time Oreogon BEWBs, who were sagging in their Spewtube show ratings. The BEWBs needed a lift and so turned to Dr Brazeere, the media mogul. It went bad.

When Dr Brazeere went on Tooter and tooted out that, after vetting the two crooks, he found them to be fake BEWBs, supporters came to their defence and burned down a few score hospitals and doctor's offices around the nation. When these peaceful protesters learned that Dr Brazeere's PhD was not in medicine, but in communications, the mindless mob began to burn down selfone antennae. People got killed over that.

Melanie had a question too. She asked, "Donut, do you always wear two-thousand-dollar suits while committing felonies?"

Loser snorted, and yellow snack cake goo shot out of his nostrils. Melanie felt her breakfast trying to escape her convulsing gut, and rising up her oesophagus. She tried not to vomit. Loser answered her question, before Donut swallowed his wad, and could reply without choking. He said, "Donut likes to be prepared in case he gets killed in action. That way he'll already be dressed for burial."

Jeemis screeched, "That's thinking ahead, and it's why he's the brains of the BEWBs."

Donut spoke up now, "They can stick me straight into the coffin, without filling me up with preservatives and all that scat, because I am totally allergic to it!"

Melanie shook her head, and said, "Crime must pay well, to afford to look like a mobster."

Donut shook his head and replied, "No; my wives work, and I've been getting unemployment checks ever since I went AWOL from the Army, and Social Justice Security pays me a disability check too."

Melanie had to ask, but she wasn't quite sure why. "How are you disabled?"

"It's for my Post Dramatic Stress Disorder. According to the Centre for Disease Patrol, a life of crime has been proven to be six times more stressful than being an author, and four times worse than being a poet!"

* * *

Barry Porter's flight to North Flatte had an ETA of 2:30 PM. He would land right on top of this breaking news story. Barry sat in a middle seat, between a newlywed man and his bride who were celebrating their honeymoon. Barry explained that he couldn't in good conscience, change seats with one of them so they could sit together, because he didn't want to confuse the stewards. The couple was going on an exciting honeymoon vacation in Guano Bay, Kewba, which had become a favourite tourist destination over the last three years, since the expansion of the prison to accommodate a heavy influx of traitors at that time.

Many past stars, from newscasters to movie moguls, and from politicians to actors were imprisoned. The inmates were allowed to earn money for food and cigarettes, by selling autographed copies of their crimes to tourists. Guano prison was a celebrity zoo. There were several busy five-star hotels and gourmet restaurants nearby, to service the prison tour trade.

Barry used his flight time in the same fashion he'd used his waiting in the concourse time, by scrolling through the many interweb newslogs. His satellite eyefone performed just fine on the airplane. He worked in the MBM industry, and so he took into account, that behind-the-scenes fiction writers, revised and rewrote all of his reports, as if his own stories weren't wild enough. So, when Barry read newslogs, he knew not to believe any of it. Nobody won a Putzer journalism award with factual stories anymore.

Currently, the news that Barry read, which competed with the alien abduction story for coverage, was President Crumm's surprise flight to Onnitt Air Power Base, which tied right back in with the aliens. The MBM was spinning in circles.

Barry's network, the Conscience Of News aka CON, reported this, "Crumm panics over TDS leaks, and flees to Onnitt APB, to ride out the fallout in a bunker. In a massive cover-up of unparalleled, unsurpassed, impeachably offensive behaviour, the president is said to be on a clean-up mission at the airbase, to destroy evidence of his collusion with aliens. Demolists call for an investigation."

According to MNBS or Mostly Non-Biased Stuff, "The president is working with the aliens to impregnate his science advisor Melanie Gryzolski, to create a super race of hybrid beings loyal to Crumm. This is part of his plan for world domination. Melanie's father, Matt, has been taken hostage, by the horny aliens as well, to force the cooperation of his daughter. Sources close to the Off White House, tell us that the three letters TDS, are code for Toxic Diet Soda.

"Stay tuned for the latest rewrites on this big, breaking news event."

Chapter 9

Pitch Al sweated with the effort. With pencil and paper, he'd created a pail list, of all the goals he wanted to achieve, over the next one hundred and fifty years. The hardest part of making these plans for his near future was prioritising them. How does one decide between becoming a Hollowood movie producer, and sailing a yacht around the world, or between having a harem on an island in the Carobean, or on an island in the Meditational Sea? He needed to take a break, and then he wanted to get fifty more years worked out for his future, before calling it a night. Al fixed himself a shot of brandy and tossed it back.

Al Darkly put his feet up on his desk and tried to clear his mind. But Al's mind never cleared completely. It was like Seaddle weather, always dripping wet. His runoff was dirty and filled with garbage, and it flowed into a sewer system which ejected from Al's mouth. It couldn't be helped. Al couldn't quit scheming, even while sound asleep. His third ex-wife said that's when he did his best thinking.

After a second shot of brandy, a plan to protect his investment formed in the bowels of his brain. Technically and financially, it was Don Crews' investment, but Crews was Al's investment, thus the kidnap was Al's investment. His brain dumped an idea out! Al knew what needed doing next. "Burnie!" he bellowed.

Torchy paused the video solitaire game, put down his bottle of beer, and made the journey to Al's desk acreage. He belched, wiped the foam from his moustache, and asked, "Whaddya want, Boss?' Torchy itched for action. His life was miserable if he wasn't making somebody's life miserable. Maybe he'd get lucky tonight at Soak and Poke, where he worked as a bouncer three nights a week. If he couldn't always find trouble at the single's bar, he knew how to make it.

"Burnie," Al said, "I want you to start making anonymous phone calls to all of the MBM, and to feed the newslogs like Bulitico and the Sludge Report. Here's what you tell them, 'The alien abduction is not a crime. The heroic

BEWBs are to the aliens, as riders are to horses. They are guiding us all to the TDS, as a boon to all mankind, ushering in a time of peace, prosperity and climate security for all."

Burnie was impressed. Al was a man of a million talents, some reputed as useful. Torchy said, "You can spin with the best of 'em, Chief. I never heard so much poking, saccharine horse scat, since the last election campaign season."

Al was touched by the praise, even if it was coming from a halfwit brute.

Torchy said in admiration, "You're a demn genius, Boss. The more positive publicity the BEWBs get, the more protection they'll have. The crooks will be the good guys. They'll be prime time darlings, and could become as famous as the double murderer Ojay Crimson. Hades, if we made a point of saying, that the BEWBs did this kidnapping to thumb their noses at Crumm, the MBM will make it a feature story. The poking Basement Elite Without Breakfasts, Boss, will be more famous than ever."

Pitch Al hadn't heard Torchy make a speech that lengthy since the last time he drank a six pack of beer at work. Al stuck a cigar between his teeth and said, "Torchy, for a muscle-headed drunk, you sometimes utter the most sensible things. That's the idea, Burnie. Be creative and I want this going out everywhere. Okay, go get 'em Torchy, and crack open another beer while you're at it".

Torchy answered, "If you say so, Boss. I'm on it."

Chapter 10

Robulus said, "Vera, I have some rather remarkable facts to divulge, and you may wish to record my words. I've told Griz some of this already, but he remains sceptical of my claims. I imagine you will disbelieve as well, but time will tell." His big voice filled the small, gravity wave powered airship to overflowing. Vera set her eyefone to record and placed it into a slot for that purpose, set into the lid of the storage bin on her left.

"Jeemis and I crash landed here on Gaia," Robulus blasted, "more than sixty-five million years ago, due to a cascading series of catastrophic synchronicities, which we call Kazooky's Conundrum. The explosion resulting from our little accident stranded us, finished off the dinosaurs and altered your planet forever."

Vera asked, "Ka who and what?"

Robulus laughed. Griz listened in silence from behind them, he'd heard this one. The alien said, "Whatever can happen, will happen, but only at the worst possible time."

"But that's Murphy's Law!" Vera objected, just as Griz had earlier.

"Yes, you call it that, "Robulus boomed. "Kazooky's Conundrum, Murphy's Law, call it what you wish. There are millions of names and labels in the multiverse for this unbreakable, inexplicable cosmic principle, but the result is always the same; a big demn mess."

Vera slid into interview mode without knowing it, because her behaviour was instinctual. As a curious youngster, on Yuletide Eve, she would sneak out of bed, and carefully open up her gifts, to learn what lay beneath the pretty wrapping paper. Then, Vera would put it all back together and return to bed. She always acted appropriately surprised when morning came, and she opened her presents. Vera asked Robulus, "Where did you come from?"

Robulus said, "We call our home planet Uzgabada, and it lies approximately seven hundred and forty million light years distant from Gaia. Jeemis and I set off from home for a holiday vacation after completing our millennial graduation.

That's when a student successfully completes ten years of advanced studies in one hundred different subjects."

Griz asked, "Does your race use a base ten math system?"

"Yes, we have ten fingers like humans." Robulus answered. "To continue; we rented a two-seater Space Scoot, which was about the size and shape of one of your school busses, but without the hideous colour. As immortals, it isn't necessary for us to eat, drink or breathe to survive, but we suffer the pangs and pains of humans if we do not. So, we took a few supplies for our ten-year romp.

"Our apparent immortality is a product of nano-technologies, and these indestructible, molecular bio-machines absorb power and receive operating energies from radiation of any and all wavelengths, and thus can operate under any conditions. When we are wounded, we heal nearly instantaneously," he said.

"The Space Scoot used a hybrid power system which incorporated fusion-drive technology with a gravity-wave translator and was capable of nearly two percent of light speed. The little scoot's main boast, was its ability to transit hyperspace, and in finding short-cuts through space-time. The spacecraft's controls could be set to any destination, and it would find the shortest route, and then travel there."

His audience of two listened raptly, wavering between doubt and acceptance. Griz found it just as implausible the second time he heard it. Robulus said, "Well, it so happened that during one such auto-controlled transit between inter-galactic points, while I was winning big from Jeemis in a card game, a malfunction in the hyperdrive, caused our ship to emerge from hyperspace in the wrong sector. A concurrent malfunction in the gravity wave translator resulted in our Space Scoot assuming an enormous artificial mass. We re-emerged into real space time, but had no control over our ship.

"Kazooky wasn't done with us yet, however," Robulus said shaking his narrow head, remembering the episode as if it happened yesterday, rather than sixty-five million years ago. "When our massive little ship emerged from hyperspace, it was in Gaia's gravity well. Within minutes, at incredible velocity, our Space Scoot entered your planet's stratosphere. The spaceship survived the heat of friction, to smash down into the area of your Yuckytan Peninsula.

"After the impact, firestorms raged for many months. It was a horrific time for an immortal. Jeemis and I were incinerated, and reconstituted thousands of times per day, until calm returned.

"Oh, my Gawd!" Vera cried, looking as if she may be sick. "I can't imagine the agony!"

"Yes well, this is immaterial, however," Robulus said. Griz thought it improbable, but Vera preferred incredible.

Robulus had more to say, "At midnight tonight, Jeemis and I will reveal the TDS to the entire world. They, or it, is a conduit of all cosmic knowledge, which arose about fourteen thousand years ago by an unknown means. Perhaps a rare convergence of alternate universes created this strange anomaly."

Griz didn't see the point of any of this. "How is this going to help Melanie? My daughter has been kidnapped!"

Vera heard the pain and strain in his voice, even if she couldn't see his face. "Yes, Robulus, what's going on with that poor woman?" she asked.

Their aircraft left behind the grey rain clouds of Nobraska and entered colourful Colorotta airspace. Vera could see nothing ahead, but beautiful blue skies and warm sunshine, all the way west to the three mile high Stony Mountains. Vera thought it gorgeous.

Robulus said, "Of course. Let's check in on Melanie, but please rest assured that no harm shall come to her. Jeemis will see to that." The alien touched a couple of keyboard symbols on the plane's computer console, and the status screen readouts were replaced by a short scene, recorded earlier by Jeemis. Griz turned around to kneel, so that he could see the central dashboard screen, over the storage bin between the two cockpit chairs. The trio watched in grim amusement as Melanie tangled with a wispy-whiskered slob, who reminded Vera of Scraggy from the Scooty-Poo cartoons. Melanie snapped his bald head back into a door that Jeemis crashed open. Both items were dented, but only one was unhinged.

Griz said her name, "Melanie."

Vera said, "Oh dear! That's your daughter? Suddenly her story seemed too much like real life. "But I know her! I interviewed her once! She's science advisor to the president! Duh; I didn't connect the pieces"

Griz recalled the interview now! It was around two years ago, soon after Melanie's appointment to her current position, and it was tastefully done. Okay, so a journalist got it right for once, and probably didn't make a second mistake. He gave Vera some credit for that much.

Griz asked, "When did that scene occur, Robulus? And where?"

Robulus boomed, "That short scene occurred in the town of Yuk, Nobraska several minutes ago. I see that your girl is tough and feisty as well as brilliant."

Vera said, "And beautiful too."

Griz smiled with pride. He said, "She's special. Always was. Nothing will keep me from her, Robulus, nothing. Whatever you're up to, whatever you need to accomplish it, as long as Melanie comes out better for it, count me in."

"Me too!" Vera chimed in enthusiastically. She was surprised by her emotions. It was strange to feel a personal connection to her news reports. They were just stories, one-minute blurbs, forgotten as soon as the next breaking news event occurred. Vera was not certain who or what this emotional connection applied to. Events were carrying her along, and she was going to go with the flow for now.

Robulus cleared his throat. It sounded like a diesel engine starting up. He said, "Vera, I want you to call your program director at No Fake News. I have a message to deliver." The alien explained to Vera what he wanted her to report, and how he'd like to see it done. She relished the idea, but she still needed to ask her boss for permission to cover the story first.

Chapter 11

President Darryl Crumm sat at the head of a rectangular conference table, in the headquarters building of Onnitt APB. Three Covert Service agents provided security for him and this meeting room. Two female agents stood outside its closed door, and one large man watched over the president, from inside the room. Crumm's chief of staff was in an adjoining room, she was working on other matters. The four not-kidnapped members of the secret inquiry panel, sat at the table with their president. They'd been kept in the dark about the day's events, because their eyefones and selfones had been collected by security. The four crusty men had been notified that Crumm was popping in to say, "Hello". They were thrilled.

Closest to the president on his right, the goose-necked Califoreignya congressman Aaron Chip sat. Fidgeting next to Aaron was the sweating Brenny Comeon, Adjunct Assistant Associate Administrative Deputy Secretary of the Federal Investigative Bureau of Bureaucracy. At Crumm's left, and sitting opposite Chip, was New Yank Senator Huck Choomor, and sitting next to him was the Berzerkley professor of weird stuff, Felix Polyplastis.

Crumm sat quietly for a couple of minutes and savoured the silence. He smelled their fear, it permeated the room. The four conspirators held their collective breath, and so the president waited to see if they exhaled or passed out first. The professor won. His marshmallow head fell forward bounced once and came to rest on the table top.

Satisfied, Crumm said, "Thank you for staying detained here to await me, I didn't want to start without you. You may or may not have noticed, but the fifth member of this secret-from-the-president investigation, Melanie Gryzolski is not here with us today. Also, there happens to be a pair of alleged aliens who couldn't make it."

"This is what we are going to do," President Crumm said. "I am going to ask what you learned in your illegal, secret inquiry into the alleged existence of alleged aliens." If the edge in the president's tone of voice was any sharper, the air would have bled. "Let's start with you Professor Plastics. What did you learn yesterday?"

The professor looked like a potato with its eyes off kilter. He adjusted his eyebrows, and replied, "That's Polyplastis, Sir. Now then, you will be pleased to learn all the relevant data I gleaned, in three simple questions."

President Crumm trusted that the questions were simple. He yawned, tapped a pencil and asked, "Is it a secret, or can you tell me?"

Irritated by the interruption, Felix frowned and said, "If you signed the No Leak Agreement, I am authorised to reveal…ooh, um; what I mean Sir, is that in three sharply focused questions…um, just take notes."

President Crumm never resorted to physical violence, and was not going to be goaded into it now, by what he described as 'aggressive stupidity'. He had inured himself to it after six years in politics. He tapped a pen on the table, expecting to be underwhelmed.

Professor Polyplastis fulfilled all of the President's lowest expectations and more. Felix felt like he had mined world shaking information from the alleged aliens. He hated Crumm, but hoped to impress him with his perspicacity. If the president was excited and stimulated by the professor's discoveries, perhaps Felix could quietly vanish afterwards, without suffering repercussions for his involvement in the inquiry. He knew that his leak had most likely led to the kidnapping, and he wished upon a star that his discharge of secret information would never be learned of. The star was Don Crews, his favourite Sacred Star Temple apostle.

Felix read to the president from his own notes, "After analysing their answers, I have concluded, that the two alleged aliens are homophobic, racist, deplorable plutocrats, who don't pay their fair share in taxes!"

Crumm started to take notes, but by the ninth word out of the professor's drooling mouth, the president tore the page from his notepad, and noisily crumpled it into a ball. He tossed it towards a distant trashcan. "Three points!" he cheered.

Professor Polyplastis felt insulted, but he had the courage to say, "Nice shot, Sir."

President Crumm looked at the scowling Senator Choomor and said, "I know it will be difficult to surpass that presentation, Huck, but be my guest and try."

The senator consulted his notes and said, "Sir, I must make this disclaimer before proceeding; I asked three questions which were meant for my wife's class, over at the school. However, you may find them interesting, if irrelevant. The first of these questions related to a woman's right to have rights. I asked these highly advanced primitives whether they supported this life-affirming issue."

President Crumm said, "Your second question."

Choomor ground his teeth in agitation, but regretted it when he nearly swallowed his dentures. He lowered his gaze and read, "My wife's second question related to women's rights and whether females earned as much as the other genders in similar jobs." He looked through his plate glass spectacles at Trapp with owlish eyes, his nose struggling under their weight. With disgust carved into his wooden face, Huck asked, "And do you know what those misogynistic, patriarchal, anti-feminist alleged aliens who probably cheat on their wives said?"

Crumm said, "No, I wasn't there. Do you?"

Senator Choomor searched his notes frantically, "It's here somewhere, Sir. I know I wrote it down."

Since leaving successful private practice behind, six years ago, to boldly enter the District of Calamity Swamp, President Crumm often felt like he'd entered an alternate universe, where up was west and down was left. He couldn't understand how people voted these same nincompoops into office, term after useless term. The denizens of a pet store would do better. Fish.

Crumm crossed his arms below his red tie and sighed. Choomor took the hint, looked at his messy notes and said, "My third question…"

Crumm finished the preamble, "…relates to women's rights."

The Senator from New Yank jerked his head up, ruddy anger flushing his grainy face. "That's impossible!" he cried. "How could you know that?"

"Spies," Trapp wisecracked.

"Oh, okay." Huck said, accepting that as normal in politics. "Well, I asked them if they would ever elect a woman for president. And get this! They answered NA, as in, no answer, not applicable. no acknowledgement, never accountable, nasty attitude, negative…"

Crumm interrupted, and said, "What do you have for me Mr Comeon? I only hope that it proves at least as valuable as the information I've already heard." The president sat forward and placed his hands, palm down on the table. In his mind Brenny Comeon was a synonym for duplicity.

"Thank you, Mr President," Comeon's voice buzzed, sounding like a cheap electric razor. He was facing in the wrong direction, but did make a course correction and found the president after a moment. He held up a piece of notepaper, waggled it in the air, and said, "What I hold here in my hand is of the highest national security important..." He stopped in mid-nonsense when the scrap slipped from his fingers, floated for half a second, then fell onto the table in front of the president.

President Crumm saw printed words, and hoped that maybe Comeon did have something secret, that he didn't want to divulge out loud. Crumm picked it up. He looked rather sad as he read it aloud, "Milk, bread, dog food, Viag, cucumbers, batteries, blindfold, duct tape, rope...This is your grocery list Brenny; what in Hades?"

"Oh wait! Here it is, Mr President. I found my other notes." Brenny Comeon had set them on his chair earlier, and had inadvertently sat on them. He pulled them out from underneath his rear, and Crumm thought, "Pulled out of his ass again."

Brenny's hard face was a geologic record worthy of future study. He said, "My first question was carefully constructed, to trick them into revealing much more than I asked them." The president perked up; perhaps something useful could, by accident, be learned after all. He listened intently and he was rewarded with Comeon announcing, "I asked them what they were doing here."

Brenny rattled papers frantically as he looked for that one which held the answer. He could not remember what they'd said, but he knew it was important. The president waited patiently, looked at his watch and began to whistle, 'She'll Be Goin Around the Mountain'.

Brenny found the answer he wanted and said, "Okay, I got it now. They said that they live here."

Crumm briefly considered offering all four of these clowns a ride on Air Power One, and then dropping them out the emergency exit at thirty-five thousand feet. He said, "Next."

Brenny took it hard. He was a reservoir of hard feelings, which held several thousand cubic feet of grudges and resentments, and was held back by a dam made of adamant ego.

Comeon never received the adulation, appreciation, attention or advancement that he deserved. People were so mean to him. This next question will blow that rat Crumm away, he thought. He said, "My next probing needle

94

jolted them good. I said if you live here, then you should pay taxes here. They said they did, but I think they should make their tax returns public. They're hiding something!"

President Crumm hadn't cancelled his busy schedule, to come out here to Onnitt APB, so that he could badger and harass the Fallacious Four. He wanted to learn all that he could about the two aliens. He wanted to know more about the TDS. It was here in Shamerica and he needed to know what it was! Crumm wanted to know where Melanie Gryzolski was being taken, too. He wasn't going to stand by and do nothing. That was never his style.

"Third question," Crumm prompted the FIBBer. Brenny shuffled his pile of papers, then cut the deck, picked the top page and read, "My final question, the most important one of all, was saved for last. I asked them what their SIGN was!" Comeon was sure this question blew away the president.

He was correct. The stupidity was mind blowing. Crumm could hardly contain his excitement as he anticipated the astounding punchline. Comeon delivered it: "They claimed both federal and state compliance with identity laws. They said that their Special Interest Group Name was LIARS."

The president scratched his chin and translated, "That's the Legal Illegal Alien Resident Squatters. This idiotic designation was created by congress, when the Demolists controlled the House. Crum looked at Congressperson Aaron Chip, and with an air of hopeless abandon, he said, "I'm your newest greatest fan Mr Chip, if you can provide even one scintilla of something, anything of use!"

Aaron licked his lips nervously. One could see a pulse pumping madly in the side of his pencilneck. His eyeballs bulged from their sockets like vanity lightbulbs, and they even radiated heat. "Well Sir," he began meekly and mildly. "Please understand when you hear my questions that I personally certified this intelligence committee hearing as being top secret, and you weren't invited. It was leaked earlier than suggested."

President Crumm was stunned that the Prince of Prevarication most likely had just told the truth, and he was thankful that this session was being recorded so he could prove it to sceptics. Crumm considered that it must have been painful for Chip to utter an honest word, and there must be good reason for it. He prepared for super lies to soon follow.

Aaron filibustered, as he was not eager to share the questions he posed, with the POTUS. He said, "I want to tell you about those too-tall belligerent, uncooperative, alleged aliens! When it was time for them to answer a simple yes or no question, they simply answered yes or no!"

"Just awful," Crumm said indifferently, as if consoling a flat tire.

Chip's eyeballs retracted back home to their sockets and he said, "My first question concerned national security, an issue of concern to us all. I wondered whether they associated with people associated with administration associations. Aaron's eyes were analogues to the nose of Spinocchio; they projected farther out with each lie.

President Crumm read between the lies. He said, "Alien collusion, Aaron? Is that it? And they said, 'No'."

Chip's neck stretched like a bungee cord, and he cried out, "How could you possibly know that! I smell collusion, Mr President! Somethings stinks…"

"Okay," Trapp said, "So you farted. Next question. Let's conclude this exercise in futility."

Subdued momentarily, Chip pulled his neck in and said, "I asked them how many they were in total, on Gaia."

Crumm said, "Now we're getting somewhere. What did they say?"

"They lied!' Aaron exclaimed. "I know it! They said it was just the two of them."

"Good, good," Trump said distractedly. He found a pen in a coat pocket and wrote a few questions down on his unused notepad. "Your third question," he prompted.

Aaron said, "My final question probed into who was financing their invasion, and they obstructed justice by denying the premise of my question."

President Darryl Crumm let the stupidity settle for a minute, while he scrutinised the four faces, one at a time. It reminded him of checking the tomatoes in a garden. These looked rotten. Finally, he said, "I appreciate all the time and effort you put into keeping this inquiry a secret from me, while leaking it to the kidnappers. I want to ask a question, and I expect participation from all of you. These two aliens, or whoever they are, probably said things that you considered insignificant and unimportant because they didn't fit your preconceptions and biases."

He asked, "Did the two alleged aliens mention how they arrived here on Gaia? Did they say when?"

Congressman Chip blurted, "That's two questions, Sir."

President Crumm thought about clearing the room, except for him and Chip. He could sell the video of the carnage after his second term ended in a couple of years. Sigh.

Polyplastis blew his cheeks out like a trumpet playing hamster, and cleared his throat with what sounded like a snow blower. "If I may say, Sir; one of them bellowed something about a crash landing awhile back. I didn't pay much attention to it, because it sounded like a bad movie of the week."

"A while back," Crumm repeated. "Nothing more specific than that, Professor Plastics?"

"Polyplastis, Sir. Something about sixty-five years, I think," Felix said.

"No," Senator Choomor objected, "It's sixty-five jillion years! They killed off Jymnastic Park."

The FIBBster, Brenny Comeon disagreed vehemently, he said, "There weren't any parks! It wasn't like on the Flintrocks cartoon back in the Rolling Stone's Age!"

Aaron Chip was the chairman of the committee and so his word was final, "He said, "It was sixty-five million years ago and they crashed into a dinosaur. Gee whiz."

President Crumm dismissed the four leaky vessels and called for Tommi Gunn, his chief of staff. The president told her, "I plan to address the nation at 7:00 PM, EST. Make ready."

Chapter 12

Melanie ate an apple that apparently came from the antique aisle of the Fas-Gas store, if the way it tasted was any indication. It seemed a better alternative to the packages of Grosstess Twinkerys and Little Webbies mini-donuts that Donut purchased. She was glad to see the rain ending as they approached Bland Island. Happily, they'd passed most of the last two hours without conversation. Unhappily, Loser had turned the radio on and crushed the silence with the mind-numbing rhythms and infantile lyrics of country western gangsta rap. It was twang with a bang, as the radio DJ called it. Melanie loathed it. Loser enjoyed it more because of that fact, and increased the volume accordingly.

He sang along with a few of the sinus-clogged country rappers who sang through their noses, like Girth Crooks and Squirrel Laggard. Loser smoked cigarette after crack hit after cigarette, and he fidgeted like a child in church. Melanie kept her window rolled down, which created a sort of tornado of trash in the back seat. Donut's empty junk food wrappers spun in circles. It wasn't easy to concentrate on her driving with two grown children in the car.

Loser shut the radio off and lit up a big fat joint now. He puffed on it twice and handed it back to Donut. Loser sipped at the cup of coffee purchased from the Fas-Gas half an hour earlier. It was finally drinkable. When purchased, the coffee was so hot that the cup's plastic lid melted. "What's your SIGN?" Loser asked Melanie.

Melanie didn't have anything to hide but she wondered what Loser was up to. She answered him and said, "MoHet, always have been and always will be."

Loser looked like he'd swallowed a sword and lost track of it. "No way!" He denied its possibility. "A hot chick like you? Ha!" Loser didn't meet a lot of Mono-Gendered Heterosexuals. Of course, spending much of his adult life in jails and prisons might explain that. He couldn't shake his disappointment. "I never figured you for a normal." He made it sound like a disease. Donut passed the reefer back to Loser.

Melanie smiled sweetly and in her melodic voice she asked him, "What's the matter Loser, normaphobic?" She laughed.

Jeemis joined in the merriment with his own ear-splitting shrieks, "Wahit! Wahit!" He brayed like a constipated jackass with hiccups. The alien hoped to deflect any rage away from Melanie when Loser lost his temper.

The top of Loser's bald head turned red, like a hot stove burner. Donut wondered if he could warm up an apple turnover on the hothead, because now he had the munchies. Before Loser's ears started to whistle like a boiling teapot, Jeemis turned down the heat. He said, "I bet I can guess your SIGN, Loser."

The ploy worked on the simpleton, his grimace transformed into a facsimile of a smile. Loser took the bait and said, "How much you wanna bet?"

Jeemis played his fish, he said, "I'll bet you our freedom."

Melanie found the alien's eyes in the rear-view mirror and it frightened her. She couldn't read them, they'd gone dark. He didn't look at her.

Loser hadn't considered such a heavy bet, he only had forty bucks. The odds were on his side however, there's no way this alien could even know all one hundred and thirty something different SIGNs, let alone guess his correctly. Not only that, but if the alien thinks I'm going to pay off if I lose, he's dumber than I am.

Loser's mind raced like a tired snail before his eyes alit on the perfect prize. He said, "I'll take that bet. Your poking freedom if you guess my SIGN, and if you're wrong, I get the girl"

Melanie wanted to spit on Loser. She wished the Tanki had a trapdoor button for the passenger seat. She'd pull in front of a tractor trailer rig and push it---- Dump…thump, thump, etc. When she heard Jeemis shriek, "You're on," she nearly pulled off the road so she could get out and kick him. She couldn't believe it!

Donut warned Loser, "Don't do it Lou! Pitch Al will kill us if we let them go!"

Loser shook his head in exasperation. He didn't understand how somebody so stupid, was looked up to as the brain of the BEWBs. He said, "Donut, are you so poking stupid as to think I would honour the poking bet? I'm a poking criminal for Al's sake!"

The sun shone brightly and warmly, and the silence inside the Tanki was painful to behold. Loser decided that he didn't want an answer to that, and tried to gloss over his error. He hurriedly shouted his challenge to Jeemis, "Okay smarty, make your best guess. What's my SIGN? Only one chance."

Jeemis wailed, "It's so obvious, you're a Bisexual Sexual Offender, a BiSOn."

Loser bellowed like a wounded moose, "You cheated! You poking foreigner!" Few others guessed. How in Hades did the alien manage it? He'd passed for a Convicted Rapist Arsonist Plunderer, CRAP, on several occasions and once as a Drug Addicted Felon Thug, or DAFT.

Jeemis shrieked, "Let's get out of here Melanie. We'll walk the rest of the way. Nice knowing you guys and good luck with the feds."

Donut threated Jeemis with his stayser. Loser said, "Like Hades! You're poking taking us to the poking TDS for that poking informality or I'll kill you, you indestructible piece of scat!"

Melanie spoke up. She said, "Loser, you earned your name, and you're going to lose big this time. My father will move Heaven and Gaia to find me.

Loser cackled like a cartoon movie villain he'd admired in the Jumbo Mermaid movie, and he mocked his victim, "Oh, I am so frightened. Big tough daddy might hurt me. Ha ha ha!" He added, "Your papa is probably playing piledriver in some motel room with a cheap whore, right this minute."

Donut was interested and he said, "I wouldn't mind getting some of that, Loser. Do you know which motel? On our way, maybe?"

"Donut?" Loser kept his voice calm.

"Yes, Loser." Donut was on his third junk food binge.

"Forget it." Loser lit a cigarette and turned the radio on. He tuned in to a news station, so he could hear about what he was doing from the media professionals.

"...an unidentified, anonymous, high-level source, who refused to divulge his identity, secretly told our undercover reporter, that an unnamed, mysterious friend of a FIBB agent's ex-wife heard from a pizza delivery boy, that one of the alleged abductors of the alleged alien was still undergoing intense interrogation. According to this report, a female suspect is giving these hard-driving agents a run for their money; their grocery money. Her alleged name is allegedly Vometta Wilde, allegedly a female, and an alleged member of the Ohaha BEWBs who allegedly kidnapped an alleged alien, this morning; allegedly.

"Alleged eyewitnesses report allegedly seeing the white Pissan Tanki allegedly driving west on I-800, and it is said to be nearing Bland Island,

Nobraska. The state police warn any and all people, to not approach this alleged vehicle. The alleged occupants are considered armed and dangerous. Now for a word from Sprout One, the natural solution for alleged ED…"

Loser turned the radio off, that Sprout One crap never worked for him. They spent the next twenty minutes in silence. If the radio had been tuned to news, instead of country western gangsta rap for the couple of hours prior to the Sprout One ad, the occupants of the Tanki would have learned what the Make-Believe Media had done, with Torchy's propaganda dump.

Torchy worked hard and he played hard. He'd gone to his office and waged the disinformation campaign that Al assigned to him, and he performed it diligently and got it done. The various news organisations and social media sites were ablaze with the sparks of nonsense he'd ignited in them. It was hilarious. Al turned on his MegaScreen TV to view the fallout, and he invited Torchy to come and enjoy the show. Pitch Al even sent out for popcorn, as long as Torchy paid for half.

Torchy fed the same bag of groceries to all the various and assorted media he contacted, but they all cooked up a different meal. Breaking news was always the most difficult for the MBM to deal with, because they didn't have time to for rewrites if they wanted to beat their competition in the ratings. The news networks were forced to hire on-air personalities, who were known for their talent at improvisation.

The virtual press like the New Yank Times, or as it was more commonly known, the NY Tripe, turned the heat up too high, and published this over cooked headline on the interweb, "HIGHWAY TO HEAVEN!"

The first paragraph read; "According to a leaking member of a government secret panel, the two immortal aliens are ushering Crumm's science advisor, Melanie Gryzolski, to the site of an actual fountain of eternal youth called the TDS. However, if you are not there, in Colorotta Springs, Colorotta, at precisely midnight tonight, you will miss out. Our fearless leaker also mentioned that there is not and has never been any intimate sexual contact between Melanie and the two male aliens. He reiterated it for us in fact, that we should make no mention of a threesome. And, so we won't"

The Swampington Post took the same ingredients and served this morsel up: "Hollowood Movie Promo Goes On The Road. Sources in the movie industry tell us that a publicity stunt went haywire this morning in Ohaha, Nobraska, when a stunt double for an alien, kidnapped Crumm's science advisor, and stole a truck. Apparently, the stuntman forgot his medication to treat schizophrenia, and some are blaming President Crumm for sending his science advisor to the movie set. The promotion was for a documentary about the aliens among us."

The prominent social media platforms like Phasebook, Soonagram and Tooter blew up with guesses, speculations, opinions and conspiracy theories so fantastically wild, that MBM newscasters and producers were jealous, and upset that they hadn't thought of it themselves.

The popular Sophisticated Conspiracy Drama Association, with its one hundred and thirty-five million viewers worldwide on its Spewtube channel claimed that, based on reliable sources, the three letters TDS belonged to the Terrorist Day Spa. If one struggled to watch further, one learned that the alleged aliens were actually members of a far-right organisation, called the Basest Racist Aces. The broadcasters claimed that, "The BRAs are supporting a pair of BEWBs in their quest for a race war. At midnight tonight, near the Colorotta city of Colorotta Springs, the Terrorist Day Spa was going to give the world, the facial from Hades. The president's science advisor, Melanie Gryzolski is in cahoots with these domestic terrorists, and is a confirmed right-wing dermatologist."

The irrelevant Hollowood nobility all made their opinions known, on the various social media platforms, seemingly unaware of the contempt that most people held for them. The near-forgotten ex-singer, ex-actress, ex-popular Bawd Medler, wrote a foul poem that she posted on Tooter. It went as follows:

'Daryl Crumm is a poking joke
He don't give a poking poke
Alien hordes invade our land
Crumm will likely just play golf'.

Another washed up relic named Tod Einer, better known as Beefhead, tooted this: 'I'm so demn mad that I could grow hair! Crumm has sold us out to Planet X for the immortality formula, so that he can rule the world forever! TDS is Timeless Deathless Serum'

Don Crews appeared on Soonagram, where he solemnly explained to his millions of fans, "The eminent Professor Felix Polyplastics, who wishes to remain anonymous, has revealed to my agent, who I won't mention, that the aliens will unleash a stupid virus on mankind, womankind and all the other genderkinds at midnight tonight. Polyplastics was on a secret panel investigating these invaders from another world, and the aliens panicked and fled, when he got too close to discovering their ulterior motives. They want human sheep, to raise for food. The TDS is the name of the alien's stupid virus, and Polyplastics said that it means Totally Darn Stupid."

Don took a sip of water, and then said, "I also wanted to update my fans on the status of my toenail fungus…"

On the sports network, ASPN, an expert was brought onto the set, to analyse the latest polls. A Mr Franky Cannoli explained what it all meant. He said, "Pollsters from all of the major Lots Bogus, Novoda casinos, give a six point edge to Trendy Desperate Sycophants over Tropical Depression System as the favoured interpretation of the letters TDS."

These stories and many others made the rounds, and they grew wilder and more frightening with each retelling, and a virtual mushroom cloud resulted, with fallout covering the entire globe. The three-day old video of the Max Beefburger shooting with the heroic aliens, went giga-spiral, with more than half a billion views in the space of a few hours!

A frightening frenzy of fear was perpetrated by CON, who spread the idea of an alien apocalypse. 'Crumm's Invasion', they called it, and MNBS speculated that TDS was a Tricky Demn Secret. Fearful people all over the planet flocked to stores to prepare for an alien invasion. They pushed, shoved and fought each other to stock up on survival goods like face masks, toilet paper and hand sanitiser. Tens of thousands of others descended onto their city's streets to peacefully protest. They were as agreeable as they could be as they looted, vandalised, and burned businesses, set cars aflame and beat people.

Young men all over Shamerica organised anti-war protests. They were not going to kill aliens! Some even chanted, "Aliens are too cute to shoot!" These protestors carried weapons and threatened to, "…blow away anyone who gets in our way!" Other ant-war protestors marched down city streets singing, "A war of the worlds we will not fight. If we submit, they'll rule us kind and right!"

Chapter 13

Melanie steered the BUV onto the I-800 exit ramp leading into Bland Island. Loser and Donut were hungry again, and Loser finally saw a likely place to eat. "Over there," he directed Melanie to the left, "At the Tricky Taco. You're gonna have to back in through the drive-up lane, so that I can order," Loser said.

The Pissan Tanki was not much smaller than a monster truck and Melanie wasn't sure if it was possible to fit the truck through the drive-up lane, forward or backward. She wasn't going to argue with the savage Loser, so she'd do as he ordered, as best she could. Melanie thought that she'd be fine, even though it had been almost two decades since she used to drive trucks and tractors for her uncle's landscaping business. She positioned the BUV, shifted it into reverse and backed up behind a tan sedan.

Loser and Donut perused the menu on an electric signboard, and made their selections. Melanie backed up so that Loser's window matched the cartoonish, talking taco ordering station.

"Welcome to Tricky Taco hombres. What can I get you?" The tacoman character said, in a voice that sounded as if Tommy Eddyson originally recorded it. It emanated from a speaker he probably made too. Donut ordered first, as arranged. He said, "I'll take the number twelve."

The scratchy voice said, "That's the Family Soapapilla Bucket. Do you want salsa with that?"

Donut answered, "Are you some kind of poking idiot? Give me the half pint of honey."

"Anything else?" the disembodied emotionless tacoman asked.

"Yes." Loser said. He ordered. "I want two chili cheese milkshakes," That was for his two prisoners. For himself, Loser ordered, "Two poking chorizo sausage and egg burritos, three poking bean and cheese tacos, plus two large poking hot fudge sundaes."

"Want any sauce with that?"

Loser said, "Yeah. Give me about two dozen poking packs of your poking Acme Hell Sauce."

The taco said, "That will be thirty-one dollars and fourteen poking cents. Please back up to the next window."

They ate or drank their items, while sitting inside the truck, parked in the farthest corner of the lot. Loser asked Jeemis a question, spattering beans, cheese and salsa, atop the crusted yellow snack cake crud sticking to the dashboard. He wondered, "Hey, um, would you mind greatly if I shot you a few times?" He pulled a pistol out of his butt crack. It still looked clean. "I've always had a hankerin' to fill someone full of lead," he said. "And you won't even feel it! It's a win-win."

Jeemis shrieked, "Oh, it hurts alright! Just as painful as if I shot you or Donut. I am repaired or reassembled almost instantaneously however."

Loser's face fell, as did more food from his mouth. Jeemis made Loser suffer for a minute, before saying, "It happens to be the case though, that I like pain. I wouldn't mind a few jolts of agony Loser."

Melanie glanced up into the rear-view mirror in alarm. She'd handed off her stomach-churning milkshake to Loser. The alien seemed to be serious. Loser spun around in his seat to face Jeemis, love in his eyes. Jeemis explained his pain fetish. He said, "After sixty-five million years marooned on your planet, I have been beaten, stabbed, shot, drowned, burned alive, guillotined, vaporised and eaten by a sabre-toothed tiger. I adopted a good attitude regarding pain, and eventually learned to embrace suffering like an old friend, to fend off boredom and depression.

Loser asked excitedly, "Is that a yes?"

Jeemis said, "Let's get this sick urge out of your twisted system, before you hurt yourself Loser." He added, "I'll get it out of my system too. It's been three days since I had a good shooting."

Melanie didn't like the sound of this at all. She said, "That's crazy! Both of you; stop it!"

Donut had to agree, "I haven't finished my lunch yet," he moaned. His face and fingers were dripping with honey, and he stuffed one Soapapilla after another into his face hole. "Give me some napkins Loser, "he said."

Loser looked down into the grocery sack of food in his lap. He dug around and finally said. "That smart ass tacoman didn't give us a single poking napkin! I oughta kill the motherpoker!"

Jeemis said, "Calm down everyone. All is well. We will find a cornfield or something nearby, and you can shoot me."

Loser's face lit up like a full moon, craters and all. Loser managed to swiftly stuff most of the rest of his meal down his throat without choking. He tossed his garbage out the window and said, "Let's go."

Melanie drove out of the lot and down the highway's service road. After a few minutes she steered the huge truck down into an abandoned quarry along the Flatte River. "Please don't do this, you guys," she begged, but the human and the alien were determined to carry out the insane stunt.

She parked the vehicle and they all climbed out. The sunshine felt warm and yellow. Loser charged the nine-millimetre pistol, and thumbed the safety off. Jeemis faced Loser, with a wall of gravely sand behind him. The alien unzipped his black coveralls to the waist and pulled his arms free, baring a skinny, hairless torso. Loser took up a shooter's stance from ten feet away.

Melanie and Donut remained close to the truck, but watched in fascination and horror, as Loser squeezed off five or six shots. Jeemis stood strong when the first two or three bullets struck, and then fell down onto his butt. but never uttered a sound. Loser walked forward and blasted as he advanced. Blood spots appeared on the alien's body to show he'd been hit, but they vanished just as quickly.

Loser finished firing bullets, and he stuck the smoking gun down the back of his shorts to inspect his victim. The hot gun barrel sizzled. Loser shouted in pain and ripped the pistol out of his butt crack, bringing fried flesh out with it. In his panic, he accidentally fired a bullet, which came within inches of hitting Donut's feet.

Melanie had run to Jeemis to see if he was truly unharmed. She'd watched him get shot in person this time, not on a video.

"Are you okay?" Melanie asked as she reached his side. Jeemis was getting to his feet. Though their ears rang with gunfire, they could still hear Donut screaming at Loser about gun safety. Jeemis answered Melanie. He said, "That was great!" But when he looked down to see a bullet hole in the right leg of his coveralls; he began to swear in anger. It was his second pair ruined in a week. He might have been alien, but Jeemis was a gentleman alien, and so cursed and swore in his native Uzgabadan, so as not to offend Melanie.

Melanie ignored his incomprehensible outburst and asked him, "Where do the bullets go?" She saw the little starbursts of blood from the bullet entry points.

"Do they pass though you?" She was a scientist after all. "Yes," he replied. "If it doesn't pass through me, my body shoves it out."

Loser was oblivious to all of it, to the entire world in fact. He couldn't hear Donut's swearing or Jeemis' swearing. He soared above the world of the senses, in euphoric ecstasy. "That was better than sex!" he yelled to the sky above. He hopped up and down like the winner of a TV game show.

Donut stopped in mid rant, and acted as if he'd suddenly turned to stone, suffering a temporary catatonia. His senses had crashed headlong into his mind, and there were casualties. His ears rang from the gunshots, and his eyes saw the alien get hit, but his mind refused their evidence. He had strict boundaries and they were constructed from strong guesses, sound feelings and solid opinions, and he couldn't wrap this event away in his mental security blanket of assumptions.

Donut knew deep down in his pastry-packed gut, that it was wrong for people not to die when they were killed. He was having second thoughts about this immortality kit, or however it came packaged. Oh yeah, immortality sounds great at first, but think of the possible ramifications. Hitmen would need to find new careers, and think of the damage to the psyches of serial killers. He shivered at the thought. Maybe social workers could help them, like set up a Frustrated Killer Hotline, or something.

Jeemis' deafening voice blasted the two crooks out of their respective delusions, "Hello!"

Loser's spirit of celebration snapped back into his body and took charge of him again. He ordered, "Let's go!"

The quartet resumed their previous seats in the big truck and Melanie drove up and out of the quarry. As she regained the service road which led to the interstate highway, Melanie noticed the red sports car fall in behind them again. Jeemis knew it was there, but the two BEWBs had no idea they were being followed. The alien knew that it was the man he'd seen at the Fas-Gas in Yuk. One follow was a good start, Jeemis thought.

* * *

A big burly, over-the-road truck driver heard a news story which identified the white Pissan Tanki kidnap vehicle, and she couldn't help but notice the BUV, as she sped past it three or four miles back. Her name was Rosie Oh, and the reporter for that story, said that the vehicle was headed to see some kind of wizard or genii, who would grant her fondest wishes.

Rosie liked that idea; it reminded her of her favourite movie, 'The Wizard Of Odds'. She had always identified with the character of the androgynous scarecrow who wanted a gender, but the cryin' lion was pathetic too! Her favourite scene featured Whorothy tossing a pail of monkey piss on the wacky witch of the West, which turned her into a ruby slipper.

Rosie yearned for a new start in life. She'd poked this one up good. This life style of hard driving, hard drinking and hard poking was become tiresome. She'd been forced to cut back to five party nights per week! She was forty-three years old for gosh sake.

Rosie wanted more however. She dreamed of a owning a beer garden in the sunny state of Floraduh, and perhaps this was her opportunity. She had been driving for twenty-one years now, and she'd had enough.

She tried to imagine what the TDS was. Maybe it was nothing more than a cosmic Anne Loonders column, solving domestic issues in two paragraphs or less, or maybe it was a pretentious god, looking to earn a few bucks in admission fees. Nothing good ever happened to her. She couldn't even win a free lottery ticket.

Rosie's current life and future prospects held no happiness for her. Seeing the white Tanki was an omen. Everything happened for a reason, and life was a long series of unlikely coincidences; she knew all the clichés. But this was real life. Speed limit signs meant nothing to her kind, but this was a sign from above; like a PSA from God. Rosie slowed the truck and gradually moved over to the right shoulder, where she stopped the big rig and flipped on the truck's hazard lights and flashers. She waited for the Pissan to catch up.

Chapter 14

Robulus' aircraft was warm, quiet and comfortable. Robulus and Griz kept quiet while Vera called her boss at NFN News. She spoke to Mortimer Ornge, the executive producer for her live news segments. Vera showed mad salesperson skills, as she spoke rapidly and convincingly, telling Mort that she'd literally bumped into the other half of the alien abduction story, and how fortunate he was, that she was at an airport she didn't belong in.

"Not only that," Vera continued her verbal assault unabated, pummelling Mort with the force, if not the logic of her attack, "But, I am high up in the sky, inside an aircraft piloted by the alien named Robulus and accompanied by the father of the kidnapped woman, and I have access to stories and videos no one else will have. If you want me to drop it and…"

"Give me a break, Vera," Mort laughed. "I'll make you a deal. You send me everything you get, and I'll kill you when you get back here. What do you have for me now?"

That went well, Vera thought. She said, "I am sending you everything that Robulus told us about this airship, the TDS and Kazooky's Conundrum. But don't go away; there's more. First, Robulus has a message to broadcast to the world. Incoming."

NFN received the alien's message, and aired it twice every hour, along with a slide show of photos of Griz, Robulus and Vera too, with the aircraft interior as backdrop. Robulus' message was this: "At midnight tonight, mountain time, on Poke's Peak, near Colorotta Springs, Colorotta, the greatest wonder of your world will be unveiled, revealed for the benefit of all mankind. Jeemis and I secreted this cosmic TDS marvel from human view fourteen thousand years ago, but now it is time. Nothing will ever be the same, and that's a wonderful thing!"

When Robulus had informed Vera what he wished to say, she'd balked, and said, "A statement like that will set people's brains on fire! Are you sure about this statement?"

Robulus had grinned and replied, without condescension, "Vera, I am slightly familiar with the human psyche. Jeemis and I built your race after all. I want people to get passionate, to get off their dead asses and come alive again!"

Griz said, "For most people, getting off their dead asses and getting passionate, means that other people will get hurt."

"What do you mean, you built us?" Vera asked.

Griz didn't much like the way his thoughts were trending. If Robulus could be believed, then his statement could mean but one thing. He said, "Logically, if you and Jeemis were on Gaia sixty-five million years ago, and we humans look suspiciously like you two guys, then only one conclusion is possible."

Vera's narrow eyebrows rose, in wide-eyed understanding. "No!" she cried. "It's monstrous!"

Robulus looked hurt. He said, "Yes, we have been disappointed in our results as well, Vera. Humans were the best we could manage. Sorry."

Chapter 15

At around the same time that the white Tanki, the red Cumaro, and Rosie Oh's silver Muck tractor trailer rig passed the town of Korny, Nobraska, Barry Porter's flight was touching down one hundred miles west in North Flatte. Barry had kept track of the progress of the great white whale of a truck while in flight, and congratulated himself on his acumen in getting out front of this breaking story.

Barry applauded his own efforts rather often. Why not? When you're a winner, pat yourself on the demn back! No one else will do it, unless you ask them half a dozen times. Porter was one, with the pop culture celebrity elite, part of the cult of the narcissist. He was well known for his CON appearances and his Sunday morning show called, 'Barry Deep', but it didn't hurt that his sister was a famous Hollowood actress. People knew her as the talented, Trans Porter who was loved for her Ashcan Award winning role in 'Fruit-Batman Hangs Around.' Barry knew her back when she was his brother Dee Porter.

Barry had served part of one term as an assemblyman in San Hosey, Califoreignya, but was forced to resign in disgrace, when videos of him having sex with the mayor and her wife were made public. This torrid episode gave him credibility, and he was soon hired by CON, where he quickly rose to prominence, and became the premier entertainment reporter and celebrity booster in the business, such as it was.

Barry had adorned himself with the Hollowood glitter, because he could sparkle too! It wasn't all about Hollowood however. Celebrities emerged in pop music and in sports also. He was a believer in the concept that celebrities are exceptional humans, that stars are special beings. That's why he worshipped at the Sacred Stars Temple. Barry was more than a member of the church; he served as Secretary-Treasurer of the Twoson, Aridzonea franchise.

The SST was founded in Loss Analyst, Califoreignya, seventeen years ago, by Elroy Humbug. Elroy had cancelled his previous religious cult called

Lyintology, which was based on his science fiction writing, and he established a new and improved cult, which worshipped those who operated the cult. The SST was now the fastest growing religion on Gaia. There were thirty-one million dues paying members world-wide. Ever since Elroy died six years ago, the Holy Temple Emperor, also known as the Emcee, had been actor Robby Indero.

Every temple was constructed as a three-sided pyramid. On Saturdays at sundown, and at midnight during full moons, customers would line up and pay a small cover charge to worship, and experience the Solemn Rite of Sacred Stars. When the doors are opened, the congregation first gathers beneath the pyramid's central peak. Three wide doorways lead to separate chapels, dedicated to the holy trinity of acting, pop music and pop sports.

The congregational customers watch in awe, as a high, High Priestess, leads her twelve temple disciples in prayer. The priestess is always a curvaceous, statuesque blonde wearing nothing but deodorant, and she raises her arms up and says loudly, "Oh Master of award ceremonies and trophies, hear our plea. We need better scripts and contracts, better coaches and better teams, better back-up bands and better tunes. Give us a poking chance, thanks."

The priestess then leads the audience from beneath the central peak of the pyramid, through one of the three doorways, swinging her hips with solemn dignity. The first hall led to the Chapel of Sports. The ornately panelled walls inside the sports chapel are plastered with photos of famous sports heroes like boxer Mack "The Rapist" Fryson. The main attraction however, was a life-size statue of football legend, Ojay Crimson. The life-sized plastic statue was wearing his signature, number 32 Bison Bills jersey. His right arm was raised high, and its gloved hand wielded a bloody knife. A small replica of a white Fard Bronc sat to one side.

The priestess and her coven of disciples each kiss the reddened, blood-soaked glove and say, "If me you love; forget the glove."

The celebrity devotees are next led to the second chapel, which is committed to the worship of pop music idols. As in the sports chapel, the walls are a photo tribute to music celebrities. The superstar, who was adored here, had a statue too. It was dressed like a colour-blind clown, in garish clothing too small for its bloated body. It sat upon a golden toilet, and wore blue suede shoes. It was Elvin Parsley, who was worshipped as the Duke of rock and roll.

The priestess and her twelve followers, each passed by the Elvin Parsley idol, and one by one, they reached into a bucket by its blue suede shoes. They all

112

pulled out big handfuls of various coloured candies, made to look like pills, and stuffed them into their mouths. Together they sang, "You ain't nothin' but a round hog, just eatin' all the time."

Before departing the chapel, each of the thirteen stopped, to kick an effigy of Meesa Larie Parsley in the butt.

Now, in the third and final chapel of the Sacred Stars Temple, there is a moment of silence in the presence of the statue of the actress Carolyn Funroe. She was displayed in her iconic pose with her skirt blowing up around her thighs; a famous scene from a shoddy movie.

The priestess says, "You are a role model, who poked truth to power in crime, and in its offshoot, politics. We aspire to your depravity and popularity, and we hope and pray for a Peeper's Choice Award."

Two large TV screens on the chapel walls, to left and right powered up to announce, "The End" and the credits rolled, while the congregation applauded. A bucket for donations is passed around and a souvenir and gift shop is opened. It was beautiful, a ceremony once seen and never forgotten, like a root canal sans anaesthesia. Barry loved it.

While waiting at the luggage carousel for his bag to turn up, Barry Porter placed a fone call to Don Crews. Porter had seen Don's Soonagram, in which Crews rambled on about Polyplastis leaking, and the TDS and a stupid virus and toenail fungus. Barry Porter had known Don since his days acting in Pop Gun, and was of the opinion that Crews couldn't play himself in a bio-flick. Barry had even written a scathing critique of Crews' acting abilities for Peeper's magazine more than thirty years ago.

Barry had won a participation trophy for it, and he could remember it nearly word for word. It went: "All humans ever born came into this world with the innate ability to mimic, to act. Pretending to be someone else, adapting your behaviour to your circumstances is as natural to our behaviour as body language. It's in our DNA. However, thirty-one years ago, a combination of genetic mutations came together to create a unique specimen, a human being who was missing the entire suite of 'acting' genes. This person is Don Crews." The two met not long after this article was published, but since Don agreed with it, there were no hard feelings, and they soon became friends.

Don answered his own selfone, because Kate Armstrong was in the gym. "Hey Barry," Don said in greeting, "What's up?" he asked.

Barry said, "Hello Don. Hey, I am working this alien abduction story, and I saw your Soonagram. You talked to Polyplastis? He was part of a secret government investigation? What's going on?"

"Slow down, man." Don was overwhelmed. "It's like this, dude; I didn't talk to Professor Plastics, I talked to Pitch Al, who talked to the professor."

"What's Al Darkly's involvement in all this?" Barry asked. He knew that people who couldn't act, couldn't lie either.

Don said, "Okay, well this is off the record and all, but I've got forty thousand dollars invested in this scheme to obtain immortality. Al said it was a cheap price."

Barry said, "Count on me, Don, I won't mention your name. I don't know if it's a crime to abet an alien abduction, but that woman is Crumm's science advisor, and she's in the truck too. Is your passport up to date? Got cash?"

Don said, "Look Barry, I didn't know anything about no abduction! I merely lent Al some money."

Barry said encouragingly, "If you kill yourself, you may end up replacing Carolyn Funroe in the temple."

"Thanks," Don said, "I'll keep that in mind."

"I'm at an airport, and I see my luggage. Gotta go. Thanks Don."

* * *

Pitch Al donned a terrycloth bathrobe with the words, 'Hihat Regency Hotels' in green letters across his chest. He cinched the belt, and his lunchmeat, a redhead sent up from HR, dressed in her clothes and returned to her job as 'looking good girl'. Al shouted for his secretary, "Torchy!"

Torchy appeared in the doorway, as silent as a wraith, and Al sometimes wondered how the big lumbering drunk managed it. It was like magic or great special effects. "Yeah, Boss," Torchy answered.

"Any new developments to report?" Al asked.

Torchy snorted and said. "The MBM stories keep morphing and mutating like a virus Al. They're getting hysterical. These guys have less ethics than a lawyer"

Al was still a member of the bar. He glared at Torchy for a moment before saying, "Good point. Now get me our Pop Gun, Don Crews on the line. And pour me a brandy. That lunch left me thirsty."

114

"You bet boss. I got thirsty watching you."

Don's eyefone rang at an inopportune moment. Kate Armstrong's hands were vigorously pumping up his smaller ego, and it was on the verge of a 'thar she blows' moment. Don inadvertently answered his eyefone when he glanced at it where it lay on the massage table next to his head. Once his fone recognised his eyes, it automatically picked up the call.

Crews was panting like an overheated dog, and would have erupted, had not Pitch Al's cackling voice turned him limp as a wet noodle in seconds. "Demn, Don!" Al ejaculated. "Can't you stop your nonsense for a minute?" he asked. Al added, "Hi Kate."

"Hello, Mr Darkly," Kate said. "Good guess." She removed her latex gloves and blindfold and ran off to the bathroom to vomit. This crap was not in her job description. Yeah, she could quit, but the money and drugs were great, and Don's private chef had a big ladle and knew how to dip it. So, she'd stay for now.

"Whaddya want now Al?" Dom demanded. Instant flaccidity. He picked up his eyefone.

Al blasted him; he said, "What in poking Hades are you poking doing? Soonagram? Tooter? This is my operation, Don!"

Don's short fuse crackled with instant flames. He retorted, "Oh yeah! Well, it's my demn money!"

"Oh yeah!" Al shouted. "Listen to me Don. Calm down. Put away your wienie, pull on some pants and pay attention."

Don donned his yoga pants and sat down in an armchair. "Go, I'm listening."

Al said, in his most suave, most patronising tone, a voice which had often swayed juries in his favour, "Dom, we need each other, like a dog needs fleas. I represent you, and you do what I say, it's a balanced relationship like that."

Dom said, "Right, I scratch your back, and you scratch thine."

"Precisely!" Al cheered. "Partners for life."

Don protested, he said, "We're not getting poking married, Al. I want to protect my investment. I want immortality too, you know. And, mostly, I want it known, that I uncovered the secret of eternal life; me, Don Crews."

Al smiled. He knew Don's weak spot. He said, "I want that for you too Don. I want to see your name in huge neon lights, on all of the marquees in Hollowood, everywhere. 'Mission Improbable: Living Forever'. So, let me run the show from behind the curtain, and later you can take the stage."

"Really Al? Promise?" Overjoyed, Dom danced around the room, in imitation of a scene he did in 'Frisky Princess'.

"I promise," Pitch Al said with crossed fingers. "Back to your poker. See ya."

Al ended the call and shook his head in dismay. It was no surprise, he thought, that Crews derailed so often, he only had a half-track mind. It would be hilarious to put Crews and Vometta Wilde in the same room together, preferably a cafeteria room. Crews would be stiff-legged for months, with his peanuts in a sling.

Darkly couldn't let Crews poke up his chance at immortality. This was Al's destiny. He needed to find a way... Then, it came to him, like a pizza delivery! He knew what he had to do! He made an expensive, but necessary decision. "Torchy!" he bellowed.

The phantom appeared and said, "Yeah Boss?"

"Call my pilot and have him make ready the company jet, and tell him to file a flight plan to Colorotta Springs. He's got two hours. Pack your beers and get ready."

Three hundred and fifty miles west of the Feenix airport where Al's jet was parked, in Loss Analyst, Califoreignya, Don Crews rang for Kate. She arrived, freshly showered and wearing a colourful kimono. "Yes?" she asked, hoping the answer wasn't too creepy.

Don said, "Call my pilot and have him get my jet ready. Have him file a flight plan to the Colorotta Springs airport. Tell him we're leaving in two hours. Pack a bag."

"Shall I pack your love doll? It's back from the cleaners."

"No, "Don said with reluctance. "I won't have time for Suckles. This is business."

* * *

The Make-Believe Media aired non-stop speculation and the wilder the tale the better. A wide variety of know-nothings, portraying themselves as know-everythings ramped up fears, fanned passions and created panic. Guest doctors ruminated about a stupidity virus, guest kidnappers debated the pros and cons of abducting an alien, and in one case a psychic known as Shookoo was consulted about the meaning of TDS. She channelled her spirit guide Sphinxy, who revealed that the three letters stood for Toby's Diaper Service, a cover name for a secret mission to infiltrate Hollowood with real people.

CON's Fredo Coma accused the kidnappers of racism, for abducting only light-skinned aliens. He ranted, "Our racist-in-chief President Crumm is behind this conspiracy to start a race war with aliens of colour!" He also said. "Mr President, little green men matter! No matter what colour or gender they are."

MNBS's Richie Madnow blustered and fumed as usual, but this time, she assured her many dozens of viewers, they could really, truly believe her news. For sure! "My facts are just as good as anyone else's," she claimed. "And Crumm will finally be going to prison where he belongs! Guaranteed." Richie had guaranteed this prison outcome many, many times over the last six years, but today was the day, she promised.

Madnow announced, "I have anonymous proof from a definite source, that a person of interest will soon reveal an actual photo of an official top-secret document, which was carelessly left unattended at the Oval Office copy machine. A super, ultra-high level administration official, right up there at the top of the heap, and real close to the president; someone almost, but not necessarily family, let me know through back-channels, that TDS means the end of life on Gaia! TDS is a massive asteroid called the Terminal Disaster Stone. After it blows up the planet, Crumm plans to start his own colony of nymphs on Mars."

Chapter 16

Barry Porter sat contentedly in a rented, blue Plummet Chugger, sipping a hot expresso at a North Flatte entrance ramp to I-800. It was 1:15 PM mountain time on the west side of North Flatte, and 2:15 PM central time on the east end of town, when a procession led by a Nobraska state patrol car, lights flashing, drove past his location. It was providing an escort to the big white Tanki, and the caravan behind it.

Barry drove down onto the highway and took up a position behind twelve other vehicles, including a red Cumaro, a tractor trailer with a silver cab, and a pair of other big rigs, two sedans, one motorcycle, a fire truck, an ambulance and two black Caddylacs, which Barry correctly identified as belonging to personal injury attorneys.

In fourth position, inside the silver truck cab, Rosie Oh was having fun! She drank beer and kept her CB radio humming, trying to recruit other weary truck drivers to the cause, whatever it was. Rosie wasn't out to save the world; she was out for the world to save her. She needed a miracle, and this was going to be it!

Melanie felt safer and more relaxed now that a police car escorted them, and the fact that a quarter mile long string of vehicles followed behind them, seemed comforting too. She kept the cruise control at seventy-two miles per hour, when she could.

Every fifteen to twenty miles, ever since passing through Winkin, one or another of the highway traffic lanes was blocked off by two or three miles of orange barrels. Red coloured speed limit signs, slowed traffic down to forty-five mph. The thousands of orange barrels looked old, dirty and battered, as if they'd been in place for years. The lonely barrels seemed to be waiting for that distant day, when half a dozen highway workers could lean back on them, while smoking cigarettes.

The Tanki inmates had experienced a difficult stretch of almost forty miles. Loser's lunch came back to haunt them. The chili-cheese milkshakes with hot sauce, topped off with hot fudge sundaes, had chemically combined in his gut to create great volumes of noxious fumes. Loser farted often, and ejected so many greenhouse gasses, that climate scientists later blamed him for a millimetre rise in sea levels. All of the windows were down, which led to a few dozen birds becoming ill and falling off the power lines they perched upon, when the toxic cloud overwhelmed them as the truck sped past.

Loser and Donut were thrilled by the police escort, even as the police presence made them twitchy nervous. The long trail of fans and admirers following behind them had the two BEWBs re-evaluating their respective places in history. In Loser's mind, this crime had elevated them to comparisons with such famous law breakers as Hooch Cassidy and the Funpants Kid, and Babywipes Nelson.

Now that he'd joined the fraternity of famous felons, Loser needed a new and improved nickname. Lou the Loser is not a name fit for neon lights or book covers. It wouldn't do at all. A new moniker needed to be catchy, but cutting-edge, a name to strike love in the hearts of women and fear in the guts of men. This would take some thinking.

Donut felt ten feet tall, yet he crouched down in the back seat so the cop wouldn't see him. He was scared but on top of the world. This entire situation was surreal! He wondered if he could still be famous, while not going out in public.

Donut couldn't handle the stress of fame, so this would be his last job! He hoped his resolution to retire after this caper, wasn't a death sentence. That's always the way it was in the movies. It was always that last job that got people killed. Donut had to quit after becoming immortal though, because a life sentence took on a whole new meaning then.

Suddenly Loser blurted out, "Shanghai Low!" Melanie tried to edge further away from the animal, squeezing up against the door. Loser was unstable, like a cow with three legs. She looked over at him to see if he was foaming at the mouth. Loser explained, he said, "Shanghai Low is me. No more Loser! He's dead and gone. It's my new identity."

Donut was impressed. He said, "That is so cool, Loser!"

"I'm not poking Loser! I am Shanghai Low!" Loser pointed at a Rest Stop exit ramp and told Melanie, "Pull off, I gotta pee."

Jeemis remarked, "Take a poo while you're at it."

Melanie switched her turn signal on, but the state trooper escorting them didn't notice, and he drove past the rest stop. He didn't realise that the big Pissan was not following behind him for thirteen minutes. The officer didn't let it bother him. The escort was only a courtesy after all. While he was out this way, it only made sense to drop in on Mrs Puller, and perform a welfare check of her privates. He hadn't seen them in weeks.

Melanie parked the Tanki in the rest stop's designated truck area, and listened to Shanghai Low threaten her with injury or death if they didn't behave. He waved his pistol around to show he meant business. Jeemis screeched, "Be cool Low! Your fans arrive."

Three cars, one I-Haul and two semi-trucks were already parked at the highway rest stop when Melanie had driven in. Melanie, Jeemis and the BEWBs exited the Tanki, and stood to watch in wonder, as the rest stop parking area began to fill up with vehicles. The convoy now numbered seventeen, with the addition of a dump truck, a ConCast service van and a school bus. Shanghai Low led Donut and their two captives, to the red brick building which housed the toilets and food vending machines.

Wayne Bruce steered his Cumaro into a parking slot at the rest area. He was terribly excited by the large group of vehicles following the Tanki. They were all stopping in! He wanted to show off his costume, and confront the kidnappers while he had an audience to perform for. He removed his custom costume bag from the trunk, and hurried off to the Men's Room. He changed out of his Wayne Bruce outfit, and into his Crime Blaster XL-5 superhero suit, while inside a locked toilet stall. He left his luggage and street clothes in the stall; it would be okay, for a few minutes of photo opportunities. He needed to build a fan base, after all.

CB XL-5 emerged from the brick building; all decked out in his red, white and blue, star-spangled costume, and his signature blue, steel-toed running shoes. His head mask was red with white star eyes, his gloves were blue and the rest of him was striped red and white, like a candy cane. He came upon an amazing sight. Scores of hopers, seekers, and dreamers were come together at the rest stop. It was a special day. These folks didn't all want to find the gold at the end of the rainbow; some just wanted to know the rainbow was still out there.

Thirty-one people crowded around the four newsmakers, but only two of the quartet were posing for pictures and signing autographs for two dollars apiece.

Melanie, and the alien, an immortal being from another planet, were ignored. Shanghai Low did ask Jeemis how to spell his new name, and he borrowed a pen.

Crime Blaster strode confidently through the small crowd, and people said ooh and aah, and made way for the colourful superhero. He marched straight up to the two crooks of the hour. CB stopped in front of the BEWBs, and stuck out a gloved right hand. "Howdy alien abductors!" He shook their hands like a politician and he said, "I am Crime Blaster XL-5, superhero. I save the world from creeps like you."

Donut pumped his hand and said, "Glad to meet you Crime Buster. I am Donut and this is Loser."

Low dropped the hideous facsimile of a smile off his face, and the top of his bald head started to resemble a sunlamp again. Spit and spume, like a heavy ocean wave sprayed from Loser's mouth, when he bellowed, "My poking name is not poking Loser you dumb poking Donut Hole! My poking name is Shanghai Poking Low!" He stomped his foot and spun in circles.

Donut wondered aloud, "When did you add a middle name?"

The crowd, without wanting to alarm the crazy man, slowly started to back away. It wasn't only Low's temper that dispersed the crowd. A nauseating stench arose, as if a graveyard had farted.

"What stinks?" Jeemis shrieked, voicing the question in all their minds. Melanie pointed to an evergreen tree six feet away where pieces of a broken sign lay beneath the limbs. Crime Blaster went over and turned the largest piece over. It read, 'Pet Ar'. A second smaller piece, facing up, had the two letters, '…ea'. CB looked down at his fancy shoes and shouted, "Oh crap!"

Jeemis said, "Yep."

People were lining up to get into the restrooms to wipe the dog poo from their shoes and to empty their bladders. Others just swore and stomped around in the 'Stay Off the Grass' area.

Shanghai Low challenged CB XL-5, he said, "When are you going to save the world from us, Superhero?"

Crime Blaster wondered what kind of idiots he was dealing with. These guys were lamer than Boll Weevil Man and Click Beetle the bug wonder; in Super-duper Tarantula Man issue #1374; 'Cotton Picking Fools'. CB answered back, he said, "Get real. Don't you know anything? If I save the world before the penultimate chapter, it messes up the whole demn plot! It's not the right time! Duh!"

Jeemis and Melanie had the same idea at the same time, "Duh!" they repeated.

Donut said, "Yeah, what the poke, Lose…Shanghai Low?"

Low said, "What in Hades kinda dumb chapter is penwhatamit?"

Low led his group to the restrooms, but waited until they were cleared of others before going inside. CB XL-5 made to do the same, when he was approached by a sharp dressed man with a Press Pass hanging around his neck. Media! Exposure! He was discovered! "I'm Crime Blaster XL-5, superhero extraordinaire," he said, offering his blue hand to the man.

"Barry Porter of CON," the man said, shaking the glove. "Nice outfit. I never met a superhero before, just actors who played them." Barry wanted to latch on to this tomato head. It would make for a great character portrayal and a second point of view, plus he wouldn't have to drive.

"I know you!" CB exclaimed. "I watch false news all the time! Hey! We should team up. We can take my car. It's a perfect deal; you cover me, and I give you somebody to cover!"

"I couldn't have phrased it better myself," Barry said.

CB said, "The red Cumaro is mine. The keys are inside, but I need to change back into my street clothes, and all my stuff is in the Men's Room."

Barry said, "Cool, I'll meet your better half. I got a bag or two in my rental car I need to grab. See ya in a sec." They went their separate ways. CB didn't notice the two kidnappers and their prisoners returning to the Tanki in the truck parking area.

Barry set his two big pieces of luggage on the walk, and got into the driver's seat of his rented Plummet Chugger. He needed to ditch the car, in a way that freed him and CON of any liability. It was charged against the company credit card. He called the toll-free number for Anis Rent-A-Car, and after several minutes of arguing with an unresponsive menu, a living human condescended to take his call.

Barry said, "Hello' Look I am a good Sumerian and see, I found this dead guy hanging out the door of one of your rental cars, at a rest stop west of North Flatte, Nobraska. You better try to get out here before the cops tow it. Hey, it's a blue Plummet Chugger. I'll leave the keys under the hood."

"Oh my. Do you know what happened; or who it is?' the lady said.

Barry said, "I think it was a heart attack. I got to him, just as he said his last words."

122

Breathless, the Anis phone operator said, "I dare not ask what he said, but, if you'd be so kind…"

Barry said, "Yes, Ma'am. The poor dying man held this car rental contract paperwork in his hands, clutching them tightly with his last bits of strength."

"Yes? Yes?"

"He choked once," Barry said, "And he grabbed my collar, and he pulled me down close to his lips. He whispered, 'My last wish is for Anis to cancel my bill.' Then he died."

The operator was audibly sobbing, she said, "It's done." The call ended.

Pleased with his performance, Barry was surprised to see the crime blaster wearing his costume, and running in an out of the red brick building. He looked frantic, as if the IRS were auditing him. Barry picked up his bags and met CB next to his sports car. "My suitcase and clothes got stolen? Did you see anyone?"

"No, I had my head down."

CB heard the Tanki horn honking, they were waiting for him! Shanghai leaned on the horn, he wanted to keep the superhero close behind, so he'd know when that pentagonal or penitentiary chapter began; whatever he said. CB and Barry got into the Cumaro. CB drove. The vehicle caravan fell in behind the Tanki, all drivers observing the courtesies and resuming their appropriate places in the train. The I-Haul truck from the Rest Area joined up, serving as the temporary caboose.

* * *

The false news media was having a field day! Sensational stories and fabulous falsehoods flew off their pages and their lips as if lying were an Olympic sport. The New Yank Times, going for a gold medal, reported in an urgent update, that, "… hundreds of aliens had carjacked cars and trucks, and they were driving west on I-800, in a locust like migration to a secret breeding ground in the Stony Mountains of Colorotta." The article went on to say, "The aliens are difficult to identify, and they differ little from humans, except that they are much taller and they drive a lot better."

On MNBS, a renowned surgeon described in gory detail, how he delivered a hybrid baby alien from a human mother, and that it was a male with a forked poker. "Thus", he explained gravely, "The best way to identify a male alien is to look down its pants." Hours later, women all across the country, were peering down men's pants.

CON aired many minutes of Barry Porter's Rest Area eyefone video, recorded with his own audio play-by-play. He'd captured the bizarre photo op and autograph session with the kidnappers and their followers. Viewers also saw a superhero, an alien, and a beautiful scientist, but had to be satisfied with Barry's description of the dog poo stench.

NFN's broadcast of Robulus's claim, which Vera sent to them from the aircraft, was picked up by other media outlets, and replayed with added commentary by experts in one field or another.

If instilling fear in people, and causing the unstable to snap, crackle and pop was the object, then the MBM could proudly boast of success. Gun stores all over Shamerica, sold out of weapons and ammo in hours; liquor stores were emptied of their booze, and grocery stores saw their water and toilet paper shelves bared. Fear is the greatest motivator of violent crimes, not rage or hate. Nothing tops fear for inspiring the unbalanced to rape, burn and kill.

Just as it only takes one match to start a conflagration, it only takes one vandal, one arsonist or one looter to start a violent mob phenomenon. A mob is an anonymous, amorphous blob of blind, mindless conduct. Jeemis had a theorem to explain mob behaviour in humans. It went: "If one person is equal to one Brain Power Unit, or BPU, then the total combined BPU shared by a mob, is inversely proportional to the number of people in said mob. Thus, a mob of two hundred people share between them, one two hundredth of one BPU." Jeemis would follow up, by remarking in an offhand fashion that, "The mob in the US Congress numbers five hundred and sixty-four people."

Social media operated like a mob. If one kook on Phasebook reported seeing a UFO, then within hours, thousands of people claimed to see unidentified flying objects. One expected to see a veritable eclipse of the sun from the vast armada of spaceships covering the skies. Each new Phasebook post or Tooter toot, had to outdo the last, and exaggerations grew like the national debt. People claimed alien abductions, cattle mutilations and crop circles.

The three letters TDS suffered such abuse as not seen before. They were beaten, tortured and mutilated by some of the best sadists in the business. Media stars and the influencers of Spewtube and Soonagram all assured their fans, that they and they alone had solved the mystery of TDS. Hundreds of the green check Tooter accounts did the same and yet, no two solutions agreed.

It was impossible to discern serious speculation from parody. A short list of the most popular of the serious guesses included, The Deep State, Tiger Dental Surgeon, Table Dancing Sluts, Triple Drop Stitch and Tiny Dance Steps. Some of the less sober ideas suggested were, Tackle Dummy Shop, Twisted Depraved Sex, and That Dog Stinks. It was as if everyone knew what TDS was about, even if they'd never seen it; very much like an Ashcan award winning movie.

Chapter 17

It was warm, sunny and sixty-eight degrees at the Colorotta Springs airport at 1:30 PM, when Robulus led Griz and Vera towards a black Range Roamer, parked on the private airfield. They'd all used the bathrooms at the private airfield offices after landing. The alien toted his black case, Vera shouldered her red purse, and Griz had his selfone and a ton of determination.

Griz noticed the many accessories on the rugged all-wheel drive Range Roamer. It was equipped for every emergency, not accounting for Murphy's Law. A heavy roll bar protected the occupants, and a floodlight bar and a cable winch perched above the front steel bumper. Two gas cans and a spare tire hung above the back bumper, and a tow ball poked out from below it.

Vera sat in the passenger seat and Griz got in back. Robulus drove his vehicle off the private airfield. He said, "Our destination is actually on Poke's Peak outside Minotaur Springs. The locals know the area; it's been under our construction for years."

Traffic was clumsy and congested, even during off-peak driving times, in this area of southbound I-250. While it proved a nerve-wracking experience, they completed the twelve-mile trip to the Minotaur Springs exit in a swift forty-five minutes. Robulus then drove west on highway 240, towards the tourist trap town, but turned off-road before they got that far. The Range Roamer bounced over rocks, crunched pine cones, and slalomed between pine trees. No one said anything as if by unspoken agreement. Griz and Vera inhaled the cool mile-high air and enjoyed the sights for now.

Robulus braked the vehicle to a halt in front of a solid, vertical wall of granite in the side of Poke's Peak. The alien pressed a button, on a small remote control hooked to his overhead visor. A panel of rock slowly slid down into a slot, like a slice of bread in a toaster, revealing a black hole. Robulus turned on the headlights, which illuminated a tunnel, and he accelerated forward. The rock panel slid shut behind them as they entered the passage. Overhead lights, spaced twenty yards apart, showed that the walls and the ceiling of the tunnel were smooth and polished, while the floor was even but rough. The tunnel led straight ahead, but tended slightly downslope.

The Roamer's bright lights illuminated a cavern ahead, and as they advanced, overhead lights came on as well, turning off behind after they'd passed. After they entered the cavern, Robulus slowed, and soon parked the Range Roamer in-between a dark green Geep, and a pair of golf carts. He blasted away the silence when he said, "Our stop."

"Where are we?" Vera inquired.

"Where are we going?" Griz asked.

"We are inside of Poke's Peak," Robulus said. "There are some things that I want to show you. We need to take the elevator."

Griz opened Vera's door and took her hand to help her down from the Roamer. She didn't need the help, but she kind of liked it. She said, "Thank you."

Griz could see that the tunnel led further on, but Robulus bought them in long swift strides, to a wall of rock with a steel door embedded in it. The alien carried the boxy, black instrument case with him. The trio stopped in front of the barrier. Robulus pushed an icon on his watch, and the door whooshed open.

They all went in, and the door shut behind them. A light and an air fan came on. Robulus said, "Our power is derived from one of our own orbiting satellites, which converts solar energies into electrical energies. Jeemis and I have sold them to your military, and this is our corporate 'test' case, so to say."

"I've read about those," Griz said. "Amazing." There seemed little point in asking questions of the alien, because he was very short on answers. He had his reasons, Griz assumed.

Three unmarked white buttons projected from a panel by the elevator door, and a handrail wrapped around the interior. "Grab the rails," Robulus said. In his best imitation of a human tour guide he added, "This elevator is our energy-saving model, and it operates strictly on gravity for its descent. An air cushion will slow, and end our descent, before the rocks below do so. We will drop nearly a mile in about seventy seconds." He pushed the lowest button. The steel cage dropped.

Vera nervously licked her lips. This was proving to be more an adventure than a story. Griz smiled at her and said, "Do you happen to have a spare chute? I seemed to have forgotten mine at home." She laughed. The elevator slowed, and came to a gentle stop. The door whooshed open. Vera unpeeled her fingers from the rail and remembered to breathe.

When she stepped outside of the elevator, she gasped, inhaling deeply. It smelled like a drive in the country after a rainfall, but looked like a scene from an old Walt Dizzy cartoon, with colourfully dressed little people employed in various activities. Some herded sheep or goats, others tended to food crops or flax. An apple orchard was even visible.

To the right a hydroelectric dam rose up, holding back a narrow lake, which was fed by mountain snow melt water. A park lay below, along the river. Small adults and their smaller offspring walked among the trees of birds and squirrels, or fished in the pond where ducks swam. It was another world, beneath the world.

Robulus stood with his two human guests atop a rock platform and they looked down at the fantastic tableau from a vantage point twenty feet above. The two humans could discern that the little 'people' possessed no hair on their heads and their exposed skin was milk white.

A yellow light, like that from a full moon, shone down from the rock ceiling four-hundred feet above, and from scores of rocky outcrops and cairns. Robulus said, "Welcome to Somtrow, which means Gawd's Throne, in Gaian, the dwarf's own language. It refers to their enclave's close proximity to the TDS, which has become an object of worship for some."

Vera, feeling as if she'd slipped into some parallel universe, asked, "Dwarfs?" She looked at Griz, in hopes he could tell her it was all an illusion. It didn't look promising, because he seemed as amazed as she.

Griz wondered for a few seconds whether Robulus may have slipped them some hallucinogens. He asked, "Where is Snow Whiteout?" He needed time to process the input captured by his five senses. Griz understood now why Robulus didn't tell them about Somtrow. It had to be experienced to be believed, and even then, it was a strain.

Robulus said, "The light is provided by bioluminescent bacteria, a species that Jeemis and I engineered many thousands of years ago. Let's go down to street level. It may not seem like much, but it has proven to be enough." The alien guided the two humans down a stone stairway to the road below. A wooden cart with ten or twelve stone blocks inside rumbled past them, towed by a dog as large as the dwarf walking next to it. The dwarf wore a tan-coloured, knee length dress. In fact, all of the dwarves wore dresses.

Now that they were at ground level, underground, the two humans could scrutinise the dwarves more closely. The adults averaged four to four and a half feet tall, with large, yellow cat-eyes, small noses and ears, and wide, smiling mouths. Their limbs, like their torsos and heads, were short and stout, with broad, splayed hands and feet.

Griz couldn't distinguish male from female at first. Both sexes were bald, and they all wore the same simple dress, but a few did wear leggings. As for shoes, wooden clogs were the current fashion for all ages and both genders. Dwarf females do not possess an hourglass figure like the humans do, and in fact they more resemble a grandfather clock. She-dwarves possessed small breasts and slight hips, as if gifts from the goddess of chastity. Griz puzzled it out however; the women had eyebrows.

"Follow me please," Robulus boomed. "We are going downriver. It's called the Woohoo River, because that's what they all scream when they get in the ice-cold water." They turned left and travelled the worn, dusty road. A rooster crowed in the distance. Vera and Griz walked side by side, behind the towering alien.

Griz asked, "Are those robots out there?" He pointed to a field on the other side of the Woohoo River. Vera saw them. They were baskets, rolling on three wheels, and with two telescoping arms, and grasping fingers that plucked apples from trees. Robulus said, "Yes, Jeemis and I have designed robots for specific operations of all kinds. In fact, as you will soon see, robots are preparing for tonight's activities."

They came to the main part of town, and trade was slow but steady, at the various shops and eateries they passed. All the dwarfs they came across greeted Robulus merrily and spoke in English to his guests.

Robulus said, "I am sure that you have many questions." His voice carried easily to Vera and Griz behind him, as the two worked to keep up with the long-legged alien.

The alien led them into a café and they seated themselves at an open table. There were several to choose from, only a few patrons were eating at this early time. All the dwarfs who were present felt it necessary to meet the two humans. It was exciting! The owner of the café came out to do the same, and asked Robulus if he wanted the usual. "Yes, and two more for our guests." The dwarf went back behind the counter and helped the chef to prepare three baked trout sandwiches.

Griz and Vera studied their surroundings and the store décor. The walls were constructed of granite blocks, like many things down here. Metal was ubiquitous too, especially iron. The café walls were hung with dozens of enlarged, framed photographs of human atrocities from the violent world above. Pictures of death camps, atomic explosions, mass graves and other horrors of war, were not appetising to look at, and Griz asked Robulus, "Why all of this?"

The alien said, "It reminds them why they shun the surface. While we await our orders, I will tell you about all of this." Griz and Vera were stupefied and incredulous, but captivated. They were all ears.

Robulus' voice filled the café, and it was impossible for the dwarf patrons and employees to not eavesdrop. They would have tried to had they needed to however, because gossip was a dwarf's best friend. He said, "Let's start with these peoples, the dwarves. The race branched off from the human tree in Yourup, about thirty-two thousand years ago. They were persecuted by your ancestors, and were pursued across Azha.

"Eventually, the last remnant of several thousand dwarves was pushed to the east coast at the Herring Strait, scant miles from the continent of North Shamerica. Their people soon crossed over the water, to reach the unknown lands here. That happened around twenty thousand years ago, and the dwarves had the continent all to themselves for four millennia, before you big guys showed up to terrorise them again.

"After humans invaded, their population in the Shamericas quickly exploded, and within a few thousand years' time, they had driven all of the mega-fauna to extinction by hunting. This caused famine amongst the dwarves, and their numbers were already depleted by the novel diseases the humans exposed them to. The humans then started preying on the dwarf race, as competitors for scarce food and for food too.

"Jeemis and I rescued the last few hundred dwarves, and bought them underground, to one of seven of our established underground research and development enclaves scattered around the globe. Jeemis and I had gone underground many millennia ago, to avoid discovery of our technologies by humans before you could use them wisely."

"What do you mean by that?" Vera asked defensively.

Robulus said, "I don't really want to get into this right now, but if you must, I will give you one example." The café manager delivered three trout sandwiches on square plates, and departed the table. The fillets were wrapped in toasted bread pockets.

"When we first introduced your race to fire," Robulus said, "you burned millions of acres of trees and grasslands, killed billions of animals and roasted many of their own relatives too."

Griz hadn't realised how hungry he was, until he started eating the delicious food. Vera was trying not to wolf down the sandwich, and forced herself to chew before swallowing; she was starving.

Griz swallowed a bite and asked Robulus, "How do the dwarfs grow food down here? Where did the soil come from?"

Robulus said, "The Woohoo River is a natural waterway. This cavern served as an underground reservoir. It was a massive lake for millions of years, and yards of silt lie beneath our feet. Jeemis and I tamed the river for power, and opened up an outlet for the accumulated water, thus draining the area that is now farmed."

Griz hadn't entirely brought the idea, that Robulus was from another galaxy, but he couldn't deny that dwarves made one demn good trout sandwich! They completed their meals and Robulus used some odd coins to pay for their food.

The tall alien, with Griz and Vera following behind, exited the café and continued downriver again, along the main street. Robulus turned left at an alley, which soon came to an end. They crossed a meadow of grasses and clover, before coming to a stop at an iron gate. Two enormous brown dogs, like hybrids between a bear and a sabre-tooth tiger, bounded towards them. The dogs patrolled inside a seven-foot-tall fence, which surrounded a low stone-block building. The dogs didn't bark as they charged the gate, but started to wag their tails and smiled when they recognised Robulus.

The tall alien said, "Open." The voice recognition system unlatched the gate and it swung open. They all entered the yard and the gate swung shut and locked behind them. The dogs mobbed the alien and he pulled some treats from a pocket, and greeted them enthusiastically. Vera asked. "What are they? And what are their names?"

Griz squatted down and the dogs allowed him to scratch behind their tall, straight ears. Robulus answered Vera, he said, "Jeemis and I call the breed, Sentries. The guy with black ear tips is Block and the other is Brick. Their mates are happily nursing litters.

"Let's go inside," Robulus said. The dogs followed them to the entry door of the stone building, which was the size of a two-car garage. A tub of fresh water for the dogs could be seen outside the entry door. A facial recognition security system matched Robulus' face, and the steel entry door unlatched and swung open.

Lights came on when they stepped inside, illuminating one large, open room. Robulus flipped a wall switch and eight steel panels slid back, bringing some light and air in through the short, rectangular windows revealed. Griz walked towards a long table with two large touch screens computer monitors built into it, which were level with its surface. A MegaScreen TV hung on the end wall, ten feet from the table. Two chairs waited for butts to warm them. A bookshelf filled with dozens of handwritten notebooks and computer printouts stood along the right wall and a closed cabinet posed on the left.

Vera wasn't certain why it was that she wanted to remain close to Griz, but she didn't delve into the reasons too deeply. It felt safe and it felt good, so she stayed with it. Robulus pulled a chair out for Vera and said, "Take a seat." Vera did and Griz sat to her left. Griz asked, "Why all the security? It's like a politician's compound."

Robulus said, "Jeemis and I design and test drones and robots at this location. Are you recording this Vera?"

"Yes," She answered. "Is it okay?"

Robulus said, "You may record, but this is off the record. The existence of the dwarves is to remain a secret. I don't want them threatened by man. There is a militant group of dwarfs who call themselves the Resistance, which has worked to thwart our Unveiling project. They worship the TDS as a god, and they do not want humans to benefit from it. They fear that your race will do what it does best and ruin it. They have broken into this building in the past, and they took everything they could haul away."

Griz was at his limit. He said, "What the poke, Robulus? The Unveiling, the TDS, dwarves, underground cities, but no Melanie; what in Hades is going on?"

Robulus walked around the table to face the humans, his back to the MegaScreen TV, which hung on the end wall. He said, "This must be heart wrenching for you Matt, but I repeat; she will come to no harm. She is one smart, tough lady, and she will overcome. She will get here safely. Jeemis will ensure it."

Vera said, "This is all so confusing, with so much impossibility to absorb, it's like a political convention."

Griz laughed. He said, "I feel so helpless."

Vera reached over and squeezed his hand. She said, "This is more than a story. I am involved and I want to help."

Robulus came back to their side of the table and touched the computer monitor screen set into the table in front of Griz. The one hundred-and forty-four-inch MegaScreen TV, which hung on the end wall, lit up, and eight separate rectangles, showing eight different camera views, in two columns of four, appeared. Robulus said, "These are live pictures."

Vera wondered, "Is that here in Minotaur Springs?"

Griz lived an hour away, south of Dunfor, and he had visited the tourist trap town of Minotaur Springs on many occasions, but not since Pamela's murder… "It looks like you're expecting a lot of company," he said.

Robulus said, "Several thousand vehicles I should think. You refer to cameras one and two. Parking lot A will hold about twelve hundred cars, and lot B can handle eight hundred more, with room for sixty to seventy truck rigs, buses and RVs too, if needed."

Vera exclaimed, "Thousands of people are coming here? Who and why?"

Griz said, "That's crazy!"

Robulus agreed. He said, "Yes, humans are nuts." He added, "Some people come with questions and some people come with dreams. The curious and the desperate come, and people who wish to change their world come."

This thought saddened Vera somewhat, she asked, "Are you offering false hopes? What do you wish to achieve?"

Robulus answered, his voice like a barrage of cannon fire, "We don't offer hope. People have enough of their own. We offer the TDS."

Griz was amazed at the number and variety of robots he saw in several of the eight camera views showing on the MegaScreen. He remarked, "Your robots are absolutely fantastic!" Robots manicured trails; concessions stands and the gift shops were being stocked with products and foodstuffs; parking lights and safety rails were tested, and other tasks done as needed.

"Thank you. We are reluctant to share our designs, but we do have patents on these models. Camera number three is a view of Gate 1, at the bottom of the trail which leads up to the TDS. In camera four you see our food court and the permanent restrooms in the concessions stands area. There are also thirty portable toilets there. Gate 2, leading uphill from the gathering area, is shown on camera five. Camera six is aimed at the third and final crowd control gate, at the top of the trail."

Vera complained that, "Camera seven is just a bullseye on a wall of rock. What's that about?

Griz asked about the view from number eight, "What's up with the tank? Water?"

The alien replied, he said, "Number seven is the rock curtain hiding the TDS, and number eight shows a tank that does not contain water, but I'll explain about that later."

"This is surreal," Vera said. "It's like you knew this moment was coming!"

"Totally prepared for opening night," Griz remarked.

Robulus answered this way: "Jeemis and I have laboured at this for the last nineteen years, and only finished our preparations five months ago. The stupidity virus has taken a severe toll on your world. The idiocy permeating Gaia has reached a tipping point, and we must take action. We had to make ourselves public, expose ourselves in a memorable way to get the media attention needed."

He added, "Jeemis and I had a few plans in the works for gaining world attention, but the murderous maniac at the burger house saved us the effort. It was a one in a billion coincidence; an opposing force to Kazooky's Conundrum, a cosmic equaliser that we call Jinksyn's Offset. It is named after the galactic race that first described it."

Vera was mesmerised by the various camera views and the robots rolling, walking or scuttling here and there making last hour preparations. She said, "What a production! This is awesome."

Griz said, "Indeed, Robulus. It looks overproduced, totally commercialised. I don't get it."

The alien responded, "Commercialised? But of course, Griz! Of course. It's the Shamerican way!"

Robulus shut the MegaScreen TV off. He said, "We're on a schedule and we have more to do. Let us go."

The trio retraced their steps and walked upriver, heading back to the elevator which bought them down here to the underground dwarf village. Robulus led with his long, quick steps. As they passed a wooded area of the park, below the dam, the tall alien suddenly spun, pivoting rapidly. His two human guests were awestruck to see Robulus snatch a flying arrow from the air, catching it by the shaft, in one hand.

Chapter 18

Donut whimpered again, "Are we almost there yet?"

Jeemis retorted, "You should have bought a colouring book at the Fas-Gas."

Shanghai laughed. He said, "We need to stop in Jewelsberg and get some fuel in this beast."

They were in Colorotta now. It was 2:30 PM mountain time, and they'd driven three hundred and sixty miles over the last seven hours. Melanie kept to a comfortable speed of seventy miles per hour. A retinue of twenty-six vehicles followed them now, and two news helicopters covered the action from above. Loser turned the radio off after listening to live coverage of their progress, mixed in with hysterical speculations and idiotic conspiracy theories. The exaggerations became absurdities, and the absurdities became drivel, and the drivel passed for news.

Shanghai Low barked at Donut, "Are you kidding me? How can you want this to end? We're on the brink of stardom and you want us to be there! We need to milk this kidnapping for every drop we can squeeze from the crime cow! Look behind us Donut! Those are our fans!"

Melanie steered the BUV onto the sole exit ramp leading into Jewelsberg, Gateway to the Stoney Mountains. There were two gas stations to choose from. Melanie drove the white Tanki into the Jewelsberg Cornoco station, and pulled up to a diesel pump. Low said, "Donut, fill it up. Then we will all go inside together. Keep your stayser handy and remember you two, I have a gun."

It had been just another slow, lazy day at the Jewelsberg Cornoco for assistant manager Orson Periwinkle. He listened to talk radio while he rotated product, dusted shelves and performed other tediums. Then, around two hours ago, his convenience store suddenly filled with his regular local customers. They were listening to the radio too, or worse, watching TV. Some feared the approach of the Pissan Tanki, others dreaded an alien invasion, or Crumm's Draconian Stormtroopers coming to rape their husbands and steal their dogs. The locals cleared Orson's shelves of popcorn, toilet paper, liquor and diapers. Some splurged-on bread and milk.

Between the exaggerated anxieties of his shoppers and the psychotic rantings of talk radio, Orson was on edge when his parking lot began to fill with cars and trucks. A line formed at his four gas pumps. He saw the white Tanki and nearly pooped his pants.

Orson didn't hesitate however; he was ready for this eventuality. While the crooks filled their half-empty tank, Orson emptied a half-full cash drawer. He wasn't going to be left behind in Jewelsberg! He was moving on to bigger and better things. This TDS was the next big thing, and he wanted in!

He heard one woman who called into the radio station earlier, who said that she saw the TDS, during a near death experience. She said, "It was orgasmic," and that, "TDS means Terrific Demn Sex." The radio host cut her off when she started explaining about the delight at the end of the tunnel. Orson liked the sound of that. The skanky, Jewelsberg town whore was like the mercy tunnel anymore, and his doctor said that Orson couldn't keep getting shots forever.

Orson stuffed all of the paper money from the cash register into his pockets, and left the coins behind. He ripped an ear off a cardboard box and used a black marker to print on it, in large block letters, all caps,' HELP YOURSELF'. He propped it on the cash register, and programmed the gas pumps to reset when the handles were hung, and the fees paid. Then he went out the back door and got into his car, just as Low, Donut, and their captives entered the store. Orson drove to the back of the line of cars, and waited for a gas pump to open up.

The Fas-Gas across the road was just as busy. Jewelsberg hadn't seen this kind of activity since the stagecoach days, when criminals were king. It seemed the locals wanted to relive those glory days of the past.

The Tanki was here in Jewelsberg! And a convoy came with them! Word spread faster than the town whore's crabs. In an eye blink, folks were setting up tables, tents and BBQ grills down on the street, between the two gas stations. By the time, Donut wheeled a hand truck loaded with pastries, chips and soda pop, out of the store, a thriving farmer's market was in operation down on the corner. Drivers, and their passengers from the vehicle caravan, were looking through the wares.

One of the two news helicopters which had followed their progress, returned to home base in Bland Island. The second chopper, carrying the Sindey, Nobraska, channel ten Skye News team, landed in an abandoned dirt lot, a couple of blocks away from the impromptu festival. In the next sixty minutes, the helicopter pilot would shell out a total of three hundred dollars, to seven different people, who claimed ownership of the land and a parking fee.

Entertainment was provided by a literal troop of talent show wannabes. First up was a ninety-seven-year-old beatnik, who played bongo drums while chanting poems about how horrible the fifties were. People threw money into his filthy, ragged straw hat in hopes that he would quit.

Low got a whiff of hamburgers cooking on a gas grill, and he decided they needed to hang around for a while. He felt as if his two prisoners were docile enough to be trusted, so after Donut unloaded his snacks into the truck, they went down to join the party. Low thought he could pick up a few bucks in the process too.

Crime Blaster XL-5 and Barry Porter were eating pieces of Mrs Applebug's homemade tomato-potato cobbler, when celebrities Shanghai Low and Donut Hole arrived in the area, with Melanie and the alien leading the way. Most of the people there were clustered around the two beer tents. Neither gas station had any beer left in the refrigerator cases. The locals had purchased it all in their panicked buying spree hours earlier, and now they were reselling it at three dollars a bottle.

The bongo beatnik had picked up the six dollars and forty-two cents from out of his hat, and got in the beer line, leaving the hat behind. Next up for their viewing displeasure, came an overweight, middle-aged woman, wearing a too-small tutu, and carrying an umbrella. She began doing a striptease to her son's sackpipe music. Low pulled out his gun, and said, "No! No poking way! Get outta here!"

It's not that he wouldn't have liked to watch it, but he could make better use of the time. Jeemis and Melanie, again stood like backdrops, as Low and Donut sucked up the approval and praise of the townsfolk. Melanie drank an energy drink and thought about the stupidity virus, as she watched the entire scene unfold. No one took Jeemis seriously as an actual alien; he wasn't cute, nor was he slaughtering people. How boring!

Shanghai Low was charging six dollars for a selfie with him, or two photos for ten bucks. Donut was undercutting him by a dollar. Crime Blaster joined in the fun and soon, he and his two avowed enemies, mugged for the crowd. CB pretended to strangle Low, as the crowd hee-hawed and shot videos. Donut was placed into a headlock for the next camera pose.

Barry Porter streamed the show back to CON engineers. These geniuses cut, edited and wrote a storyline that seemed to show a real life and death struggle, between a super-hero and the two celebrity criminals. The two figures in the background; Melanie and Jeemis, were excised, and replaced with a painting of a flying saucer.

The channel ten Skye News team used similar video footage, but created an entirely different story. It focused on Jeemis and Melanie, and reported this: "Look at these two sinister figures, who lurk in the background, as if uninvolved, when it is they who are the masterminds, they who compose, orchestrate and conduct this madcap Crumm opera of world domination, known as The Dark Side; TDS."

People, who saw the contrary CON and the Skye News' stories describing the same incident, were often able to believe both lies simultaneously. As one wise father explained to his confused children, "The aliens are distorting reality and altering space-time. It will all make sense, after we all die together in the conflagration when worlds collide." One of those confused children replied, "Dad, are you drinking again?"

Rosie Oh topped off her big rig with fuel, and went inside the abandoned Jewelsberg convenience store. She stuffed four pounds of beef jerky down her bra, and looked through the condoms. She saw one package with three condoms called the Friday Night size, and a second package with five prophylactics called the Family Size. She didn't want to dwell on that. The next larger package with nine condoms was the Party Pak, but she chose the fifteen-count, Orgy Box. A girl could dream. Plus, she had a trailer full of refrigerated beer, and gals all look good after three or four. Well, maybe six or eight.

Chapter 19

The Emcee, and High Priest and Prophet of the Sacred Star Temple Inc., Robby Indero, called the emergency meeting to order. He slapped the coffee table with a ping-pong paddle. Eight of the twelve temple apostles were assembled here in his mom's basement, including him. Bawd Medler was missing, for one. Apparently, she'd recently taken a part time job, working as a buoy for the Harbour Authority.

The odour down here, where Bobby spent most of his time since his last wife kicked him out, rivalled that of an outhouse full of smelly socks after a chili cook-off. The assembled temple elders, sat at an odd assortment of arm chairs, lawn chairs, beanbag chairs and one high chair, all of which were last dusted and wiped clean, sometime in the past century. Several of the celebrities present, wore face masks drenched with perfume, to assuage the basement stench.

Robby stepped atop a stage, made of three stacked car tires with a piece of warped plywood balanced atop them, to address his friends and temple co-worshippers. "You all know," he said, "why in the poking Hades I called this scat smoking, butt poking meeting. The poking aliens! The dumb-clucking, crotch sucking news is non-stop, poking aliens!"

Seven heads belonging to one of four men or three women, including five actors, one pop singer and an athlete, bobbed up and down like apples in a tub of water, but with less seeming intelligence. They knew how to decode Robby's meaning, automatically separating the meaningful words from his profanity. They were well practiced in the art; his weekly temple sermons were masterpieces. None of them wanted to be a target of his mouth, so they agreed with him. It was safer.

Indero grew more agitated with every sentence he spoke, as if he was pissing himself off. "We are facing an ass jacking, butt packing, nut cracking, and religious poking crisis! Our poke stroking, rectum reaming way of life, is poking threatened by these upstart aliens!

"Thus, it is up to us father-poking, sons of whore ass, rich, famous, poking, temple apostles to do something about these aliens trying to spread their TDS cult crap! It could cost us millions…of souls, I mean."

Okra Wipmee, the apostle of diversity, had spread her wide self across two folding chair seats. She spoke up, saying, "I make a motion that we do something."

If she made a motion, she'd fall her fat ass out of her chair, thought the rapper Arti P, apostle of morality, who said, "I second the emotion."

"Sold!" Indero shouted. He jumped down from his tire tiered stage, to whack the coffee table with his ping pong paddle.

Robby resumed his plywood stage again, and said. "Now, the second poking item on our hose-choking, crotch soaking agenda, is what poking action, do we poking take? But wait! Have no poking fear. I have it under poking control. In this throat-gagging, ass sagging, ball dragging regard, I have poking prepared, a butt humping, stump pumping survey.

"But first," Indero said, "I want you to poking listen to this finger popping, hole hopping, poke slopping fone conversation I had, with that bad acting, jack-assing, ball-waxing Don Crews, our esteemed poking apostle of doctrine," he sneered.

He stepped down off the plywood, to confront a short silver cylinder on the coffee table. He spoke at it, "Hey Perplexa," he addressed it. "Wake the poke up and play that nose picking, butt licking, teeth kicking fone call I had with Don Crews."

The little machine talked back in a digitalised woman's voice, "Here is the replay, you pus drinking, poke shrinking old buzzard."

The call began with Don's voice; he said, "Hey, Bobby! I'm calling to ask if you've been following this TDS hullaballoon stuff going on out there in Colorotta. So are ya?"

"Of course, I poking am, Don. In fact, I was just calling around, to all of you scat eating, wife beating, dog cheating apostles. I am calling a poking emergency, poking meeting."

"I'll have to give you a rain coat on that Bobby. I am being driven out to my personal jet at this time, and I'm in a hurry, "Dom had replied.

Bobby asked, "Where the poke, Don? What's more poking important than the future of our temple bank accounts?"

Crews replied, "It's like this; I have to go to Colorotta Springs to see that TDS dude. I've got an investment to protect. I need to be first in line for the immortality vaccine, or pill, or whatever in Hades it is," Don said, defensively. "Plus," he added, "There should be a lot of cameras, photographers and peppernazis there for me to pose for, and interview with. PR is always good Robby."

Robby snarled viciously, "It's not peppernazis, you poking idiot! You mean papa-rotseas! And you're already immortalised you poking nitwit! You're practically an SST saint!"

"I am talking about living forever! Physical immortality! I need this, Robby! There are seven more Mission Improbable scripts out there and two for Grand-Pop Gun."

Robby raged, "You lousy poking piece of rat scat, heretic son of a septic snatch, trailer trash, sore sailor ass, slop of sperm! You can't go to this alien god, this TDS! You are the poking Apostle of poking Doctrine!"

"You've got it all wrong," Crews whined. "I'm just picking up my immortality and then I'm coming straight home! No TDS temptations will deter my faith! I am SST, not TDS."

"You know that it means Temple of Death Sacrifices, right?" Indero said.

Crews replied, "You said a whole sentence without profanity! Are you well?"

"It's a poking emergency!"

"I know right."

"Look Dom, you will have to be our point man out there in Colorotta. Cancel the TDS! We're depending on you," Indero replied.

"Call ended," said Perplexa. Indero cracked the ping pong paddle onto the table as an audible exclamation mark, and Perplexa fell over, rolled off the table and, crashed onto the concrete floor. "Ouch!" the soft female voice cried. "Watch it, you dumb ass-grabbing, mouth-blabbing, clumsy poke!"

Six pairs of blank eyes stared into space, as if studying dust motes. One set of eyes, however noticed that Perplexa was in distress. The eyes' owner, netball star Labrat Jades accused, "You killed her!" He ran over to the cylinder's side and helped her to her foot. Then he carefully placed her back onto the coffee table.

Perplexa said. "Thank you Labrat. Come up and see me sometime."

That bought a smile to Robby's face. He pulled a folder out from under a sofa pillow and said, "I took it upon myself to create this poking, short, one-question survey. Please read it poking carefully, and choose one of my multiple poking answers." Robby Indero pulled a dozen pieces of paper from the folder and gave ten to Lonny Doop and said, "Pass these around." Robby had three pencil stubs for them all to share.

The survey question asked, 'What action or actions should we or our hired help take, to exterminate these evil alien religious imposters who threaten the future earnings of our church, and who will most likely, also accelerate climate change?' The three answers to choose from were these: 'A. Quarantine; B. File bankruptcy; and C. Call the Dunfor, Colorotta branch of the Sacred Star Temple, and make their members deal with it'.

The seven Sacred Star Temple apostles thought long and hard before making their choices and they passed the pencil stubs around until all of the ballots were completed. It seemed obvious that either Robby's lawyer or his mother had written and typed out the survey, since not one shred of profanity was found.

Indero collected the ballots. He looked though them quickly, and stepped up onto his tire and plywood stage to announce the results. He said, "Who in poking Hades, is the one poking, anus snacking, nut cracking, bass turd, who answered A? Everyone else knew that C was the correct poking answer! Who?"

The apostle of investments and finance, Pike Flea raised his hand and said, "It's safer to shelter in place until this all goes away."

Indero said, "I should skip over you when I hand out refreshments later, Poop Dogg."

"I'm Pike Flea! Not Poop Dogg!"

Indero said, "Alright then, we are unanimously agreed that I call up the Dunfor SST, and have them confront this menace from outer space."

A woman's voice yelled down from the top of the basement stairway, "Oh Robby! I'm home with your poking beer!"

"Okay. Thanks Ma!" Indero hollered. He climbed a few steps up, to meet his ninety-six-year-old mother halfway. He complained, "Demmit Mom! You only poking bought a poking twelve poking pack!"

Mom ascended to the top step, then turned to say, "Poke you Bobby, and poke your crooked poking church!" Then the door slammed shut.

The ten apostles laughed and laughed. Robby joined in, thinking they made fun of his mother. He said, "She's always poking kidding like that." He handed out one beer for every two people and told them to share. Robby gave one entire beer to Arti P. He popped open one of the remaining cans of beer and took a long swig.

Then he spoke to the silver cylinder again, which had been restored to the coffee table by James. Indero said, "Hey Dyslexia! Call the poking Dunfor temple and get poking Lem Kerry on the poking line."

The instrument replied, "Placing a poking call to poking Lem Kerry; standby."

Lem Kerry, the Dunfor, Colorotta temple High Priest, was a disappointing comedian and a dismal artist who thrived in the SST religion. Phoniness paid dividends in the SST, which is why celebrities flourished there. He answered his temple office fone. "Hello Robby. I was sort of expecting a call from you. The end of the world is nigh. Should I halt all further tours until after the apocalypse?"

"Yes," DiZero replied. "Put the closed for poking business sign up. How many poking apostles are there with you?"

Kerry said, "I got four here. What do you want us to do?"

"You guys have to get on down to the poking Colorotta Springs airport to meet Don Crews. The poking TDS must go back to its own poking planet! Make sure it does. Thanks. End the poking call Dyslexia."

Bobby ascended the tires to address his apostles. He said, "Apostles dismissed. Okay, just go on back to your normal daily tasks. Everything is handled."

Indero's mom's basement emptied out, and the pampered celebrities all got into their separate chauffeured cars, which had been waiting out on the street. Robby said, "Hey Perplexa; call my poking pilot. I need this poking immortality."

"Get my poking name right asshole! It's Exlaxa!"

Seven other celebrity apostles, secretly placed calls from their limousine fones, to their respective personal pilots, and told them to prepare to fly to Colorotta Springs. These entitled people were not going to be left out of the immortality sweepstakes at midnight. No way.

Chapter 20

The white Pissan Tanki passed through Ft. Boragain, Colorotta at 5:58 PM, pulling a train of thirty-six cars behind it. Melanie was tired. She'd been driving for over ten hours, under severe stress. It was only about one hundred and fifty miles more to Minotaur Springs. With luck they could make that in two and a half to three hours, even considering the heavy traffic around Dunfor. She could do that easily!

Low played a game on his selfone, and Donut texted his two wives about his wanted status. They were proud of him. Melanie took the opportunity to engage Jeemis. She looked up into the rear-view mirror and happily caught his attention. She said, "Jeemis, you and Robulus wrote this play, didn't you?"

Jeemis smiled bigly. He answered in his ear shattering voice, "Excellent deduction my dear. Well done!"

Melanie grinned in return. She said, "You said much more than you needed to at the panel inquiry. I see now, that you led me to the questions that I asked."

"It's a script with tons of impromptu mixed in," Jeemis said.

Melanie said, "Well, acts one and two have been fun, but I bet that act three is a real doozy."

"Impressive," Jeemis remarked in his blasting shriek.

Melanie posed another question, by making a statement. She said, "Evolutionary theory explains in fairly simple terms, that a race of aliens from another planet cannot possibly resemble humans as closely as you do. You and Robulus are too human by far. This isn't Star Dreck or another fake sci-fi television show."

Jeemis replied, "You're not going to like the answer, Melanie." The alien saw that he need say no more. The look of shock in Melanie's eyes, seen from his vantage of the rear-view mirror, showed that she wanted him to reconsider.

Some sound, perhaps a word or its tone or volume, triggered a mental shotgun blast that blew holes in Low's video-absorbed mind. He departed game land and re-entered reality with a sense of pain, and his brain bled sense from a score of holes. He wailed, "I heard that! What are you playing?" He pulled a long hatpin from a sandal and thrust it towards Melanie's eye.

Jeemis screeched, "Not a good idea at seventy miles per hour."

Donut said, "They're planning an escape, Loser."

"If you call me Loser one more demn time…"

"I'm sorry Shanghai Low, it's just that you've been a loser as long as I've known you," Donut said.

Realising that it was not smart to jab the driver in the eye with a hatpin, Low turned around and buried it in Jeemis' thigh. "Wow! Thanks!" Jeemis shrieked.

Elated, and in a good spirit again, Low tried to make polite conversation with his captives. "The news people said you are a scientist advisor for Crumm. I know science, like quantum fizzies."

"Oh really, do tell, "Melanie replied. "I need to brush up on that."

Low smiled, happy to be taken seriously. He said, "Yeah, so like this dude named Schroeder had this cat, see. And if you couldn't smell its litterbox, then it hadn't crapped yet. Get it?"

Donut shook his head and dared to correct Low. He said, "That's not how it goes, Shanghai. It's like this, man; Schroeder lost his cat in the woods, and no one could find it, which meant that it never existed at all. See, if I go somewhere and no one sees me, then I never went there, unless I left my DNA."

Jeemis screeched, "I see why Donut is the brains of your outfit."

Low was tired of it. He turned on the radio, and soon found a Dunfor talk station. "Line two, Fungus in Flakewood, you're talking to Gabby Prattle. Tell us what TDS means to you."

"It's Fergus, Grabby. I have it on excellent authority, that these three letters represent the merging of our planet's three most dangerous and most powerful forces for evil; the Illuminati, the Tri-lateral Commission and the Pope, all rolled up into one large flour tortilla called the Trap Door Spider.

"That's a mixed metaphor Fergie."

"No, I don't drink so much anymore, ever since that…"

"Who is your excellent authority?"

"Who do ya think? My cat of course. She's from…"

"One line is open at 555-Gabb. Gym Scarey from Dunfor on line two; go ahead sir."

"It's Kerry, Lem Kerry; Gumby. I'm sure you must know who I am. I am the super-iconic comedian from such hit movies as… Well, I am him. Anyway, I am not calling you as the famous Hollowood celebrity, but as the High Priest of the Sacred Star Temple in Dunfor."

Gabby needed to set down some stricter rules for her call screener. He apparently still thinks, 'the kookier the better'. She had to ask though, "Okay Grim Cherry; what does the high, um, High Priest of Dunfor, think of all this?"

"It's Lem Kerry, Grubby. Listen to me! These TDS are The Dark Saints, and it ain't no racial thing…"

"One line open at 555-GABB. Hello Shanghai Low calling from a car. You're gabbing with Gabby. What do you have for us?" Low had punched in the fone number during that last crazy call, and had passed the screener. He had been put on hold, and he turned the radio off as instructed. Low turned on his fone's loudspeaker.

With his new handle and notoriety, Low took on airs. He said, "Hey Gabsy doodle baby. Me and my BEWB brother Donut Hole are riding inside a white Pissan Tanki, with a loud tall alien and some chick named Melanie."

Gabby couldn't help correcting poor grammar. She said, "My boob brother and I." She wasn't sure how breasts found their way onto her show, but, learn English!

Low was surprised that she was one of them. "I'd love to meet your BEWBs and you can see mine."

Gabby changed her mind about discussing rules with her call screener. There was a gun in her purse. She went to end the call, but there was something here, maybe. She said, "You're the fourth kidnapper riding in a white Tanki, to call in and confess this afternoon. But at least the previous ones all had the same moniker of Loser."

"That's all behind me now. Soon you will know the names Shanghai Low and Donut Hole better than your own, Gabster."

"It sounds more like a breakfast order from Skorbucks, than names for two desperadoes. Since you are riding with the alien, you can tell us what TDS means. You have ten seconds," Gabby said.

Shanghai Low deserved more than this sort of treatment. Outraged, he shouted, "Ten demn seconds!"

"That's not the worst solution I've heard today. One line is open…"

Low shouted at dead air, "That wasn't my poking answer!" He threw his selfone on the floor mat and turned the radio on. He heard Gabby reading off a short list. "Transylvanian Death Stare, Tangerine Deodorant Soap, Tacky Designer Shoes, Topless Dancing Seniors, Trolls Don't Sweat, Teenage Delinquent Slut, Tone Deaf Singer, Toothless Drunk Stoner and Talking Dragon Statue. And now a word from…"

Low turned the radio off, moving in dazed, slow motion. He said, "Mine was Torturous Deafening Shrieks!" He sounded as if he might cry. Jeemis laughed, "Wahit! Wahit!"

Chapter 21

Griz reacted quickly, and he wrapped Vera up in a hug, and turned his back to the area from whence the arrow came. Robulus walked back to them. He said, "That's all. It's only a warning." Griz released his embrace, much to Vera's relief because she could breathe again. It did feel good though.

Robulus handed the arrow to Griz, and said, "Look at the feathers."

Griz held the arrow by the shaft and held it so that Vera could read the blood red words on the three, white chicken feathers. They were written in dwarfish Gaian, and Robulus translated, "We. Will. Resist."

Vera's adrenalin or something was making her feel warm. She asked the alien "How did you do that?"

Robulus grinned. He said, "Senses made more acute with nano-technology. I heard the rustle of clothes and the twang of the bowstring, the flight of the arrow. There were three dwarves."

Griz was angered. "I seemed to have missed the memo, where you warned Vera that her life was in danger, in this nutty plan of yours. My daughter is out there, so I don't give a scat for the risks, but this ain't right!"

Robulus acknowledged Griz's concerns. He said, "Vera, Griz is right. If you wish to depart, tell me now, because we are going to the elevator depot."

Never at a loss for words, Vera, answered without hesitation. She said, "Life is a risk, and I am living. Let's go!" She took Griz's big arm and Robulus led them back to where they'd entered this improbable underworld. They ascended the stairs and entered the elevator. Once inside the capsule, Robulus pressed the centre button and they rose on a cushion of air. A parallel sealed tube was connected with theirs, and as it filled with water it pushed the capsule up, in this far skinnier air tube.

They rose more slowly than they'd dropped and Vera made conversation. She asked, "Where are we going; one level up, to a town of gnomes or trolls?"

Robulus said, "We are ascending to another part of the mountain."

Griz said, "I want to know more about this dwarf resistance group. How dangerous are they? How determined are they, to stop the Unveiling?"

Robulus' voice was like a sledgehammer to their eardrums inside the small elevator enclosure when he said, "That's a fair question. The leader of the Resistance is Cynna Spoile, the wealthiest dwarf in the seven colonies. He's gained that wealth in crime, and by exploiting the followers of the TDS religious cult. He has convinced his hard-core nexus of followers, that Jeemis and I are betraying their race to humans, and exploiting their idol. There are forty dwarves who support his Resistance in this colony, but only a handful of them are violent."

Griz said, "It only takes one."

"We have taken precautions for tonight. Our robots can detect gunpowder and flammable materials and they will be everywhere. Drones have swept the area, and will continue to do so."

The lift came to a gentle stop and the door slid open. They exited the car, and clusters of LED lights illuminated a garage-sized cavern. A dark tunnel led from it, and two small carts, akin to golf carts were parked nearby, plugged into an outlet in a rock wall, to charge their batteries.

Griz asked "How did you drill these shafts and tunnels? This is unreal!" He and Vera followed Robulus to the wall of rock where the two carts were parked. The alien touched the wall and a door popped open. The alien said, "No drilling was done. We use gravity wave pulse cannons. You will see one in action later tonight. Come on in to one of our broadcast studios."

Hot, bright overhead TV lights came on when they entered, illuminating a small stage. Two rolling cameras pointed towards the stage as well. Vera marvelled at the set-up and asked, "Can you broadcast from down here?"

Robulus' face wore a scat-eating grin. He said, "Yes indeed. We soon will." The tall slender alien walked through the room, turning on equipment. He said, "In fact, I can pirate communication satellites, and force them to broadcast the signal I send. I can air a program all over the planet, and that's precisely what we shall do."

"No way!" Vera exclaimed.

Griz smiled. "Bravo!" He said. "Air-jacking the Make-Believe Media, I love it!"

Vera looked askance at the two. She wasn't certain that it was wise to season the fake news meat with facts. "Have you done it before?" she asked.

"We've been sorely tempted, but have only performed operational tests, until now." He added, "If you're up for it Vera."

Vera protested, "You want me to throw my career away. You are asking me, to be the face that breaks across regular programming around the world, and deliver a message for you."

Griz answered her. He said, "This is more than a job. I'm in this."

That hurt. Her own words echoed. She needed that jolt. It put things back into perspective. "What would you have me do?" she asked meekly.

Griz kissed her on the forehead and said, "Thank you, Vera."

Vera blushed and to cover, she said. "It's nearly 6:00 PM on the east coast; prime time viewing."

"Precisely," Robulus said. "Once we air our announcements, I will set up our comments to play on a loop, once every hour. Okay, come on up here. Face the camera. The monitor is to the left. All three of us will be in the shots, but the speaker will take one step closer to the camera."

Robulus guided Vera to where he wanted her to stand. He told her, "You will speak first and introduce me. I will say my piece and intro Griz. Griz, say what you will, and then bring Vera in. Got it? Any questions?"

"Sounds good," Griz replied.

Robulus asked Vera, "Do you need time to prepare?"

She laughed, "Are you kidding? I do this for a living. I'm always ready." She was nervous, but pushing ahead.

Robulus said, "Broadcasting will begin on my voice command. 3…2…1… you're on."

"Hello and good evening. I am Vera Fynne. We are interrupting your regular programming and replacing your false news with a large dose of reality. We are in Minotaur Springs, Colorotta, and tonight the world enters a new era. Let me introduce you to the long, tall, immortal alien standing behind me, Robulus, who will usher in this new golden age for all Mankind."

The alien stepped forward, as Melanie stepped back. He said, "I, Robulus and my fellow alien, Jeemis, will unveil the TDS at midnight, mountain time." His powerful, deep voice blasted forth like a force of nature. "This," he continued, "will herald a future where all things are possible. In eight hours, Gaia will know the greatest boon to civilisation ever conceived."

"Behind me, on my right, stands Matt Gryzolski, father to President Crumm's science advisor, Melanie, who was kidnapped this morning; Griz."

Robulus stayed in place and Griz came up to stand next to him, on his right, and Vera came with him and held his right hand. Griz said, "I am here for my daughter and I will get her back, whatever it takes, even if I have to help these two aliens save civilisation in the process. I don't know what the TDS is, but if I didn't trust Robulus, I wouldn't be here. I suggest we all trust the aliens."

"Cut!" Robulus said, ending the broadcast transmission, and allowing the various television satellites to resume control. The entire broadcast lasted a total of twenty-four seconds, but the way that the media reacted was worthy of a supernova. Blame radiated outward like gamma rays, roasting all peons and underlings in its scorching path, but leaving the high paid talent unscathed. Major media outlets, on two hundred and eighty channels, in one hundred and eighteen countries unwillingly aired that live clip. Engineers and producers scrambled to learn its origin and struggled to stop the interference.

It added another dimension to the wild conspiracy theories abounding on the interweb and in the media. It was another subject about which to speculate and analyse, if they ran out of other nonsense. After the brief interruption, CON anchor Dee Rainge interviewed the distinguished Professor Felix Polyplastis, who was making the rounds on MBM tonight. After the introduction, Dee prompted him, "You actually interviewed these power-crazed aliens. Tell us your impression of these demented invaders."

Felix sat in his home library, wearing a fancy white bathrobe from the Hiltop Hotel, and he smoked a pipe of something with an odour reminiscent of burning tires. His jowls were something that mastiffs could only dream of, but he drooled more. He wiped his mouth with a sleeve. He replied to Dee Rainge, saying, "These two charlatans are mentally deranged, insane maniacs, freshly escaped from a maximum-security nuthouse. These two psychopaths are more dangerous than a Shynese virus laboratory, Dee."

Dee said, "Professor Polyplastics, you must know what this TDS mystery is all about. And what in Hades are you smoking?"

The professor corrected Dee. He said, "It's Polyplastis! But you are correct Dee. I do know the secret of the TDS, Typical Deplorable Scum. I think some of my students replaced my tobacco with cow scat again. Not much difference.' His facial acreage shook like pudding in a gaiaquake as he spoke.

Dee was deeply disappointed by his answers. She was hoping that the professor would indict President Crumm. She redirected him. "Perhaps you meant, Traitor Demolishes Shamerica. They do sound alike," Dee said. "Could you possibly have misunderstood?" she suggested. Her tailored eyebrows formed pointed daggers on her forehead, like a threat.

Polyplastis nodded his dumpling head, saliva dripping like gravy from his sagging lower lip. He said, "You may be right Dee. Listen: Typical Deplorable Scum and Traitor Demolishes Shamerica. The more I consider it, the more I think you hit the bullseye in the heart. They sound almost exactly the same!"

Dee decided that this was the perfect ending. She said, "Thank you Professor Polyplastics."

Polly Wag was the hostess of the MNBS primetime views-cast. This big-chested blonde, was highly admired by the Demolists and other liberals, who appreciated her talents and skills, at mangling words and sentences. Her gaffes were nearly as famous as those of one-time presidential candidate Jepsteen Baboo, who now spent his days in federal prison, making paper airplanes containing messages claiming he never killed himself. Baboo enjoyed sailing the paper planes over the prison walls.

Polly Wagg's guest expert of the night was psychologist Dr Salamanderful Bagavaardingbatoodicus. She introduced him as Dr Salamander and asked him, in her convoluted language, "What do you make of the menstrual malfeasance of alien faeces, who could pirate my telecastanet, and plagiarise nearly half a minute of my face time, Doctor? I mean, who does that?"

The doctor replied in a thick accent, "If I misunderstand you correctly, Pollywog, you are referring to a narcissistic sociopathic disorder often found in celebrities and TV news anchors."

Dee said, "Doctor my ass! Probably manages a 7-12 store."

In the United Queendom, the British Bloviating Quackers, or BBQ, featured a philosopher who was famous for having an actual job as a philosopher. Dr Shal Oh opined that TDS was a Terrible Drug Smuggling cartel, which operated between Gaia and Venus, and that the aliens were sex-change surgeons addicted to coffee.

Due to fear-mongering stories, and their own mental horror shows, people either isolated in their basements, or they ran amok, burning and looting in peaceful protests. Stores were vandalised and looted, and vicious battles for toilet paper and hand sanitiser broke out. It looked as violent as the fans at an Inglish soccer tournament.

In the US, tens of thousands of 9-1-1 calls were logged, as people foned in to say that their neighbours were aliens, or confess that they were an alien.

Emergency operators and police forces were overwhelmed. One of those 9-1-1 calls was posted on social media and went spiral, with more than ten million views, and it went as follows:

"Hello, this is 911, what is your emergency?"

"Hey Lady; see, it's the people next door. Their dog house is the mothership for alien fleas and…"

"I'm sorry sir, but our entire police force has been beamed up Uranus. Thank you, call again."

* * *

At 6: 18 PM Eastern Time, President Crumm's press conference, followed the segment of Robulus, Vera and Griz, and it was carried live on national television, from Onnitt Air Power base. In his usual blunt, positive manner, the president calmed fears, offered hope and even bragged that the United States was blessed to possess the TDS, but he didn't know what it meant. He also said, "Melanie; we're bringing you back, alive and well."

Then he took a few questions from some of the esteemed journalists of the Off-White House press corps, who'd accompanied him on this trip. The first question was posed by Jip Icostya of CON. He asked, "Why do you refuse to put a halt to this criminal escapade, Sir? It's as if you condone the kidnapping of your science advisor. Some say that this amounts to aiding and abetting a federal crime which is an impeachable offense and a felony. How do you answer to their charges?"

"Jip," the president said, "You would have been the kind of person, to stop the midnight ride of Paul Severe because of noise violations. Some say this, some say that, and some say you are a journalist, but we can't take such talk seriously Jip. We must deal with facts."

The president pointed to ABS newsman Teeter Jennies. Teeter asked, "Some say that you should shut the country down for at least fifteen days, and perhaps, up to four hundred and nine days, until you finally implement a national plan to save lives."

"Was there a question in there somewhere, Teeter?"

"Yes Mr President. Let me clarify. Is the FIBB Hostage Rescue Squad headed to the Air Power Academy in Colorotta Springs?"

President Crumm said, "I'm not shutting the country down for eight hours or eight seconds. Last question."

He chose Hoeda Kob. "Thank you, Mr President. Some say that calling aliens, aliens, is xenophobic. How do you respond to this fact?"

Chapter 22

Nine members of the notorious Dunfor motorcycle club, formerly known as the Sons of Satan's Cousin Fred, were drinking pitchers of beer at their favourite hangout, Damage Control. They all seemed to be clones of the other, from their long hair and beards to their tattoos and their grease-stained fingers. They even wore the same clothes; dirty denims, filthy vests and black boots; a uniform of sorts. They all boycotted dentists too, as one noticed when they smiled, their remaining teeth blended in with their grey beards.

"Are we jist gonna poking sit here and let aliens infringe on our poking territory? "Melvin Grubb, leader of the newly renamed Mel's Angels, asked rhetorically. The nonet surrounded a large roundtable, and often imagined themselves knights who rode iron horses. Melvin was no King Esther however.

Their sergeant-at-arms, Bruce Joyce, answered. He said, "Hades no! Did we let that Mejican motorcycle club steal our customers?"

"Ha!" Brad Crum laughed. He said, "The Pandexos? We burned their clubhouse, then raped their women and smashed up their hogs!"

Craig Slyst said, "It was hard tellin' them apart too!"

Mel asked, "So what are we gonna do about it, fellas?"

The brain of the group, Brad Crum said, "If we only knew what the TDS was, we could more easily defeat it, or them. Know your enemy!"

Bruce Joyce said, "I think it means Tattoo Design Studios. I'm thinking about getting a tatt on my poking forehead, of a snowman, right; with the poking words, 'White Powder' underneath it."

Mel shook his head in dismay and said, "That's dumber than a poking acorn, Brucie."

Bruce slammed his beer pitcher down on the table and stood up. He shouted, "Don't poking call me poking Brucie!"

"Sorry, Joyce," Mel said. They all laughed, except for Bruce Joyce.

Craig Slyst offered up his wisdom. He said, "I think that TDS is like a climate change thing meaning, Terrific Dust Storms."

Brad said, "You just made an acorn look like a poking genius."

"So, what's your idea, smartass?" Craig retorted.

"That's easy, sleazy." Brad said smugly. He hoisted his pitcher and drained the last of it. Then he held up his middle finger to beckon the cocktail waitress, who had a suspicious five o'clock shadow. When 'she' arrived at the scarred, abused table, Brad ordered, "Another round of pitchers; Poor's Light."

Brad folded his thick, hairy arms across his broad chest and said, "It's a simple matter of inductive logic, you see. It's like solving a Pubik's Cube while handcuffed and blindfolded, underwater."

Mel growled, "I'm gonna kick your poking ass!"

"Chill bro!" Brad said calmly. "Here it is; Terror. Drugs. Sex. It's either a vice squad sting or it's our competition."

Nine knuckleheads set down their beer pitchers, their faces set in grim contortions of hate and disgust. Those three words were their business philosophy! This meant war!

Mel said, "Let's ride!"

Nine pitchers were raised in solidarity with this righteous suggestion. "Right after we have one more round of pitchers!" They roared, "Yeah!"

Mel's Angels wasn't the only group going to Minotaur Springs. Parties came from every direction and by every conveyance, their goal; the TDS. Something big was going down, and folks wanted to be a part of something big. For instance, a charter bus, carrying a marching band made up of college students, was driving north on I-250, from the Tejas College of Useful Degrees, in Dullass, to a Battle of the Bands in Shyanne, Whyome. The bandleader, a Miss Balmy and the bus driver Mr Doomie, decided it would be great to let the kids practice their routine at the TDS event, while the two of them kept the bus secure.

A sun-baked, Winabagel RV with Misery plates, rolled east on I-700 through the Stony Mountains, driving back to St Loozus, from a convention in Loss Analysts. The driver was the disbarred lawyer, Mikul Imanasti. He made an announcement to the five prostitutes riding in the back. "Hey girls! We're stopping in Minotaur Springs tonight to party!" He figured they could earn a couple hundred bucks each for him. The whores all cheered and drank a slug of Johnny Stagger Back whiskey. Sounded fun.

Driving behind them, and returning from a Retreat in Steambath Springs, were five nuns from the Little Sisters of the Pork, so called because of the pig farms on their convent grounds. They supported their mission by selling bacon, under the label, 'Heavenly Hog'. Sister Shaymon Yew said, "I believe that aliens have souls too, after all, they are creatures of God." She drove a Fard Accident, which sat them all comfortably, and wished she could pass the junk bucket RV in front of them.

Sister Egsan Hamm agreed, and said, "Aliens must need saving. What if they're liberals?"

"They can be saved too. Let us pray."

"Amen."

And so it went, minute by minute; people changed plans, or changed directions to make the pilgrimage to the TDS. It mattered not, that no one knew exactly why they were going. Some thought it something like the premiere of a new movie or the opening of a Broodway play. Others imagined it to be the Superball of tailgate parties, with alien entertainment, like from Hollowood. Another type hoped to see flying saucers and little green men.

Chapter 23

It was quarter to eight, when Melanie finally left I-800 behind, and steered the big Tanki onto southbound I-250. Dunfor traffic was stacked, packed and backed up like never before, even surpassing the traffic for Bunco football home games. Melanie occupied her time by trying to imagine world events that moved more slowly than the traffic. Evolution came to mind, as did plate tectonics, climate change and the justice department.

Shanghai Low smoked one cigarette after another, and he was as jumpy as a kangaroo doing ecstasy on a trampoline. He ranted and raved like a lunatic, intruding on Melanie's musings. "We're supposed to be the lead vehicle!" He pounded on the food-encrusted dashboard. "We'll never poking get there!"

Donut tried to cheer him up. He'd seen Low in full mania and it wasn't a happy sight; like watching a Superball halftime show. It was at such crucial times, that Donut took over as Low's, 'designated thinker'. He said, in his bird chirp-like voice. "Relax Loser! You're still the headliner here. Nobody can find the TDS except for Jeemis."

"Quit poking calling me poking Loser, you poking donut poker!"

Melanie said, "Look behind us, on the right shoulder."

The two crooks twisted their heads half-off, and they saw two Colorotta State Highway patrol cars, coming up quickly from behind, driving on the right shoulder with overhead lights flashing, but no sirens. Fear turned their faces the colour of snow, tinted by dog. Low's brain cells formed into a foetal position, and he cried out in fearful confusion, "What the poke?"

Jeemis screeched, "It's another escort, Low. A star is born."

Donut said, "Two stars!"

Melanie felt overjoyed. An escort would mean a quicker conclusion to this endless drive! She said, "We can be the lead car again," as if she spoke to an insane child.

Low puffed out his chest and held his head high. His brain cells recovered their composure and took naps, at peace with the silence. Donut fantasised about all the crime groupies he would attract; women who appreciated a good smack, gals who loved the limelight and a hard kick.

One of the two state trooper escort cars, pulled ahead of the white Tanki, and slowed down to match its speed. The second officer held back, leaving Melanie a slot in-between the two. Melanie pulled over onto the shoulder and the white Tanki became the filling, in a cop car sandwich. They accelerated, passing by the sluggish traffic on the left. Crime Blaster XL-5 pulled his car behind the second trooper's car, and Rosie Oh steered her big rig onto the shoulder behind him. It became a new lane and soon filled with vehicles.

Shanghai Low wished he had friends who could see him now! They'd be so jealous. He laughed to think how Buster Monk had missed out on all this, because of a poking toothache. He said, "You know we are going down in poking history, right Donut? And we didn't have to kill no one to poking do it!"

Melanie was tired of Low and his filthy mouth. She said, "You're going down alright Low, down for a long prison sentence."

Donut feared jail was in their future too, and not Hollowood stardom or a reality television show, unless it was on Courtroom TV. He declared, "We will make history, as receiving the longest prison sentence ever, Low."

Low wasn't going to let these negative people bring him low. He fantasised about his legacy, his place in history. He almost envied the schoolchildren of the future, sitting at their tiny Shynese plastic desks, and learning about the famous alien abductor, Shanghai Low.

Everyone knows that all heroes worth their saltpetre, whether good or evil, had a sidekick. It was a tradition lost in the mists of crime. The Alone Ranger had Blotto, and Bratman had Goblin, and Carly Brown had Stoopy. He thought that Shanghai Low and Donut Hole was a winning combination.

Melanie felt like a wreck. Her curly hair hung limply on her neck, and her eyeballs burned as if floating in acid. Her tired shoulders ached. She was not a quitter however. There were no I-give-up genes in her DNA. She was a fighter, like her late mother, and a landslide, like her father. She was going to be in this tale's epilogue.

The speedy advantage provided by driving on the shoulder with a police escort, didn't last long. The police escort soon caught up with a traffic jam on the shoulder. Apparently, some time back, an impatient driver had veered onto the shoulder, and like beads on a string, hundreds followed his lead.

Other drivers had chosen the sunken median between opposite directions of travel, as an extra traffic lane. It was now littered with their cars and trucks which were mired in the loose sand, amongst the hubcaps, panties, beer cans and a shoe. The lead state trooper escort vehicle left the highway to attend to a serious traffic accident down in the median. The cop car following behind them left a minute later to attend to another crash elsewhere. Their police escort had lasted nearly four minutes.

Donut was falling apart. He trembled. The stress was eating away at the fibres of sanity and reason, like insects chewing on his brain. He could hear them. He shrivelled up inside his psyche, and regretted being a BEWB, except for his time with the sperm whale. Donut saw no honour, no dignity and no future, as the second most famous prisoner in a maximum-security prison.

There was a way to put an end to this charade however, and to become the number one hero of this story. Donut Hole saves the day, sounded better than Donut Hole in jail today. He had a stayser, fully charged. If he staysed Shanghai and incapacitated him, Donut felt certain that Jeemis and Melanie would be only too happy to push Low out the door of the truck. For now, he would bide his time and look for a good time to strike.

* * *

Traffic jams proved to be no problem for the nine members of the Mel's Angels motorcycle club. They slalomed through and around traffic, and were rarely forced to slow down. At some point, they adopted the right shoulder of I-250 as their assigned lane, and were soon speeding along at sixty mph. Mel and the gang caught up to a line of cars blocking their paths there, and once again, they were forced to drive along the dotted white lines dividing the lanes of traffic.

Mel and Bruce spotted the white Pissan Tanki at the same moment. Ha! It was as if the heavens had opened up and rained beer! This story was going to end right here, and Mel's Angels were writing the last chapter! It was a huge bonus that four helicopters flew overhead and followed the action, representing the big four of Dunfor television stations. The bikers would gain maximum coverage! It was awesome, and would prove a great recruiting tool.

Chapter 24

Robulus drove a quiet golf cart up the tunnel inside of Poke's Peak. Vera sat next to him and Griz squeezed up against her on the front bench seat. The cart's bright headlights illuminated the path ahead. Water seeped through the rock, and ran down the smooth tunnel walls. The ceiling rose more than seven feet above the road. Griz noticed drainage holes on the wet tunnel floor, which was humped in the centre, and air flowed uphill too, going their way.

Robulus said, "It's about four and a half miles of curves and upward climb to the TDS location. "His voice echoed through the tunnel. "I will tell you how the TDS entity came to be, and how it operates, how it accesses cosmic knowledge."

Vera asked, "May I record this?"

"Absolutely," Robulus thundered.

The alien said, "Thoughts and ideas are forms of energy. This energy persists for eternity in a non-dimensional point outside of space-time, which I refer to as the Omnivoid. Every fantasy, every dream, every iota of intelligent mental activity that has ever occurred, by a reasoning sapient being throughout time, in all the multiverse, exists in the non-there of the Omnivoid. The TDS can access this well of cosmic knowledge."

Griz said, "But there is no where there."

Vera added, "And no when."

Griz protested, "There must be countless thoughts, without number! How can this TDS thing, find one needle, in a galaxy-sized haystack?"

Robulus said, "It is a difficult concept to process, but thoughts are not things like needles, nor is the Omnivoid an enormous haystack, because no space is taken up by it. Access to those thoughts, for the TDS is instantaneous, of course."

Griz said, "In that case, it will be as if it can read your mind."

Vera remarked, "Oh! That's right!"

Robulus acknowledged the point, he said, "It's the closest thing to telepathy, to exist anywhere."

Their cart rounded a hairpin turn in the dim tunnel, and then Robulus slammed on the brakes and swore, "Scat!" All three of them sat in helpless fear as the cart broke through a tripwire strung across their path. The tunnel ceiling blasted down upon the cart, tons of granite torn from above by powerful explosives.

Chapter 25

Pitch Al and Torchy sat in the private lounge of the private airport in Colorotta Springs, drinking eleven-dollar bottles of luke-cold beer. The twelve empty bottles on their table, attested to the ninety minutes they'd sat there, waiting for Don Crews to arrive. Al had found out from Torchy that Crews was flying in.

After they'd landed here, Torchy told Al that Kate Armstrong had texted him about Don's imminent arrival. The information angered Al. He'd told Crews that he was in charge of this operation! So, they waited for Don to show up.

Al adjudged it a bad idea to let Crews run loose. There was no telling what Don might let slip out, about the kidnapping and Al's involvement in the crime. Don needed a guide dog of sorts, so that he didn't trip over his ambitions. Al had filled that position for decades, keeping Don from falling off the path to stardom.

However, after five beers and over an hour of sitting on hard, plastic chairs, angry Al, transformed into the guide dog from Hades, when he learned there were no rental cars available. The beer foam on his upper lip simulated rabies, and he was angry enough to bite. Don Crews could be torn to bits when he walked in.

"I can't believe it!" Al snarled. "No rental cars, no cabs, no hotel shuttles, no limos or oober! It's just not possible!" he complained for the seventeenth time. Torchy kept score on a napkin.

The big lug shook his head in dismay. According to everybody that Torchy called, once he could actually reach someone instead of hearing a busy signal, traffic was backed up, and an unprecedented number of airport passengers had changed their plans, to stay in town, and go see the TDS in Minotaur Springs. The twelve miles separating them from the TDS was too demn far to walk. So here they sat and drank beer.

Al faced the entry door from the airstrip, so he saw Don Crews and his attendant Kate Armstrong, when they entered the common area. Kate struggled beneath the weight of a luggage bag larger than she was on her bent back, and she pulled another bag behind her which was no larger than a refrigerator. This excess of excessiveness was another hot button for Al, and Torchy watched in awe as Al turned into Pitch Darkly. It reminded him of those campy wolf man movies, where humans became animals. Torchy always found it strange, that wherever those stricken wolf men lived, every night was a full moon there. The townsfolk never stood a chance.

Don didn't get a chance either. Al jumped up hollering, "You have enough poking luggage there, for a poking safari! Are you poking moving in, or what?"

Don wasn't expecting to see Al. He was actually hoping to avoid him, but he had a story prepared, just in case. He said, "Well, what a coincidence seeing you here Al. You are close in your surmise. I decided to come to colourful Colorotta for a vacation. You know, get away from things and relax for a few weeks. What are you doing here?"

Don hated being seen in public with Al. Don wore tailored suits and shiny shoes, while Al looked like a vegetable salad; greens and reds and oranges with bleu cheese dressing. Plus, the caveman tagged along with him, and Don didn't trust Torchy.

Kate set down her burden and she greeted Torchy and Al. Lounge customers were leaving the area, not appreciative of Al's loud, foul mouth. One young boy, maybe nine or ten years old, who was with his parents, paused by Al's table. He looked at the short, shabby man and he said, "Do you know who that is you're talking to like that? That's Don Crews! He's a famous poking comedian!"

Al said, "Real funny, kid"

Don's selfone trilled. He sat down in a chair at the beer bottle littered table, and removed the fone from his coat pocket. He handed it to Kate. She answered, "Hello, you have reached the headquarters of Don Crews Enterprises, Kate speaking; how can I help you?"

"I'm Lem Kerry! The high priest of the Dunfor SST! Don should have me in his poking contacts!" He did, but Kate had a job to do. "That's nice," She said. "And how may I direct your call, sir?"

Lem grumbled, "Where in Hades is that nincompoop?"

"It's for you," Kate said, handing the fone to Don.

Don took the fone and asked, "What?"

"What what, Don?" Lem replied. "I'm waiting in the Colorotta Springs airport with three other temple apostles. Indero told us to come meet you here. We flew in, because of the impassable traffic southbound on I-250."

Don's face scrunched up in puzzlement. He asked, "Who is this again?"

"Lem Kerry! The famous comedian!"

Don said, "Oh yeah! You were in 'Blazing Poodles'! What can I do for you? I'm all the way out in Colorotta Springs, at an airport."

Lem said, "We are too! We're looking for you!"

Don didn't like this one bit; it was too much interference. He couldn't escape it though, and needed to deal with it. First Al, and now the Dunfor temple crew; what else could happen to screw up his plans? He said, "Okay, alright. I will come to you. Where you at?"

Lem said, "We're in B concourse, drinking ten-dollar beers at the Poor's Light Pub. It's got a Burger Jack on one side and a Grubway across the hall."

"Okay, I'll be there in a jiffy." Don replied. He ended the call. He stood up and meekly said, in a barely audible voice, "I gotta go now."

Pitch Al sharpened a riposte, but before he could slice Don into Crews cutlets, Robby Indero entered the lounge area from the tarmac outside. He was without his personal attendant, because his mom said that her back ached, and she'd stayed home.

When Al and Don and Robby all caught sight of the other, a veritable swearstorm inundated the lounge. Loud profanity poured forth from three directions in a deluge of filthy fury. The cocktail waitress quit and fled in tears. Even the mice and cockroaches left and took their offspring on field trips to the Bagel House across the aisle.

After they ran out of expletives, a recognisable sentence was spoken. Robby Indero asked, "Don, have you poking heard from those poking Dunfor temple pokers?" If Robby's eyes had been lasers, Dom would have been lobotomised.

Kate, in her ever-helpful way asked, "Is that who called, Don? Somebody named Kerry, I think."

They were in public, so Don couldn't kill Kate. He hadn't rehearsed a scene such as this before, and so he didn't know what to say, but help arrived; in a sense. Before he could lamely reply to Robby, two celebrities entered the lounge from outside. Lonny Doop and Tod Einer traipsed in.

The ensuing outrage and surprise was mutual. Each knew that the other was here for the immortality. They were here for the same reason, but they each thought poorly of the other for it. Almost in unison, four voices accused with a question, "What the poke are you doing here?"

Don's selfone rang some more. Robby continued to berate the two new entries, using what he termed, 'creative cursing', or 'poetic profanity'.

Torchy took advantage of the diversions to make a suggestion to Al. He said, "You can't overwhelm stupidity with sense, Boss. You gotta go with the slow."

Pitch Al's fake smile almost looked real for a second. He said. "Torchy that almost made sense. Sometimes stupidity takes a holiday. I saw that in you when no one else did, and I hired you away from those personal injury attorneys you broke legs for."

"I always appreciated it Boss. I hated the begging and crying clients."

Don was yelling at his fone. "I said, wait! We're coming! Keep your poking bra on Lem! Who's the bigger star here? Who waits for whom?" He dropped the shouting, but added, "Me!"

Lem Kerry said, "Poke you, Don! You are quite funny, when you're serious!"

Don went for the knockout blow; he said, "Indero is in the house." Crews didn't need to count to ten, the bout was decided. Call ended. Don pocketed the fone. He looked like a sheep, embarrassed; right after it's been sheared of its wool.

Indero had paused halfway through a very artistic profanity tirade, to listen to Don yelling into his fone. Robby said, "That was the poking Dunfor SST! Let's meet up with them. We'll go in force to send the TDS back to its home galaxy. Let's rent us some limos and smash the TDS!"

Okra Wipmee waddled in and Arti P bounced into the airport lounge, followed by Pike Flea and Labrat Jakes. After several minutes of spewing profanity-laced invective, in way of greeting, Indero absolved the celebrities of their selfish desires. He said, "We all poking came here to save our temple, and that's exactly what we are going to poking do! We will not let some upstart alien celebrities into our pantheon! Never!"

Al's beer-addled brain, slowly absorbed what Torchy meant when he said, don't fight stupidity, and to, '...go with the slow'. Few were slower than those in this group. He needed to keep Don attached at his hip, and the only way to do that was to go along with this temple nonsense. After they reached the site of the TDS, he would find a way to ditch Indero and his cult buddies. In the meantime, he'd take charge.

Al got out of his chair and stood wobbling for a moment before the world rebalanced. No one much noticed that he had stood up, as there was little change in height. Torchy rose also though, and then everyone quit swearing at each other to see what was going on. Al said. "Look, I don't know if all the members of your cul..., I mean church, are here or not, but apparently some of the Dunfor temple crew is in the main airport. Let's go join them and work together."

Indero hissed like a leaky tire. He said. "You are not poking involved Al! You don't even poking belong, to our crack-smoking, ass-poking, throat-choking cul...I mean church!"

Torchy cracked his knuckles. It sounded like a tree falling over. Al waved him off. He and Torchy knew how to work useful idiots. Al said, "You are poking right Robby, as poking usual. That's why you are the poking face and voice of the SST around the poking globe." One thing that Al knew about narcissists is that, like children, they should be fed sugar in small doses. If one erred, and served up too much sweetness, one created monsters. Al swore heavily too, so as to bond with Robby.

Indero looked around to make certain that everyone was paying attention to Al's wise words. Al put the finishing touches on his masterpiece of bullscat. He said, "I regret never joining your churc...I mean cult, and I support your mission here today. I also represent my client, Don Crews, and am here to protect his interests." Torchy remained as stone-faced as a judge. He no longer broke out in laughter during Al's sales pitches.

Lonny Doop offered his opinion. He said, "It wouldn't hurt to have a crooked lawyer along, Robby."

Don's selfone jangled. Crews muttered, "I bet it's that demn Lem Kerry again!" He pulled it out of his pocket, and Indero snatched the fone from Dom's soft hand. He said, "Let me set this poking unfunny man straight!" Robby, as alpha male, needed to constantly reassert his authority. He answered the call, "Listen here, you stupid, poking, impatient, scat-brained jester; sit the poke down and shut the poke up and poking wait! We are on our poking way!"

Robby listened for meek assent, but he heard the end of a telemarketer's scripted spiel. These types heard nothing, and only continued to mechanically read, as if paid by the spoken word. The disembodied voice said,"...and nearly eighteen cents of every dollar contributed will go directly to the Tranny Scouts of America, to provide tampons, birth control, and feminine hygiene products..."

"Tranny Scouts? Wrong number?" Indero asked.

"Yeah; never heard of them." Don kicked himself for forgetting to send the scouts money this month.

The eight members of the city of Loss Analysts Sacred Stars Temple took a secret vote about whether Al should join them or not, using pub napkins as ballots. One pen was passed around. The votes were tallied, and there were four yays, two nays and two abstentions. Al would accompany them. Torchy wasn't voted on, but no one told him he couldn't come.

The eleven people packed into a shuttle train, and were transported from the private airfield to the main airport. Once there, Robby Indero led the group in through the main entrance, and he marched straight up to the information desk. Pitch Al and Torchy hung back. Kate trailed behind too, lugging a huge trunk on her back, and dragging a second bag with pneumatic tires behind her.

A young woman with a mocha-coloured complexion, and wearing a white turban atop her head, sat at the help desk. When Indero arrived at the service counter, the woman asked, "Can I help you then sir?" in a far-eastern accent.

"Don't you poking recognise me you dumb poking, tea-drinking, cow worshipping, pagan ass, poking Hindoo?"

The lady smiled sweetly. She didn't recognise the withered; slobbering fool's wrinkled face, but his profanity struck a chord. "You're Robby Indero! Take the escalators behind me. Go up one floor, turn left and two blocks down on your right, you'll find your people at the Poor's Light Pub. Thank you."

Indero glared at her and snarled, "I think you're lying to get rid of us? How could you possibly poking know where in poking…?"

Her desk fone rang. She picked it up and handed it to Robby, "It's him again; for you."

The Poor's Light Pub was filled to capacity with stranded passengers, who had no ride to leave the airport grounds. Lem Kerry had arrived with two of the Dunfor apostles, including Harley Skeen, an actor with a passion for whores, and the morbidly obese, mockumentary film maker Syko More.

When Robby and eleven more people arrived in the pub, the walls bulged, but after Lem Kerry gave Indero the news that no rental cars existed, and that they were all stuck at the airport, Indero managed to empty the place out in less than two minutes with his profanities, including the employees.

Al smiled. This is where he took over. If anyone could find or finagle a ride, it was Pitch Darkly. "Follow me," he said.

Chapter 26

"It looks like we've got company!" Jeemis trumpeted. Donut turned to look, and nearly wet himself. Melanie looked into her mirrors and swore, "Scat! They're coming for us!" Mel's Angels were riding up on the slow crawling Tanki. Donut cried out, "We're safe!" He added, "All the doors are locked!"

Shanghai Low swore loudly and exclaimed, "They'll never take me alive!"

Suddenly, they were boxed in by nine bikers. Three stopped in front of them, two on each side, and two behind. Melanie was forced to stop the big truck. Low shouted, "Stayser, Donut!" Low pulled his Schlock 9 mm pistol out of his burnt butt crack. He ejected the magazine, and counted two rounds remaining, plus one in the chamber. He snapped the magazine back into place.

The biker's plan, decided on by a majority of drunks during the second to last pitcher of beer, was simply this: the two bikers on either side of the Tanki, would pull the three humans and one alien out of it; one man, one door. The Angels each carried a couple of zipbands, which they would use to cuff and shackle the BEWBs. The girl and the alien were coming back to the clubhouse with them, willingly or not. They had voted against keeping the big Pissan BUV. They thought it was cool, but it wasn't a hog. The two BEWB's would be left behind too.

Mel and Bruce were on the victim's side of the BUV with Melanie and the alien, while Craig and Brad were on the BEWB's side of the truck. The four bikers dismounted and tried to open the Pissan's locked doors. Then they pulled revolvers from their belts, and hammered the butts against the window glass until they broke it in. Four thick hairy arms entered through four broken windows reaching for four door handles.

Melanie leaned down and bit Bruce's tattooed limb, which had poked through her window. Jeemis grabbed the hand that invaded his space and in one swift move, he broke Mel's wrist. Low shot a hole in the arm snaking through his window.

Donut felt as if he were being ripped in half. The angel on his left shoulder, wanted him to stayse Shanghai Low, while on his right shoulder, there perched a devil, who said, "Listen up Scatbreath, that's a real stupid move. These bikers will be on you in one second, and having you grab your ankles in two. You're a BEWB! Act like one!"

Donut was going for the glory. He shoved open his door hard, causing Brad Crum to shoot himself in the foot. Donut hopped out of the Tanki and Brad just hopped, screaming in pain. With desperation masquerading as courage, Donut marched forward, towards the three bikes which were blocking the Tanki's forward progress. He wore his Max Stayser gloves.

The three bikers faced him, because they'd turned their bikes around to watch the festivities. The three men were laughing uproariously at their wounded brothers, hopping about in pain and screaming in agony. They watched with astonishment and wonder as this little runt, with a sickly smile painted on his face, strode towards them.

Four breathless newscasters reported live, from four hovering helicopters, and they panted through this news story of violence and injury. They couldn't hear what happened below, but they provided play by play, like sports broadcasters.

The trio of bikers taunted and teased Donut as he neared. Once within six feet, he staysed the middle man, who fell over. His heavy motorcycle fell atop him, and the hot exhaust pipe seared his leg. Donut looked to his right.

Low poked his pistol out the hole in his window, and shot his last two bullets in the general direction of the two upright bikers blocking their forward progress. One bullet hit Donut's spine and he dropped instantly. One bullet blew a hole in the front tire of the right-hand bike and then flew harmlessly until it eventually struck a shoe on the side of the road.

Low slid hard to his left on the front seat of the truck, and he slammed Melanie up against her door. He slapped the truck into drive and stomped the accelerator.

Melanie screamed in horror, and grabbed at the wheel, and beat, slugged and pushed against Low to no avail. He would not be stopped. The big Pissan Tanki rolled over Donut and two motorcyclists, and the bikes they rode in on.

Jeemis grabbed Low by the nape of the neck with one hand, and pulled him off the front seat, nearly yanking him over the top of it. Melanie slammed on the brake pedal, stopping the Tanki, only yards from the slow-moving car ahead of them.

Donut had died instantly. His spine shattered, so he didn't feel the truck tires roll over him. Two Angels died in the collision too. Another pair suffered bullet wounds, and Mel had a broken wrist. Seven motorcycles were still operable, but only four of Mel's boys could operate them, so three of the wounded bodies, piled on behind their less injured pals, and all seven of the living Angels escaped the bad scene, leaving behind their two dead comrades and three bikes.

They could never escape the abysmal humiliation of their failure though, which was captured on camera for the entire world to see. The Mel's Angels Motorcycle Club was a national object of scorn and derision, and six months later, depressed and disillusioned, they disbanded the club and, as one, turned themselves into authorities and confessed to all their crimes.

Shanghai Low slobbered and slathered like a Hollowood monster, as if possessed. He was in the front passenger seat next to Melanie, and he slashed at invisible enemies with a cigarette butt. Melanie was screaming and pounding the steering wheel, and tears flowed down her cheeks. "You killed him. You killed people! Murderer! Kidnapper! Lunatic!"

Melanie undid her seatbelt, and pulled her door handle; she was outta here. Low swiftly regained his senses. The switchblade was suddenly in his right hand and he poked it into her, under her ear, drawing blood. His left hand grabbed her earring and he pulled her back in by it. Jeemis wanted to backhand Low, but he knew that Melanie would pay the price for his intervention.

Yes, the alien could put a stop to this debacle, anytime that he wished. He thought about putting an end to Low, but he decided to let human nature take its course. The Unveiling took precedence over his rash behaviour after all. There still might be some advantage to letting this play out. Jeemis needed to make Low back off, that's all. He shrieked, "At least now, in the movie version, you won't have to share top billing with anyone else."

Melanie was horrified by the alien's remark, but was relieved at the result, when Shanghai let go of her. He fell back against his seat, and lapsed into a dreamlike mental state, a delta wave neutral gear. Low coasted on the lovely thoughts. No costar! Wow. Low felt as light as a feather, things couldn't get much better. He said." At least he's dressed for his funeral."

Jeemis said, "We can't help them now Melanie. You are doing great. Get us there."

She compressed her lips in grim determination and nodded her head. Traffic rolled slowly.

Chapter 27

Smoke and dust filled the dark tunnel. Flames from several small fires burned here and there, giving glimpses, like a flickering fluorescent bulb, of the rubble littering the tunnel floor. Griz coughed and choked. He shook his head as if to dislodge the loud, echoing "Boom!" inside of it. He was lying face down, on the rock floor of the tunnel. He got up to his knees and coughed hard. Debris rolled off his back. Stabbing pains pierced his left chest cavity. He'd broken two ribs in the explosion. He panted in short sharp breaths, and he smelled the burning tire rubber permeating the tunnel with its black stench. Dust filled the air.

Griz didn't move for a moment, still, on his hands and knees. He listened. Bits and pieces of stone and gravel fell from the tunnel ceiling, and rattled onto the rock floor below. Flames crackled faintly. He heard a sound, a cry, a woman's voice. Vera!

Using the tunnel wall for support, Griz stood up. He could see the floor area dimly, thanks to a few sputtering flames. But floating dust and black-smoking tires obscured much of that. The wreckage of the cart sat amongst rocks and stones. He saw a bare foot and then found the body attached to it.

Vera was flat on her back. He put a hand on her shoulder. She opened her eyes wide, and jerked away, then moaned and coughed.

Griz said loudly. "It's me; Griz." He knelt down beside her to pick stones, and to brush dirt from her body. He helped her sit up, bracing her back, up against the tunnel wall. Vera choked on the foul air. Griz stood again, holding an arm tight against his ribs. "My hand!" Vera mewed. She held it against her side, and remained seated.

"Is it broken?"

Vera shook her head and said, "No, it feels crushed, but my wrist is okay, I think."

The last fluttering flames died out and darkness engulfed them. It was as black as the inside of a coffin in the tunnel. Vera hoped it didn't become hers. A narrow ray of light penetrated the darkness, inches above the floor. Griz saw Robulus' leg and foot illuminated as the light beam passed by it.

"We'll be right there, Robulus!" Griz yelled loudly. "He must be pinned or something," he said to Vera. "Can you get up?"

"Yes, I think so. It's my hand that hurts."

Griz said, "Well then, stand on your legs instead." He was glad to be alive, and a grim joke didn't seem out of place. Vera didn't laugh.

Griz squatted down next to her, and put an arm around her back at waist height, and he helped her stand. He held her for a moment until she got her bearings. The beam of light along the tunnel floor helped them to see where they stepped, as they made their way to its source.

Griz bent down and removed a small flashlight from Robulus' hand, which was stretched out next to his leg. Griz aimed the light at the alien. Vera gasped in horror. Robulus lay face down, a large granite slab sat atop his back, covering him from his shoulder blades to the back of his knees.

Griz went to Robulus' head and got down on his knees, bending low to look into the alien's face. Robulus left eye looked up at Griz and he struggled to whisper, "Can you move it?" Griz could see the agony on Robulus' face, but the alien died for a split second. He was revitalised, to die a few seconds later again. Over and over.

Griz answered, "Of course, we can move it," he assured the alien. "Hang in there." That sounded rather dumb, he thought after saying it. The guy is immortal, and had no choice but to hang in there. Griz stood and used the flashlight to inspect the boulder.

The rock chunk from the tunnel ceiling looked like an upside-down cupcake, but was the size of a washing machine, and weighed more than a quarter ton. Vera took the flashlight from Griz. Griz put his hands against the boulder and gave it a hard, exploratory shove. It didn't budge; but it thought about it.

Griz stepped back and considered the situation. Vera could help push with one good hand, but Griz didn't think that was going to work. He would look for something he could use as a lever, in whatever remained of the cart they'd rode in on.

Griz took the flashlight back and asked Vera if she would sit with the alien, while he searched for tools. "Yes, of course," she replied. Griz gave her a smooch on the forehead and went on his hunt. Vera sat down next to the alien's head, and touched the wet, warm spot on her own head. She put her good hand on Robulus' face, and told him that he'd be free soon. She hoped she was right.

Griz surveyed the wreckage of the cart and the locations of the major pieces. From what he saw, the explosion blew the ceiling down in front of the cart. Robulus' timely braking had saved them from being crushed. The cart was tossed backwards and broken to pieces. They were banged up, but had fared better than the cart. Fire and heat had burned and melted the plastics and the tires for the most part. The front, drive axle was bent and twisted, but a few yards away, Griz found the rear cart axle. A wheel clung to one end, but the other end was lacking its wheel. Amazingly, the steel rod was unbent.

The axle was only about a yard long and it was clumsy, but it was the only lever available. He hauled that back to where the alien lay, pinned by a boulder. Griz returned to the hunt, this time looking for a couple of blocky stones. There were many to choose from and he picked up a ten-pound chunk to use as a fulcrum and a smaller stone to use as a chock block.

His broken ribs were stabbing pains in his side, but he wouldn't notice it much until after Robulus was freed. Griz was focused. "Vera, hold the flashlight for me," he said. She stood and took it from him and aimed it at the base of the problem rock. Robulus lay at a sixty-degree angle to the tunnel wall, and his feet were downhill of his head.

Griz set his fulcrum on the tunnel floor, on the alien's uphill side so as to roll the rock downhill. There wasn't much of a slope to the tunnel, but gravity was a force he didn't want to fight. "Vera; I need you to do something else," he said.

Griz saw her nodding her head. She said, "Yes, anything! We have to hurry."

He pointed to the brick-sized chock block and said, "You'll have to be brave Vera. When I leverage this boulder over, inch by inch; I need you to push that block beneath it to hold it in place. Then, when I move the fulcrum, I can get a new bite with the lever and repeat. Can you, do it?"

Griz was fortunate not to see the expression of abject horror and disgust on Vera's face, as she understood his sadistic suggestion. It would have scared him. The flashlight beam made the picture clearer in her mind's eye too it seemed. She raised her voice and said, "Are you heartless? Do you know what you're asking me to do?"

Griz picked up the unwieldy axle and said, "I'm ready." Robulus groaned, right on cue. Vera groaned too. She wasn't squeamish, but this was too much. Griz and Robulus were counting on her. She had to do this. Vera got down on the tunnel floor. She held the flashlight in her damaged hand, and picked up the chock block rock in the other. She aimed the flashlight at the base of the boulder. A lip of the big rock, of five- or six-inches width, hung out past Robulus' crushed side.

Griz knew that every second of this attempted rescue, would cause the alien more suffering and pain than did the boulder. He couldn't think about anyone's pain. He had a job to do. Griz jabbed the end of the axle under the boulder. The fulcrum was set as close as he could get it to the boulder. He had the wheel on his end of the axle.

"Ready! Set! Heave!" Griz yelled, as much for his own efforts, as to prepare Vera for them. The boulder budged; barely. Vera couldn't do anything with that. Griz inhaled, and exhaled in short pants. Vera asked, "Are you okay?"

Griz said, "Never better. Just testing." It was heavier than he'd bargained for, and it sat on a flattish base too. He thought about Melanie for added motivation. Robulus suffered untold agonies too. Griz's anger flooded his tissues with hormones, and he could actually feel the rush. Griz shoved the axle as far under the boulder as he could jam it. The cart wheel, which was attached, wasn't much above waist height for Griz on its short axle.

Griz used every bit of leverage, the tunnel's slope, all of his weight and his tremendous strength in his next attempt, and the rock moved! In fact, he'd gained about seven inches. Vera pushed the block in as far as she could, and it held the boulder in place. The block sat atop the alien's back close to his spine. She saw the alien's body compress, and she felt ill.

Griz moved the big fulcrum stone onto the alien. He picked up the axle, and thrust it into place, digging it into the alien's back, to get a good bite under the boulder. Demn, his ribs were going to hurt when he was done! Demn!

Once again, Griz shoved down hard, practically lunging atop his lever. The result was spectacular! The boulder fell off Robulus' back, teetered for a moment, and then toppled over. It rolled slowly, hit the side of the tunnel and came to a halt five feet away. Griz's momentum took him down to his knees. He stayed there. Vera shouted with surprise and joy, "You did it! Oh, my Gawd! You did it!" She scooted to his side and kissed his cheek twice quickly.

When she turned around to see about Robulus, he was standing up behind her brushing the dust from his black coveralls. His booming voice rang out, "Griz! Are you alright?"

"My ribs!" he groaned." I think I fractured one or three"

"Oh no!" Vera cried. "Sit down. We have to wrap your chest."

Robulus boomed, "I'll hold the flashlight; you bandage him. Thank you for the rescue. In all honesty, that sucked."

"I don't think I can manage it: my hand," Vera said. She held it up. It looked as swollen as a wet sponge.

Robulus said, "Yes, I better do it."

Griz, moving gingerly, removed his jacket and shirt. They were ripped and torn in places, and his chest was lacerated and streaked with blood. Robulus wrapped the shirt around Griz's torso, and used the long sleeves to tie it snugly. He draped the jacket over Griz's back.

Robulus said in his earth-shaking voice, "Okay, we have work to do." Vera and Griz looked at the immortal with murder in their hearts. He could see it. He explained, and said, "We have two miles of an uphill trek ahead of us, and this flashlight is starting to dim already. I think we can construct a lantern from cart parts."

Vera wasn't ready. She was still shaking from the experience of nearly being killed, for some crazy reason. Robulus didn't have to worry about that! Griz was furious. If not for needing to rely on Robulus to get the Hades out of this mess alive, he would have unleashed a torrent of verbal abuse upon the alien.

Griz said, "We apologise for our mortality. If we die in the next attempt on our lives, you won't have to bother with us."

Robulus frowned, but thought better of saying anything.

Vera spoke up too. She said, "That came courtesy of the Dwarf Resistance, I suppose. A peaceful protest perhaps?"

Griz snorted in derision.

Robulus regretted the danger and injuries the two humans sustained, but he had no qualms about pushing them onward. He replied, his voice rumbling the tunnel walls, "Your apology is accepted Griz. Vera, zealotry is the idea that bad deeds done in the name of goodness, is a blessed thing, so the Resistance is capable of anything. Shall we try to build a lantern?"

Robulus found one of the cart's intact tail lights, and six batteries were scattered about the tunnel floor. He found electrical wires too. Griz helped the alien assemble a working lantern. The contraption was awkward however, and consisted of a twelve-pound battery, a bare light bulb and a couple of strands of wire connecting the two. Griz considered the problem for a few seconds before a solution became apparent. He said to Vera, "Your purse; where's your purse?"

Vera was befuddled by the question, but she recovered quickly, and said, "Demn it! Somehow, I must have forgotten to grab it before the explosion."

If Griz were made of less sturdier stuff, he may have fallen in love with Vera at that moment. Dry, sarcastic wit, was a work of linguistic art, and he loved it. He smiled and said, "Women!" He took the flashlight and went back to the area where he'd found Vera. She smiled and went along with him on his quest for her purse.

They first found her missing tennis shoe, and she bent to add it onto her foot. The purse was nearby. Its red handle strap protruded from beneath a rock, which resembled half of a sockher ball. Griz removed the stone from atop the two-thousand-dollar Pucci purse and he handed it to Vera. The outer leather was scratched, but intact. It was as flat as roadkill and she didn't bother to look inside of it. Instead, Vera shook it. It sounded like castanets in a tornado.

Vera turned the purse upside down and pulled it open. Griz showed the lightbeam down onto the tunnel floor, and watched as the jumble of selfone parts, some change, broken mirror glass, a shattered hairbrush and a wallet, all smeared ruby red by crushed lipstick tubes, poured onto the ground. Vera picked the red wallet out of the pile and said, "What a mess."

Griz answered, and said, "Look on the bright side; at least everything matches red."

Vera reflexively gave him a playful slap in the shoulder and cried, "Ouch! My hand!"

Robulus thundered, "Anytime, children."

"Are we on a schedule, Boss?" Griz asked sharply. The shirt bandage helped with his pain somewhat, and it was less agonising to breathe, but he wasn't in the best of moods. He was injured, in a dark tunnel, inside of Poke's Peak with an immortal alien, and his daughter was a kidnap victim. Griz was an optimist at heart, but when your glass was half full of piss, all the cheerfulness in the world wasn't going to make it taste good.

The two humans returned to where Robulus waited, next to their lantern. He said, "I think your idea will work Griz, but those purse handles won't carry the weight." Griz handed the purse to the alien, because he was the one with tools. Robulus reached into a side pocket on his coveralls, and produced a pair of scissors. He cut a hole in one end of the rectangle shaped purse, for the light bulb to look out of. Griz stretched the purse open and the alien managed to slide the battery down inside of it. The snug battery, held the bulb in place, by pressing against it. Robulus had placed a piece of foam from the cart's seat, between the battery and the bulb, for protection against the jostling it was sure to bear once they were underway. He pushed the wires into the purse.

Robulus tried to lift the heavy thing by its red leather handle. The purse was sad to see its handle take off into the air, while it obeyed gravity and stayed on the floor. It looked like they were splits. Vera swore, "Scat!" She was upset that it hadn't held. She had already written off the purse, and was wondering if No Fake News would cover the loss, since she was on the job when it occurred.

All three of them had a 'Now what?' look in their eyes. Griz visualised a possible resolution to the problem of toting the lantern. He asked Robulus, "Can I borrow your scissors? Robulus dug them from one of the numerous pouches and pockets in his coveralls and handed them to the human.

Griz sat down and first cut one, then the other leg from his jeans, leaving him with tattered shorts to wear. He said, "We can use these as slings under the bottom of the purse. I'll carry one side and Robulus; you are stuck with the other."

Robulus said, "Griz, Jeemis and I are always looking for good engineers. Let's try it out." Griz laid the two pant legs down on the tunnel floor, side by side. Robulus set the battery-stuffed purse, on top of the pant legs, leaving an equal nine inches of denim on either side for them to hold onto. They each picked up the heavy lantern by the two-pant leg ends in their hands.

They started to walk side-by-side, up the tunnel, with the lantern pointing ahead of them to light the way. It looked as awkward as two people joined at the hip, who'd never met before. Once they actually began to walk in-step however, it looked more graceful, like a giraffe and a rhino swinging a square bowling ball between them. They turned around and came back down the tunnel to where Vera awaited their verdict.

She offered her own critique of the test walk. She said, "And that was our coordinated dance team Bumble Bear and his side-kick alien, Long Legs Loudmouth. For our next act…"

Griz said, "Vera, for our next act, we need something to keep these pant legs from sliding around as we walk. May we borrow your bra?"

Robulus nearly spat out his teeth and laughed out loud, in spite of his best attempt at restraint. Vera was as startled by the question, as she was embarrassed by it. She filed a sharp retort, but sheathed it. Vera had watched the test walk and had seen the problem that Griz referred to.

She sighed in resignation, turned her back and removed her brassiere. Vera bypassed Griz and handed it to the alien. Griz thought better of estimating the cup size out loud, and he allowed Robulus the honours of winding the brassiere around the purse and pant legs twice, and snapping the straps together.

The test walk went much smoother the second time around. Robulus adjusted his stride and the lantern swung in regular oscillations, the beam of light rising and dipping with each step. Once again, they returned to Vera's location. They set the lantern down on the tunnel floor. The light shined up towards the tunnel ceiling. Illumination spilled around them. They looked at each other closely, and at themselves for the first time since the explosion.

Griz was blackened and sooty. His ragged shirt wrapped his chest and his jean shorts looked cut by a rat's teeth. Vera's red blouse was torn open above her left breast, and part of her nipple peaked through. Her jeans were dirty and torn open in places. Griz tried not to notice the boob. Vera appreciated that more than he could ever know. Robulus looked sooty and his hair was singed. All in all, they looked like chimney sweeps that had formed a punk rock band.

Griz laughed first. Vera soon joined in, and even the tall alien began to laugh. The trio rapidly devolved into hysterics, until tears rolled down their cheeks.

Chapter 28

"Good evening liberals and gentlemen, I am Chuck Wod, and you are watching CON. We have breaking news concerning the alien abduction. One of the kidnappers is dead at this hour, after a massed assault by the notorious far right motorcycle club, Mel's Angels, which left three people dead and four injured. Witnesses say that it was the evil genius, Ido Notno, who was behind this world-shattering kidnapping. Ido, also known as Donut Hole, was lost to us tonight. He played the duo role of criminal and victim in today's historic action.

"Tonight, to help us make sense of this dark episode in Crumm's presidency, we have with us, the iconic Professor Felix Polyplastics. Welcome."

"It's Polyplastis!" He was swaddled in a pink terrycloth bathrobe that read 'HERS' in bold black letters across the front.

Chuck said, "Earlier today, you courageously revealed to the world, that the three letters TDS, referred to a massive asteroid known as the Tartarus Death Star, which will strike Gaia at midnight, annihilating all life on the planet. This vital information has led to violence, suicides, plus fires and riots all over the world. Now that the human race has only three hours left before our extinction, what more can be said?"

The professor drank from a brandy glass before answering. He laughed and cackled for a moment and then said, "Well, I'm glad that you brought that up Chuck. Due to a slight error, I would like to retract that translation of the TDS. According to my latest analysis of this mystery, I am now led to the conclusion that TDS really just means, Trendy Department Store and is nothing to be concerned about. Sorry for the confusion."

"Good evening; this is Jake Dapper and you're watching MNBS news. Looting and riots continue tonight, as xenophobic, white supremacists take to the streets, to protest the presence of aliens in Shamerica. Clearly, President Crumm is up to his eyebrows in this crime of the century. As you can clearly see, in this clearly disturbing video footage, the president's own science advisor, Melanie

Gryzolski is clearly driving the white Tanki, and she deliberately mowed down several, far left bikers, who were clearly out for a peaceful night's ride.

"Here with us tonight is trusted leaker of the House, Aaron Chip. What do you make of all this Congressperson?" Jake asked.

"The real question that should be weighing heavily on all our minds is this, Jake; where is the second alien?" Aaron asked. He went on, "The kidnapping is a distraction, a sleight of hand, to hide the evil deeds of the other missing alien. He vanished from the air power base in Ohaha, at the time the fake kidnapping occurred. And listen to this; Melanie's father disappeared too! Think of the significance of it! The science advisor to the president is involved!"

That was Jake's cue. He said, "Exactly! Climate Change!"

Aaron was pleased. He read off the next line, "You guessed it. TDS is a sinister plan to control world climate, with the aliens and Crumm colluding to destroy Gaia. It means Temperature Disruption Sequence."

"Good evening Shamerica. This is Jordge Stuphitupyeras and this is an SBC Special Rendition. Tonight, we are fortunate enough to have with us, the estimable Gill Bates. Gill, what can you tell us about the alleged stupidity virus? A hoax?"

Gill adjusted his spectacles and replied, "If there was a real stupidity virus, wouldn't we have been smart enough to have discovered it by now? I probably have a vaccine for it, sitting around somewhere anyway. So, no big deal Jordge."

Jordge nodded sagely. He then asked his guest, "What is your take on this TDS nonsense? Should we be out burning and looting, or cowering in terror down in our basements?"

"That's a tough one, even for me." Gill said. He added, "I channelled my spirit guide, Socks, and she revealed to me that TDS had one of two possible meanings. The first is Tongue Depressor Stick, and the second more concerning idea, is that it may mean, Transcendental Douchebag Spectre. According to Socks, this epithet refers to a supernatural asshat, who gads about in the celestial ether, pulling feathers from angel wings, and vandalising their harps when they're not looking."

"This is Jill Terr, for KRAT TV in Ohaha, Nobraska. I am coming to you live, from the dumpsters behind the local FIBB office building, in downtown Ohaha. You can see what long hours they put in, and how hard these twenty-two agents, men and women alike are working, to solve today's kidnapping, by the amount of food containers in these two overflowing dumpsters, which were emptied earlier today.

"The FIBB have one female in custody. Her name is Vometta Wilde, aka the Sperm Whale, and she is allegedly, a vital component of the self-described, but alleged, domestic crime family of BEWBs. These dedicated agents of FIBB, are drilling this alleged kidnapper relentlessly. Many had lined up for hours, just so they could interrogate her too, each carrying huge tubs of chicken, and with boxes of pizzas and donuts in hand. Every agent wants a piece of this alleged crook! I haven't observed anyone going into the FIBB building with sushi or fish, but a flock of inland seagulls are circling above me. And why do they call her the Sperm Whale? I don't get it."

Jammy Kamel announced, "Tonight on the Early Late Show, my guest is the iconic astrologer, Mewant Yerwallat. Let's all welcome Mewant!"

Host Jammy Kamel stood, as the sage astrologer Mewant strode barefoot onstage. The studio audience applauded when cued to do so, and this cue came late, but the crowd eventually caught up to the moment. The usual cue-master had not come in to work tonight, and the custodian was working the keyboard in his absence. She was playing on her selfone too, and this television program was interfering with that pursuit.

Mewant had cultured his appearance to fit a certain stereotype. It was good for business. His hair, beard, moustache and eyebrows were so brightly white, that new fallen snow looked grey by contrast. Each of these hair growths were of equal length, at about three feet. One wondered about his pubic hair.

Mewant sat in the chair next to Jammy's desk, and Kamel took his seat behind it. Jammy said, "Mewant, you have made more than one hundred accurate forecasts, including predicting that last winter would be cold, and that a lot of people would vote in the last election. Isn't that amazing folk?" The crowd was mistakenly cued to say, 'Boo!' instead of the whistles and applaud signal they should have been given.

Jammy Kamel frowned for a second, but made a joke out of it to save the moment. He said, "It's not Holloweenie yet people. That's next month." The studio audience was confused. The neon cue-board sign was flashing between, 'Standing Ovation' and 'Piss Off' now. The spectators stood up and applauded while chanting, "Piss off! Piss off!"

Kamel shouted, "Shut up!" He turned to his guest and asked him, "Mewant, what can you tell us about tonight's mysterious Unveiling of the TDS?"

Mewant wore something resembling a white sheet with holes for arms and head, like a kid's ghost costume. He said, "Well, it's like this man; when I was chilling in them Himalyin mountains in Nippal and Yabet, with them Boohiss worshippers, and fighting off Yitis and climbing up Sheepas, I took time to study the planets, stars and all them other objects floating around in space up there, and I observed the perfect alignment of some sort, which was a cosmic code that I deciphered, and there's like this whole story up there, written about the aliens and it was like a movie, albeit a silent foreign film."

Jammy asked, obviously awed, "Was that all one sentence?"

"I'll have to get back to you on that," the astrology guru replied. "Let me tell you what the stars revealed," he said. "Those crazy celestial objects may be scores of light years away, but I have a direct line to them, and what was the question again?"

"The TDS, the Unveiling of the TDS," Jammy reminded his guest.

The audience cheered and applauded as the neon cue-board instructed.

Mewant said, "Yeah, right, okay, sit tight dude. I'm gonna lay it on you right now. The aliens are alcoholics see, and TDS is Trader Duck's Scootch. But looking from another angle, it could be Taco Deluxe Salad."

A standing ovation ensued; the studio audience went wild.

"This is Harry Hogshed of BBQ world news in Undun, Ingland. Capital cities around the world are burning. Massive, friendly riots are peacefully raging, in at least seven world capitals and thirty other, major metropolitan areas, including Pairass, Franz; Undun, Ingland; Hurlin, Germy and Hamsterland in the Neitherlands. As per usual in Terrorhan, Irun, the populace is out in the streets chanting 'Death to Shamerica' and burning their latest shipment of Shamerican flags."

* * *

President Crumm was flying in Air Power One, one hour away from his Colorotta Springs destination. He sat in a comfortable easy chair, and trolled the MBM on Tooter, with several toots that alleged to decipher or reveal the meaning of TDS. He posted different versions at ten-minute intervals. The first read, 'Tie-Dyed Shirts'. This was followed by, 'Triple Decker Sandwich', 'Top Demn Secret' and 'Truck Driving School'.

185

It worked; it always did. The media mob went mad. Crumm loved it. They were easier to bait than starving hyenas. He kicked back and watched them go nuts.

Chapter 29

Pitch Al Darkly led Torchy, and Kate Armstrong along. The eleven members of the Sacred Star Temple followed behind him too, as if he were the second coming of Elvin Parsley. Robby Indero fumed and steamed like an angry volcano. He was the proper leader of this cult! Not Al, the self-appointed messiah.

Robby occupied his mind, by creating and forming novel strings of profanities to use in the appropriate circumstances. He needed to stay at peak performance. One never knew when a long, drawn out, chain of oaths was needed, and it paid to be prepared.

The fourteen people stood outside the airport now. The sun had set, and a slight breeze wafted from the west, but it was a pleasant sixty degrees. The eleven saints of the Sacred Star Temple each towed one piece of luggage behind them. Kate laboured under the weight of Don's bulky trunk; the smaller bag was stored inside an airport locker. No cabs idled at the curbs; no hotel shuttles waited for clients. Not one hotel room sat vacant tonight.

The bright cluster of stars were dumbfounded that they, of all people, were left stranded. They followed Al, not because they looked up to him, but because he was so beneath them. If a ride for fourteen people was needed, Al would find one. Celebrities used charm and finesse to manipulate others, while Al was more suited to cunning and wile. Torchy added muscle.

Al turned and announced to his flock, "We will comb the parking lots for suitable transportation. Any questions?"

Tod Eiiner protested. He said, "We can't steal someone's poking car! We could get in big trouble, arrested even!" He snivelled.

Robby Indero snarled, "Shut up meatface! Are you some kind of brain dead-o, lousy pedo, poking butt miner? Arrested? Really? Think about who we are! If any nosy, poking cop shows up, give them an autograph to their poor Aunt Leaky, and they're happy! We're on a mission from Carolyn Funroe, Elvin Parsley and Ojay Crimson!"

Torchy suggested to Al, that they check the long-term parking lots. A vehicle removed from that area wouldn't be noticed right away. The group of brightly dressed, jewellery clad celebrities resembled a cluster of Christmas ornaments, as they paraded past the short-term parking, beneath the overhead security lights. After a long walk, they climbed up a series of stairs, until they had ascended to the uppermost parking lot, five stories above the tarmac below. Syko More took the elevator.

Floodlights illuminated several score vehicles, and an acre of empty pavement. Torchy and Al saw their dream vehicle! It was extraordinary! Transportation for all of them, as if made to order! A grimy, white and orange moving truck, a rental from I-Haul, sat under a bright light, and looked as if it had been there for weeks.

"There it is!" Al exclaimed.

"It's perfect!" Torchy agreed. He added, "It may even be stolen already, and therefore empty!"

Kate swiftly assessed the situation, and then yelled, "Shotgun!"

The eleven celebrities, were slower on the uptake, but like a school of fish, saw the danger simultaneously. They reacted as one, with a chorus of diverse moans, groans, curses, and oaths. Arti P went so far, as to squat down and urinate a pentagram diagram on the pavement, so that she could cast a death spell on Al from inside of it.

In the meantime, Torchy walked around the truck. He found the two doors and windows secured, and the back lift gate was padlocked shut. He pulled a contrivance, which he called a 'locksmith', from a vest pocket. It consisted of a steel ball attached to an elastic loop. Torchy slipped the loop over his middle finger and cupped the ball in the palm of his hand. He stood an arm's length away from the driver's door held his arm at window height and flicked his wrist. He opened his hand and the steel sphere whipped out to crash against the glass, shattering it.

He reached his thick tattooed arm inside the cab, and unlocked the door. In less than thirty seconds, Torchy found a set of ignition keys under a floor mat, with the padlock key lying next to them. He handed the padlock key out to Al. Torchy started the truck with his second attempt, and was pleased to see the fuel gauge read half a tank of gas. He let the engine idle and went back to see if Al had the back gate opened.

Pitch Al walked past the celebrity eleven. Every last one of them swore they would never ride in the back of the box truck, and cursed his ancestors for their DNA. Al used the key and pulled the lock from the door. Dom Crews, Kate, Bobby and the rest, crowded around Al, saying silent prayers to their idols, which often meant themselves, as he lifted up the cargo door.

Suddenly, the hills were alive with songs of profanity. Voices were raised high in condemnation, and denial of what they saw inside. The truck was filled end to end, and top to bottom with furniture and household goods. When Torchy came around to the back of the truck, and saw the problem, he returned to the cab and got inside.

Torchy poked his head out the broken-out window and yelled, "Clear!" He was grouchy. He hadn't drunk a beer in ages; not since this morning even! Torchy drove the truck slowly forward for twenty yards. Next, he shifted into reverse and accelerated. The truck bogged down initially, but then picked up speed. When the truck approached its original departure point, Torchy slammed on the brakes.

The truck slid and skidded to a stop, but the items in the cargo box did not. Two bicycles, a lawnmower, a concrete birdbath and a rolling toolbox, spewed from the truck's rear end like projectile diarrhoea. Torchy drove the truck forward a few feet, and turned off the ignition. He rejoined Al and the popstars, who circled around aimlessly, like dizzy hamsters. All of the celebrities were suitably impressed, by Torchy's bold actions without a script!

Torchy and Al climbed up inside the truck, which was still more than three quarters full of stuff, and started throwing it out; clothes, chairs, mirrors, pictures, mattresses and every household need. The celebrities watched the unidentified flying objects launching out of the truck, and the subsequent crash landings, in fixed stupefaction for a few brain idling seconds, before they realised that they were missing out on all the fun.

Kate stood back for safety, when the celebrity saints rushed the cargo box, as if free drinks were on offer. They pushed and shoved each other, and climbed and clambered up inside of the truck. Lem Kerry was dazed momentarily, when his head collided with a barbell that Torchy was heaving out of the truck. Syko More was grounded. He couldn't manage the battle against gravity to elevate so high.

It seemed metaphysical, that thirteen rampaging people, could cram themselves into a truck loaded with furniture and appliances, and still manage to move, but move they did! Within minutes, the parking lot looked like a garage sale after a windstorm.

Torchy had to drive the truck forward every few minutes, as the discarded items piled up behind it. A small audience of curious spectators, drawn by the commotion, started to form. Selfones were pulled out of pockets and purses, and the spectators began to record the carnage. One nosy, but courageous woman, using a sofa cushion as a shield, got close enough to the projectiles shooting out of the truck, to recognise Don Crews.

She shrieked, "Oh my Gawd! It's Pop Gun!"

The spectators surged forward in a gush of adoration. Some hopped up into the truck, and one unlucky fellow was struck by a lamp in flight. Then, as other celebrities were recognised, the cries of love rose up to the heavens above. One lady fainted. The names of the celebrities were whispered as prayers.

Kate Armstrong knew this drill. She performed like a drill sergeant, and one by one, she lined up the celebrity worshippers in single file, with promises of one-on-one time with 'Pop Gun'. Don Crews came off the truck on cue. Kate collected five dollars, and Don autographed their grocery receipts, their money, or their arms, whatever they offered up. A few had him sign objects they'd collected from the pile of stuff at the rear of the truck.

Robby Indero provided entertainment. He exited the truck, to pour out a foul stream of invectives that stirred and inspired his many admirers. He was a role model for the swearing masses, and the mascot for the Cuss Club, an international gentlemen's lodge of excellence in profanity.

One lady dared Robby's contempt, and approached him for an autograph. By way of breaking his train of filth, she said, "I loved you in Raging Taxi, where you beat that little girl to death in the boxing ring. Would you sign this to my grandson? I named him after you! Robby Expletive Smith is his full name."

Indero was both honoured and touched by this woman's honesty and taste. He nearly brought his profanity to an end and spoke English. Her homage had humbled him. Humility was one thing, but Bobby couldn't show any weakness. He was a tough guy after all. So, he took the piece of proffered cardboard from her, which she had torn from a box, and pulled a pen from his coat pocket. He wrote, "Poke you Robby, you dumb son of a poking sow. Love Robby Indero." She cried.

One man found a yearbook in the growing pile of discards, and offered that up to be autographed. All the stars stood in line, behind Don and Robby, and the people could go from one star to the next; cash only. Some of the pop stars, charged only three dollars for their signatures, and Lem Kerry offered up a dollar for anyone who would take his. There were no takers.

Torchy and Al pushed, heaved and tossed items off the truck, while the rich and famous folk, earned some spare change. Torchy grew grumpier, by the second. He couldn't bear these phony, condescending narcissists, and he really wanted a poking beer! When the last bed rails and headboards were jettisoned, and the truck was emptied of stuff, Al and Torchy exited it.

The pop stars had tired of their fans, who'd run out of money, and the celebrities were now picking through the pile of stuff they'd tossed onto the pavement. Al's and Torchy's moods worsened at the sight of the aristocracy, behaving like homeless people.

Torchy made an announcement. He bellowed, "We're leaving in three minutes! Get in the back, or stay here. I don't give a cat's scat which." He turned and walked to the truck cab. He got inside, and started the ignition. Al laughed, heartily. He told Kate, that she could ride up in the cab, with Torchy and him. He also suggested that she bring one of the pillows they'd tossed out of the truck.

They waited, and watched the temple saints pile, first their luggage, and then themselves, into the back of the truck. As much as they loathed the very idea of such degradation, none wished to be left behind or to be tongue-lashed by Indero. The loading ramp was pulled down, and after a struggle, Syko More successfully ascended it. Once they were all inside, Al pulled the door down, but left it slightly open. The crack let in some moonlight, so that the celebs were not in complete darkness. Later, Al would claim that it was Kate's idea to give them air and some light, because he would have closed the door and padlocked it shut.

Kate sat in the middle of Torchy and Al, on the cab's bench seat. Torchy shifted the I-Haul truck into drive, and they were on their way to Minotaur Springs. It was 10:03 PM.

Chapter 30

Shanghai Low was pleased at how well things were working out. He didn't need Donut. Sidekicks were over-rated. Besides, he had this under control. The girl behaved, so that he wouldn't carve her face up. And the loud-mouthed alien minded his manners for the same reason. Low controlled his own destiny now. He believed that Donut's death would be poignant, and add a tear-jerker moment to the movie version of this grand caper.

Melanie had tired of the sluggish pace of the traffic and the danger too. The big white Pissan Tanki stood out like an honest politician. It was a bright neon sign. People threw bottles and shoes at them and cursed and spit and swore at them too. Others threw words of support and encouragement her way, but she preferred not to deal with any of it. She had gradually steered the massive BUV across three lanes of jam-packed vehicles, to access the deep, weedy median which split oncoming traffic.

Other vehicles had tried the same shortcut, and without fail, so it seemed, they'd all become stuck in the soft sand. She powered the truck through the weeds, around the mired vehicles and the people hanging around them. Every few minutes, Melanie peered up into the rear-view mirror, looking to Jeemis for encouragement and approval. He was always looking back at her. They were less than five miles away from the I-250 interchange with state highway 240, which led west into Minotaur Springs, when she caught his eye again. The alien cupped his ear and looked up. Melanie listened. It was an absence of noise from outside the vehicle that confused her.

She looked up to the mirror again and Jeemis pointed a finger up towards the ceiling and swirled it around in a circle. Melanie got it! The four news helicopters whirring above them for hours were gone! They'd all left at once. She wondered what that boded. It was 10: 14 PM.

Low ruined her concentration. He'd twisted around in his seat to ask Jeemis, "Hey; how demn long does that immortality stuff last for anyway?" He lit a cigarette. Low was losing touch with reality.

Melanie enjoyed that, and she laughed loud and long. Jeemis didn't want to spoil her fun, so he let her answer in her own time. She took advantage, and mocked the big BEWB, "What's the matter Hi-Lo? Are you afraid that a life sentence may mean what it says? Ha ha! Hilarious!"

Shanghai Low gulped. Jeemis added to the crook's discomfort. He shrieked, "Everyone in prison will try to kill you; shivs in the throat, broomsticks up your ass, drug overdoses. But you'll be like new in seconds and ready for more." The alien laughed, "Wahit! Wahit!"

Low was rethinking the entire immortality lifestyle when a black helicopter, descended from the moonlit sky. It landed a couple of hundred yards ahead of them on one of the emergency service roads, which cut across the median and connected the opposing traffic lanes. Four tall streetlights shed yellow sodium rays on the area, but the descending chopper whipped dust and trash up into the air, obscuring its identity.

Melanie depressed the brake pedal as they drew nearer to the chopper. Low correctly assumed that the helicopter's black colour was a bad sign. Melanie stopped the Tanki and shifted the truck into Park, at a distance of fifty or sixty yards from the whirring blades. The copter landed.

Three dark figures exited the ominous aircraft in front of them, and approached their location. Dust settled as the spinning blades slowed, and now white letters could be seen on the helicopter. The acronym 'F.I.B.B.' sat atop the words 'Hostage Rescue Squad'.

Shanghai Low pulled out his little .22 pistol, with its empty magazine. Jeemis plucked it out of his hands. The BEWB squealed like a constipated pig, and angrily reached down into an orange sock and pulled out his switchblade. Low quickly pressed the blade under Melanie's ear. Jeemis tried to calm the maniac. He said, "They're probably here to give us a ride to the TDS, you idiot! Calm down and get a grip, Low!"

Melanie remained calm. She saw where Jeemis was going, and she contributed. She told the loser, "You're a celebrity, and these guys just want to be part of the show Low."

Her words were like a kick in his demn head! Duh! How could he have not predicted this scene? It was so obvious now! Every good crime thriller had a cop scene in it. The crook gets arrested, and then his fans mob the jailhouse and break him loose. Duh. Okay, he knew the dialogue for this bit too! Ha!

Jeemis screeched, "They wouldn't dare arrest you Low! It would be like arresting Ojay Crimson during his slow ride in the Fard Bronc"

That idiotic comment would haunt Low for many long, suffering years to come. He never quite figured out what in Hades the alien meant by it, but he pondered it for many years, from behind his prison walls on quiet nights.

Shanghai Low dropped the switchblade into the truck console, and divested himself of three other weapons too, including a sharpened screwdriver, an ice-pick and a hatchet. He donned a pair of sunglasses, put an unlit cigarette in a corner of his frowning mouth, and said, "Let's go meet them dudes, and don't forget that I am still in charge here, even if I can't kill you. We're making history, Gotta do it right, cuz you only get a chance like this once in a lifetime"

Jeemis shrieked, "Unless you're immortal that is."

Melanie felt like collapsing. It was all over! In a few short minutes she would be freed of Low. She exited the vehicle, and Jeemis got out behind her. She left the headlights on, but turned off the ignition and tossed the keys into the weeds. Shanghai got out front and said, loudly, "Get behind me, and be cool."

The three figures from the helicopter became clearer as they drew nearer. Their group was in a similar formation to that of Low's group; one person led, and two followed behind, like an arrowhead. They were dressed casually in blue jeans, dark sweat shirts and wore no visible weapons. Once this trio of FIBB rescue squad agents had come within ten yards of Low's group, they came to a halt. They would let the kidnapper decide on whether he wished to close the distance between them or not.

Shanghai Low was eager to demonstrate his absolute domination of his captives, now that these FIBBers were near enough to hear him. Low was also well aware that dozens, perhaps scores of people stuck in traffic, were recording this entire episode. This confrontation may be his biggest scene! He had to shine. He yelled like an army drill sergeant, "Alright, you two worthless, poking victims! Behave your poking wimpy asses!" He screamed louder, "I'm in charge of this brilliant crime! Me! Shanghai Low!"

Low strutted forward boldly, confidently, and he advanced right on up to the six-foot, criminal-distancing guidelines set by Congress, before he stopped. Shanghai Low faced a man, whose shiny black hair, looked as if it was sculpted from obsidian. His face was pink marble. The man spoke first. He said, "I'm

194

Special Agent Rocky Stones, and I am looking for a guy named Loser, not Shynese takeout."

Low puffed out his chest, raised his chin defiantly, and scowled for the cameras. He loudly proclaimed, "I am he whom you seek. Loser is no more. I have evolved and am now the great Shanghai Low, abductor of aliens."

Rocky's left eyebrow may have moved. He answered nonchalantly, "Sounds like a circus act."

Low was on top of his game. This blockhead couldn't topple him. He said, "And I'm the ringmaster. So, what the poke do you want?" Low adjusted his shades and chewed his cigarette once or twice for effect.

Special Agent Rocky knew and understood now, what kind of BEWB he was playing with. This was going to be easy. He could take down this halfwit hoodlum, anytime that he wished. He wanted to play first, like a cat with a retarded mouse. Shanghai wants a show, and I'll oblige him, he thought, his lips straining at a smile.

A waxing, three quarter moon hung in the clear, starry skies, casting shadows in the weedy median, where the two parties of three faced off. Rocky, as rigid as a statue, his arms hanging loosely at his sides, said, "We want to give you a lift in our helicopter. You can skip the vehicle traffic altogether. We are here to help you get to your destination."

Shanghai Low was too smart for this ruse. He said, "Sure, right, like I am going to get into a helicopter with three FIBB rescue squadders, who don't even know where in Hades my destination is! "After a second, he added, "You think I am stupid!"

Unfazed, Rocky simply replied, "I didn't know you could read minds." Low was processing that remark, when Agent Rocky said, "What we figured, you see, is that if you knew where you were going, you could give us directions, and then we could kind of drop you off wherever you wished."

Low suspected treachery. He said, "Yeah, you just wanna know where the TDS is. You can't fool me."

Melanie and Jeemis were listening to the idiotic exchange between Rocky and Low, but they were taking the visual measure of the two idle agents, who stood shoulder to shoulder, behind their leader. One of the two, was a tall, thin man, wearing a Sad Fandisco Sixty-Niners, baseball cap, atop his blonde-haired head, and on his left side, a muscular woman stood, her arms folded across her hard chest.

Shanghai dialled down his tough guy act from level nine to level four, as seen in the popular Mobster Mowdown Showdown video game, which Low had mastered a few months back. Rocky was like a Boss, and when Low got past him, he'd be up to the next level. He reflected for a moment before he said, "I'm going for immortality man. You can't win more lives than that!"

Shanghai Low was losing it, but didn't see it. It was so easy to slip into fantasies, in which he always won in the end. It just took practice. He had this. Low turned his back on his new friend, to face his captives. He said, "Okay kiddies, we get to ride in a fancy government helicopter! How cool is that?"

Rocky struck as quick as a cobra. He had Shanghai handcuffed, and face down on the ground, before Low knew he'd been bit. Rocky grinned as his two partners ran forward to assist him. He said, "How cool is that?" The three FIBB agents yanked Low to his feet and pulled his pockets inside out, looking for weapons.

Low snarled, "What the poke are you poking doing! Do you know who I am?"

Rocky said, "You're under arrest, Loser."

Low gave up and hung his head in defeat. This wasn't how it was supposed to go! What went wrong? Rocky read Low his rights, none of which included future movie royalties. Melanie and Jeemis approached the agents. Rocky noticed, and told his two team members to hold up with the prisoner for a minute.

Jeemis screeched, "Sir, I believe it would be appropriate to allow Melanie to say goodbye to Low."

Rocky's face cracked slightly, his lips nearly forming into a smile. His two co-workers were astonished by such an embarrassing display of emotion on his part. They'd never seen anything like it. Rocky looked Jeemis up and down, then he said, "You're awfully snarky for an alien." He turned to his partners and said, "Bring the prisoner forward. Miss Melanie wants a last look at our celebrity."

Melanie was grateful to Jeemis for giving her this opportunity. Tears of thanksgiving welled up in her tired eyes, and she hugged the alien. Jeemis was surprised, but touched by her response. He held her for a while, and then turned her around to face Low, and the two agents who held him in place. The cigarette and sunglasses were missing from Low's haggard face.

Melanie walked closer, her clenched fists held at waist level. She let pent up anger, and a flood of other emotions build strength into her revenge muscles. She took one measured step backwards. Shanghai Low had just thought of something clever to say, when Melanie, stepping into it, threw a hard right fist into Low's throat.

Jeemis was impressed. Rocky's face altered not, but tears of mirth in his eyes, were discerned by at least one witness, and Low was in tears too, although he was choking and gagging. The two agents led and dragged Low away towards the waiting helicopter.

Rocky had business with Melanie and the alien. Melanie could feel it. She asked, "What about us?"

Rocky said, "That's above my paygrade, Miss Melanie. I didn't talk to your boss, directly, Ma'am, but my boss did, and the President sends a message."

Melanie was plumb out of adrenaline, and so she barely reacted to the report. Jeemis filled in. He shrieked, "We go forward."

Rocky gritted his teeth in irritation. It sounded like a hail storm. He wasn't pleased that the alien stole his thunder and ruined the surprise. "That is correct," he said, the words squeezed out between his clenched teeth. He loosened his jaw, so that he could add this, "You are the Presidential Science Advisor after all."

Melanie saw the picture now! Yes! It was like the Blewus and Clank expedition! She was on a presidential quest for the advancement of science! She felt renewed and rejuvenated. She and Jeemis were pioneers, crossing into a new frontier. They would walk the last six miles to the TDS. It was night-time, and they would be strolling on a highway, but they would be moving as fast, if not faster than the traffic around them. They'd be safe. Jeemis would protect them both if need be.

Agent Rocky asked Jeemis about that, "Can you protect her? Are you armed?"

Jeemis screeched, "Yes Sir! I've got two arms."

Rocky didn't blink. He said, "President Crumm wishes you good luck, as do I." He reached out to shake both of their hands. He was thrilled, but didn't show it. He could brag that he'd touched an alien and didn't get anally probed to do it.

There was one tragic accident that occurred during the arrest of Shanghai Low. A certain Karen O'Ceedee of Dunfor fell out of the bed of a pickup truck. She had been standing up in the moving vehicle, while filming the arrest, when she toppled out. A personal injury attorney in a black Caddylac just happened to be in the area, and soon made her acquaintance. Karen suffered from wounded feelings and emotional distress, and she sued the state for making their highways hard, and solid and hurtful to people who fell out of trucks.

Melanie and Jeemis watched the FIBB helicopter lift off, and fly away before they continued their journey on foot. They faced a half mile trek to the I-250 and Colorotta State Highway 240 interchange leading into Minotaur Springs. It was another five miles into town after that. The moon seemed to show a spotlight upon them as they walked through the median.

* * *

Rosie Oh snaked her big rig through the hesitant traffic like a sidewinder with a blast-horn, keeping mostly to the shoulder and far right lane. She flashed the truck headlights, blasted the horn, and revved the powerful diesel engine, to frighten drivers and force them off the road. Rosie knew, was certain in fact, deep down in her ample gut; she and her trailer of cold beer were essential to a proper Unveiling. She had a mission, a purpose beyond her own cravings, and nothing would stand in her way.

The poking, red Cumaro riding her tail like a second trailer irritated her sensibilities. The little sports car had been in front of her for much of the trip, but now he rode her like a cowboy. Maybe they were on a sacred mission like she was. She pondered that idea, for a few precious seconds of brain time.

Rosie Oh had seen the two men in that red sports car in Jewelsberg, but Barry Porter of CON News was as much a stranger to her, as the superhero who drove. She didn't watch the movies or its sibling the news. Her brain was mushy enough already, she figured.

Crime Blaster XL-5 was pumped! He was as excited as a whore on factory payday. Following a crazy driving tractor trailer, as closely as he dared through this horrible traffic, had paid off. He was getting close, in distance and time, to the world saving climax of this adventure.

CB estimated that he was six miles and eighty-five minutes away, from pop culture immortality. After he saved the world, in front of the whole world, he would claim his rightful place in comic book and video game history forever. All he needed now for icing on the cake, was a nice fat cheeseburger. He scolded himself for the mixed metaphor, but he was poking hungry!

CB felt like he'd recovered from the horror of the dead Donut story. Barry had broken the news to him without ever looking up from his demn selfone. The reporter had interrupted the silence by saying, "Donut is dead."

Crime Blaster almost lost his mind for a moment. His reason nearly died with Donut. It was devastating to realise, that only one dastardly villain remained for him to vanquish and bring to justice. At first it appeared that he may only reap half as much glory as previous, but after he studied the matter, CB realised that he still had an entire world to save, and two important personages to rescue, including an alien and a beautiful damsel in distress.

CB calmed himself with deep, slow breaths. He thought that he could manage to understand and accept the present reality. CB was sick and tired of thinking now; sometimes thoughts pissed him off. He needed a diversion. He attempted a conversation with the selfone-absorbed reporter riding in his passenger seat. CB tried to disconnect Barry Porter from his newslogs, and so he asked him a question, "Hey; do you think the woman ran over those bikers and that BEWB on purpose?"

To his credit, Barry actually looked up from his selfone to reply. He said, "Even a mouse will bite when backed into a corner."

CB chewed on that, in lieu of a cheeseburger. Before he could swallow it however, Barry said something that made him lose his appetite, as well as his mind. Porter announced, "The FIBB has just arrested Lou Snert, aka Loser, aka Shanghai Low."

Barry innocently continued his report, unaware of its potential perilous effect on the operator of the vehicle he rode in. "It says here, "Barry twisted the knife in, "that eyewitnesses described a black helicopter, with mysterious lettering on it, which plucked the poor man out of the Tanki at top speed, and kidnapped him. The mysterious chopper rapidly disappeared into the darkness, leaving the truck, the alien, the woman, and one, lone, unmatched shoe behind in the median."

The shock of the news bought out Wayne Bruce for a spell, and the Crime Blaster XL-5 persona was subsumed and submerged, until more favourable circumstances returned in a future occasion. Wayne Bruce resumed his normal duties, in place of CB. He reached down deep, and loudly screamed, "No!" He stomped his foot, and it landed on the accelerator. The turbo-charged Mid-Life Crisis Vehicle, leapt forward, and Wayne wrenched the steering wheel to the left. The MLCV surged out of the right traffic lane, and created a new lane, which cut across the other two, by smashing and crashing through any cars in its path. The red Cumaro ricocheted, then jerked hard and left the road, It shot over the embankment and plunged down into the sunken median below and kept going!

Barry prayed to Elvin Parsley and dropped his eyefone, which for Barry, was akin in trauma to a divorce. It was all over now. His number had been called. Barry's IRA flashed before his eyes. Wild thoughts ran amok in his head; his bathroom was a mess and his yard needed mowing! How embarrassing. He could hear it now, his boss, Mr Bleeker, giving the eulogy at his funeral, "Barry's bathroom smelled like death. Maybe it was an omen, and the lazy bass turd left his yard a mess too!" Demn his poking boss! What kind of a lowlife would say such a thing? He'd get his boss back for that, even if he had to reincarnate as a virus to do it! All these thoughts and more spun through his head like a whirlwind as the car sped towards destruction.

Barry grabbed at the ignition keys but Wayne slapped his hand away. The car began to bog down and its engine started smoking. It ran up the other side of the median and hit the edge of a concrete base holding up a towering streetlight. The car's momentum caused it to spin out into oncoming traffic where, with perfect Inglish, like a well hit cue ball, the Cumaro sent the cars it struck into other cars. A total of twenty-seven insurance claims were later filed as a result of it. Two black Caddylacs, driven by personal injury attorneys, were only minutes away.

The Cumaro's airbags deployed and it came to rest, in the centre lane of I-250 northbound traffic. The passenger airbag planted Barry's selfone into the middle of his forehead, and the pain of it made him think that he might still be alive. The fone's logo of an eggplant, with a bite out of it, was permanently etched into his head. He shook like a leaf and climbed out of the window of the passenger door. The door was stuck and the glass was missing. He fell out onto the ground and sat up, breathing. Barry removed the fone from his forehead to check for service. It peeled off in small pieces.

Wayne Bruce had exited the car, and he moved like an automaton, his eyes fixed and unfocussed. He was like a somnambulist on acid, and when Barry saw him march around the crushed front end of the car, he nearly pooped his pants in fear at the sight. Wayne's eyes were as empty as a used car salesman's. Barry nearly blurted out, "I'll buy it," in hopes that Wayne would turn his head and smile. He'd seen eyes like that once before, when his pet lizard died.

Horns tooted and honked, people shouted, screamed, swore, cursed and cried. Barry and Wayne remained oblivious to it. They remained outside of that world. They'd closed it out for the moment, and had other matters to attend to.

Barry Porter's fear and terror soon faded out, to be replaced by anger. Barry gave in to its demands, and he spewed forth with volcanic verbal abuse. The swearing and cursing flowed from him as if he were a born rapper. He didn't know he had it in him.

This story wasn't the first time he'd been exposed to danger as a reporter. When he had covered the grand opening of the world's first Sacred Stars Temple in LA, for example, a streaker raced through, and ripped down the ceremonial ribbon; and once, when in Hollowood for the premiere of 'Super Puppy Versus the Squeak Toy Killers', he witnessed a woman throw her popcorn onto her boyfriend. He'd seen danger alright, but this level of comic book insanity required hazard pay!

Wayne Bruce stood facing the ranting raving reporter, with a blank look on his ashen face. Barry concluded his oral arguments. He kept his eyes on Wayne and backed slowly away. He started to whistle a happy tune and continued in reverse. After he'd established a safe distance, Barry turned around and ran faster than since that time in high school, when he'd squeezed a cheerleader's boob and it was a guy who didn't appreciate it. The dude had beaten him up with pom-poms.

Wayne Bruce, costumed as Crime Blaster XL-5, turned towards the not-too-distant lights of Minotaur Springs, and mechanically, started plodding in that direction, unaware of the derisive shouts and jeers flung at him from stranded and injured motorists.

* * *

Mikul Imanasti listened to Christian talk radio, as he drove the Winabagel RV of prostitutes to Minotaur Springs. The whores drank booze and played cards in the back of the RV, while listening to country western gangsta rap.

Mikul was an ironic sort of guy. He'd fought against temptations his entire life, and was proud to have beaten the worst of them; working for a living. Driving and pimping provided great money and constant sex for him, and he had the diseases and infections to prove it. His doctor always joked, that his blood was one part haemoglobin and two parts penicillin.

A frantic preacher shouted at Mikul from the RV's radio speaker. In fact, the man sounded absolutely hysterical. Mikul couldn't discern whether it was religious fervour or fear that drove the sermon. The radio preacher's voice rose and fell in tone and volume as he cried out to his audience; "There are no aliens, brethren. Aliens are not mentioned in the Biblo! Therefore, they do not exist my friends! However, pay attentions brothas and sistas, because we ain't in that Garden of Eatin' no more! Ava ate the forbidden eggplant and sold her soul for a hay roll. We can't swallow it!

"These two fake aliens, who promise everlasting life, are truly the spawn of that poki...the serpent! I can prove that Beastijeus, and his public relations managers are involved in this devilish scheme. Listen children, listen to me now!" The preacher was losing his voice, and it sounded scratchy and worn, like an old vinyl record.

He testified with fervour, "The diabolic duo of aliens, is unveiling the hole leading down to Hades, in the mountain called Poke's Peak. This phallic mountain leads to Perdition and I will prove it! Get yourself a pad of paper and a pencil and follow my logic. Write out the words Poke's Peak. Now, assign a number to each letter, according to its place in the alphabet. For example, the letter A equals one, and B is two and so on.

"Once you have done this, add together the numbers in each separate word. As you will observe, the letters in Poke's adds to 66 and the letters in Peak add to 33. If we add the pair of threes our third and final six is discovered and thus, we have the number of Beastijeus—666! "And now for a word from our loyal sponsor, Personal Injury Attorney, Sue M. Aul..."

Mikul turned the radio off, and hollered to the sex workers in the back, "Hey did yawl hear that girls? We is descendin' into Pahditchin."

The head whore took the cigar out of her mouth and bellowed, "I thought we wuz goin" ta Mini-Toe Springs!"

The Little Sisters of the Pork, by happenstance, rolled directly behind the battered Winabagel RV and were listening to the same maniacal radio preacher as Mikul. An ad played now, "...she will get you every dollar you deserve or don't deserve! "Then a jingle: "Remember; when you get hurt or when you fall, blame someone else and then you call, Sue M. Aul."

Sister Shaymon Yew mocked the ad and she sang in a tenor, "You make my skin crawl, Miss Sue M. Aul."

Sister Gottel Gitchya laughed and she sang out in a similar manner, "I saw her name on a bathroom wall, for a good time call, Sue M. Aul."

The carload of nuns was a joyful group, and Sister Egsan Hamm added some lyrics of her own, and she belted out the words, "This lawyer chick just loves to ball; when you get horny Sue M Aul."

Sister Shaymon was at the wheel and she drove the Fard Accident, as if she were operating a tank again, like when she served in the army, in Laughgasintan and Eyerack. She'd blasted many of the enemy into the next world, and had always prayed that the fire was hot there. She wished she could pass the RV, but doing so on the curvy, two-lane, steep mountain highway, was unsafe, even with Gawd on your side.

The Five Sisters of the Pork had discussed the pros and cons of Gawd creating aliens, and keeping it a secret from Mankind. They'd concluded, with one dissenting opinion, that Gawd created the aliens as a back-up species, just in case humans wiped themselves out. Sister Gottel objected, preferring to see them as a dress rehearsal, for making Man.

Chapter 31

The makeshift lantern swung to and fro in step with Robulus and Griz, its light beam alternating between the tunnel floor and the ceiling. They walked side by side, sharing the burden, carrying the weighty lantern by the pant leg slings. Vera followed closely behind the lantern bearers. There wasn't room for three abreast in the tunnel, and this was easier, because she could see where they stepped.

Their pace was slow, and it took time for Griz and the long-legged alien to learn to walk in step together. Griz struggled. His cracked ribs were agony, and he panted in short shallow breaths that were sharp as knives. Periodically, Griz needed to switch sides with Robulus, when one arm tired of the lantern's weight. He could catch his breath too.

Warm air flowed upslope, and pushed them forward, like a ghost assisting their progress. The tunnel trended uphill, with hairpin turns interwoven between level areas. Robulus, Griz and Vera were all on the alert for trip wires, and further adventures with explosives. None wanted a repeat.

Robulus spoke up, his deep voice rumbling the rock walls of the tunnel. He said, "We should reach our destination in less than an hour."

Vera asked, "The TDS?"

"No," Robulus replied. He added, "We must air the Unveiling; broadcast it to the world. Another production studio lies ahead. It is quite close to the surface and the TDS. You have a part to play, both of you do."

Griz pondered other matters. He said, "These dwarfs of the Resistance aren't done yet Robulus. Fanatics don't give up. You've underestimated them, and my daughter, and hundreds, perhaps thousands of people are going to be out there to view your 'Unveiling' tonight. What are you going to do about it?" It was painful to speak, but sometimes life just poking hurt.

Vera thought that Griz was right, but that his language and tone were unnecessarily aggressive. But, then again, she didn't have a kidnapped daughter to worry about.

Robulus thundered an answer. He said, "Jeemis and I have taken security very seriously. Drones are flying over the area constantly, and the robo-staff of parking attendants, guides and concessionaires, can all detect the presence of gunpowder, and most can detain a human and disarm him or her as well.

Griz's left arm needed a rest, and so did he. "Break!" he called. Robulus stopped and they set the lantern down on the tunnel floor. They switched sides, but Griz wasn't ready yet, he was only human. His lips were dry and he wished for a cold beer. Vera drew near. She could tell that Griz had more to say. He wore it like a bell, and it rang loud and clear.

After he caught his breath, Griz asked the alien, "Do you know everything that will happen tonight? You may have this production running on schedule, but you can't control everything."

Robulus thought about that before answering. He said, "Much has happened already that was not accounted for. Many things are happening now that we are unaware of." His voice was a battering ram against their eardrums. He continued, and said, "We have exploited to our best advantage, every circumstance that has so far arisen."

Griz growled, and said, "Yeah, exploited; that's the idea."

Vera agreed, but saw the need. She said, "Absolutely! We're up to our necks, but there ain't no going back!"

Griz said, "You betchya! It's like jumping off a cliff; you can't change your mind halfway down."

Vera laughed. She said, "Things could always be worse. We could be in some crazy alternate universe, where people are stupid without the assistance of a virus."

Robulus and Griz appreciated the cheerful thought.

"Shall we? "Griz looked to Robulus, and bent to retrieve the lantern slings. He was ready to resume their trek."

He and Robulus hefted the lantern, and the group was on the move again. The alien boomed, "One can never prepare for Kazooky's Conundrum. The little rascal is always about, just waiting for the opportunity to make a mess of things."

Griz and Vera both appreciated a bit of levity, and both were familiar with the workings of Kazooky, aka Murphy. Griz made conversation, but with a purpose. He said, "Robulus, you have told us little of the TDS, for you wish to be mysterious. I am going to make some assertions regarding it, and I want you to either confirm them or deny them."

Vera scooted up closer behind them; this could be interesting. Robulus thought so too. He said, "Let's give it a try."

Griz caught his breath and said, "Obviously, the TDS is a living entity of one sort or another. You have referred to it in both the singular and in plural terms. It seems credible to suppose, that a trio of entities, is represented by the three letters, TDS."

Robulus replied, and said, "A credible supposition indeed, but incorrect nonetheless. The TDS is one biological lifeform, created from a unification of six individual entities, one of those, is not of this planet. But we are unsure of its origins. Do you have more?"

"Yes," Griz answered. "One more. You said that the TDS can access some cosmic thought point and communicate. Does it have other powers? Can it perform miracles worthy of dwarf worship?"

Vera piped up. She said, "Good question, because if it does magical things, then we humans will worship it too."

The three hiked steadily, Griz and Vera hoped to see a light at the end of the tunnel. Robulus knew better. The lantern would suffice.

Robulus answered Vera first. He blasted, "Humans worship cows. Unveiling the TDS does carry this risk, and has caused Jeemis and I some concern, but its advantages to man outweigh these issues. As to your question Griz, there was one occasion when something inexplicable may have occurred.

"It happened approximately fourteen thousand years ago," Robulus boomed, "prior to the building of Somtrow. The dwarves of North Shamerica lived in the nearby underground village of Tregan, and they were stricken with an aggressive virus, which took Jeemis and me completely by surprise. We learned later, that the germ crossed the species barrier, from a breed of bantam chickens they raised. Jeemis and I isolated the germ in our lab, and worked literally, around the clock to learn the virus, and devise a treatment approach.

"At the peak of the disease, which caused high fevers and severe diarrhoea, often leading to death, Tregan's Chief Felbar, called a meeting of town elders. After a short speech to many mourning and fearful parents, he led a delegation of several dozen of them on the five hour journey aboveground, up to the TDS. All their questions would be answered there.

"Once the group had arrived at their TDS destination, Chief Felbar ascended to a block of rock called the Altar of Inquiry. According to oral legend, the chief was inebriated. He had drunk a flask of a type of vodka on the journey, and he addressed the TDS this way, he said, 'Lishen to me, you foolish woman! If I want to go out drinking with the boys, then I sure as…' Apparently, at that point, his mistress shouted, 'It's not your wife! It's Emulda!'

"Chief Felbar had stopped in mid-abuse at the interruption, to take stock of his surroundings. He coughed. He shook it off, like a wet dog flings away water, and he addressed the TDS, which they had named Emulda, after a popular girl at the dwarf single's bars. He said, "Emulsha, I have written an exshecutive order requiring you, in the futsure, to warn us of a pandemic, and I asksh you now, in the name of all that is horny…I mean holy, how can we cure this thickness?' Many of the attending dwarves had bought protest signs along, and they now marched back and forth, in front of Emulda, chanting 'Dwarf Lives Matter'."

Griz needed another break from carrying the lantern, and he had to trade sides with the tireless alien too. They stopped and set the heavy contraption down. When Vera came closer to the light, Griz noticed that her fashionably shredded jeans were soaked in blood, on her left leg. "What in Hades, Vera?" He asked in wonder. "Why didn't you say something?"

Bewildered, Vera looked down, and was surprised by all the blood. The wound stung, but she didn't think it so serious. She said, "I did say something; I told the demn thing to quit bleeding."

Robulus looked concerned. He said, "You humans are so fragile. Vera, if you sit down, I will stitch that up."

Vera sat down in front of the narrow light beam thrown by the lantern, with her back against the cool tunnel wall. She said, "Go on. What happened next?"

Robulus squatted down beside Vera, and took out a compact sewing kit from his coveralls. He selected needle and thread, and went to work. The alien first used scissors to cut away her left pant leg. While he cleaned the wound, with liquid from a bottle he'd scrounged from another pocket, he continued his tale. Robulus said, "Legend records that many dwarves witnessed what happened next. As per usual, eyewitnesses rarely agree on much, but we can ascertain that the TDS did change colour and became much darker. It changed shape too, before releasing a golden-brown cloud, of dust-like motes into the surrounding area, enveloping the dwarves in a dense fog.

"Within minutes it was said, all of the dwarfs present, who were feverish and ill, began to feel relief. The legend goes on to say, that when these villagers returned home, their very presence bought about the healing of others who ailed. And so, as the pandemic ended, the worship began."

Robulus completed stitching Vera's wound; a long, shallow slice in her thigh. He completed his tale too. He said, "Jeemis and I found no explanation for this alleged phenomena, but we found antibodies to the virus in all the dwarfs we tested."

He stood up and helped Vera to her feet. Griz asked, "Did you check the dwarves for nano technology?"

Robulus looked startled by the question and replied, "Of course not. It seemed likely to us that the dwarfs had acquired herd immunity. However, a mythology arose as a result of this 'event', and a religion was constructed to fit the beliefs."

Vera said, "Thank you Robulus. I'm ready, if you and Griz are." Griz was impressed by her resilience and her attitude. Vera was a journalist now, but she would always have some Aowa, farm girl tomboy in her. Blood and guts didn't bother her much. She thought of herself as tough, but tender; hardy, but hearty. "Demn! That was corny!" she scolded her thoughts.

The two males, one human, one not, picked up the lantern assemblage by the pant leg slings under Vera's purse, and continued their hike. "Twenty more minutes," Robulus said.

Chapter 32

Melanie and Jeemis walked briskly together, along the right shoulder of highway 240. It was unpaved and skinny. The shoulder consisted of a narrow band of gravel and then it slanted sharply down into a dark ditch of weeds. Jeemis walked on the inside, closest to the sluggish traffic, but that left Melanie liable to a spill. She held onto the alien's hand with hers, and he helped keep her upright.

Melanie liked the feel of his long, soft fingers. She liked Jeemis. It was so strange. He was not of Gaia, was inhuman, and yet she felt a deeper connection to him than she did the creeps from yesterday's secret inquiry. Demn! Was that only yesterday? It seemed like another age.

Four miles separated them from Poke's Peak, and they'd only been pelted with oaths and shoes twice, when a horrendous commotion erupted from behind them. They turned around to see and hear a silver tractor trailer rig flashing its headlights, racing its engine and blasting its infernal horn. It bore down hard on the vehicles in front of it and sent them darting off in different directions to avoid the onslaught.

Rosie Oh laughed in glee, as vehicle after vehicle plunged off the roadside to avoid the truck as she barrelled down on them, rumbling and roaring at five or six miles per hour! As she lifted a fifth can of beer to her lips, she spotted two individuals walking along the road.

Rosie knew immediately who they were. Not only had she heard about Donut's violent death, and Low's arrest, she'd seen the carcass of the abandoned Pissan Tanki in the median of the interstate. In the span of thirty-six minutes, the BUV was stripped down to its frame. Souvenir and trophy hunters removed and hauled or sold off, the wheels, seats, and steering wheel and engine parts. The simple pieces such as hub caps and windshield wipers had disappeared before the FIBB chopper lifted off. When Rosie had passed the area, serious mechanics with tool boxes were on site.

Rosie expected to see scammers selling these 'Alien Abduction' truck pieces and parts on FeeBay in the next few days. She imagined that dozens of copies of each part would be offered up. Who wouldn't want all ninety-nine wheels? Collector's items!

Rosie also recognised the tall pale alien and the attractive woman looking back at her in amazement, because she'd seen them at the gas station in Jewelsberg. She applied the airbrakes and brought the big rig to a halt, next to the two hikers. She lowered the passenger window with the push of a button and bellowed like a wounded buffalo, "Hey Handsome! Climb on in! You and your lady friend! Ride in style with Rosie Oh. Odd Style." She belched. "Beer is what's for dinner. Ha Ha." Belch.

Jeemis pulled the door open. He helped Melanie up and in. She wrinkled her nose up in disgust, at the odour of belched beer, which permeated the truck cab. A cloud of the noxious gas escaped out the open door, and made a small bird drunk, when it flew into the cloud. Jeemis climbed up and took a seat in the truck. He said, "That's Odd Style alright," he said after a whiff of the atmosphere. He pulled the door shut.

"Welcome aboard!" Rosie shouted. She put the truck in gear and blew the horn. They were on the move. Rosie was so excited! "I can't believe it! "She exclaimed. "This is like one of those weird synchronicity things, like in the movies! By the way, I am Rosie Oh and we are rolling with a trailer full of beer! I've been following you guys for the last four hundred miles, you know!"

Rosie wasn't drunk, she was happy high, and she was surging with enthusiasm. The very fact that she was chauffeuring an alien in her truck was proof positive that it was meant to be, that she was doing the right thing. She couldn't stop talking; there was so much to say. "I never met an alien before. Well, actually, there was this one guy and his poker was…oh, you don't want to hear that. I feel like I already know you dudes! Melanie and Jeemis, right? Are you really an alien? Is your poker all…wait. What I mean is; did you guys run Donut down on purpose? I would have! Demn right. Wanna beer?"

Rosie couldn't continue to jabber and drink beer at the same time for fear of choking. While she drank, Jeemis answered her question. He shrieked, "Yeah, I'll have an Odd Style." He pulled a can of the beer from a Styrofoam cooler that sat on the floor between the cab's two seats and popped the top. Melanie shared the seat with Jeemis.

Melanie said, "Hi Rosie. I saw your truck behind us and I noticed you at the rest stop. What ever happened to that costumed character in the red Cumaro?" she asked.

Rosie blasted the horn, and the flashers were on nonstop. She continued wending the truck through the traffic, like a lion cutting through a herd of wildebeest. She replied to Melanie, eager to speak again after the ten second lapse. She said, "Oh, yeah, that crazy Captain Shamerican character man! He was up in my fat ass like a suppository, but then, poof! He was gone."

Jeemis screeched, "The comic book man was in it for fun and fame. Once he learned that the two crooks were unavailable for further pictures, the super-goofball packed it in, and went back home. That's my guess."

* * *

Crime Blaster XL-5, the re-altered ego of naïve, cuckolded Wayne Bruce of the Winkin, Nobraska police force, stood along the shoulder of Highway 240 to Minotaur Springs. He faced the crawling traffic and poked a thumb out. Drivers and passengers alike, gazed at him in astonishment, as they crept past him at half the speed he could walk. Some of the people were rude. One told him, that he must be the famous superhero known as Icantwalkman.

CB ignored the mocking taunts and the sarcastic jeers cast at him. They didn't understand. The life of a superhero wasn't entirely like in the comic books or the movies. Crime Blaster XL-5 never had any witty dialogue going while kicking the enemy's ass, for one thing, and for another, he never really kicked any ass at all.

Those make-believe superheroes never had to contend with Murphy's poking Law! Things couldn't possibly be worse! His two foes were vanquished already, and the damsel was no longer distressed! CB's plans to thwart the criminals had been thwarted by the law! The law screwed it all up this time! The law is supposed to show up after, they aren't needed anymore! Everyone knew that!

CB had nearly turned in his superhero badge when he realised that he wasn't needed, and the world no longer required saving. He went into an internal exile, to contemplate mailing his costume in to the League of Concerned Superheroes, and resigning from the profession altogether. He had put Wayne Bruce in charge of matters, while he meditated on his future.

There would be no comic books, or video games, no movies or action figures. No Spewtube channel, no CB XL-5 socks or pyjamas! It was too much to bear. He'd steered his thoughts down a different lane. Perhaps he had missed something.

Then it hit him! CB experienced an epiphany. It was a rush, like a snort of his wife's powdered 'sinus medicine'. He was given a sign, like a personal text from Super Everything, the god of superheroes everywhere, and then CB knew what he had to do.

He was needed! This story hadn't yet ended! CB felt so stupid for not seeing the obvious! It was a superhero rule so obvious and apparent, that no one ever thought about it. It was a given, a truism, just as much as Murphy's Law was.

Destiny! It was really that demn simple; Destiny. In its most generic terms, the unspoken 'Destiny Rule' for superheroes was this: 'Where ever in the world, a superhero happens to be, that's the place, where the world will need to be saved'.

It was uncanny, but true. Imminent death and destruction followed superheroes around like stalkers. A new crisis was always right around the corner. Enemies such as plagues, climate change, asteroids, droughts, floods, liberals, earthquakes and world-ending toilet paper shortages, clung to his species like lovers.

CB XL-5 felt recharged! He needed to get his costumed super-ass to the TDS site right away! CB restored himself, and sent Wayne Bruce packing for the duration. The guy was a nut anyway. He sometimes wondered if Claire Kent and her alter ego Super Mom ever argued.

When he returned from his short hiatus, CB found that Wayne had been walking west on state highway 240 leading into Minotaur Springs. He stopped in his tracks and stuck out his thumb. Walking didn't seem sufficiently dignified for a superhero.

Crime Blaster had conversations with some of the people in the cars that inched past him. He explained that he hitchhiked because he didn't want his costume to get dirty. He wondered briefly, whether he would have had a better chance at a ride, if his costume had a cape.

A dusty black Caddylac moved towards him so slowly as to make him wonder whether time had stopped. It followed a green Hoaxwagon, but nearly two car lengths separated the two vehicles. He urged the Caddy forward with his thoughts, as if they might speed the car's progress. He discerned a woman driver behind the dusty, dirty windshield.

CB was inexplicably invested in this sad Caddylac's forward advance. He used both of his blue-gloved hands and arms, to wave the air forward, swimming in place, thinking that the slight vacuum in front of the car would assist its motion.

After an eternity or six, the black Caddylac reached his location. The passenger window slid down and the woman driver leaned across the seat to say, "Come on! Hop in!" Her voice sounded as if it resonated from deep within an echoing sinus cavity, and a nasty odour emanated from within the car. The stench reminded him of the dumpster behind the police station where Wayne worked.

CB thought he might regret it, but he stepped over and pulled the passenger side door open. The sight reminded him of the dumpster behind the police station. The floors, the seats and the dashboard were a three-dimensional collage of drink containers, bags, napkins, wrappers, straws, sauce packets and mummified fries. It was slop art.

The woman used her arm, to brush the trash off the seat and onto the floor. "Sit down," she said. "Just pack it down with your feet." CB edged his butt onto the seat and lifted his knees high and swung his legs into the car. He pulled the door shut and stomped his feet down, compacting the rubbish enough for his knees to be lower than his chin.

The driver accelerated for a few inches, to catch up to the Hoaxwagon in front of her. She wore a blue and orange smock and a pair of fluffy slippers with rabbit ears on them. "Hi! How ya doin'?" She said. She turned her head and added, "I am Sue M. Aul, personal injury attorney. Are you hurt?"

Crime Blaster XL-5 knew a few of her radio advertisements. He said, "Had a fall, call Aul."

Sue eagerly responded, "Did you have a fall?"

"Unfortunately," CB said, "I didn't, sorry."

"That's fine; we'll work something out. Do you superhero for a living or is it a hobby? Do you have hobby insurance? I know a good person in the business."

CB was not going to let this situation make him suicidal again. He kept repeating his new mantra: 'Things could always be worse'.

Chapter 33

Torchy was an impatient driver by nature. His great thirst and the unmoving traffic only added to his agitation. He drove the I-Haul truck as if it were an emergency vehicle, honking its horn and operating its flashers. He bellowed out his glassless window too, "Get out of the way! My wife is having her baby!"

Kate Armstrong was standing up, with her head and torso protruding from the passenger window. The pillow under her blouse gave the illusion of pregnancy, and her shrieks of agony were meant to express her labour pains. The ruse was discontinued after poor results. Rude drivers and their families, shouted and yelled back at them, with irrelevant comments such as, "You're going the wrong way, you poking idiots!" and, "The poking hospital is north of here! ".

A normal person in Al's position, would have blown up, when seeing the stripped skeleton of the white Pissan Tanki in the median. But Al wasn't exactly normal. He needed more information before he blew up. Torchy was so disturbed by the sight, he forgot about beer for a while. Kate returned to her seat in the cab, had her baby, and pitched the pillow out the window.

Al turned on the truck's radio, and Kate searched for facts on her selfone, but all she could find was CON and MNBS. Al flipped through the AM and the FM dials, and every last station, no matter their regular format, was doing TDS news! The world had gone crazier! In record time too! Al settled on a radio station, and those in the cab learned, that one of the BEWBs was dead, and the other one was in custody of the FIBB. The kidnap victims had been unbelievably set free! Apparently, the alien and the woman were on foot now.

Al was dismayed that Loser Low was taken alive. The idiot would tie him to the crime. Pitch Al Darkly Esquire would prevail in the end however. He and his team of lawyers would make slush of all that crime nonsense easy enough. District attorneys were for sale, and he would buy the one he needed.

Even if he was charged with a serious crime, and had to defend himself in court, it was so easy to trick jurors into making leaps of faith that Al worried not.

Most of the dummies, who served on juries, were raised by their family television, and they believed that all crimes and court cases were wrapped up in sixty minutes time, not counting commercials. When he was a practicing attorney, Al simply copied television when he presented a case. He mesmerised jurors. Al would use the same teevee script strategy again, if he was ever a defendant.

Al still had a chance at immortality! The alien and the scientist must be going to the TDS! There was no reason for the feds to let the alien go, except for his knowledge of the TDS location. The government, or the military, or maybe even the president, wanted the secret too.

Al had to get there before the feds assumed control of it and closed it off to the public. He needed to win. He imagined being the first person at the counter, when the TDS opened for business at midnight, placing his order, and destroying the joint after he was served, but before anyone else was. He also considered planting a flag on the TDS and declaring it as his. He could patent it and sell the rights.

Al turned off the radio, and he addressed Torchy and Kate about another matter. He said, "We need to keep this information secret from Don Crews. He doesn't know about the BEWB failure, and he will freak out about his investment."

Kate agreed. She said, "He won't think to look on his selfone for news. That's just for business calls and porn."

The demn stifling traffic and his beer withdrawals, combined to create a noxious miasma in Torchy. His ugly mood continued its descent, until it arrived in the pits of misery. He wanted company there, and there were enough people for a party in the truck's cargo box. A smile appeared between his moustache and beard, a smile that chilled Kate's blood when she happened to look at him.

Torchy said, "Hang on, the truck is running rough."

Al and Kate didn't know what he referred to, but Al knew Torchy well enough to prepare. He pulled on his seat belt and told Kate, "Buckle up, Honey." She did.

Torchy stomped on the accelerator, and rapidly closed the two car lengths, between the I-Haul and the car in front of it. He slammed on the brakes, and skidded to an abrupt halt. Torchy waited for the tan sedan ahead of them to gain some space, before he repeated the action. Al was laughing so hard that tears poured down his face. His ribs ached as he howled in delight.

Kate too, laughed and laughed and laughed some more. Torchy was enjoying himself immensely. The star temple celebrities in the back of the truck, must be rolling around and bouncing off the walls and each other, like rag dolls in a clothes dryer.

Chapter 34

"This is the Late Story on CON, and I'm Pixie Dixie with breaking news. Tonight, one of the alleged kidnappers, was kidnapped by the unidentified occupants of a mysterious black helicopter, that witnesses say descended out of the dark skies of Colorotta Springs, to whisk away the BEWB, allegedly identified variously as Lou Snert, Loser and Shanghai Low, leaving behind, a mutilated white Pissan Tanki truck, which allegedly served as the kidnapper's criminal transport vehicle, while allowing Melanie Gryzolski, the presidential science advisor and the formerly abducted alien Jeemis, to go free."

Pixie placed an oxygen mask over her mouth and nose, and inhaled deeply several times before attempting her next sentence. She said, "This incident proves positively, absolutely, unequivocally and uncontestably, and now is certain beyond any shadow of a reasonable doubt, and must therefore convince every rational person and their pets, that President Crumm, was and still is, colluding with alleged aliens, to accelerate climate change, and use their advanced, alien, military technologies and weapons to invade Greenland, and transform it into his own private eighteen-hundred-hole golf course with casinos!"

Pixie nearly fainted from lack of oxygen before she completed that sentence, and she required an extra breath from her tank before she recovered. Her producer insisted that breathing in the middle of a sentence was gross, and so prohibited it. She was proud of herself for getting through the entire thing. Her writer always challenged her to dig deep.

"Good evening, America! This is Blondie Blundi for 'I Witnessed News' on KRAQ TV in Ohaha, Nobraska. I am standing outside, at the downtown FIBB office building, where I can count the cars of eighteen dedicated, tireless men and women who remain on top of this investigation. They have been pounding away at the alleged accomplice Vometta Wilde, with one agent after another, going one on one with her, using deep, probing interrogation techniques to reveal her deepest secrets.

"The overflowing dumpsters you see behind me are a testament to these hard driving agents. Every empty pizza box, all of the many chicken carcasses and the innumerable donut boxes that you see piled high, tell the tale, of how much time and effort is being pumped into this investigation. These devoted servants will be humping and sweating through the night, if need be, while we sleep safely in our beds. We owe them our thanks."

Vometta Wilde listened to the report, while she entertained one of those hard-driving agents. His wife watched. One smoked ham, and two dozen assorted donuts lay on the interrogation mattress, next to her. She was chewing the last chicken wing, from a carton. She swallowed, belched and said, "Fwakis." The agent's wife climbed in.

"Tonight, on NBS news with your host Ide Rather, we delve into the alien abduction hoax, starring President Darryl K. Crumm. The president's predicted future attempt, to cover-up this criminal behaviour, will certainly, and finally, be enough to expel this traitor from office! It has been reliably leaked to us by our usual unidentified, nameless, anonymous secret source, that at midnight tonight, the alleged aliens will call down millions upon millions of their invisible spaceships, and turn Gaia into their own world's Trash Disposal Service. That's the TDS!

"Peaceful protests, in at least thirty cities tonight, have resulted in seventy deaths and untold billions of dollars, in burned and looted businesses. Some of these demonstrations included rapes and robberies as part of their message. Police went into hiding and made no arrests.

"Unfortunately, some cops stayed on the job. In one case a friendly neighbourhood shootout between a happy drunk, and one murderous cop, ended in tragedy, when the heavily armed drunk man's defences were breached, and he was seriously murdered by the wounded police officer. The National Guard was put on high alert by seven Demolist governors, and then sent back to bed."

"This is the BBQ. First, in royal news, the queen celebrated her one hundred and nineteenth birthday today, and hardly looked a day over a hundred and ten. She proclaimed that, from this day forward, September third, be forever known as Great Brital's National 'Act Stupid Day'.

"In alien abduction news, we have it on no authority, that four cruise ships at sea have suffered mutinies, or attempted mutinies by passengers and, or staff,

218

due to fear and panic, related to our reports. One cruise ship captain was reportedly forced to walk the plank into shark-infested waters off the coast of Oz. He is feared lost at sea.

"We have also learned that long lines have formed at traditional suicide sites, such as the Golden Glut Bridge, Viagran Falls and the Great Canyon. Vultures are on standby. Ammunition and gun sales skyrocketed today in the United States, and the stock market plummeted, as people prepared for the coming apocalypse. Gun shops have been cleaned out across the pond, by shoppers and looters alike."

"Good evening; this is Woof Blister with breaking news. Tonight, in Destroyt, several police cars were set on fire by a far-right wing, extremist group, calling themselves People for the Ethical Treatment of Aliens. Spokesperson for the group, Comet Rider, said the burning cop cars were to serve as landing lights for the spaceships.

"Comet Rider was heard to say, 'People are scared as Hades! It's like electing a liberal; you know it's going to hurt somewhere, but you're just not sure where'."

"Good evening. I am Keuwa Knon and, you're watching 'Conspiracy Television', the show that knows. So, let me break it down for you. This is all about the stupidity virus. The TDS is the drawing card; it's the bait, to gather thousands of people together. People from all around the country will be crowded close together in one small area.

"The aliens will then use a bioweapon, perhaps some kind of germ which they designed in a laboratory, to cure humans of stupidity. The bioweapon must be able to infect or attach to others, and like ripples in a pond, the effects will spread outward, and we will be whole again!

"Why would alleged aliens do this? Why would a pair of unidentified foreign outlaws, want to cure the human race of the effects of the SV? Think. Follow me. It's simple; they are sick and tired of living on a planet full of poking idiots!"

Chapter 35

Their awkward lantern sat on the tunnel floor, aimed at Robulus. Griz and Vera waited while the alien opened a heavy iron door set into the tunnel wall. Robulus pushed it open, and then entered his underground broadcast studio. Overhead lights came on automatically. Griz and Vera followed him inside.

Griz dimly heard a generator's chugging noise. He asked, "You have an uninterrupted power supply?"

Robulus replied, his booming voice an aural a-bomb, "Indeed. It exhausts outside the mountain, after passing through a series of cooling filters." He walked around turning equipment on. He directed the two worn and wounded humans to a pair of chairs. The sound stage was set up similar to the one down in Somtrow. Their chairs faced a MegaScreen TV on the end wall. The screen lit up now, and it was divided into eight smaller rectangles, as was the one down below in the dwarf town.

Vera and Griz were amazed. "Look at the cars and the people!" Vera exclaimed. Parking lot A was filled to capacity and B was nearly full as well, and cars still poured in. Thousands of animated people stood in line behind Gate 1, or milled about in the parking lots.

Griz asked, "Is Melanie out there somewhere, with the kidnappers?"

Robulus said, "Negative. If they were present, my sentry drones would have alerted me. I have a spare eyefone up here. I will check it for news."

Vera asked, "Are you directing the Unveiling, from inside this tunnel lair of yours?

Griz answered, "He's going to broadcast it to the world from here."

Robulus read the latest news on his eyefone quickly, and then, without batting an eye, he said, "Melanie and Jeemis are free. Donut is dead and Loser is locked up. Jeemis sent me a message that they are well, and on their way here." His thunderous voice overpowered the cheers from Griz and Vera. The two humans came out of their chairs to share their joy. Vera and Griz hugged each other.

Robulus waited for them to pull apart before he said, "The Unveiling will be broadcast to the world live, just as you said, Griz."

Griz and Vera sat down in their viewing chairs, to face the MegaScreen. Griz's ribs were regretting the tight hug with Vera, but he thought it well worth the pain. Vera felt a warm thrill inside, and she admonished her heart for beating such a dangerous rhythm, especially for a man; and one she met less than twelve hours ago!

It was all the excitement, and the strain of the shared adventures, that had her behaving like a silly, young girl. It would pass, she told herself. She redirected her attention to the matter at hand. The Unveiling was less than an hour away.

Robulus stood behind a podium, upon which sat a computer. The loud tall alien was to the left of the two humans, and he faced the MegaScreen too. He said, "Any more questions? We have a few minutes, before we go live on television."

Griz deferred to Vera, "Ladies first, "he said.

Vera thanked him, and said, "If I understand you Robulus, that tank is filled with mega-doses of an anti-stupidity virus bug. That bothers me, Robulus. What is really going on?"

Robulus said, "You will notice that the tank overlooks the concession area, which can contain up to eight hundred people. I will show you how the infecting will be done."

He spoke to his computer, "Blipey, zoom in on camera eight, to the dispersion unit." The aliens named their artificial intelligence Blipey, in honour of the scientist on Uzgabada who invented true artificial intelligence.

The stationary camera zoomed in to a boxy structure beneath the grey tank, and between its four spidery legs. The six-foot square box was closed in on the sides, but open front and back like a huge fan, which is basically what it was. A spinning propeller forced air through the box, which was honeycombed somewhat like a car radiator. The front of the box flared outward towards the concession area, about thirty feet away.

Robulus explained, "This diffuser unit is fed the bacterial solution via pump, from the tank above. Three sprayers, then blow the fluid though the diffuser unit, and the powerful fan behind it, blows a mist into the people in the concession area."

Vera asked her follow up question, "Are you just going to infect everyone with this respiratory bacterium of yours, without any consent?"

Griz commented, "Briefly; the TDS is the draw, to attract crowds of people, and then you simply douse them with whatever, and de-stupefy them. Correct?"

Robulus skipped over their moral concerns. He and Jeemis had debated the subject for many months, and the argument of the greater good won out. Ridding the planet of human idiocy, overcame the ethics of the process. He said, "I mentioned before, that this bacterial infection has two side effects on humans. You recall that after I told you that the common cold would vanish as one result of our Bugsy bacterium, I was interrupted before I could tell you the second strange side effect.

Griz said, "That's right. Is it important?"

Robulus boomed, "It could have enormous implications for the human population."

Vera wondered about the alien's use of the word 'population', and began to ask him a question, when Blipey announced, "Alert! Please acknowledge. Alert!" Blipey's voice was that of the famous western movie actress, Joan Wayne, and to Griz's ears, a computer with a cute drawl, made a crisis sound amusing.

Robulus said, "Acknowledged; details please."

Blipey announced, "Jeemis has entered the area. Look to camera number two. You will see a tractor-trailer rig, with a silver cab and a trailer advertising Odd Style beer. It seems that he is accompanied by two humans, one a female and the other of unidentified gender."

Robulus said, "Enlarge camera two. Seven of the eight camera views vanished from the MegaScreen, and the picture from camera two showing the truck in parking lot B, now filled the entire screen. Griz rose from his chair, and approached it to enlarge his view further. The big rig was parked in the vicinity of a raggedy Winabagel RV, which had a line of men outside of it, who looked like they wanted in.

The two humans and the alien kept their eyes focused on the occupants of the truck. They exited the truck cab. Jeemis first, followed by Melanie, stepped down from the passenger's side, and Rosie Oh came from the driver's side. Griz nearly wept with relief to see his daughter walking, talking and smiling.

The trio in the tunnel lair watched as Jeemis and Vera shook hands with the big androgynous driver, and departed the area. They began walking towards a robot barn at the end of lot A. Rosie Oh went to the rear of her trailer, broke the seal and opened its doors.

Robulus told Blipey, "Go pick them up." All of the hundreds of robots in operation on site, were extensions of Blipey, and thus, all of the connected devices were addressed the same. Blipey rolled out of the barn as a robocart, and went out to pick up Jeemis and Melanie. It weaved through and amongst the people. It also had to avoid vehicles that cruised back and forth, with their drivers looking for spaces to park.

Jeemis smiled when he recognised the cart coming towards Melanie and him. It resembled an all-terrain vehicle without a steering wheel. The single bench seat was positioned over the rear tires, and was elevated, so that the passengers sat high and visible. A pair of bright lights looked out from the front of the cart, and illuminated the ground ahead of it.

Blipey-cart stopped in front of Melanie and Jeemis, and said, "Please be seated." Melanie laughed when she recognised the voice of Joan Wayne. They climbed up and were seated behind a steel bar, which gave them something to hold on to. She was fatigued, and her shoulders drooped. She was happy to have her blue windbreaker; the night was cool and clear.

Jeemis said, "Robulus sent the cart. If he's here, so is your father." The robocart set off across the parking lot and angled towards the lower end. Melanie grabbed the alien's arm and pulled him around to face her. "What?" She exclaimed. "My father is here? With Robulus? I don't know whether to kick you or kiss you, you lousy alien!"

Jeemis said, "Kick me hard! You know how much I love pain."

Melanie stood up, and held onto the bar, turned and kicked Jeemis. He sighed dramatically and said, "We're a match made in Heaven."

"Where are they?" Melanie asked. "I want to see my dad."

Jeemis said, "Blipey stop. Back up to the light pole we just passed by, with camera two on top." The vehicle did as instructed. When they were about fifty feet away from the streetlamp, Jeemis told the cart to stop. He pointed up to where the tiny camera was situated, twenty feet above them. He said, "Wave to your father, Melanie!"

The two bright lights projecting from the lamppost blinded Melanie, but she smiled hugely and waved at the sky. A few blocks away, under the rock of Poke's Peak, Griz saw the wave and he asked Robulus, "Can I speak to her?"

Robulus answered him, "Absolutely. Come up to the podium. Blipey, patch Griz through to the cart speaker."

Griz jumped to his feet, and his ribs sharply reminded him to behave. He went to the dais and said, "Hey Lady! You're a trooper alright, and you have a proud father!"

Melanie thought that she'd never heard a sweeter sound, and tears arose in the corners of her blue eyes. She clenched both fists, and thrust them above her head in salute. Suddenly she didn't feel tired anymore. Dad shed a few tears too.

Jeemis told Blipey to transport them to Gate 2, above the concessions area. Two routes to that area existed. Only one path was open to the public however, and that's where people lined up, ten deep, waiting for Gate 1 to open. Blipey would take the alternate route to the upper gate, thus bypassing the waiting lines of people.

The moon and the stars shone down, competing with the many lamps and lights, and thus little was left in shadows. Two drones patrolled silently above the people, and scores of robots kept watch, and provided other services on the ground. Some people thought the parking-bots, and guide/info-bots were for their amusements and tried to push them over or steal them. Each robot delivered a powerful static electric discharge, when someone approached within ten inches, and thus discouraged most. Others required a second stiffer jolt.

Blipey drove Melanie and Jeemis towards the second road, which lay at the far west end of parking lot B. An iron gate opened, when the robocart approached. The entry gate and the high fence it hung on, wore square, yellow signs that warned, in bold black letters, "DANGER! DO NOT ENTER!" They rode past and the gate shut and locked behind them.

The steep road led them, in a series of hairpin turns, directly beneath a bulge in the mountainside. Jeemis remarked on it to Melanie. He said, "The TDS is directly above us here, hidden behind a veil of rock." His shrieking voice scared off a foraging chipmunk.

Melanie gazed up at the bulge. A ten-foot diameter white bullseye was chalked onto the rock. She asked, "And at midnight, you will unveil it, and remove tons of rock?" She was a sceptic prior to becoming a world-renowned scientist, and Melanie's education had only reinforced her doubting instincts.

The robocart rolled up the smooth road of planed rock quietly. The outside temperature seemed fixed at fifty-eight degrees. Jeemis screeched, "The face of rock protecting the TDS from humans was constructed by me and Robulus fourteen thousand years ago. We fabricated the lightweight, durable material. It contains a strong honeycomb interior structure, and withstands contraction, expansion and erosion. The Unveiling will amaze you; I think."

Melanie said, "Tell me about the TDS." The robocart completed its climb, and now approached Gate 2, from behind it. The cart reached the gate and came to a stop there. It was twelve minutes after eleven. Jeemis said, "Blipey, open Gate 1, and the concessions." The gates were constructed of steel tubes, and they reached across the twelve-foot-wide roads they blocked. Gate 1 swung open, inwards.

Gate number one, lay about a third of a mile downhill from Jeemis' and Melanie's position behind Gate 2 but, with the surfeit of lights, it was easy to see the flood of people pouring through the lower gate when it opened.

A mass of people surged ahead, running enthusiastically up the high mountain trail. The leading ranks of runners thinned out rapidly, their fervour waned when their oxygen did, and after thirty yards, the frontrunners were reduced to a gasping, stumbling walk.

The concessionaire robots were open for business, and were selling TDS T-shirts, and hats, water, soda pop and short order food items, like beefburgers and hotdoggies. Two thousand gallons of bacterial solution, hung above the people who were starting to enter the concessions area. The big grey tank, standing on four skeletal legs, held the Bugsy bacterium cure to human stupidity, endemic in the world population for nineteen idiotic years. Jeemis told Melanie about the TDS.

Chapter 36

"You're listening to CON, and I'm your host, Reelie Impoartint, with breaking news! Anonymous sources have informed us that President Darryl Crumm, who went off the reservation and trashed the American people's day with his wasted flight to Onnitt Air Power Base, to harangue and harass some brave, but leaky public servants, has landed, in Air Power One, at the Air Power Academy, in Colorotta Springs! What the maniac of the Off-White House is up to, is anyone's guess, but Gawd help us all!"

"This is Iggy Bliss of MNBS, and we have breaking news to bring you! As we reported earlier, the President made an unscheduled stop at Onnitt Air Power Base. This president is unprecedented in his unpresidentialness. He has now sent Air Power One, to the Air Power Academy in Colorotta Springs, while he secretly remained in the nuclear bunker beneath Onnitt APB. Crumm plans to use nuclear missiles to blast the alien invaders from the skies, but the aliens are wise to that, and plan to invade Cooba and not the United States, because they like cigars, so it is said."

"I'm your host, Pam Spray, with KNOW in Colorotta Springs, and I am coming to you live, from one of two, overflowing parking lots, below the looming Poke's Peak Mountain near Minotaur Springs. As you can see, as Zoey pans the camera, we are surrounded by thousands of cars. Flocks, herds and packs of people, of every age, sex, race, criminal record, and profession are here for the great Unveiling of the mysterious TDS, thirty-six minutes from now.

"Let's talk to a few of the people, and find out what motivated them to come here tonight. I find it curious to see a moving truck, pulling in to the lot, and I think it might be interesting to talk to the occupants. Zoey, let's get their story, they're parking."

Torchy parked the I-Haul, facing the silver cab of a big rig. He turned off the ignition and exited the truck cab. His boss, Pitch Al followed Kate out the passenger door. All three were awed at the spectacle, the crowds, and the lights.

The excitement was growing, it was palpable. One could see it, in hopeful faces and hear it in happy voices. It was like a Crumm rally.

Torchy smelled something too. A scent of beer wafted up to his quivering nostrils, and it wasn't his body odour. Neurons fired, synapses snapped, and an answer appeared in his taste memory; Odd Style! Ding! Ding! His jaw trembled. His tongue sat up and begged. The tractor trailer! He knew what he had to do, but he had to bide his time for few minutes. He needed to hear from his passengers first. They might want to say, 'Thanks for the ride'.

Eleven angry, dishevelled celebrities tumbled, and crawled out of the truck's cargo box. Syko More seemed to have sprung a leak, he was flat, and he rolled out a few minutes later, after re-inflating. The stars were a mess. The stop and go ride, had them doing somersaults in the back of the truck. Their perfect hair, clothing and accessories looked awful. Their luggage had beaten them up in the turbulence, and some bags had popped open, strewing clothes and toiletry items all over the place. Obscenities and profanities erupted from the stars, lifting up to the stars. It was like Hade's Choir practice. Voices high and low sung out long strings of hate and abuse, and the pop stars serenaded Torchy.

Torchy absorbed the verbal assault and swelled up like a proud father. A scat-eating grin divided his moustache from his beard. He was enjoying this immensely. Robby Indero was on his game. He was an impresario of expletives, a master of the art, and he'd saved his best for Torchy. Torchy was honoured.

Indero pointed a gnarled finger at the big guy, and bravely let loose with a string of invectives to make one's ears curl. "You stinkin' drinkin', no-good drivin', butthole divin', rectum wreckin', poker peckin', cooch chewin', moo screwin', doggie doin', son of a stenchy wench! How dare you!"

The other ten Temple Stars, just couldn't keep up with Robby, and they gave up after a few cursory curses, to attend to straightening out their clothes, hair, jewellery and makeup, without a trailer to do it in.

Pitch Al was so impressed, by Indero's Ashcan winning performance, that he remarked, "You improve all the time Robby. That was museum quality. Stakespeare, roll over and all that."

Local television reporter, Pam Spray and her cameraman Zoey, had captured it all, and they hoped that their viewers could appreciate Indero's diversity of profanity. He was a true impresario.

Even tough guy actor Robby Indero, had a soft spot for flattery, and, with a hint of something approaching civility, he told Al, "Poking practice, makes father poking, ass smoking perfect."

The parking lots were awash with hordes of people wandering hither and thither, or running to get in the growing line of dreamers trying to reach the crowded concession area, while waiting for gate number two to swing open. A half mile long line of excited people snaked up the mountain road.

The celebrities were soon spotted by a passer-by. Her shout went up, followed by dozens more, as others recognised the stars who'd fallen to Gaia. People began to crowd around the dirty almost dozen of pop idols, to take pictures and record their profanities.

Kate Armstrong knew what to do. She collected Don Crews, and set up the autograph line again. She raised the price to six dollars per this time around, without telling Crews. Bobby knew what to do too; there was a camera rolling. He turned to his collection of mumbling, grumbling, distressed temple saints and said, "Follow me and line up behind me so you all get seen."

Robby led his flock towards the camera. To see the famous Robby Indero approach her for an interview, was beyond anything that Pam Spray could have ever hoped for, but here he was. She nodded to Zoey and began her spiel. "Look who has come to Minotaur Springs, to celebrate the unveiling of the TDS. It is an honour Mr Indero. Would you mind telling us why you and your celebrity entourage are here today?"

Robby stepped up to the microphone. He barely glanced at Pam. He glared and scowled at the camera though, before replying to the question. Then he said, "We are here, to stop this unholy unveiling! This blasphemous alien god must be smashed!" The actor started to tremble and shake. The strain of uttering an entire sentence, without a word of profanity in it, had weakened him, and he didn't know if he had another one in him. He was tough though. He could do this.

Robby took a deep breath, refocused and explained. He said, "I am the head priest of the Sacred Stars Temple and these are my apostles. This alien TDS deity is a heretic, and must be cancelled." Sweat beaded on his brow. His lips were dry. His fingertips felt numb and tingly. He didn't know how much more polite conversation he could make.

Miss Pam Spray erred at this point, and asked a question that caused all of the actor's prior restraint to vanish. She asked, "Why does your church, use an I-Haul moving truck for transporting its apostles?"

The near coven of celebrity apostles, endeared some of their fans with their angry replies, but repelled others. All of the stars were eager to answer the TV reporter's question, and they erupted as one, spewing profanities and raving like lunatics, except for Don Crews who was signing autographs. The KNOW television station quickly broke for a few commercial advertisements. Pam Spray escaped the area as quickly as she could in high heels.

Al was tired of the nonsense and he announced, "I need to be the first person in line, so I'm heading on up." He didn't want the temple saints slowing him down. It would be difficult enough to cut in line a couple thousand times, without a train following behind. Don was not going to let Al beat him to the head of the line! He had an investment to protect, and he didn't care what Indero said. He and Kate closed the autograph business, and hurried to Al's side.

Torchy was telling Al, "I'm taking the rest of the night off Boss. I got some beer drinking to catch up on, and I see a long line stretching behind the beer hauling rig in front of us." Then he turned to Kate, and said, "You can handle this one, better than me. Help them to the front of the line. I'm outta here."

Al, Kate and Don strode off, heading towards the lines of people leading up the mountain road. Robby Indero let blast with another flurry of filth, as he and his temple of stars hurried to catch up with them. Don Crews used his charm and fame, to cut past one row after another, of eager excited people. Al and Kate used Don. Robby used his charm and fame too, but his charm was expressed in different terms. Terms such as, "Get outta my poking way! I'm a poking tough poking guy! Move!" Nine entitled celebs followed him.

Al and Kate stayed back, and let Crews do his schmooze. It was highly successful for the most part, until they were about halfway up to Gate 2 and the concessions area. They were blocked by a giant of a person, half as big as Poke's Peak. Her brother was even bigger, and together the two blocked the wide road leading up the mountainside. Don Crews smiled up at them and ducked beneath the woman's legs to cut ahead of the pair.

The hulking mass of muscular masculinity looked down with amusement at the little darling and so did her brother. The man laid a huge heavy hand atop Crews' head, to hold the rascal in place, like a kid with a beetle, and he said,

"The line starts at the back, not the front." His deep voice thundered from above, like a god's.

Don couldn't look up, to see what was holding him in place, but he shouted, "Do you know who I am?"

The mountainous man said, "No. Do you?"

His huge sister said, "Perhaps if you have some identification, we can help you." The two giants sounded alike too.

Don Crews would have rolled his eyes, if the downward pressure on his head hadn't been so fierce. His neck bent into a vee shape and his knees quivered. He forced from his constricted throat, the name of his biggest movie draw, as a form of ID. "Pop Gun!" he cried out. Al and Kate watched with amusement.

The giant said, "Okay then Pop, get thee behind me."

Kate Armstrong stepped forward at this point. She posed in the basic Kung Frute martial art fighting stance, and she said, "Now, that wasn't very neighbourly of you folks." Kate was a fifty-eight-degree, black hole belt in Kung Frute.

The pair of colossi was astounded! Both of them were thirty-three-degree black hole belts in Kung Frute! The woman giant bellowed, "We're like family!" She and her brother posed in the identical fight stance, with one clawed hand outstretched, to rip the gonads off with, and with pursed lips, to spit in the foe's eyes.

Kate couldn't believe their luck! There were less than three dozen Kung Frute masters in the entire world, so meeting two of them was beyond chance, like what happens in movies. She dropped her claw and swallowed her spit. "We are needed at the front of the line," she hollered up to them. The giants nodded their heads, causing a slight downdraft. The male pointed to Pitch Al Darkly and asked, "Him too?" He wrinkled up his nose as if he smelled something rotten.

Kate said, "Him too."

The female giant farted, and a couple of miles away, a tree that took the brunt of it, died. The trio was allowed to pass, and continued up the road, coaxing, cajoling and autographing their way ahead. Robby Indero had observed the entire ordeal between Kate and the two big people, and he knew what to do to pass them. He looked back at his faithful flock of sainted sheep and said, "Watch this."

Robby loved crowds. Performing meant nothing, without masses of adoring fans, fainting at one's famous feet. Indero's acolytes pushed in closer to see their hero in action. Robby strutted confidently forward, and made as if ready to pass the two supersized siblings. Then he walked between the brother giant's legs, and cut in line ahead of the pair. The sister growled, "Beat it, pipsqueak."

Indero tried to cheat the easy way first, and he said, "Look at us! We are poking, big name, poking celebrities on a poking big mission from Elvin poking Parsley!"

The two biggies looked behind and down, and they scanned the blank faces of the ten pop stars. It seemed obvious to them, that these nuts were filled with a religious fervour. The big brother looked disappointed after his brief visual survey. He said, "And I'm just poking big. Get outta here!"

Robby played his trump card. He assumed the Kung Frute fighting position that he'd seen demonstrated and said loudly, "That wasn't very neighbourly of you folks," exactly as Kate had done.

A hush fell over the crowd. Hundreds of people were mesmerised, by the performance which unfolded before them. It was like a movie, and they watched with intensity. Popcorn seemed to appear from nowhere and was chomped ferociously. Selfones recorded all the action.

The male giant aped Indero, and he posed in the extremely rare martial art form known as Kung Frute, which is taught in only one small village in Outer Mongoland. Then, quick as a serpent, he struck. He spat a pint-sized glob of saliva into Indero's eyes and clawed Robby's scrotum hard, lifting him from the ground.

Robby was tossed to the hard rock ground, and landed on his butt. No one laughed. No one made a sound. No one wanted to miss a single blistering profanity laced tirade. They would delay their gratification, and laugh later. Robby was smart though, and he quickly recovered from his unseemly treatment. He rolled to his feet with a big fat smile plastered across his face and yelled, "Cut!"

The mood of the crowd transformed from jollity, to wonder and amazement. They were watching a movie being filmed! Robby Indero was acting! The giants were actors! This was awesome. Applause broke out, with cheers and whistles.

Indero was brushing the dust from his nine-hundred-dollar jeans when he saw another road winding up the mountainside, half a mile away. He recalled seeing a cart going up that path. He kicked himself. Demn! That's the back entrance for the talent! That was how the VIPs got to the stage without passing through the fans. They were VIPs.

Robby Indero, like a modern-day prophet turned to his flock and said, "That poking way!" Bobby pointed to the alternate road, which would be their personal backstage pass. Lem Kerry squealed, "What about Don Crews? He's way up ahead."

Beyondme, Arti P, Harley Skeen, Pike Flea and the rest of the star temple saints were all thinking the same thought; "Kill Lem Kerry". It was too late though. Indero answered the question, and there was nothing they could do about it, but listen to his swearing and learn. They followed Robby at a distance however, as he led them to the lower end of parking lot B, because he was cursing Crews with every step.

The stars marched onward, never stopping to pose for worshipping fans, who wanted a photo, autographed panties or a signed beer can. Syko More moved like a tank without treads, and even trailed far behind Okra Wipmee.

The celebs stopped in front of the secured gate, which barred further progress. They waited until Syko More caught up with them. He panted and wheezed and gasped for breath, like an engine starving for air. The gate was decked with warning signs and danger signs, and do not enter signs and was made of iron pipe. Indero knew that the signs did not apply to the talent. They were meant to keep out the riff raff. So, he bent down and slid his head and torso between the pipes and pulled his legs up and through. "It's a cinch," he announced.

It proved to be a simple feat for everyone, except for two of the stars. Okra Wipmee got herself stuck, with one thick leg and one fat boob on either side of the pipe. Labrat Jakes pulled on her leg and Tod Einer pulled on her hair. Her hair proved to be a wig, which came off her bald head. Einer fell on his ass. Okra cursed and swore and screamed. With each word she expelled more breath, and by the time she finished her expletive filled rant, she was so deflated, that she fell through the gate.

More imagination was needed however, to find some method, by which a five-foot-thick package could be forced to pass a three-foot opening, and get Syko More on the other side of the gate. When Harley Skeen explained his solution, Indero was so overjoyed, he nearly smiled! The others saw the genius of the idea, but it didn't seem right somehow.

Robby organised a work crew and spurred them to action. He assigned Tod, Labrat and Lonny Doop their tasks and they obeyed for fear of a profanity attack.

Those three men slipped back through the pipes to the other side, where Syko nervously awaited their help.

Indero donned his director's hat and began the scene. "Lower your head More! You are a battering ram! You are breaching the walls of your alien masters! If you fail, well then poke you. We'll leave your fat poking ass here. Is that motivation?"

Director Indero now spoke to the three extras, he said, "I want all six of your hands pushing that fat poking butt, through the gate and across the poking finish line. When I say 'action' I want Syko More, to keep his head down and start rushing the gate, like a raging bull, and I want you three assistants to push from behind with all of your combined might."

The scene was a cut on the third attempt, and now their pilgrimage could continue. The damaged gate they left behind could now admit a small car between its bent and twisted pipes. Syko dented his head slightly, but it was nothing serious.

At around the same time that Indero had been playing at Kung Frute master, a dusty black Caddylac rolled into lot A, where Pam Spray and Zoey of KNOW TV were live, on the air, doing interviews with interesting looking people. Crime Blaster XL-5 was overjoyed that his ride in the Caddy had come to an end. CB had been forced to escape into his colourful fantasy life, to block out the non-stop jabbering of personal injury attorney, Sue M. Aul. She discharged more tired clichés from her mouth, than a worn politician while she drove.

CB XL-5 knew that Destiny would wait for his arrival, before any serious trouble popped up. That's always the way it was for superheroes; they were needed most, whenever they got there. He exited the Caddylac trashcan quickly, once Sue parked it. He had to pee!

CB filled his lungs with fresh mountain air, hoping to rid his nostrils of the car's stench. In fact, CB felt some concern that his olfactory nerves may have suffered a post traumatic stench syndrome, which could plague Wayne Bruce for many years to come. Sue M. Aul was happy to part ways with the weirdo in the patriotic costume. She had to seek out the hurt and the injured anyway, and give them one of her business cards.

Crime Blaster was walking quickly towards a row of handipottis edging the parking lot, so that he could pee, when he was stopped by a lady with a microphone. A cameraman accompanied her. She said, "Good evening, I am Pam Spray and we're live on KNOW TV in Colorotta Springs. I like your fancy getup. What's the story behind your costume, and what is its significance tonight?"

Crime Blaster looked up to the heavens, and thanked Super-Everything, the god of superheroes. CB's ride with the lawsuit lawyer had been providential after all, and had led him here, to this time and place in front of a camera! He pulled in his stomach, puffed his chest out, and replied in a deep superhero voice, with a hint of humour in the tone.

He said, "Thank you for asking Miss Spray. I am Crime Blaster XL-5, and I am here to save the world in the nick of time, from the evil…something or others." His bladder was near to bursting, but he had to have his say while he had the chance. He started to rock on his heels, as if that would assuage the pressure on his bladder.

Pam smiled lamely, as if she knew exactly what he was talking about. She skipped over it all, as if it needed no follow-up or explanation and she asked, "Crime Blaster XL-5; is that like your superhero name or something? Maybe you're with the movie stars that passed by five minutes earlier?"

He said, "There's no doubt about it. I'm a superhero, and it is time I took my leave, midnight approaches." CB scratched his masked chin and asked, "Who do you think should play me in the movie version?" He hoped that one of his superpowers involved not peeing himself in public. His heel rocking had become more frantic, but he stopped when the urine waves crashed against his bladder walls.

Pam said, "Most real superheroes have better dialogue, with corny jokes. What is the evil you save us from tonight?"

He said, "Most superheroes have better writers. Look, I have yet to identify the evil foe I face, but things could always be worse; I might be stuck in traffic with Sue M Aul. Now I must go!" He couldn't run or hurry to the handipotti, it was too risky. He waddled away as if he were holding a wet bar of soap in his rectum. He made it in time and took a deep breath before he entered one of the portable toilet facilities.

CB XL-5's costume, unlike those worn by most superheroes, had a built-in zipper. He assumed that most superheroes never peed at all. When he exited the unit, he walked away from the parking lot to consider his next move. The world didn't have much time.

He scanned the mountainside, and looked for a sign.

It came, just like he knew it would. It didn't have a choice. Rules are rules.

As he was searching with his eyes, he'd seen a glint of something in the moonlight. He kept his eyes focused on the spot, and he saw the glimmer again. Someone was up on a dark ridge, a couple hundred yards to his southwest, in an area nowhere near the forthcoming TDS festivities.

Crime Blaster knew that this was the menace that must be destroyed. It was trouble, superhero-sized. He used the moonlight, to make his way through the pine trees, and up the rocky slopes towards the area he'd seen. He stopped to take his bearings from time to time and look up to the dark ridge. Once, he saw five heads bobbing around up there. Yes!

As he grew closer, CB used boulders and trees, to cover his silent approach. While hiking and clambering up to the dark ledge, he considered a title for his future comic book, but realised that he needed the measure of his enemies first. CB circled around their position, so he could approach them from behind.

Chapter 37

Cynna Spoile, the leader of the Dwarf Resistance, trembled with anticipation. It was almost midnight. He and four of his closest and most loyal associate terrorists, huddled on a dark ledge, looking down on the concession area and it's hundreds of excited human occupants. A projecting tongue of rock overhung their position on a hidden ledge, and they'd avoided discovery by the sentry drones of the two treacherous aliens.

Cynna Spoile was a middle-aged dwarf, with a pronounced overhang at his waistline, like a marsupial with a full pouch. He'd once been a contented chicken rancher in Somtrow, with a pretty wife and a young daughter. Two years ago, he contracted mid-life crisis syndrome.

He treated the illness by various means. For example, he built a sporty red he-shed to escape to, and for entertaining his drinking and gambling friends. This device only addressed his symptoms and not the underlying sickness, so he indulged in a series of adulterous affairs, in hopes of alleviating this crisis of health and well-being.

These frantic sexual antics brought immediate relief, but it was like going to a dwarf chiropractor, and one had to keep returning for another adjustment. All of the positive health benefits of these dalliances, were seriously unappreciated by his nagging wife. Since she no longer supported him in his ventures, he split… her open with an axe. Cynna didn't want his thirteen-year-old daughter, to grow up without a mother to guide the way, so he chopped her up too.

Cynna Spoile was sick of his life, sick of the stench of chicken scat, sick of poking working! He was going to turn over a new leaf. Cynna's Uncle Flynch was a onetime mayor of Somtrow, and so he had loyal friends in the small, but persistent dwarf under-underworld. Flynch had introduced his chicken rancher nephew Cynna to his criminal support team, prior to the mayor's arrest and conviction on charges of graft.

Cynna's status as a wanted, double murderer, although looked down upon by members of his diet club, gave him instant credibility with the crime gang. His enrolment application was marked for immediate approval. In two short years, he had reached the pinnacle of crime stardom, and was made chief of thugs.

His rise to power often came as the result of fatal accidents to those above him in the criminal hierarchy. One unsolved death was the result of Cynna's dinner guest drowning in his chicken soup. Cyn's tale, that the man was searching for a missing cracker, and had forgotten to come up for air, was accepted without question by authorities.

Once he achieved outlaw royalty status, Cynna took the opportunity to reorganise the criminal enterprise, and he transformed the club of petty rapists and muggers, into a well-trained terrorist cell called the Resistance. Initially, the Resistance had no target in mind to fight against; however, they didn't let this small stumbling block deter them from their goals, which they hadn't yet defined. Their purpose became clear, when Robulus and Jeemis announced that they planned to commercialise the TDS as a gift to the human race.

Cynna peered down towards the concessions area through a pair of night vision binoculars, focusing his attention on the ugly grey tank of Bugsy bacterium standing there. According to his scopes, the tank was ENE of them, and situated four hundred and sixty-five feet away, with a one hundred-and twenty-two-foot drop in elevation.

His four terrorist cohorts wore matching grey uniforms, with a black beret to cover their bald heads. Cyn wore the hat, but his outfit consisted of his signature suspenders, which used cables to hold his gut off the ground. Two drones and their associated controls occupied spaces on the hidden ledge too. The drones were armed with explosive missiles.

The drones and the NV gear, came courtesy of a daring burglary, which Cyn and six dwarf accomplices had pulled off, when they broke into the alien's Research and Development lab, prior to the addition of the two dogs as extra security. The job had taken a lot of planning and training, but the burglars still tripped an alarm when they entered the building.

The dwarves had acquired two drones, their associated controls, and made their getaway before the robocops could respond. An appropriate diversion at the other end of Somtrow had kept the law busy. Tonight's mission was the culmination of that earlier burglary. The five dwarves on the ledge had trained and rehearsed for this night for many months. Everyone knew that Robulus and Jeemis were going to go public with the TDS, but no one knew when.

Cynna and his squad had only learned of this night's Unveiling a mere ten hours ago, when word came that Robulus was in Somtrow with two humans. The five dwarves scrambled to get their gear out of hiding and set up on this ledge of rock before dark, undetected.

Cynna hoped that he and his crew could cancel or at least postpone the aliens' plan. The Resistance knew that the tunnel explosion couldn't kill the immortal alien, and they cared not about the humans, because Robulus would be blamed. The dwarves assumed that if the humans lived, they'd be too injured and crippled to carry on. They were disgusted that the Unveiling was to go on, but they could still ruin the big night.

The timing in this military operation was as important as its goal. No humans were supposed to die, because the dwarves needed to remain a secret from the maniacal killer race of humans. If they were ever discovered, there would soon be nothing left of dwarves, except for relics in a museum display.

Cynna whispered words of encouragement to his troops. He said, "Destroying the tank of anti-stupidity bacterium will cause maximum psychological damage to the dumdums, once they learn they are stuck in their mentally deficient state." Dumdum was their term for a human. Cyn had always been a big admirer of his own words of wisdom, and added a memorable one now, drawn from his ranching experience. He said, "The aliens' plan will explode like a chicken with diarrhoea!"

The apprentice terrorist, Dworkum Slaug quietly remarked, "It's too bad that we can't explode the humans like that."

A grizzled elder dwarf, Wahz Ooh, drank down another big slug of homemade liquor called cornpop, and his shiny flask sparkled in the moonlight. He slurred rather loudly, "Kill 'em all! Blow 'em to thsmithereens! Thow no merthy!"

"Put that booze away, Wahz!" Cynna bawled, "I told you no drinking on this mission! And pipe down!" he yelled quietly. Sometimes he felt like a babysitter for children whose parents were never coming back home again. Whenever Robulus started to broadcast tonight's sacrilegious event, that's when they would blow the tank up. They would launch both of their drones, armed with missiles. The two missiles were programmed to target the grey tank, and the drones were mere launching platforms for them. It wouldn't be long now.

One third of a mile east of the five dwarves of the Resistance, on the far side of the two parking lots, a lone gunman adjusted himself in the branches of the pine tree he'd lain in for the last six and a half hours. It wasn't comfortable, but he had a great shot from his vantage point. His NV rifle scope, made the target look less than sixty feet distant, rather than the six hundred yards that actually lay between him and it. His job could hardly have been made any easier! There was a large white bullseye for him to zero in on.

The hitman was Bosco Jacobi, better known in the trade as the Jackalope, because of his rapid exits after his jobs. His record of kills, was admired by many an aspiring hit-person. Bosco didn't know who had hired him for this job and he didn't want to know. Most of his clients found him through his ad on Dregslist. All the arrangements were done online, and his fees were collected through his PayUpPal account.

Jackalope's current employers called themselves SwampLife, and they paid him twice his usual fee, because he kept a strict twenty-four-hour notice policy. SwampLife missed the deadline by fourteen hours, but Bosco lived only an hour away, so he took the job. His hitman unemployment insurance had nearly run its course, and he needed the work.

Bosco's assassination contract, called for him to kill whatever lived behind the wall of rock with the bullseye on it. The instructions made no sense when he first read them, and things became no clearer when he reached this site. He'd been paid a lot of money, so he would stay until midnight and see what opened up.

* * *

Robulus told Griz and Vera all about the TDS, while they sat and people-watched the eight views on the MegaScreen TV. Robulus used almost the same words as did Jeemis, who was telling Melanie the story at nearly the same time. Jeemis and Melanie sat next to each other under the stars in the Blipey robocart. The narrative was the TDS genesis story, which was taught to all dwarf children and was featured in their picture books.

The fourteen-thousand-year-old legend was called; The Fusion and it went like this:

Once upon a time, in the underworld village of Ventchly, there lived two upstanding dwarf families. One of the families was burdened with three teenagers at once; two boys and a girl. The oldest son was named Laboyba, his younger brother was Gajoyba, and the youngest was sister Grinkoyba. In the neighbouring house dwelt the twin, hormone-addled, adolescent males, Pblalb and Gdalb.

One day the five young friends and playmates, on impulse, journeyed to the forbidden upper crust. They'd heard tales of the delicious berries that could be found on the bright surface, and it sounded like an adventure. Their parents thought they were playing ballkick at the park.

When the five teenage dwarflings did not come home for the evening meal, their folks started to worry. When their kids hadn't returned by bedtime, the two sets of parents joined forces to double the power of anxiety.

The four adult dwarves tried to explain the mystery of their missing children, and their imaginations ran wild, creating frightening horror stories. They immediately conjectured that the five had gone to the upper crust. After that correct assumption, their reason abandoned them. Blagma, the mother of the twins Pblalb and Gdalb, made the suggestion that a small group of gay humans had kidnapped the five children to establish a homo-harem. The girl, Grinkoyba, would be the harem guard.

Korsly, who was Mom to the two boys Laboyba and Gajoyba, and daughter Grinkoyba, groaned and said, "That is the most grossly idiotic nonsense I have ever heard, Blagma! It's much more likely that the humans, who captured them, are grilling them for a feast."

Blagma's plump, stumpy husband, Smapa, came to his overbearing wife's defence. He didn't appreciate the hostility from Korsly. He raised his chins up, one by one, and said, "You must be as stupid as a dumdum, Korsly! Don't you know anything about humans? They eat dwarfs raw. Korsly, you are letting hormones and emotions drive your story.

"We must be thoughtful and rational," Smapa explained. "I use the science of logic, combined with wise common sense, and I have reached the inescapable conclusion, that your daughter Grinkoyba, has seduced our twin boys and your two sons are watching the orgy. They may even get drawn into their sister's depravity and, you know…"

Grinkoyba's father, Flubko simmered slowly, his eyeballs sautéed in hot blood. Veins popped. He clenched his fists, and used them each once, to punch his neighbour Smapa, in the mouth. Flubko's wife Korsly laughed hysterically

240

at the violence. Blagma pulled Korsly's hair, bending her head back, and then stuck two fingers up her nose.

Smapa wiped the blood from his lips, and clapped his hands on Flubko's ears, turning his head into a hand sandwich. When the battles ended and the sex began was difficult to determine, but clothes were ripped off, body parts exposed, and it wasn't long before Flubko was poking Smapa's wife and vice versa.

A nosy neighbour, investigating the source of the screams, came over for a welfare check. In absolute shock and awe, she watched the live pornography show for several long minutes, before removing her clothing and joining in the perversions.

The mailman, and a survey taker in the neighbourhood, soon joined the festivities. A pair of Shuvova Witnesses, who were proselytising nearby, also jumped into the fray. Somehow or another, most of the adult population of the village, came to the home of these worried and distressed parents, to help console them about their missing children.

At some, much later point, the sore, stiff-legged villagers formed a search party. Assignments were made, and organisers led volunteers through the house and yard, until everyone's clothing was found and returned to the original owners.

Finally, it was time to hunt for the five naughty young dwarf brats. After an uphill hike of five hours duration, fourteen adult dwarves emerged onto the upper crust. Several minutes elapsed, before their eyes adjusted to the bright sunlight aboveground.

The pure, fresh, mountain air tasted wonderful. The sky was clear and it was rather too cold for the clothes they'd worn, but they didn't let that deter them from their task. They hadn't taken weather into consideration. They didn't experience the four seasons in the underworld. The dwarves loved the outer world, but they couldn't live up here, because the savage humans, who dwelled here, didn't believe in coexistence. They all fervently hoped and prayed that the teenagers had not become victims of that murderous race.

The fourteen dwarves organised into smaller search parties, with three sets of four members each, and a pair of alert dwarves to stand security watch. Blagma and her husband were in one group, and Korsly and her mate in another. Areas were assigned, search patterns defined, and then the dozen dwarfs began to comb the mountainside for any traces of the youngsters.

Less than an hour after the hunt began, four voices rose up in yells. These were not shouts of discovery, but shrieks of horror! The other two groups of dwarves and the sentinels too, ran towards the source of the screams. The howls originated in an alcove, cut by nature into the face of a sheer wall of rock, accessible by a narrow ledge. One by one, as dwarfs arrived in the alcove, new shrieks and screams of revulsion and disgust erupted.

The repellent sight that elicited their horrified reactions was a hot brand, which scarred their brains, and burned for as long as they lived. No two dwarves ever described the thing in the same manner. It seemed to defy oral description, and had to be seen to be believed. One needed to experience it to comprehend its horror.

An enormous toadstool stood in the alcove, nearly filling the space. The fungi towered more than six feet tall, and its one-foot thick, fleshy white stem, held aloft a ten-foot diameter cap. The giant toadstool resembled a fly agaric; a fairy toadstool, and its sloping cap was a bright orange-red colour, mottled with splotches of white.

The horror of the fairy toadstool lay not in its size, however, but in its custom accessories. The umbrella-shaped hood of the giant toadstool seemed to have a half face atop it. One very large eye seemed to look out over a huge nose. One great ear stuck out and a pair of enormous lips finished the picture. None of these body parts moved, but they were recognisable, to four of the dwarfs there.

Blagma and Smapa could distinguish Gdalb's enlarged left ear, and Pblalb's fattened nose. Korsly and Flubko knew the big grey eye of Gajoyba and the gargantuan lips of his older brother, Laboyba. There was nothing of the girl, Grinkoyba. It was unthinkable.

Blagma dropped to her knees on the rock ground, and she cried out in grief and pain, "What are you? Where are my children?"

"I am the gateway to all multiversal thought," it replied in the light, melodic voice of Grinkoyba. Her voice seemed to emanate from the unmoving lips of Laboyba. Fear drove the dwarves out of the alcove in a mad flurry, and they bashed into and fell over each other. Two wet themselves.

It was madness! None of them felt brave enough to converse with a haunted toadstool, and so, distraught and confused, they found their secret entrance, returned down their tunnel, and went home to their little village. The ten dwarves who helped the parents' with the search, all swore secrecy. They would protect and honour the memories of the five kids. They would blame the humans for their disappearance.

The sacred secret never even made it into the village as a stranger. Several of the dwarves returning with the search party, ran ahead of the main group, and shouted out the terrible news like the heralds of Hades. Within a span of mere minutes, the secret was as popular as the town whore.

Robulus concluded by saying, "That's the legend."

Vera felt like she was living in an alternate universe, where reality warped, twisted and folded like a heap of lies. She didn't trust it. Blow on the legend and it would break apart and drift away like smoke.

Griz recovered from the bizarre tale more quickly than she, and he also deciphered the meaning of TDS. He blurted out the three words, "Toadstool Dwarf Symbiosis."

Robulus was well pleased and boomed, "Bravo!"

Melanie was even quicker than her father; to decode the three letters TDS. She was a biologist after all. She asked Jeemis, "And then you walled up the TDS. Was that to protect it from us, or to protect us from it?"

Jeemis screeched, "We encased it in rock, yes." He added, "To protect the dwarves when they came to consult the TDS. Jeemis and I created interior access for them, so the dwarves never had to expose themselves to outer world dangers. We installed lighting and ventilation too."

Melanie had more questions. She asked Jeemis, "And it has survived, unchanged, for over fourteen thousand years!"

Jeemis shook his head and shrieked, "It survives, but changes. The TDS is your planet's oldest living organism, other than Robulus and me, and is also the largest. Rope-thick hyphae and flat straps of rhizomorphs reach for more than a half mile radius in all directions, penetrating rock and soil."

Robulus said, "It's time! It is twenty minutes to midnight, and is time to open Gate 2, and to begin our pirate, round the world satellite broadcast." He walked over to a counter, and returned with a microphone headset with ear bud, for Griz and one for Vera. He said, "All three of us will participate, so speak up whenever you want to say something. The camera view currently airing, will be the one outlined in red on the MegaScreen. Any questions?"

Griz and Vera shook their heads, but Griz remarked that, "This setup reminds me of those hokey Harvestday parades with the floats and balloons."

Vera cocked her head, her singed, dirty black hair fell across one eye, and she looked at Griz, with feigned injury. She said, "But those parades are hosted by dull, boring people, repeating the most worn, banal clichés…wait."

They all laughed.

Robulus turned on the PA system and announced, "Gate 2 will open in thirty seconds. Please proceed in an orderly fashion up to Gate 3." The distance between the two gates was only a hundred and fifty yards. One side of the upsloping road leading to Gate 3 was bordered by the mountainside. On the opposite side of the road, a waist-high, iron fence kept people from falling down the rocky slope below it. The road narrowed as it approached the uppermost portal of Gate 3, eventually funnelling the people into a single file line, before reaching a turnstile there.

Jeemis asked the Blipey cart to retreat, to remove Melanie and him from the immediate area before the gate opened. The robocart zipped them up the road to Gate 3.

Melanie and Jeemis stepped down out of the cart, and looked down the sloping road at the stampede pounding towards them. Mad beasts on two legs raced for the gold medal first place finish. Melanie saw the cart blocking the gate and asked Jeemis, "What about Blipey?"

Jeemis smiled and said, "Blipey let's get in place, and get your camera rolling." The cart stood up on its front wheels, a small third wheel projected from the front grill area for balance. The back wheels turned in and the Blipey-cart unfolded a camera, from under the seat. It led Jeemis and Melanie through the turnstile, and into an open area where they could view the road below. People no longer charged up the road, they had slowed to a walk, gasping for air.

Griz and Vera could see all of the action, in the eight camera views, but the picture on the MegaScreen which was outlined in red, showed the concessions area and the grey tank behind it. That is the view that would open the big show.

Robulus said, "We're on the air, in three, two, and one."

"Hello Gaia!" Robulus' voice boomed around the world, and blasted out of the PA system loudspeakers on Poke's Peak. "I am Robulus, a long-time resident of your planet, here from another galaxy. You are watching the pre-Unveiling show; live from Poke's Peak in Minotaur Springs, Colorotta. Thousands of people are here to see the wonderful and amazing TDS, which will be revealed to the world eighteen minutes from now."

More than one and a half billion humans were watching or listening to the alien, on one medium or another. Another couple million people were too busy burning, looting and partying to bother with it. Robulus thundered, "My partner from another planet is Jeemis, who you will meet later. There are a couple of your fellow human beings with me here tonight. I'll let them introduce themselves."

All over the world, thousands of engineers and hundreds of on-air talents, news directors and programmers lost their collective minds, at the second signal interruption of the day. It was apocalyptic, and many experienced psychological issues for years to come.

Griz pointed at Vera, and indicated that she go first. Vera appreciated the gesture, and she said to the world, "Hi there! I am Vera Fynne, recently of No Fake News, and I sure am glad you can't see me." She looked down at her torn, sooty clothes with one boob peeking out, and Vera knew that her face was cut and scratched, and her hair a dirty, tangled mess.

She shook her head in resignation, and said, "I am in Colorotta, sitting inside the mountain called Poke's Peak, with Robulus and the brave, ingenious father of the kidnapped scientist, Melanie Gryzolski. Tell them Griz."

Griz wanted to kiss her. He said, "Thank you Vera. You're a warrior. And thank you Robulus and Jeemis for bringing my daughter back to me safely! I am Matt Gryzolski, and that's my girl down there with Jeemis."

The Blipey-cam indicator light blinked red and Jeemis directed Melanie's attention to the camera. He said, "We're on. Hello Gaia; I am Jeemis," he screeched loudly. He added, "This is one spunky woman next to me, and I am proud to know her."

Melanie blushed at all the praise and she said, "Hi Dad, hello Robulus. Hi Vera, we've met, I believe."

Jeemis noticed that the TV news helicopters, which had been circling above them like flying sharks, had suddenly all departed the airspace at once. That was curious, and he wondered what it portended. A few minutes later, he wondered more so, when a big black helicopter flew into the area, and began whirling overhead.

Robulus' powerful, forceful voice was a sound quake, which sent tremors through the skull. He resumed speaking, and said, "In a few minutes, you will see something remarkable and inexplicable, which will change the world forever.

You will never be the same again and that's a good thing! The TDS is a lifeform known nowhere else. It is unique in the universe."

Robulus poked a button on his podium computer keyboard, and changed the MegaScreen camera view. A large white bullseye, chalked onto a rock face was shown. He explained, "The TDS came to be, more than fourteen thousand years ago, and this seamless, rock wall was built around it, encasing it in stone, to protect it from harm and danger. Perhaps it can defend itself. I do not know."

Robulus switched the on-air camera view again. This new picture came courtesy of a roving drone, which was programmed to find interesting activities in the great crowds of people. The main attraction seemed to be centred on a silver tractor trailer rig. The Odd Style logo and a can of beer were painted on the side of the trailer.

Torchy and Rosie Oh presided like royalty there. A half-dozen, half-drunk servants, laboured at the honoured duty of hauling cases of beer out of the refrigerated truck trailer. The king and queen then handed out the beer to their happy subjects. They passed out six packs of cold brew, to all who presented themselves, and many came to offer their respects for free beer.

The drone beamed out a picture, which showed scores of people in various activities, some of which would have made Dionysius sick. One drunken man pissed on a drunken woman as she vomited, and an amorous couple poked underneath the beer truck. A naked guy who identified as a squirrel fell out of a pine tree, and coincidentally landed near a nude woman who thought she was pinion nut. They were made for each other.

Between the beer, the thin mountain air, the night sky and the fearful, hopeful excitement of the moment, so much sex was taking place behind bushes or rocks, under trees, in cars and out in the open parking lot, that business dropped off completely at the nearby Winabagel RV whore wagon. The head prostitute, Aunt Yomama, was so disgusted that she hung out the 'Closed' sign, and told her co-whores, "Let's make the best of it girls. We can just act normal for a change, get drunk and poke for free, like everyone else!" They cheered and jumped for joy. Imanasti, their bus driver pimp, joined them at the back of the beer truck trailer, grabbed a six pack, and looked for a drunken horny stranger to poke.

Robulus switched the camera view back to the big white bullseye on the rock. He glossed over the beer orgy and said, "We will soon remove this wall of rock to unveil the TDS, and return it to the surface of Gaia. It is a boon for all mankind, and will prove as beneficial as when Jeemis and I taught your race to speak. The

TDS can access all universal knowledge; everything ever learned or discovered, every thought made by an intelligent lifeform. All of man's questions answered, all of your ills cured, and all of your conspiracy theories laid to rest."

The alien again switched the camera view, this time to show the crowded concessions area and the ugly grey tank. He said, "This great TDS fountain of knowledge is of little use however, if a race is too stupid to use it appropriately. After tonight, the human race will begin to be cured of the mental debility caused by the endemic stupidity virus! The grey tank you are looking at contains a cure, which we will distribute as a breathable mist. Do not be afraid! The only two side effects are the extermination of the common cold, and…" Boom!

An explosion interrupted his disclaimer.

* * *

Cynna Spoile and his merry dwarves of the Resistance had been waiting for the broadcast to begin. They wanted the grey tank of contagious medicine to be showing on air, when they blew it up. They were certain that the humans would panic, resulting in many casualties and, perhaps even a postponement of the Unveiling altogether.

Cyn would operate one of the armed drones, and it sat next to him on the ledge, the controls at his fingertips. The five dwarves on the rock ledge lay on their bellies, watching the despised humans below. A seasoned criminal dwarf named Orfo would operate the second drone weapon system.

Crime Blaster XL-5 stood as still as the pine tree he hid behind. He'd studied the five dwarves. They faced away from him, at about 1 o'clock relative to him. The superhero had circled around to come up from behind the dwarves, and had observed them for several minutes. The little people, reminded him of the Dung Beetle gang, in Super-duper Tarantula Man, issue #6738, who wanted to turn humans into turdballs, and roll them down into the sea. CB couldn't understand the strange language of these little world destroyers either. He couldn't learn the plans of his small bald enemy.

Super-duper Tarantula Man never faced such foes as these, who spoke in strange tongues. One of the five dwarves, wearing suspenders, seemed to be lying atop a large beach ball, but then CB realised it was just his gut. CB was on his own now. Tarantula Man couldn't help him, and it was almost the 'nick of time' too. He could feel it.

The scenario he faced, also contained some elements from Issue #3451, in which TM found himself up against the far-right extremist gang, Tommy Termite and the Cockroach Girls. The bug-supremacists were on the verge of using insect-like drones, to spray a deadly humanicide poison called Rayd, over the planet Gaia, and cause human extinction. In the nick of time, Tarantula Man put an end to their plans, by stepping on them, eight at once!

Crime Blaster's enemies were little, but he didn't think he could squash them like bugs. He armed himself with a thick tree branch in one hand, and a heavy rock in the other. He wished he had eight limbs like Tarantula Man did.

Saving the world was not a learned skill. It was innate, part of one's DNA. Superheroes were born, not made. Destiny was made for superheroes.

It was twelve minutes to midnight, when Cynna and Orfo powered up their respective drone units. As in rehearsals for this moment, the two dwarves moved in synchrony. The drone missile platforms, rose slowly off the rock ledge, and hovered in place. After their attack, the dwarves would seek temporary refuge in a nearby den, which they'd dug out months ago in preparation for this day. It was stocked with supplies, and they would make their way back to the underworld at a later time, when safe.

It was then, when all five dwarfs were distracted by the drones hovering above them, when Crime Blaster XL-5 struck. First blood splashed, when the rock he hurled, merged with a dwarf's skull. He rushed upon the others, bashing and crunching furiously with his wooden club.

Cynna didn't think. He acted, and fired the drone's missile manually, smashing his thumb onto the red button. The rocket was programmed to hit its target, no matter where it was launched from, and it shot off towards the grey tank. The exhausting backfire from the missile, set Cynna Spoile and Wahz Ooh afire and blasted at CB's legs.

Orfo was slower than Cyn, but he had the same idea, and his finger was descending towards the red 'Launch' button, when CB, his legs ablaze, leapt onto the hovering drone. He brought it down, landing atop it. Orfo's finger hit the wrong button, and the white, self-destruct button was accidentally depressed.

Chapter 38

Air Power One landed at the Colorotta Springs airport at 11:29 PM that night. The presidential ground detail consisted of four motorcycles and three long black limousines. Several Covert Service agents were already on the Poke's Peak site, and had been there for hours. A black helicopter staffed with two spotters and a sniper, now circled over the TDS area too.

President Crumm's impulsive decision to come out here, and give his science advisor a ride back to the DC swamp, had left his staff scrambling. His press secretary was besieged by demands from the press corps, and his Chief of Staff was trying to argue him out of the trip. The president wanted to go, and to be on time to watch the Unveiling however, and so all the arrangements were made. Whatever the TDS was, it was on Shamerican soil, and it was his responsibility. Also, if it had any possible use to the military, President Crumm needed to protect it from them. The TDS could be a national treasure.

The president's entourage was nine minutes away from the Poke's Peak area, and he was poring over reports of a brewing, fifth impeachment investigation by the frustrated Demolist party, when his car-fone rang. His chief of staff, Tommi Gunn picked up the line and listened. She hung up the fone, and told the president, "An explosion at the TDS location has been reported, Sir. This is a no go; we must turn around."

The president said, "tell me the rest of it. The threat is over; correct?"

"Ostensibly, Sir," she replied. Tommi added, "The perpetrators have apparently blown themselves up, but I suggest…"

"Other casualties?"

"Yes, certainly, Sir."

"Well then, in that case, I'm going in for sure" President Crumm averred. He added, "This isn't about me, Miss Gunn, this is about Shamerica first."

Chapter 39

The resulting fiery blast on the dark ledge, and the rising flames there, caused seven thousand, six hundred and eleven people to look up to the southwest from whence came the commotion. A few couples were focused on more explosive matters, and didn't notice. Most people saw the fire and heard the distant screams. Then they also noticed a flaming rocket headed in their direction. Many wondered if it was another gender-reveal party gone badly.

Robulus' security drones barely had time to announce, "Incoming!" before the missile impacted the grey tank. It was 11:49 PM. The ground shook with the explosion, causing a woman under a man under a bush, to remark, "Wow; you rocked my world." They tried for a repeat.

All of the anti-SV bacterium, Bugsy, was instantly vaporised in the fiery heat of the blast. People screamed and ran and fell over each other in their mindless rush to escape the area. More people were injured in the short-frenzied run to safety, than from the blast.

Robulus pled for calm, "Be still! The danger has passed! First responder-bots are on the way to the injured! Be calm!" His massive voice crashed through the noisy chaos like a cannon through paper and shredded people's fear. They halted in mid-step as if they'd run into a wall of sound.

Drones dropped fire suppression chemicals onto the small fires, which burned around the shards of the shattered metal tank. Robulus' spirit wasn't shattered, but his enthusiasm had cracked. Privately, he remarked to Vera and Griz, "Kazooky's Conundrum"

Vera added her voice to the alien's and called for calm. Her voice projected from the PA system, "Stop where you are! Stay in place! You are safe now!" She trusted Robulus that it was so. Vera wanted to cheer up the alien, so she tried to put a happy face on the sad situation. She said, "Things could always be worse."

Griz groaned. "The Resistance, I presume," he said, with anger in his voice.

One of the security drones flew to the source of the missile, where six, charred bodies lay atop a ledge, smoking and still. It sent a video feed back to Blipey-control, and the picture appeared on one of the eight MegaScreen views. Robulus remarked on the carnage, "Five dwarves and one human, very odd." Although distraught at the loss of the Bugsy solution, Robulus continued with the program.

People were still frightened and uneasy, so the danger they posed to themselves had not yet passed. Robulus had to manage their anxieties, distract them. He spoke through the PA system, "Look to the bullseye! It is TDS time! The Unveiling is arrived!" His voice reverberated in their skulls and the crazed mob slowly dissolved into rational individuals again, although the smell of burning adrenaline remained in the air.

People couldn't move far without bumping into someone, so when they ran in different directions, they collided after a step and cancelled each other out, and so the short mad rush to nowhere ended as quickly as it had begun.

There were several doctors in the mass of people, who assisted the first responder robots with injuries. Two women with simple fractures were being splinted, and some contusions, lacerations and burns were treated too, but nothing serious. Sue M. Aul was consulting with one of the injured parties.

Robulus went on as if nothing had happened. He didn't even address the loss of the stupidity-defeating Bugsy bacterium to the watching world. Curing humans of this malady would be delayed. The show must go on.

It was time for the Unveiling. Robulus said, "Look at the white bullseye!" Four powerful floodlights brightened the target on the rock face. Billions of eyes stared at the view. Those four lights went dark, at the same time that a pair of white lights came on from the opposite side of the two parking lots, a hundred yards away. A tracked vehicle sat atop a ridge, and supported two bright lamps, and moonlight shone upon it as well. A contraption sat atop it, but it was too distant for people to see its details, even with the lighting.

Robulus said, "You are looking at a tool which will revolutionise engineering projects around the world. It is a gravity wave pulse cannon." The item looked like a cement mixer and it sat atop the tracked vehicle.

Robulus relit the bullseye lights and said, "The TDS lies behind this honeycombed wall, which is only two inches thick. The pulse cannon will turn the wall into several tons of powder, and unveil the TDS."

Jeemis and Melanie were closer than anybody else to the target of the cannon. He assured her that they were all safe. He shrieked, "Listen to Robulus' instructions." She nodded and held onto his arm.

Robulus announced to the crowd, and to the watching world, "You must protect your eyes and lungs from any rock powder that may result, so when I say 'go', take a deep breath, and close your eyes. Then, count to ten, before you take a peek or breathe."

Griz and Vera watched the MegaScreen intently, not worrying about rock dust in the underground broadcast studio. Robulus said, "Go!' his voice echoed around the mountainside.

At the word 'go', Blipey spun up the pulse cannon to the required intensity, and fired. A 'woof' emitted, like a cough. The target wall of rock, converted to powder in an instant, and an eighty-foot-wide swath, ten feet high opened up in the mountain. Pink dust puffed up and out, but soon dropped down out of the air, rolling and tumbling down the mountainside like an avalanche. A camera-bearing drone sent a picture of the resulting dust slide, to Robulus' MegaScreen TV.

Griz, Vera and the alien were horrified, to see a train of a dozen or so people on the slope, looking up at the pink wave of rock dust crashing down upon them. The alien couldn't understand what kind of idiots would have ignored the fence, the gate and the warning signs, to ascend the back road. He sent the drone in for a closer look, to check for casualties. Robulus hoped the fools were uninjured.

The current on-air TV picture came from the Blipey-cam, which stood next to Melanie and Jeemis. When the dust fell out of the air, and slowly cleared away, the TDS gradually came into view. The four flood lamps focused on the TDS, which most resembled a thick post with a large, inverted bowl, balanced on top. The alcove was fully exposed to its original condition, except for the roof covering, which would be removed at a later time, in a different fashion.

Robulus told the world what they were seeing. His deep voice pounded out of billions of speakers; he said, "This is the TDS, the Toadstool Dwarf Symbiosis. The dwarves were a race of little people that roamed this part of North Shamerica fourteen thousand years ago, when this entity was formed. This race of small humans, were wiped from the face of your planet, by a more lethal race of larger humans."

Robulus saw on the MegaScreen, that whoever had been traveling up the back access road was now all covered in pink powdered rock, but they seemed unhurt, so he continued his explanation of the TDS. His audience was agape at the ghastly beauty of the thing. He said, "It so happened that one day, five adolescent dwarves were incorporated, into the flowering body of a toadstool fungus. We ascertain that the spore, which grew in this rocky plot, came to Gaia from outer space."

People in the Poke's Peak crowd, as well as all around the planet, reacted in predictable, though in some cases, diametrically opposed manners. Shouts of "Cool!" and "Awesome!" were interspersed with terrified screams like, "It's an abomination!", and "What the poke?" One loud mouthed jerk standing first in line at the turnstile gate was heard to holler, "It's my mother in-law!"

Pitch Al laughed at his little joke. He waited at the Gate 3 turnstile, and was first in line, followed by Don Crews and Kate Armstrong. The trio had coaxed, bullied, pushed, prodded and paid people to reach the head of the line where they belonged. Crews couldn't have been more pleased, and his faith in Pitch Al was restored. Promises made, promises kept.

Robulus said, "The eye, ear, nose and lips do not function of course, and are much enlarged, but they were recognisable to the poor, grief-stricken parents as belonging to the four boys who were incorporated into this being. They symbolise the entity's ability to hear all, see all, smell all, and also to speak all. The fifth dwarf was a young female, and it is her voice that emanates from the TDS.

"Jeemis and Melanie will soon open Gate 3, which allows a single file stream of people to enter the upper viewing plaza. Please do not climb over the inner rail or try to touch the TDS. Walkways surround the TDS, and the exit trail circles around to connect back with the road you came up on. About three hundred people at a time can fit in the viewing gallery."

"Once you enter the gate, Jeemis and Melanie will conduct parties up into the docket. Five people at a time can stand in the docket, but only one person will be allowed, to pose one question to the TDS. It will not debate you nor make conversation in the ordinary way however."

Just as he readied to tell Jeemis to open Gate 3, Robulus saw something on one of the eight MegaScreen camera views that made him pause. He hadn't seen it earlier, but now a large black helicopter descended closer to the ground, and hovered above the crowd. Jeemis had identified it as Covert Service, but said nothing to Melanie. He wanted her to be surprised. She was.

The entire crowd was silenced, and the world watched another historic moment. They weren't watching the chopper. There was a commotion at the entry road.

Tears came to Melanie's eyes; when she recognised the Presidential motorcade entering the parking lot below. Two motorcycles led, and two more followed the three long black limousines, which rolled towards the lowest gate.

Chapter 40

Bosco 'Jackalope' Jacobi wasn't certain that he could fulfil his contract. He was supposed to kill the TDS, but he'd never assassinated a fungus before! He had standards and principles! Bosco wasn't a heartless hitman. He'd never even carved a pumpkin! Using a weed-whipper to kill dandelions was the worst he was guilty of. He was a vegan for Gawd's sake!

The Jackalope studied the toadstool monster through his night vision rifle scope, searching for the proper place for a kill shot. He first considered shooting the thing right between the eyes, but it only had one. He looked at the ear next, but wasn't sure the bullet would penetrate to the toadstool's brain, if it had one. Jackalope settled on shooting its fat, ugly nose off. Bosco didn't know if he could go through with it. His palms were sweaty. He took a sip of water from his canteen, and tried to think calming thoughts, like shooting people.

It was then, that the hitman gods blessed him with a priceless target. President Crumm arrived! Assassinating a president was the dream of every professional killer; a never-ending fantasy. A successful hit on Crumm would be a gold star on the hit charts! It was like winning the slaughtery. Bosco started to scan the crowd for the undercover security, which he knew must be in attendance.

Robulus saw the presidential motorcade come to a stop, at the bottom of the crowded road leading up to the TDS. He shouted, "Let's give a loud, warm welcome to the President of the United States of Shamerica, Darryl K. Crumm!"

A Covert Service agent opened the president's car door, and the POTUS exited the armoured vehicle. People began to chant, "Crumm! Crumm!" The president looked up at the TDS, and surveyed the road filled with people, which led up to it. Without hesitation, the president, walked over to an escort motorcycle and hopped on it, sitting behind its driver. His Chief of Staff did the same on a second bike.

The four motorcycle escort cops drove in single file up the road to the TDS, with the president of the US riding on the second bike in line. People crowded close together, and backed up against a rail on one side of the road, or the mountain on the other side, leaving an open path in its centre, like a gauntlet.

Bosco spotted a few suspected Covert Security agents here and there, but saw nothing to change his mind about killing the president. It was a once in a lifetime opportunity. A successful kill, would make him a nationally recognised figure. The name Bosco Rotini Jacobi would be written in history books, school kids would learn about him. He would be in the Hitman Hall of Fame, next to such memorable president slayers as John Fones Booth, and Flea Larvae Ozwalled.

President Crumm risked all for his country, he appreciated the cheers of the crowd, and he enjoyed the motorcycle ride up the mountain road as well. He and two of the escorts dismounted at the top of the road, before it narrowed to a path, and two stayed behind with the four motorcycles, as did Tommi Gunn.

Robulus greeted the new arrival via PA system. He said, "Welcome to the Toadstool Dwarf Symbiosis, Mr President!"

The President staggered slightly at the verbal onslaught, but he continued walking towards the Gate 3 turnstile, between a pair of Covert Service agents. Melanie waited on the far side of the gate, eager to greet her beloved boss. Jeemis too, was honoured at the surprise visit by the leader of the free world. The Blipey-cam captured the audio and video of the president's grand entrance, and Robulus broadcast it to the world.

Everyone parted to make way for the president, and his two-person security detail. The party encountered three people at the front of the line, who were unwilling to move. The lead agent, Mr Spladders spoke to the recalcitrant trio. He said, "Please let the President proceed."

Pitch Al looked at the agent lowered his thin eyebrows and scowled. He said, with a dose of indignation in his snivelling voice, "Do you know who this is?" He jerked a thumb in the direction of Don Crews, who knew instinctually that he was on camera.

President Crumm gently pulled back on Agent Spladders' arm, and said with a smile, "I'll take it from here." He stepped forward, looked at Pitch Al, and said, "No, I don't! Do you perhaps recognise the President of the United States?"

A great consternation arose from a short way down the road behind them. People broke out in uproarious squeals of laughter, and unrestrained glee, causing the President's security detail to brace for trouble. What they saw approaching them, in the open path between the people, had them clutching their bellies in laughter too.

Ten people of indeterminate form, who were thickly coated in pink rock dust, slogged their way forward, as if every step was ordained by script or scripture. The pink pilgrims were stopped by presidential security. The president looked at them and they glared back. The pink creature at the head of the pack spoke. He said, "What in the Crumm-crappin', ass-slappin', lip-flappin', puppy pokin' Hades, are you doing here?"

President Crumm cocked his head, as if studying an insect, and he replied, "Are you filming a movie sequel to The Cotton Candy Zombies?" He turned his back on the Sacred Stars Temple saints, and returned to the turnstile entry gate. Mr Spladders had cleared the way, paying Pitch Al to move, with the eighty-seven cents he'd found in his pocket.

Jeemis opened the gate for the president and his two security men, and fastened it behind them. Melanie greeted the president, her smile as big as the sky. He hugged her warmly. "Are you okay, Miss Gryzolski?" he asked. "You've been through an awful ordeal, but I assumed that you would want to finish the day with a win."

Melanie stepped back and nodded her head; tears clouded her eyes. She said, "Thank you Mr President, I did indeed!"

President Crumm turned his attention to the very tall alien standing next to his science advisor. He looked up at Jeemis and said, "You don't look anything like the Hollowood aliens! You're neither cute and adorable, nor hideous and deadly." He shook hands with Jeemis, and said, "Glad to meet you, I run this country."

Jeemis said, "It is an honour to meet you Sir, and I run my mouth." His loud screeching voice caused the president to cringe. The alien shrieked, saying, "I am Jeemis. My pal Robulus and me are aliens sure enough, but we are one hundred percent Shamerican patriots!"

Jeemis took Melanie's arm and addressed the president and the two Covert Service agents with him. He said, "The docket is this way, Sir. You can ask the TDS a question from there." He led the way, and the Blipey-cam moved with them, capturing everything that occurred.

Bosco 'Jackalope' Jacobi was ecstatic! Crumm was in his sights! The president stood with two others, right in front of the TDS, as if posing for him.

He had a perfect shot, at the back of Crumm's head. It couldn't have been any easier. Bosco took a deep breath, and slowly began to squeeze the trigger of his rifle.

Bosco was not destined for the history books however, nor would his bust be in the Hitman Hall of Fame. He would remain anonymous to the conspiracy theorists too, and in fact, his quick quiet death went completely unnoticed.

The great, old pine tree whose branches he perched on started shaking, though no wind blew. Pine needles and cones fell from quaking limbs. Bosco dropped his rifle, and fell out of his nest, crashing down through the branches until he smacked onto the ground, flat on his broken back.

The ground beneath his tree ripped open and fat ropy tendrils of fungal hyphae reached out for him. Bosco's neck, torso and legs were wrapped and then, like a boa constrictor, the tentacles gradually squeezed tighter, and tried pulling him under the soil.

Unaware of his close call with death, the president addressed the world through the services of the Blipey-cam, and the satellite pirate broadcast of it. "Hello Colorotta! ", Crumm yelled. The crowd cheered. He went on, "Can you imagine it! I just shook hands with an alien! How about that?" He gestured towards Jeemis, who stood behind the president with Melanie. Jeemis grinned and took an exaggerated bow. More cheers.

After the applause faded, the president said, "And what about my brave, gutsy Science Advisor, Melanie Gryzolski? She's got b...b...b...brains!" That remark elicited laughs and applause.

Now he turned his attention to the TDS. He said, "So, this grotesque monstrosity rising up from the rock is a boon to the human race? This is the TDS that has the world doing cartwheels? I am not much impressed. It reminds me of Bawd Medler.

"So, what should I ask this photo-shopped hoax of a talking toadstool?" he asked the crowd. People shouted, yelled and bellowed out all sorts of the usual nonsense, like, "Who will win the World Series?", and, "Is my wife cheating on me with you?"

In a very short time, the chaotic crowd noise evolved into a chant of, "TDS! TDS!"

President Trapp said, "Okay, alright, we all have a million questions. I'll warm it up with an easy one."

Robulus's voice blasted from the PA speakers. "It won't hold a conversation, Sir, but ask it something and it will answer."

The president nodded in understanding, turned his back to the camera and mounted the Docket, accompanied by his two security agents. He faced the hideous fungal being, poised to frame his question, when the voice of a young girl emanated from it.

"Welcome, Mr President, "the voice said. "This unimpressive, grotesque monstrosity is honoured by your presence. Thank you for coming. Shall I answer your question?"

When one and a half billion awed and amazed people, all gasped at once and inhaled deeply, simultaneously; a partial vacuum was created in the atmosphere, and for a moment, Gaia truly sucked. President Trapp was as astonished as anybody, at the petite, girlish voice.

He said, "Not conversational, eh? A teenage monster with a sense of humour; I like it."

The TDS replied, "We are teens no longer. To be precise, we are clustered around fourteen thousand and sixty-one years of age. The answer to your question, to be polite, waits the asking, Sir."

The president, with a dramatic flair, said, "Oh, pardon me! Let me not keep the great and mighty wizard waiting. Answer me this; how many sentient civilisations exist in the universe?"

The TDS answered, "Excluding alternate universes, 13,721,864 identifiable thoughtprints are discernible, indicating sentient species."

Gaia observed a moment of silence, as it digested this information. The Poke's Peak crowd was as still and quiet, as a discussion about the positive attributes of socialism.

As per usual, the president, quick on his feet, announced, "Thank you TDS. Welcome to the United States National Park Service, effective immediately by executive order."

The gathering of thousands cheered madly as the POTUS waved goodbye. He and his pair of officers returned to the escort motorcycles, below Gate 3. They mounted, and returned down the road to the armoured limousines.

After the red tail lights of the presidential detail, finally vanished into the night, Robulus announced the opening of Gate 3. He was stunned at the sudden verbosity of the TDS. It was a wonderful development! "Open the gate!" he roared. The line thickened as people closed ranks.

Jeemis and Melanie stood at the turnstile to greet people, and escort them to the query docket. Pitch Al, Dom Crews, Kate Armstrong and ten pink blobs of powdered rock waited anxiously to enter. The SST apostles looked like a batch of cookies.

Robby Indero and Don Crews were arguing. Don shouted, "You're not the boss of me!"

Robby spat and snarled like a foul-mouthed cat. "This isn't about you! Think of the poking temple, you lousy, traitorous son of a sow's incestuous, mother poking, toadstool humping cousin!" Clouds of pink dust fell from Indero with each word and gesture, leaving a pile growing around his shoes.

Jeemis opened the gate and people began to stream inside, one by one to see the TDS up close! The temple saints all hung close together, and Don and Robby continued their argument as they walked towards the docket. Melanie accompanied them, and could hear every word. The Blipey-cam aired the celebrity footage too.

Pitch Al should have seen it coming and he had no excuse for not jamming a rock in Don's mouth to prevent it. The 'Days of Blunder' actor got defensive with Indero, and retorted, "I have forty thousand dollars invested in this kidnapping scheme! I won't let the poking temple down! I just want to get my immortality first."

Griz jumped out of his chair, his face darkened with anger and he clenched his fists tightly. "I'll kill him!" he shouted. He wasn't actually threatening homicide; at least he didn't think so.

Vera was surprised and dismayed, "I can't believe that even he, was so stupid!"

Robulus said, "Be charitable, the stupidity virus is to blame remember."

Pitch Al and Kate, tried to fade back into the crowd, and move away from the Don Crews zone. Don hadn't yet realised his error, and in fact, he doubled down on his stupidity and said, "Isn't that right Al?" while looking over at Pitch Darkly. "But we don't have to pay them BEWBs forty thousand dollars, because where are they Al?"

Robby Indero dug a hole next to the one Don Crews had excavated. He said, "Forty poking thousand dollars ain't scat! We can take that amount out of the poking temple treasury, and not a single poking idiot would notice or care!" He knew he was on camera, but didn't much care. He was a tough guy after all.

The delicate, musical voice of Grinkoyba sang out from the TDS, "Hooray for Hollowood."

Melanie stepped in front of Don Crews and said, "Hey Pop Gun!" and she spit in his face."

Robby broke from the group, and climbed over the rail which encircled the TDS. He yelled, "I'm gonna turn you into a poking salad!" He charged at the toadstool, pulled a knife from a pocket, opened the blade and started hacking at the TDS.

The TDS said, "Poke you Bobby!"

It was said later, that laughter was heard round the world. 911 operators reported scores of calls, regarding possible deaths by laughter; including falls, chokings and asphyxiations.

The enormous toadstool quivered and trembled; rocks fell and rolled, and Robby did too, landing on his butt. People held onto rails and each other. The ground throbbed and vibrated, and a whistling sound erupted from the TDS. It grew in shrill intensity and volume. The gills which hung underneath the toadstool's cap turned dark, and flared outward.

Frightened, but entranced, people were shocked at what happened next. The TDS seemed to squat down slightly and a massive black cloud whooshed from under its cap. A second whoosh and then a third blew out, before stillness and quietude ensued, as if it were all a mistake.

Trillions upon trillions of black spores filled the air and coated the mountainside, and all the people on it. People inhaled them and swallowed them and wore them. Everyone was suddenly wearing black-face and black hands and clothing too.

Robulus did not know what had happened, but he didn't need people freaking out. He yelled, "Please, remain in place! Do not panic!"

Jeemis was choking and coughing, and Melanie was trying to clean the black stuff from her eyes with a tissue she'd pulled from her windbreaker's pocket. People couldn't easily act crazy and panic like idiots, until they could see and breathe, and people were having difficulty with both.

Griz paced, worried about Melanie. "What in Hades happened?" he shouted. "And don't blame Murphy's Law!"

Vera walked closer to the MegaScreen, as if in a trance. She said, "Wait."

Griz turned to look at the on-air picture that caught her attention. Robulus did too. "What the poke?" the alien swore.

Melanie and Jeemis saw and heard it too. People were shouting in joy and crying happy tears, and yelling euphorically, as if their most fervent wish had come true. Folks raised their arms to the sky, and hugged each other. Some hopped up and down, as if they had just won a hundred dollars on the Price Is High game show.

Robulus said, "Let us go out there and see what has occurred. A robocart sits outside the door here." Vera, Griz and Robulus exited the underground facility and each took a seat in the cart. They rode up the tunnel, and emerged above ground from behind the TDS. The cart took them through the jubilant crowd to where Jeemis and Melanie stood, awed as was everyone by the development.

"It's a miracle!" people screamed to the world. Fogs lifted and minds cleared! Stupidity was cured! Strangers hugged each other. It was miraculous!

Griz, Melanie, Vera, and the two aliens hugged and laughed and introduced each other. Pitch Al, with Don Crews and Kate Armstrong in tow, snuck past the reunion party and hustled up into the docket. They were blobs of blackness.

Pitch Al knew they were busted, but he'd come a long way and trampled over a lot of people to get here, and he wasn't leaving until he got his immortality! The trio stood at the rail. Al turned to Don and said, "I'll ask for both of us."

Don replied, "Well, alright, but I get the last word! I wanna tear this mushroom a new asshole!"

In its soft girl voice, the huge TDS said, "Speaking of assholes, aren't you Don Crews? And with Pitch Al Darkly too. Nice examples, both."

Al spoke up. "I appreciate that, but see, we're just here for the immortality. That Indero guy swearing loudly in the background wants a second go at you. So, how much?"

Kate rolled her eyes. The TDS would have rolled one too, if it could have. The light voice of Grinkoyba answered him. It said, "About eighty to one hundred years, I would guess. Humans should have the necessary nanotechnologies available in that time span. Your prison sentence should be over by then."

Epilogue

One year later...

The one-year anniversary of the Unveiling of the TDS was celebrated the world over, as International Stexit Day or Exit Stupidity Day. Gaia was a much less stupid world. Pets, like dogs, cats, birds and mice, were surprised by the marked improvement in the intelligence of their owners.

The billions of spores ejected by the TDS one year ago on Poke's Peak were found to be precise replicas of the Bugsy bacteria, created by the Nobells Prize winning aliens Robulus and Jeemis. The immediate cure however, was inexplicable. There was no physiological pathway that could explain the instantaneous cure of idiocy.

Even more remarkable was the ease of transmission and the precipitous infection rate of the TDS spore bacterium. Four out of every five people on the planet were cured of their stupidity in twelve months! It was truly remarkable, and many called it a miracle.

People aided the spread of the sickness. They held anti-stupidity parties in hopes of catching the illness. Most people wanted to catch the 'Bugsy Bug', to undo their stupidity, but not everyone.

A group called #MeStupid had grown into a major political movement. Their adherents wore masks, and practiced 'intelligence distancing' to preserve their stupidity. They were known for their propensity to hoard certain items, including vast amounts of toilet paper.

There was also a section of the populace, which was incurable and stuck in stupidity forever. It was learned that a small percentage of the world's population, was immune to the infection. Hollowood was the poster-town for this particular malady it seemed, because the movies they put out never improved.

Many of the entertainers, and Hollowood celebrities had no reason to celebrate the first International Exit Stupidity Day, especially those pop stars who attended the Unveiling. Some said they were all cursed by the TDS, and they would be haunted for the rest of their miserable lives.

Apparently, Tod Einer and Okra Wipmee believed in the curse, because they resigned from their apostleship in the Sacred Stars Temple, to become certified Witch Doctors at the Institute for Advanced Primitiveness in Loss Analyst. The SST as an entity was jinxed, according to Professor Felix Polyplastis of the College of Conspiracy Theories in Berzerkley.

The Sacred Stars Temple suffered a catastrophic crash in popularity. Membership numbers declined and congregations shrunk, and more than a dozen temple franchise locations had closed and were converted into massage parlours. People who once worshipped at the altars of the rich and famous had found better ways to spend their time and money. Robby Indero had become a pariah. He'd seriously damaged the church and his reputation with his comments about raiding the temple treasury.

Robby's ego suffered severe trauma, after being ostracised by his co-narcissists in Hollowood and shunned by the public. He never recovered enough, to ever again swear in such pretty phrases as in days past. This cussed failure, cost him his gig at the Poetic Profanity Institute, and he wound up owning and operating one of the aforementioned massage parlours. It was said that the germ to cure stupidity came by to infect him, but was sworn at and cursed out, until it turned around and left, never to return again. Robby Indero's massages were like his acting; tough.

The TDS National Park, served more than eight million visitors in its first year, and tourists and researchers from around the world were eager to see the symbiont, and ask their question of it. Physicists, chemists, biologists and many other scientists flocked in by the thousands, and many mysteries were solved. As usual, each solution created more mysteries for the TDS to unravel at future visits.

A ten-foot-tall monument to Crime Blaster XL-5 rose up in the place where the grey tank of Bugsy solution once stood. His uniform was recreated to perfection, thanks to photographs taken by scores of people that fateful day. His heroic story was pieced together from details, provided by his grieving wife Moon Bruce, Sue M. Aul and Pam Spray among others.

The base of the majestic statue of CB XL-5 was enshrined, with the iconic words of Super-duper Tarantula Man Issue #1147, when he faced Germiny Cricket and the Notsee Chirpers. In the last possible second, an instant before the

Germiny gang, and every last cricket on the globe chirped in unison, to set off earthquakes, landslides and TV reruns all over the world, Tarantula Man said, "Things could always be worse," and then he got them all drunk and they drowned in the hot tub.

The BEWBs were a flat bust. The national headquarters of the Basement Elite Without Breakfasts, decided that they were tired of going without the most important meal of the day, so they disbanded. Of the three living ex-members of the Ohaha chapter of the sagging BEWBs, Shanghai Low was spending his days and nights in a federal penitentiary. He'd been moved to an isolation block; due to the many death threats he'd received. There wasn't a single convict who could bear to hear one more time, the 'I abducted an alien and shot him' story. They wouldn't stand for it.

Vometta Wilde and Buster Monk, ratted out everyone involved in the kidnap scheme in a plea deal, and they walked away from court with a lifetime probation sentence. Vometta was now a professional wrestler, known as Bubble Wrap, and Buster was her alleged manager. Bubble Wrap was famous for her grease paint ring garb, and for her face splashes, in which she pinned her opponent by sitting on his face, while she devoured a pizza.

Al Darkly once again evaded justice and avoided prison. He knew too much about too many important people. He was shattered to learn that immortality didn't come in a pill or a do-it-yourself kit. When the TDS told him and tens of thousands of other, equally shallow people, that it projected that immortality for humans, was still a few decades in the future, he became despondent and donated his office desk to a senior centre as a dance floor. He sold Darkly Cinemas to Syko More, who made a documentary film about his experience tumbling around in the back of a moving truck called 'Body Surfing An I-Haul'. Al played golf now.

Torchy and Rosie Oh lived in a van down by the river. The van was parked by the Flatte River near Bland Island, Nebraska. They were broke. Rosie was ordered to pay $80,000 restitution to the Blight Trucking Company for lost beer revenues. Lawyer bills also stretched their budget. Their meagre income was derived from selling a line of perfumes, colognes, deodorant products and candles made with beer, which they sold on Shamazon. Success seemed to be right around the corner, with cleverly marketed brands like 'Bar Bathroom', 'Stand Stout', and 'Rosie's Ale de parfum'.

Barry Porter was found in a Dunfor, Colorotta homeless camp, after several months had elapsed. He'd been arrested for prostitution and was entered into a drug rehab centre for an addiction to heroin.

Don Crews was set to star in 'Donnie Does Dallas', his first porn flick.

Matt Gryzolski and Vera Fyne live together in a Colorotta Springs ranch house now, and they have recently published the first in a series of books called, 'The Stupid Awards; The Dumbest Questions Ever Posed To The TDS'. Griz also consulted as an engineer for R&J Enterprises Incorporated, in the Colorotta Springs area. Vera had resigned from her position at No Fake News; and her split from Terry had been amicable.

Melanie Gryzolski resigned her position as presidential science advisor, and had begun going to church again. Melanie and Jeemis were romantically involved. She was not sadistic however, so Jeemis attended to his own needs. He loved pain and had a strange routine that took some getting used to for Melanie.

Jeemis had a Spewtube channel and was popular on Soonagram too. His most popularly viewed show featured him running through his homemade obstacle course. The tall alien's first obstacle was the 'tiger death pit". The deep hole was festooned with dozens of dagger sharp bamboo spears. Other obstacles included a mine field, a pond with crocodiles, and a bonfire.

President Crumm had famously nicknamed the TDS conglomerate entity, 'Shroomie', and he came to Poke's Peak, to celebrate the one-year anniversary of the Unveiling on September third. He held a press conference there on that day. Many of the people who experienced the Unveiling, had returned for this special day, including Melanie, Griz, Vera and, of course the two aliens, Robulus and Jeemis. It was a grand spectacle. CB action figures and comic books were sold.

The Make-Believe Media conglomerate stayed stupid, but people who were cured of their idiocy could now see through the dense wall of false news lies, and they turned it off.

The cure for the common cold was a spectacular side effect of the Bugsy bacterium clone released by the TDS. There was a second side effect, which began to cause considerable alarm to the usual fear mongers. Its effect was immediate, but the results of the effect, only began to appear nine months later in maternity wards all over the world.

The side effect in question happened to induce extreme horniness in people, for a period of ten to fourteen days and nights.

END

CPSIA information can be obtained
at www.ICGtesting.com
Printed in the USA
BVHW032255061222
653631BV00006B/43